The orchestra struck up a waltz.

Jason pulled her closer until they were touching from shoulder to thigh. "You clod, this is a ballroom, not a bedroom," she snarled. "Don't hold me so vulgarly."

Jason squeezed her roughly for a moment, then loosened his hold. "You're quite right, my dear," he agreed pleasantly. "Your punishment must be in private."

Her eyes reminded him of a furious cat's. "My punishment?" she hissed. "After your behavior today? If there was ever any doubt that ours is a normal marriage, you have laid it at rest."

"Indeed, my precious, ours is *not* a normal marriage." The leer was replaced by a frown so fierce Leanna was alarmed. "But no one else will taste of the fruit you withhold from me. Is that understood, wife?"

Wild Heart Tamed

Colleen Shannon

Ⓒ

CHARTER BOOKS, NEW YORK

*To Vi Lea, chief critic, biggest fan,
sister and always a friend.*

WILD HEART TAMED

A Charter Book / published by arrangement with
the author

PRINTING HISTORY
Charter edition / June 1986

ISBN: 0-441-88813-5

Charter Books are published by The Berkley Publishing Group,
200 Madison Avenue, New York, New. York 10016.
PRINTED IN THE UNITED STATES OF AMERICA

PART ONE

"There's a divinity that shapes our ends, rough-hew them how we will."
—Shakespeare, *Hamlet*, Act V, Scene II

Chapter One

THE CONSPIRATORS MADE an odd pair in the silent, gaudily furnished room. The candles caught the pale locks of the nobleman and cast a halo about his beautiful features, accentuating the contrast he made to the tall, garishly dressed woman. The flattering light should have lent an angelic expression to his face, but the strong emotion evident in his bored features made even the madam uneasy.

A white hand plunked two sacks of gold on the hideous, lion-footed table. "Absolutely *no one* must get wind of this."

The madam opened the heaviest sack, upended the contents, and counted the guineas carefully while the small, slim man surveyed the room with a shudder of distaste. Heavy purple drapes, sumptuous gold carpet, and ornately tapestried furniture endowed the room with an opulence that oppressed rather than appealed to the senses.

The twist of contempt on his well-shaped mouth eased somewhat when he looked back at the woman. He watched with

1

narrow eyes as she pocketed the sack and smiled with satisfaction. She nodded cordially. "I'll fetch the chit tomorrow morning. Might I ask why you want her saved for Blaine?"

The gentleman's long-lashed blue eyes flamed with hatred for an unguarded moment, then his eyelids dropped and doused the fire. He replied in a deep, mellifluous voice, "Let's just say I have an old score to settle."

He rose decisively and walked with easy, athletic grace to the door, where he pulled his cravat up to hide his face. His eyes glittered a warning above the mask. "I want no mistakes, do you understand?"

The madam opened her mouth to retort, but the arctic gleam in his stare froze the words on her lips. His condescension grated, but it was too soon yet to defy him. Later, he would find she had plans of her own. She nodded shortly. The exquisite man bowed mockingly and left the room in eerie silence.

"Leanna!" Edith's querulous voice shrilled through the crisp morning air as she made her way into the garden.

The slender figure perched precariously high in the old oak made a face, clamped her lips together, and defiantly swung her slim legs. Her mulish expression emphasized her firm chin and stubborn jaw in a way that heightened rather than detracted from her delicate beauty.

"Bother, Edith!" the girl muttered under her breath. She was tired of the constant attendance she was expected to play on her cousin. Mend this dress, air my bed, fix my poultice! Well, she would not play the role of unpaid companion today. She would spend this day as she pleased and she cared not if Edith had apoplexy.

The small, plump woman snapped her head from side to side as she searched for her charge. Leanna was not ashamed of her uncharitable thought: She looks like a fat vulture searching for a meal.

Edith spied a flash above the ground and she gasped in shock and outrage when she saw it was Leanna's indecently exposed legs flicking impudently back and forth. Her round face darkened, and she slapped her hands together with anger.

"Come down this instant, you ungrateful chit. Exposing yourself like a hussy. I always knew there was a wild streak in you. Serve you right if you fell—"

Edith's tirade was halted when the old butler shuffled into the garden and droned, "There is a guest to see Miss Leanna, ma'am."

Edith's eyes widened and Leanna jumped in surprise. Their eyes met as, for once, a mutual thought struck them. Leanna knew of only one person who would visit her. "The earl," she breathed.

Edith's little hands fluttered in sudden agitation as she patted her elaborate coiffure. "Clean up and be quick about it!" she snapped at Leanna. She turned and scurried as fast as her plump legs could carry her back to the house.

Leanna jumped down from her perch nimbly, then sped to her room where she combed and repinned her hair. Her thoughts raced. She had become the ward of Jason Arthur Blaine, the wealthy Earl of Sherringham, upon the death of her parents in a freak carriage accident two years earlier. She had never met her guardian, for he had sent her to live with her cousin Edith until his "pressing business commitments" allowed him to devote time to her debut into London society. He had pleaded the same excuse almost a year ago when she wrote and asked when she would be allowed to go to London. His indifference rankled, and the first seed of resentment toward her guardian was planted.

However, even his reluctant attention was welcome if it would free her from Edith's dreary house and even more depressing presence. She had lived in the country all her sheltered young life, but the solitude of country living had never bored her until she was forced to live under Edith's strict discipline.

As the daughter of the Duke of Chester's tutor, Leanna's position in society had always been nebulous at best. Neither servant nor aristocrat, she was accepted by neither the working class nor the aristocracy. Nevertheless, until two years ago her world had been a happy one, despite the fact that it consisted of little but her studies and her parents.

When her parents died she was shrouded by grief so strong,

she cared little where she lived or what happened to her. Her loss was doubly hard because she had no other close relatives.

She was even too grief-stricken to resent her spinster cousin's patronizing attitude. But only at first. The natural resiliency of youth and her own innate strength helped her subdue the painful memories, treasure the happy ones, and begin to enjoy life once again. She chafed at her quiet confinement so that even her books were no longer a comfort.

For months she endured her cousin's constant strictures of propriety. She quietly sat through interminable tea parties with Edith's equally narrow-minded cronies until, one day not long ago, Leanna overheard a conversation that so enraged her she decided to seek employment rather than remain with her cousin.

"Such a shame, my dear," Edith simpered to one of her friends. "She's a real beauty, but without a feather to fly with. Poor cousin Charles never had much sense and he barely made enough at that demeaning job to keep them fed."

Leanna's fists clenched and she was on the verge of entering the drawing room to confront her cousin when Edith continued, "Why, I haven't a notion what would have happened to the child if Blaine hadn't been such good friends with Charles at Oxford and consented to be her guardian. I fear he's her only hope now, but I doubt he'll settle much on her. The pittance he gives me barely keeps her clothed and fed. I can't say I blame him for not sending for her. Well, really, a *tutor's* daughter! And while the Hardwicke family lineage is respectable, I would hardly call it assurance of entree into *London* society. Yes, now I am afraid her beauty can only cause trouble."

Leanna retreated silently, tears in her eyes, when Edith switched subjects. For a moment she longed for her mother's arms so fiercely she could almost feel them around her. Then her pride, which was to be a help and a hindrance in the future, reasserted itself. She straightened her spine, pressed her lips together, and marched upstairs to pen a letter to the Duke of Chester, requesting he recommend her for a position as a governess or teacher. Better to be alone and independent than an unwanted burden, she reasoned.

Now, Leanna glanced in the tiny mirror and straightened a

last rebellious lock of hair. Her mobile face set grimly as she promised herself she would escape, with or without her guardian's assistance. There was a wide, fascinating world to be seen, and she was eager to see it.

When she entered the salon, she was surprised to see a thin, brown-haired woman sitting next to her cousin. Edith sniffed when she saw Leanna, and her voice was cool. "Leanna, child, this is Mrs. Horton. She has been sent by your guardian to escort you to London."

Leanna heaved a sigh of relief and her wary look shattered into radiance. "London at last," she breathed. She smiled warmly at the visitor, but she was puzzled when Mrs. Horton subjected her to a close scrutiny that verged on the improper. She shifted under the woman's close examination. She would have been even more uncomfortable had she been able to read Mrs. Horton's mind.

The girl would be popular with even our most demanding clientele, the woman thought. She'll remain when Gavin's done with her, whether he wishes it or not. Though why he wants to involve her with Blaine is beyond my imagining. Mrs. Horton surveyed Leanna once again from head to foot.

From the top of her burnished golden head to the tips of her dainty feet, Leanna seemed to radiate beauty and innocence. Her bountiful bright golden hair made a fitting frame for her fair, silky complexion. Her nose was small and finely molded, emphasizing the elegant bone structure of her face. Her dimpled chin drew attention to the determined slant of her jaw and the slenderness of her long swan's neck. Her mouth was full and oddly bold-looking in such an innocent face. But it was her eyes that arrested and captivated the appraiser. Large, slightly slanted, and framed in dark curling lashes, they were a clear emerald green that lightened or darkened with her moods. Her petite figure was slender, small-boned, and tiny-waisted. Her breasts were full for a woman of such small stature.

Mrs. Horton's face smoothed into a proper smile when she met Leanna's eyes. She walked forward with lithe grace and held out her hand. "How do you do, Leanna. I am delighted to meet you. Your guardian speaks most highly of you. If you'll pack your things, we can leave without delay."

Reassured by the woman's courtesy, Leanna smiled. "I'll pack at once, ma'am. I shall not be long." She ran out. Edith watched her retreating back with hard eyes, then she turned to the silent woman at her side.

"I'll be glad to be rid of her, I can tell you. She's an imperious little snit, daring to put on airs with me in my own house. It's not as though Sherringham is paying me enough to make it worth my while." Her shrill voice lowered with bitter satisfaction. "He's shown little enough interest in the girl. Why, he's never even troubled to meet her. Hasn't seen her since she was a babe. He just foisted her off on me—"

Mrs. Horton smoothly cut in. "Yes, his lordship understands the trouble you've been caused. That's why he's authorized me to give you this." A small, heavy sack of gold clanked as Mrs. Horton placed it in Edith's eager hand with a cynical smile.

Edith pocketed the sack and gave it a satisfied pat. She smothered the further complaints she longed to make and ordered tea. Her smile was ingratiating as she poured the woman a cup. "Do tell me the latest *on-dits*. I declare, it's been an age since I was in London, even though I don't live far away."

Mrs. Horton took a small sip of tea, then disguised her shudder of distaste with difficulty.

She set the cup down on the spindly table next to her brocaded chair. "It is not my function to gossip about the *beau monde*. A chaperone must set a proper example in order to discourage hoydenish behavior in her charge." She looked at Edith with a supercilious, raised brow.

Leanna entered in time to hear this remark, and she looked at Edith's red face almost sympathetically. Now that she was leaving, she could find compassion in her generous heart for this bitter, unhappy spinster.

Mrs. Horton rose as soon as she saw Leanna. "Are you ready to leave, my dear?" she asked with visible relief.

Leanna nodded. Then, looking at Edith, she hesitated. Her cousin had not been kind to her, but parting with bitterness would serve no purpose. Leanna held out her hand. Her voice was sweet and pleading. "Thank you for taking me into your home, Edith. I hope you'll come to see me in London. I'd appreciate it if you'd have my mail sent on."

Edith nodded coldly, her gray eyes as hard as pebbles. She ignored the outstretched hand. Leanna flushed and stepped back. She tilted her chin. "I'm ready, ma'am." She pulled her cloak about her and stepped out the door, never dreaming that in that moment she was setting in motion a momentous wheel of events.

Mrs. Horton nodded at Edith shortly. "Good day. Thank you for the tea." She followed Leanna into the weak sunshine.

Leanna was surprised to see a hired carriage awaiting them. She accepted the coachman's eager hand thoughtfully as she allowed him to assist her into the plain but comfortable interior. She missed the man's bemused look as he gaped at her face. When Mrs. Horton was aboard and the coach had swayed into motion, Leanna asked with a puzzled frown, "Mrs. Horton, did my guardian tell you why he didn't send his own carriage for me?"

"Why yes, my dear," Mrs. Horton replied after the barest of pauses. "His coachman is refurbishing the earl's carriages, as he usually does at this time of year. His lordship exempted only his perch phaeton, and I'm sure you realize *that* would be totally unsuitable for you to ride in."

Leanna nodded, but she felt the first niggling sense of unease. Still, the explanation seemed reasonable, so she sat back and once more gave rein to her anticipation. She had never visited London, and the excitement of seeing the world's largest city at last seemed even more thrilling than the glittering round of social events scheduled for her.

Some of her excitement dimmed as she thought of the man who would sponsor her. She fervently hoped Sherringham's sense of consequence would be too great to foist her off with a hastily arranged debut. Leanna did not deceive herself that Sherringham was arranging her debut out of kindness. More than likely the earl wished to rid himself of her. He loomed ever larger in her mind as a cold, commanding figure who had more concern for his wealth and position in society than for the orphaned girl he had adopted.

Briefly, she wondered why he had not bothered to inform her about his decision to send for her. Her mouth twisted bitterly as she decided his "pressing business commitments" probably didn't allow him time for such a courtesy.

Leanna bit her lip. Her unseeing gaze roamed over the rolling countryside outside her window. It irked her to be so dependent on a man who seemed indifferent to her welfare. She was doubly glad, now, that she had written to the duke. If living with the cold earl was as unpleasant as she suspected it might be, it would be easier to seek employment in London. Her nineteen years of age would be a handicap, but she hoped the duke's recommendation, coupled with her unusually broad education, would overcome that obstacle.

She had been allowed to study with the duke's sons until she blossomed at the age of fifteen, when her father withdrew her from his pupils' roaming eyes to tutor her privately. She was a joy to teach, for she had inherited Charles's indefatigable curiosity and thirst for knowledge. She was tutored in Latin, mathematics, the classics, and political history, despite her mother's protests that she was being educated as a boy rather than a girl. To appease Clarice, her mother, Leanna diligently studied the topics which her parent thought suitable: sketching, sewing, etiquette, and the pianoforte.

However, diligence could not replace talent. When her finest efforts resulted in mangled sketches, tangled embroidery, and jangled sonatas, Clarice threw up her hands in defeat and protested no more.

Leanna's favorite subject was literature. She had been allowed free rein of the duke's library and she spent hours poring over Milton, Scott, and Cervantes. Her greatest literary love, however, was Shakespeare. She had read all of his plays several times and most of his sonnets.

Her forays in the library also introduced her to writings her parents were not aware of: highly erotic poetry and works such as *The History of Tom Jones, a Foundling*.

Leanna's unusual childhood and broad education had melded an odd personality for a young English lady of nineteen. She was a complex mixture of wisdom and innocence, knowledge and ignorance, and independence and vulnerability. It was her independence that made it so hard for Leanna to accept her cousin's grudging charity and the earl's reluctant patronage.

Mrs. Horton seemed disinclined to talk, so Leanna passed the brief journey squirming in her seat with increasing impatience. Soon the traffic thickened and she realized they had reached the outskirts of London at last.

Leanna sat with her nose pressed to the window of the swaying carriage. The roiling cauldron of humanity that was London in 1805 exploded into her senses. The dreariness of her life the past two years had so sensitized Leanna's stifled curiosity that she now drank in the sights, sounds, and smells like ambrosia. The Industrial Revolution had brought an enormous influx of people into London. Their characters and stations were vastly different, but their goals were similar: They sought work, excitement, and, above all, profit. If financial advantage could not be had legitimately, then it would be had illegally. London's habitants were as diverse in their way of life as they were in their mode of dress.

Shabby street peddlers hawked their wares as shopkeepers, servants, factory and dock workers hurried past. Filthy chimney sweeps and street urchins gawked at elegant gentlemen, chaperoned ladies, and affluent merchants as they strode arrogantly by. Carriages of every description jockeyed for position in the crowded streets with battered hacks, delivery wagons, and loaded mail coaches.

A parade of shops lined the streets—jewelers, boot-makers, apothecaries, book-sellers, goldsmiths, tailors, and dressmakers. Leanna itched to join the throng of people and explore the streets.

She finally turned shining eyes back to her fellow traveler. "Mrs. Horton, do we go directly to my guardian's, or must we stop at an inn to change coaches?"

"We proceed directly to your guardian's, of course." Mrs. Horton's voice was easy, but Leanna's attentive ear caught an undercurrent of nervousness. Why would the woman be nervous? Leanna frowned and examined Mrs. Horton with care, but the coach lurched dangerously and stopped suddenly. As she landed in a flurry of skirts on top of Mrs. Horton, she could have sworn she heard the woman curse. The carriage door swung open and Leanna looked up to see a strange gentleman extending a hand.

Leanna accepted and was lifted into the arms of the large, heavy, red-headed man, who then set her down on the cobbled street. She adjusted her wide-brimmed hat, which had tilted forward over her face, and smiled up at the gentleman sweetly. "Thank you so much, sir. Could you please assist my companion also?"

The man's merry blue eyes widened when he saw her face. For a moment he looked stunned as his gaze traveled from her eyes to her mouth, down her figure, and back again. Puzzled, Leanna repeated, "Sir, my companion needs assistance."

He flinched, flushed, and said with embarrassment, "Certainly, ma'am." He once again leaned down inside the carriage and leant a hand to an angry Mrs. Horton. Her thin cheeks red, the woman emerged awkwardly.

She strode over to the coachman, who was examining the broken axle, and snapped, "Fine carriage you have for hire. We're late already. I fully expect compensation for your clumsiness." As she continued to berate the sullen driver, Leanna was beginning to feel uncomfortable under the eagerness of her rescuer's gaze. Her experience with the opposite sex was extremely limited.

Sensing her unease, he offered gallantly, "May I present myself, my lady? Harry Jeffries is the name. I'm delighted to be at your service. May I convey you to your destination in my carriage?"

Mrs. Horton stopped haranguing the coachman. She responded coolly, "Thank you for your offer, sir, but it would not be proper for us to accept. The coachman has sent for another carriage. Thank you for your assistance. Good day." She grabbed Leanna's arm and pulled her behind the carriage.

To Mrs. Horton's annoyance, Mr. Jeffries followed them and requested Leanna's place of lodging. Before Leanna could answer, Mrs. Horton intervened rudely, "Really, sir, your services are no longer required. Now *good day!*" She spied the approaching carriage with relief. As it jerked to a stop, she hastily bundled Leanna inside. Harry watched wistfully as the coachman loaded up the baggage and signaled the other driver to pull away.

Leanna leaned out the retreating carriage to call, "Thank you again for your help, Mr. Jeffries."

Mr. Jeffries waved back and turned to his carriage, though he saw nothing but the smiling visage of the angel who had captured his heart.

Inside the hired coach, Leanna expostulated, "Really, ma'am, was it necessary to be so rude? He was only being helpful."

Mrs. Horton's voice was dry. "When you've been longer in London, child, you'll discover that for your own safety you should not converse with strange gentlemen. He might have seemed harmless, but he could well be London's biggest rake-hell, for all we know."

Leanna absorbed her lecture in silence and conceded the point, but she was still perturbed at the woman's harshness. She examined Mrs. Horton carefully, again noting the tenseness in her thin figure. Leanna's smooth brow wrinkled as she recalled the suspected muffled curse. She could not dispel the instinct that something was wrong; she was beginning to suspect the woman was hiding something.

Leanna tried to reassure herself that her guardian would not have sent anyone disreputable to collect her, but she was not totally convincing. His former indifference to her well-being did not instill her with a great deal of confidence in him.

The carriage swayed from side to side as it maneuvered dangerously the crowded streets. Leanna heard the whip crack as the driver urged the horses to a canter.

She was puzzled at the urgency of the trip and Mrs. Horton's tense manner. "Is something wrong, ma'am? Why are we in such a hurry?"

The woman laughed at the question. "We are later than I expected and I fear his lordship will be worried if we don't arrive soon."

The answer was feasible enough, but Leanna's earlier sense of unease returned. The evasiveness in Mrs. Horton's answer

made her appear suddenly menacing to Leanna. She sat tensely
next to Mrs. Horton as they withdrew from the main thorough-
fare and began traveling through residential streets.

They pulled to a halt with a jolt, and Leanna, her heart
beating fast with instinctive alarm, watched as Mrs. Horton
relaxed with a visible sigh of relief.

"We've arrived at last, child." Mrs. Horton stepped down
and held the door for Leanna to do likewise. "Are you ready
to meet your guardian?" she queried as she waited. Leanna
hesitated in the carriage, though she really had little choice but
to trust the woman. She hadn't even enough coin for a night's
lodging. Sighing, Leanna nodded and descended.

She examined the edifice in front of her. Built of gray brick
and few windows, it had an ornate stone portico flanked by
Corinthian columns. The grounds were immaculate, but the
surrounding houses were not as neat. It was a handsome man-
sion, but it was smaller than she had expected. It was certainly
an unpretentious residence for a wealthy earl.

She turned to question Mrs. Horton again, but the woman
was already beckoning impatiently to her from the door.
Leanna's steps dragged as she climbed the stairs. She stifled
the foolish urge to call for help and forced her laggard feet up
the steps. Mrs. Horton gripped her arm to impel her through
the door. Leanna stiffened and tried to pull away, but it was
too late. The heavy door slammed behind her before she could
escape the woman's grasp.

The man who let them in was enormous and coarse-looking,
an impression intensified by the elegant purple and gold livery
he wore. Leanna paid him scant attention because she was
stunned by her surroundings. They confirmed that she had been
duped.

She was in a spacious, domed antechamber that was carpeted
in virulent purple and papered in gold damask. The pictures
hanging around the room made Leanna blush. Leering satyrs
pursued naked nymphs on the ceiling above her head. An ornately carved staircase led to closed doors above. Their purpose
was painfully obvious, even to Leanna's innocence.

She collected her scattered senses and turned to flee, only

to find her way blocked by the enormous servant and a maliciously triumphant Mrs. Horton.

"You began to suspect me, didn't you, dearie?" the madam mocked in a voice that no longer affected respectability. "That's why I rushed you here. But don't worry, we have quite a treat in store for you. Now, go with Beekins, and if you know what's good for you, you'll cooperate. He would derive great satisfaction in disciplining you."

Leanna listened to her taunting voice in silence, too filled with terror and fury at her own stupidity to take much notice. When Beekins, leering, grabbed her arm, she kicked him in the shin as hard as she could. Without hesitation, he slapped her viciously across the cheek. Through the ringing in her ears she vaguely registered Mrs. Horton's sharp reproof. "Be careful, you fool, do you want to bruise her? She must be ready for tonight."

When her ears stopped ringing, Leanna drew herself up to her full height, and with a dignity somewhat pathetic because of her trembling, she warned, "You'll never get away with this. My cousin knows you came for me and she'll inform the earl when she doesn't hear from me. He'll find me somehow."

Mrs. Horton laughed harshly. "That old crone? She couldn't see the back of you quick enough. As for the earl, he's shown how concerned he is about you in the past, hasn't he, dearie?"

Leanna whitened at the cruel words and bit her lip to keep from begging for release. With an extreme effort she subdued her rising panic by admonishing herself: You got yourself into this mess, my girl, and it's up to you to get yourself out of it. As usual, you can depend on no one else.

Leanna held on to this grim determination with bitter clarity, and without another word, she allowed Beekins to push her roughly up the garish staircase.

Chapter
Two

ON THE PREVIOUS evening in that October of 1805, in a more exclusive part of London, Jason Arthur Blaine, sixth Earl of Sherringham, slumped in his chair as he brooded into his brandy. He was a large, good-looking man with thick black hair and pale blue eyes that normally glowed with geniality and joie de vivre but which now were somewhat dimmed. He had just returned from the War Office with news that weighed heavily on him.

Napoleon amassed his navy to once again attempt an invasion of England. The earl was weary of war, as were all his countrymen. Except for a brief period of peace following the Treaty of Amiens in 1802, England had been at war with France since 1793.

The conflict was a continual, increasing drain on the economy, particularly since England had recently had no ally but Portugal until Pitt's diplomacy finally persuaded Austria and Russia to her side. The war had dragged on interminably, a stalemate between Napoleon's superior land forces and England's mighty navy. While Napoleon's string of victories on the continent attested to his brilliant land campaigns, his naval successes were another matter. The British lion was indeed the master of the seas. The earl smiled as he recalled a comment made by Lord St. Vincent: "I don't say the French can't come; I say they can't come by sea."

England's primary defense was the naval blockade, a tactic that had so far failed to drive France to her knees, for what she couldn't smuggle from England, she bought from America. The upstart "neutral" Americans had enraged the British government by reaping large profits in trade with both countries. Harsh measures were being considered to abort American trade with France, or the war could drag on and totter England's shaky economy. Internal revolt could then vanquish England as Napoleon had been unable to.

Th earl was jolted from his gloom by a loud commotion in the hall. Sounds of scuffling and cursing ensued, then a loud crack rang out. The earl jerked open the door. "What the devil is going on—" Astonishment choked off his words. An angry young man wearing the rough clothing of a seaman was struggling in the grip of several footmen. Hastings, the butler, was coming groggily to his feet as he rubbed his aching jaw.

In other circumstances, Sherringham might have laughed at the novel sight of his prim and proper butler so discomposed, but he recognized the face of the young man still struggling with the footmen.

The participants in the scene saw him at the same time. "Sir, I demand to speak with you!" said the angry man in an American accent.

"Your lordship! This . . . person forced his way in despite my refusal to admit him," stuttered Hastings, his face red with chagrin.

And from one of the footmen: "Cor, they's as alike as two peas in a pod!" He looked from Sherringham back to the other man with astonishment.

The earl walked up to the American and extended his hand. "Release him," he said to the mystified footmen.

As they shook hands, he smiled. "You must be my cousin Jason from America. I am delighted to meet you at last. I can see you are a Blaine to your toes, as Uncle Thomas suggested in a recent letter. Come into my study and tell me what I can do for you."

The earl strode toward his study but stopped and turned toward his startled butler. "By the way," he teased. "Hastings, say the word and I'll have Jackson give you pugilism lessons. I believe your guard could stand some improving." Sherringham then turned to lead his visitor into the study, leaving the affronted butler to take out his frustrations on his underlings.

Sherringham seated his guest, poured them both a brandy, and returned to his chair before the fire. He ignored the young man's obvious impatience while he took a calm sip of his drink and studied the other man.

He was a strapping fellow, lean and muscular, with a lithe grace that seemed unusual in such a large man. He looked to be about thirty. His thick, black hair curled tumultuously around a bronzed face. The aristocratic nose was just saved from over-prominence by the wide, full-lipped mouth and broad cheekbones that were at the moment flushed with anger. The eyes were the deep, turbulent blue-gray of the Channel on a stormy day. He had long, curling lashes that would have looked ridiculous on a less masculine man, but which served to emphasize his rugged good looks.

"Suit you, I trust?" he inquired sarcastically.

Sherringham laughed. "Sorry, Cousin, but you must admit the likeness is amazing. Your eyes are darker and you're somewhat taller, but other than that I feel as though I'm looking at myself ten years past. Quite gives me an eerie feeling. Now, what can I do for you?"

"You can get my ship back!" he snapped. "It's been confiscated for carrying contraband." He snorted in disgust, "Contraband! My only cargo is good Georgian cotton and rice, some of it from my own grandfather's plantation. We're neutral, remember? Not content with kidnaping our seamen, now you take our ships as well."

Sherringham was unsurprised; he'd heard such a policy was

under consideration to thwart American trade with the French. However, he'd understood confiscation would be attempted only from those ships that carried goods from France, her allies, or protectorates such as the West Indies, or on those ships bound for a French port.

"Indeed, I'm sorry to hear that. I assure you I'll do everything in my power to get your ship released. Where are you berthed?"

Some of the tension left Jason. "The London dock. She's a Virginia-built, sharp model schooner, the *Savannah.*"

"I'll go to the War Office in the morning and obtain a release. Don't worry, you'll get your ship back," the earl said in a soothing voice. Jason thanked him sincerely and sat back, exhausted, to sip his brandy.

"When did you dock?"

"Several days ago. Our cargo was completely unloaded and I was ashore with some of my men, enjoying...uh..." Jason reddened slightly, "London's diversions. When I returned this evening I found her chained off. They wouldn't even let me aboard. I remembered Grandfather speaking of you, so I decided to ask for your help." He smiled for the first time that evening, revealing a crease in each cheek. "I'm very grateful for your intervention. I apologize for my rudeness earlier, but your man wouldn't let me in. This was my vessel's maiden voyage and all of my funds and a good part of my grandfather's money is tied up in her. It is imperative I get her back."

"Certainly it is. Don't worry about Hastings." The earl grinned mischievously. "I quite enjoyed seeing the old curmudgeon so discomfitted. No doubt you don't suit his ideas of propriety in your present attire."

Jason surveyed himself ruefully. "My clothes are aboard the *Savannah.*"

"You can wear some of mine for this evening." The earl held up a hand as Jason started to protest. "No, I insist you stay. For shame, Cousin: You hadn't planned to call on me, had you?"

Jason's averted look was answer enough.

Sherringham's handsome face saddened. "I had hoped the

animosities within our family died long ago. How is Uncle Thomas, by the way?"

"Fine. He manages Whispering Oaks, our plantation, while I handle the shipping part of the business."

"It's a pity my father never forgave him for emigrating to America. I believe the final break that severed their relationship was Uncle Thomas's support of the American revolution. Father also never understood why he insisted on leaving. Younger son or not, he still had opportunities aplenty in England."

"No opportunities to match what he found in America. The land around Savannah is beautiful beyond your wildest imaginings, and our plantation is one of the largest in Georgia." Jason fidgeted in his chair. Raking over the ancient family schisms made him uncomfortable. "I know Grandfather is grieved your father died before they reconciled. He encouraged me to visit you, but I had planned a brief stay. I still have a deal to accomplish."

The earl gave an understanding nod. "I hope that now we've met, you will lodge here for the remainder of your stay. I'd welcome the company and the opportunity to catch up on family history. I'm to be married soon and one of my friends is having a birthday party tomorrow evening that will be the last of its kind I'll experience. It will indeed be one of London's finer diversions. You are, or course, invited."

Sherringham laughed and a tender look softened his face. "I'm afraid my betrothed will not be a compliant wife. She'll countenance no straying." He mused thoughtfully, "Still, I'd wager I'm getting the best of the bargain. I suspect there is enough passion in her slender form to keep three men happy."

As Jason reddened, the earl rose and slapped him on the back, laughing. "Didn't mean to embarrass you, old fellow. I'm not usually maudlin. If you find a woman to love half as much as I love my Abby, perhaps you'll understand one day."

Jason's lip curled. "I doubt that I shall, cousin. I've never found a woman who could be called endearing. In their place they can be quite entertaining, but let them get too close and they smother a man. No, I'll never let a woman become necessary to me." He rose and turned away to stare into the fire.

His shoulders were rigid with some strong emotion Sherringham couldn't quite define.

He sounded so set in his opinion that the earl was loath to disagree. Nevertheless, he felt sure Jason's solid certainty was bound to be shaken one day. He knew Jason's childhood had lacked a gentle influence because he had been reared by his grandfather after the death of his father. Of his mother, Sherringham knew little, except that she was a Boston girl of good family. He would have inquired further, but he sensed a deep, cankering wound in Jason that was too painful to touch. So, with the tact that was second nature to him, he said nothing.

He tapped Jason's arm gently. "Why don't you get cleaned up, cousin. You look tired. I'll have Mrs. Jory show you to your room and send Astin, my valet, with a change of clothing. Then we'll sit down to dinner and talk some more."

Jason made no response, so Sherringham tugged the elaborate bellpull beside the fire. When Hastings entered a few moments later, he commanded, "Have Mrs. Jory prepare the oriental room for our guest. He wishes to bathe. Please tell Astin to take a complete suit of clothing to his room. We are about the same size." The butler nodded, his face wooden, and exited as quietly as he had entered.

The earl turned again to Jason and inquired, "Would you care for another brandy?"

Jason did not reply for a moment, then he visibly shook himself and moved away from the fire. "No thank you, I believe I'll go straight to my room. I am indeed weary. Perhaps a bath and a change of clothing will revive me."

He started for the door, but not before Sherringham caught a glimpse of pain in the younger man's eyes. There was more to this striking American relative than one would guess, and Sherringham was resolved to know him better.

They met the housekeeper as they left the study. She greeted Jason politely and escorted him up the enormous curving staircase.

Jason had not had time earlier to absorb his surroundings, so he paused on the landing to look about. He was impressed by the spacious hall, tiled in black and white Italian marble.

Glittering crystal chandeliers and wall sconces reflected off the polished surface. Two Louis XIV chairs sat against the wall, flanked by ornate gilded mirrors and a handsome inlaid oriental escritoire.

The housekeeper opened the third door on what seemed an endless corridor. Inside, the bedchamber proved a triumph of colors and elegance, from soft yellow damask papering the walls to the luxurious oriental rug covering the floor. An enormous four-poster bed sat on a raised dais, its bed hangings of scarlet and yellow silk brocade embroidered with dragons and cherry blossoms. Best of all, a steaming tub stood before a fire, and a suit of clothes lay neatly on the bed.

"If we can serve you further, sir, just ring." The housekeeper indicated the pull beside the bed and left the room.

Jason wearily stripped and stepped into the deep brass tub. He leaned back with a sigh and let the steam seep into his tired bones, relaxing him. He wished his unhappy memories could be shed as easily.

The news of his mother's remarriage had reopened wounds he thought long healed. The earl's obvious happiness about his impending marriage had irritated them until he could no longer repress his thoughts.

He remembered his mother as a light-hearted, loving, laughing presence that permeated his home with the soft glow only a well-loved woman gives off. Gradually over the years, the glow was muted to a glimmer as fights erupted between her and his father, Andrew.

Finally, when Jason was twelve, the glimmer died entirely when she—Bella—departed, leaving an embittered husband and grieving son behind. When a bewildered Jason pleaded with his father to bring her back, he met with cold rage. His father forbade him to mention her again and told him from that day forward, he had no mother. Jason heard Andrew mention her name only once again: when his father was in his cups and unaware that Jason was listening. His voice betrayed such anguish and longing that tears came to Jason's eyes.

Two years passed as he watched his father change from a hard but vigorous man into a drunkard. Gradually, his former love for his mother changed, first into resentment, then into a hatred all the more intense because of the love that had preceded it.

Jason's grandfather saw the anguish building in him and tried to intervene, but the damage was done. The boy was deaf to Thomas's explanation that his mother was unhappy in the wilds of Georgia. He added that Andrew's preoccupation with the plantation further strained their marriage. In addition, Andrew was arrogant, and his domination did not set well with his independent wife. Finally, in desperation, Thomas told Jason as delicately as possible about his father's mulatto mistress and how his mother's pride and love had been unable to sustain this final blow.

Indifferent to the reasons for his mother's departure, Jason was aware of only one fact: She deserted them when they both needed her. When Thomas's angry appeals finally pierced his son's melancholy, Andrew awoke to the realization of what his pain had done to his son. He tried to make amends by explaining the situation himself, but he was no more successful than Thomas had been. The world is black and white to a proud and passionate fourteen-year-old.

Jason and his father gradually patched up their former close relationship, but Jason's old admiration for Andrew had waned. Andrew once again took command of the plantation and tried to resume his former existence and regain his son's respect. He was unsuccessful in both attempts. When he decided to join an expedition exploring France's Louisiana Territory, Jason was almost relieved. When they received notice of Andrew's death eight months later, the final brick was set in the wall Jason had built around his emotions. The last residue of longing for his mother was vanquished as he resolved to never love a woman so he would never experience the desolation his father suffered.

As the years passed, Jason matured into an intelligent, strong man who was capable of giving and receiving great loyalty. However, he found strong emotions difficult to deal with, so he usually masked his feelings with cool indifference or anger. His mother's unanswered letters and invitations to visit Boston dwindled and finally ceased entirely.

Now, at thirty, Jason was a handsome man with a slight element of cruelty in his demeanor that piqued women's interest and drew them in swarms, with hopes of being the one to capture him. He flirted mercilessly with the belles of Savannah's fledgling society, deriving amusement at their humiliation when he turned his attention from one to another. His relief was found with whores and widows when opportunity arose, though he was not a constant seeker of such diversions. He felt one overriding emotion for all women, lady and harlot alike: contempt. He had yet to meet one he respected other than his old English nanny, long dead, and the mulatto housekeeper—at their plantation.

As Jason completed his ablutions, he deliberately cleared his mind of everything but eagerness for the night's event. He had spent a couple of moderately enjoyable evenings ashore with his men, gambling, drinking, and womanizing. However, he'd found their taste for hells and brothels a bit rough for his liking. He was certain the earl patronized much more select establishments. He preferred his women fresh and lovely, qualities usually found only in London's most exclusive brothels.

He felt most rejuvenated as he dressed in an exquisitely tailored wine velvet coat and nankeen trousers. Tying the cravat at his neck in a simple fall, he slipped into his leather shoes and mimed a mocking bow to his reflection. Then he quit the room his usual confident, arrogant self.

Sherringham spent the time before dinner working in his study. When he opened his desk drawer to search for a document, he came across the one and only letter he had ever received from his ward, Leanna. The handwriting was flowing and strong, but the wording was stilted and formal as she asked when she would be allowed to come to London. She made no mention of being unhappy in the country, but it was obvious she wanted to escape her cousin Edith's chaperonage.

Sherringham felt a twinge of guilt as he remembered he had put her off and then promptly forgot the matter. That was almost a year ago. Sighing, he admitted he had neglected his ward. He thought of her only on those occasions when his agent informed him the usual generous quarterly stipend had been sent to Edith. As he straightened his desk and locked his papers away, he resolved to send for her soon and have Abby introduce her to society. It was the least he could do for the poor child.

Jason and Sherringham met in the hall. As the earl led the way to the dining room, he complimented, "By Jove, Cousin, you look a different man! It's amazing what a bath and clean clothes will do for a fellow. How is the fit?"

"The coat is a mite short in the sleeves and large in the waist, but otherwise everything fits as though it were made for me. And I *feel* a different man, the important thing," Jason replied.

As they seated themselves a footman served the first dish. As course followed course and the wine flowed freely, Jason lost all stiffness and talked to the earl easily.

"Grandfather is having a fine time running the plantation while I control the shipping end. Savannah's port is small and primitive by London's standards, but it's growing. Since Whitney invented the cotton gin in '93, cotton has become a much more profitable crop. We have our own merchants' exchange on a bluff overlooking the river." He shrugged his broad shoulders. "Our society is still small and backward by eastern standards, but since trade has become more lucrative, we're importing more luxuries."

"Your profit could lead to England's doom," Sherringham said dryly.

Jason stiffened. "What do you mean by that, sir?"

"Come, Cousin," the earl chided, "you must know that our French ports blockade is ineffectual as long as you still trade under your so-called neutrality. As long as France receives steady supplies she'll be much harder to conquer. So unless you admittedly ingenious Americans at least moderate your trade with her, Boney will continue to terrorize the continent."

"May I remind you, Cousin," Jason's voice dripped ice, "that this war is not of our making? We'll trade with whomever we please as is our right. Your country lost the right to dictate to us when we won our freedom. All we want is to be left alone. But if you don't quit impressing our seamen, you'll have another enemy besides France to deal with."

They glared at each other angrily. Sherringham replied with equal ire. "Your government has not the right to shield our deserters. England must have enough sailors to man her fleets or the war is lost."

"If your countrymen desire to become Americans, we're happy to have them. Despite the claims of your government, they do not remain Britons until they die. Not to mention the number of Americans born and bred you've kidnaped in your search for 'deserters.'" Jason's voice calmed somewhat as his anger began to abate. "Besides, our seamen sail under much better conditions. If you Limeys would treat your sailors as men instead of animals, perhaps you'd have fewer deserters."

The earl's face darkened at the sarcasm, but he merely retaliated: "I concede our conditions at sea are not as easy. But dash it, man, we're at war! Our officers are not pampered either. Until this conflict is resolved we cannot spare sadly-needed funds to make conditions more comfortable."

With an effort, the earl smiled. "But come, Cousin, let us not discuss politics further. That's not why you're here. What is your full name? I assume you're named after Father?"

Jason readily agreed to the change of topic. "Indeed I am, but my middle name is Andrew instead of Arthur."

"Luckily my friends call me Sherry, otherwise it could become quite confusing," he smiled. "We are going to visit La Bianca's tomorrow evening, one of the most select brothels in London. We have quite a party planned. And of course in the afternoon we will visit White's, my club. If you desire to have clothes made, I suggest you visit Weston's early tomorrow while I'm at the War Office. No one can cut a coat like him."

"I'll be glad to join the celebration," Jason responded. "But the next day I must attend to business matters. I'd like to sail by early November."

He yawned, excused himself, and said, "You'll pardon me if I forgo the port and retire?"

Sherry nodded. "Certainly. I, too, am tired. Besides, we'll have an exhausting day tomorrow and had best be hale and hearty for the evening." He dropped a suggestive wink and grinned.

Jason laughed and rose. They bade one another good night and parted at the top of the stairs, Sherry to dream of his betrothed, and Jason to sleep unaware that his well-charted life was about to have its course abruptly and forever altered.

Chapter
Three

THE NEXT AFTERNOON, Jason strolled to White's with Sherry. He had spent an enjoyable and productive morning at Weston's ordering a new wardrobe for himself and his grandfather. While Savannah's stock of tradesmen was expanding, the city as yet could boast no tailors of Weston's caliber. He had also ordered dishes, silver, and elegant Chippendale furniture to take back to Whispering Oaks. As the plantation became more profitable, Thomas had slowly redecorated the house until its beauty rivaled any around Savannah. He had given Jason a specific order of items to purchase that were as yet unavailable or of inferior quality in Georgia. Jason felt he had ordered goods his grandfather would be pleased with.

His satisfaction was complete when Sherry met him with the news that his ship was released. In a harmonious and gratified mood he entered that most hallowed of gentlemen's clubs, White's.

The interior was subdued and quiet at this early time of the day. A few gentlemen sat about, smoking, reading, or quietly playing cards. The rooms were permeated with the smell of cigar smoke, expensive brandy, and good leather. The exclusive atmosphere trumpeted the wealth of its patrons.

Sherry was greeted by numerous friends, to whom he in turn introduced Jason. He was especially warm to the gentleman who hailed him from a corner table. "Sherry, old fellow, well met! I was about to call on you to finalize our plans for this evening."

The earl smiled and waved. "Harry, how good to see you! I, too, need to discuss our plans. May I present my cousin Jason Blaine?"

Jason shook hands with the hefty, red-headed gentleman of about his own age. He looked humored. "By Jove, it's obvious you're related to Sherry," he said. "Gave me a start when you entered. Glad to meet you. Harry Jeffries is the name. Are you one of the relatives from America?"

He didn't give Jason an opportunity to reply. "Never thought there would be another fellow as handsome as Sherry. Devil take it, we finally get him leg-shackled and demmed if his cousin don't show up as more competition. Plan on staying long?"

It was impossible for Jason to take offense at the question because it was asked jokingly, in the manner of a child about to have a long-desired treat snatched away.

Before Harry could draw breath and continue, Sherry interjected. "Excuse him, cousin—he's not as dim-witted as he seems. You'll find the only way to deal with Harry is to interrupt loudly when you have something to say."

Jason laughed as Harry playfully poked Sherry in the ribs. He listened as the amiable banter continued between the two friends. They sat down and ordered drinks, then concluded their plans for the evening.

"Right, then, we'll meet at La Bianca's at nine o'clock to celebrate Harry's birthday," Sherry said, taking a sip of his wine.

Harry also took a sip, then he amused Sherry by rhapsodizing about a girl he had met that day. He said dreamily, "She was the most beautiful angel I've ever seen. Hair as golden as new-minted guineas and the figure and eyes of a goddess. But dash it, the old gorgon she was with sent me off before I could discover her lodgings."

Sherry inserted laughingly, "In love again, old fellow? I hope you'll let us meet this mystery goddess, when you find her."

Neither of them noticed Jason's disdainfully curled lip. He thought the wench was probably as treacherous as she was beautiful. Most likely she'd engineered the meeting in an attempt to catch a wealthy husband. She'd avoided him, in order to pique Harry's interest. She would now plan another "accidental" meeting. Jason preferred an honest whore over a deceitful society bitch any time.

None of these thoughts were expressed as he listened to Harry moan. "I'm looking for her, Sherry. I've met the perfect woman this time."

Sherry shook his head in despair. "That's what you said about the Devon chit, the Haviland girl...." Sherry's words trailed off as he glanced up and met the gaze of the gentleman who had just entered. Jason saw his animation fade. He followed Sherry's eyes and saw a small exquisite blond gliding gracefully toward them.

He had the most perfect features Jason had ever seen on a man. Indeed, in different clothes and with longer hair, he could have passed for a beautiful woman. He approached their table, shattering the impression of femininity when he spoke in the deepest, smoothest voice Jason had ever heard. The velvet tones made Jason uneasy. They could be likened to a dangerous sheet of ice that would break and drown a man lest he trod warily.

"Greetings, Sherringham, Jeffries. I understand you're planning a little celebration tonight." His limpid blue eyes narrowed when he saw Jason, and for a moment he looked startled. Then he sneered, "Quite burning the candle at both ends, aren't you, Sherringham? Of course, if I were about to wed, I'd probably do the same. Even the fair Abby will become less than exciting after the novelty has worn off and her, er, freshness has diminished. But then, one would still have all those lovely golden guineas to comfort one, eh?"

Sherry jumped to his feet, enraged, but the golden-haired

man retreated with a jeering laugh. Sherry would have followed, but Harry grabbed his arm and spoke quietly, his manner for once serious and determined.

"Sherry, it will only be food for gossip if you retaliate. Everyone knows you have no need of Abby's fortune. He's only trying to provoke you into a challenge. You know dueling is forbidden. Besides, he would stand a good chance of killing you. Fop he might be, but he's deadly with a pistol. Nor is it beyond his means to fire early. And if you killed him you'd have to flee England." His voice lightened as he teased, "I'm sure Abby would enjoy her honeymoon on the continent, but not quite in those circumstances, what?"

Sherry's arm went flaccid and he reseated himself, muttering, "You're right, Harry." His voice became fierce again as he added, "But by God, some day that bastard will overstep himself. I'll bide my time, but I'll catch him at his dirty dealings somehow."

Sherry turned to Jason with a hooded look. He seemed to be torn between anger, regret, and sadness as he explained, "It was not always thus between us. Once, we were very close." He stared into the distance as though searching the past.

"Our estates bordered as boys, and all through our years at Eton, we were the best of friends. Now, I realize there was always a streak of cruelty and ruthlessness in him. But he didn't become the way he is until his mother died and his father lost their estates. Gavin began drinking and gambling in an effort to forget his problems, but naturally, his activities only increased his difficulties."

Sherry shook his head, a frown creasing his strong mouth. "I did what I could, but he saw my advice as interference. He barely made it into Oxford. Because of his late nights, he began cheating on exams. We had drifted apart before this time. One night in our second term, he came to me to plead for my help in writing a history paper. I refused, of course. He was expelled for cheating soon afterward, and from that time onward, we became bitter enemies."

Sherry gulped his brandy as though to rinse a sour taste from his mouth. "He had an influential uncle who finally obtained his readmission when I was in my final year. I was involved in athletics, my marks were high, my family was wealthy, and I was reasonably successful with women."

Harry laughed heartily at this understatement. "Fess up, old boy, you were a regular devil. Still would be, if it weren't for Abby."

Sherry spread his hands as though to say "What else is a man to do?" Jason laughed. Sherry finished as if eager to get the unpleasant task over with. "Gavin was jealous of what he thought was my greater advantage in life. When his uncle disinherited him because of his libertine ways, I think Gavin blamed me for that, too."

Sherry sighed. "He was one of Abby's many suitors. She never seriously considered him, though his vanity wouldn't let him believe it. Now I have won Abby from under his nose, I'm afraid he'll hate me more than ever." The table was grim and silent for some time.

Suddenly, Sherry burst out with a bitter laugh and turned to Jason. "Sorry you had to sit through that, Cousin. As you can see, Sir Gavin Redfern would like nothing better than to rid the world of me and comfort Abby in my stead. If he doesn't settle his debts soon, he'll end in debtor's jail."

Jason spoke quietly. "I quite understand, Cousin. I've got my fair share of enemies. I would agree with Harry. Nothing would delight him more than to provoke you into a duel. I'd hazard a guess that the best way to deal with him is to ignore him entirely."

"I agree, Sherry," Harry nodded. "That will make him madder than anything else you could do. 'Tis a fitting revenge."

"I guess you're both right," Sherry conceded reluctantly. "But it goes against the grain letting him insult Abby without retaliation. Well, let's forget the matter." Grinning to ease the tension in the air, he joked, "Damn me, Harry, I've never seen you so serious. I thought we came here to play cards. Let's see if I can fleece you as usual."

His companions smiled and settled down at a green baize table to while away the afternoon in several enjoyable games of faro.

* * *

As Jason spent the afternoon in masculine pursuits, Leanna trembled with a fear only a woman alone and afraid of violation can know. After she was roughly shoved inside an obscenely plush bedchamber, she stood in the middle of the room, her surroundings heightening her fears.

The purple and gold theme downstairs echoed throughout this chamber. An embossed gold design papered the walls and purple and gold fabrics carpeted the floor. Naked marble figurines in wall alcoves reflected obscenely in the large mirrors that surrounded the room. The vast mahogany bed was carved with mythological scenes such as Hades abducting Persephone and Zeus as a swan seducing Leda. The fact that Leanna knew the stories behind the scenes reinforced her fear.

She stumbled to a gold velvet tasseled sofa by the marble fireplace and sat down. She tried to subdue her rising panic, but her thoughts were too disjointed. All she could think was, How could I have been so blind?

Like all girls, Leanna had dreamed of winning a handsome husband. She pictured him as tall and kind, the image of her father. Her parents' happy union became the model upon which she fashioned her ideas about marriage. She knew when she finally married the man of her dreams, their vows would be founded on the same love and respect that formed her parents' happiness.

She had never thought much about the sex act. She was vaguely familiar with the process from her readings and the animals on the duke's estate. Unlike most ladies of her age, she had no fear of it, for her mother had taken pains to inform her of its beauty when performed between two people in love.

Now Leanna feared that unless she could escape, all her chances for a happy marriage would shatter with her lost maidenhead. It meant social ostracism for a young gentlewoman to lose her virginity before marriage.

Leanna clenched her teeth and tried to think calmly. It was indeed likely that Edith would not question the lack of correspondence. When the earl received her reply from the Duke of Chester concerning her request for a job, he would doubtless question her whereabouts, but she couldn't wait that long if she was to save herself. A deep anger began to build in her toward the earl, an anger that overshadowed her former resentment. If he had shown more concern for her happiness, she would not be here. The ire she felt acted on her like a tonic, subduing her panic, and she looked about her for a means of escape.

She examined the room for windows, but could find none. The door was locked and appeared to be the only exit from the room. Her only option, it seemed, was to find some sort of weapon, render her captor unconscious as he entered the room, and flee while the door was open.

A little calmer now that she chose an action, Leanna walked over to one of the marble figurines and attempted to lift it. It was far too heavy. She looked at the fireplace, but there were no flanking andirons, nor were there logs in the empty grate. In desperation, she circled the room again and stopped when she spied a gold ormolu clock on a table by the bed. She lifted it experimentally, grunting. It was heavy and unwieldy, but it should wield considerable force if she could heave it in the right direction. She pulled a chair close to the door, cradled the clock in her lap, and waited in grim silence.

Before thirty minutes had passed, she heard a key rattle in the lock. She quickly leaped behind the door. She lifted the clock with some difficulty over her head and brought it down with all the strength she could muster on the frizzy brown head of Mrs. Horton. As the woman fell unconscious to the floor, Leanna jumped over her and out the door—straight into the iron arms of Beekins. She had barely registered the fact before he raised his huge fist and hit her in the jaw. She collapsed into a heap beside Mrs. Horton.

When she recovered consciousness hours later, she was lying on the bed, once again alone. She looked around for a moment, disoriented, then remembered in a rush. She buried her aching head in the pillow and sobbed, no longer able to hold her fear at bay.

The door opened and Mrs. Horton entered. Beekins followed. Leanna stiffened, surreptitiously wiping her cheeks, and tried to look composed. For the first time she noticed the noisy music and laughter floating up from downstairs. The sounds were muted as the door closed. Mrs. Horton advanced to the bed, an ugly look on her face.

Leanna lifted her chin as she met the irate gaze. Terrified she might be, but she would not give her jailers the satisfaction of seeing it.

Her cheeks flushed with anger, Mrs. Horton spoke. "If I didn't stand to gain a tidy little profit on your innocence, bitch, I'd let Beekins initiate you as he does all my girls." Her thin lips stretched into a sly smile. "But when Sir Gavin is finished with you, I think you'll find that Beekins is mild in comparison."

Leanna's face paled, delineating the bruise on her jaw in sharp relief. She noticed Beekins's eyes raking her body and saw him lick his fat lips in excitement. She followed his gaze and gasped in horror. Her sober morning dress had vanished and she was now clothed in a sheer black lace nightdress. She jerked the covers up the shield herself.

Mrs. Horton laughed harshly and Beekins's eyes glowed brighter. "Modest miss, ain't she, Beekins?" she jeered. "You'll not have reason to be modest after tonight, gal." She pulled a small brown bottle from the pocket of her dress and uncapped the lid, then she climbed on the bed to straddle Leanna's legs.

"Hold her," she commanded the servant. As he crushed Leanna's arms above her head, Mrs. Horton muttered, "You'll not hold your tongue without a little assistance. We can't have you ruining our tidy little plan, now can we, dearie?"

Leanna struggled in fury to no avail. Her nose was held and her jaw was pried open. She gagged as a bitter liquid was poured down her throat. She was forced to swallow or strangle. Mrs. Horton roughly jerked her off the bed, pulled a brush from a drawer and yanked it through her hair.

Beekins rearranged the covers and folded them back neatly. Leanna swayed as the medicine began to take effect. Mrs. Horton shoved her back on the bed and fanned her hair out over the pillow. She jerked Leanna's face around and bent down to hiss, "If you struggle, you'll only make it hard on yourself. I wouldn't tell the gentleman you're being held against your will, either. The gentry have odd ideas of entertainment and he might think you're inviting him to play a little game." She smiled maliciously. "A little game I'm sure you wouldn't like."

"Have fun, my dear," she finished with relish. She beckoned to Beekins, who followed her reluctantly from the room. Leanna rose in an effort to reach the door, then grabbed the bedpost as the floor swayed under her feet. She crumpled back onto the bed and lay there weakly, too physically enervated to cry and too frightened to do anything but tremble.

Downstairs, Jason was having a delightful time. He cuddled a petite redhead in his arms and laughed as he watched Harry dance drunkenly down the table with a voluptuous blonde clad in a sheer chemise and stockings.

The party had been boisterous, but was gradually winding down now that the cake had been cut and gallons of champagne consumed. Jason surveyed the couples around him, each individual in various stages of deshabille, and smiled regretfully as he thought of Sherry, called away to the War Office right before their departure. He was doubtless ensconced in some dusty office, listening to the latest gloomy report.

Jason toasted his absent cousin, drank the last of his champagne, and patted the redhead on her shapely thigh, intending to rise and follow his fellow revelers up the stairs. Just then, a thin, sallow-faced woman descended like an angry hornet and pulled the girl from Jason's lap, snapping, "Bessie, I told you not to come back until you'd seen a doctor. Sorry, your lordship, the girl is not clean."

Bessie, obviously bewildered, protested, "But mum, I ain't had the—" The woman slapped her before she could finish, then commanded roughly, "Be gone! And don't come back until you're healed!" She pushed the girl out the door and groveled an apology to Jason.

"My lord, I have a girl upstairs who should suit your taste better than Bessie," she grinned obsequiously. Jason started to correct her in the use of the title, then shrugged his shoulders as she continued before he could speak. "She's our newest girl and is fresh as a daisy."

The woman was escorting him up the stairs as she spoke

and she continued to praise the unknown girl. Jason followed readily enough. What difference did it make? A woman was a woman, after all. This wench would probably suit him just as well as the other.

She opened a door at the end of the corridor, unlocking it first. Jason thought it a bit odd that the girl was locked in, but when the woman pushed him inside and shut the door behind him, all thought fled at the sight before him.

A girl was reclining on the bed. She was dressed in a black lace nightdress with a deeply scooped neckline that revealed a lovely expanse of white, silky skin. The straight gown was slit up the sides, displaying a rich thigh invitingly. The lacy material clung to rather than concealed her lush curves, titillating his already aroused senses.

Her bountiful golden locks were spread over the pillow and over the edge of the bed, almost reaching the floor. Her small features were the loveliest he had ever seen, with fine-textured skin glowing a soft, creamy peach. Her full pink lips drew him like a magnet as he walked closer to the bed. He had never seen such a sensuous mouth.

He sat down on the bed beside her and asked softly, "What is your name?"

For the first time her eyes opened and his captivation was complete when he gazed into green depths as unfathomable as a primeval forest. Her lips moved softly and he had to bend his head to hear the words, "No, no, please . . ." The words faded and she sighed, as though the effort of speaking drained her. He scrutinized her coloring and for the first time realized that the flush in her cheeks might be due to drink.

"Lovely lady, it seems we've both imbibed too freely this evening," he laughed softly, beginning to undress. Her eyes widened as she watched, and Jason thought he saw fear in her gaze.

"Don't be afraid. My tastes are quite normal. I promise you I'll be as gentle as possible," he comforted as he peeled off the last of his garments and lay down beside her. "My name is Jason Blaine," he murmured, drawing her gently to him.

Leanna's heart was beating like the wings of a hummingbird,

and when she got her first glimpse of a naked, aroused male, all her instincts clamored for escape. The only movement she could manage, however, was a restless shaking of her head. She would wonder later why his name didn't alert her, but her terror was too great to allow for calm thought.

He stroked her cheek gently, trying to soothe her fears. He grazed her brow with light kisses and his hands wandered leisurely over her shoulders, easing the neckline down until her full breasts were revealed in all their beauty. He groaned in passion and began to kiss her heatedly, savoring the sweet moistness of her mouth and the round, satiny flesh of her body.

Leanna yielded helplessly, too weak to struggle. The heated assault on her senses terrified her, especially when he forced her mouth open and thrust his tongue within. He explored her there as languorously as his hands caressed her body. He was slowly sliding up the hem of the gown until it bunched around her waist. His mouth left a trail of fire as he traversed her neck and journeyed around one full breast. He finally drew the soft nipple into his mouth and sucked until he felt it harden.

Leanna gasped at the sensation spinning through her body and some of his passion communicated itself to her. When he raised himself to devour her mouth, she responded hesitantly until she felt his probing fingers stroking the inside of her thighs, when she gasped and tried to push him away.

He growled deep in his throat and pulled the gown over her head, no obstacle now barring him from his goal as he parted her thighs with his knee and lowered his body over hers. Her terror returned when she felt his hardness probing high between her legs. She tried again to push him away and struggled to get words past her dry throat, but all she could muster was a faint moan.

Her terror failed to penetrate his senses, which were befuddled by champagne and passion. He was aware only of her beauty beneath him and the throbbing of his manhood that wanted release within the soft warmth of her body.

He set himself firmly against her and thrust as gently as his passion would allow between her legs. She gasped in pain and opened her mouth to scream when he thrust again, deeper, but the sound was muffled against his mouth as he once more drank from her lips. He thrust again, harder, and when he could still not enter he pulled back in puzzlement. She was white, biting her lip in pain, and abruptly he realized that she was untouched.

He was both startled and obscurely pleased. He had never bedded a virgin before, and somehow it seemed totally fitting that he should be the first man with this beautiful creature. He once again started to kiss her when he sensed her relax as the pain faded.

He probed her small ear with his tongue, then fastened his mouth over hers as his desire reached a peak. He groaned, "I can't wait any longer," caught her buttocks in his hands and drove deep, momentarily uncaring of the pain he caused her.

She sobbed as she felt a fiery sword pierce her to the quick. He thrust faster and faster, nearing completion, her tight softness arousing him unbearably. Abruptly he rammed as deeply as she would allow, then he tensed and shuddered as the most pleasurable spasms he had ever felt coursed through his body.

Leanna knew what was happening as she felt the warm liquid filling her. She stiffened in revulsion, but it was far too late. As he relaxed above her, spent, she was torn between hatred of him, herself for being such a fool, and the earl for letting his neglect bring her to such ruin.

Jason withdrew with a gentleness that came too late and apologized softly, "I could not contain my passions longer. I'm sorry I hurt you, but you have a beauty that drives a man wild. I'll make it worth your while." When she didn't respond, but lay with her eyes shut, he collapsed beside her, exhausted, and slept soundly.

Leanna cried until her pillow was saturated, moved as far to the edge of the bed as her aching body and the dregs of the drug would allow and slept restlessly.

She bolted awake sometime later at the sound of voices and opened her eyes to see an enraged blond-haired man standing at the side of the bed. He snarled, "You fool, that's the ward of the Earl of Sherringham you've just bedded," to the man still lying beside her. The man whitened and turned to glare at her.

"Is that true?" he barked, his eyes narrow with suspicion. She glared back, then nodded silently.

Jason stared at the angry figure before them. He purred, "And how do you know who she is? Could it be you planned for someone else to be in this bed rather than me?"

The man looked at him haughtily. "Certainly not! I've only seen the girl once. It's pure chance that I entered this room by mistake." His white teeth gleamed in a malicious smile. "But it's your mistake I should be worried about, if I were you. Sherringham will not be pleased when he finds out you've ravished his ward." He gave them both a last withering look and wheeled abruptly from the room.

Jason leaped out of bed, jerked on his breeches, eased out the door, and stealthily followed Sir Gavin down the stairs. The sallow-faced woman met him at the bottom. Sir Gavin spit at her furiously, "God dammit, you bitch, that's Sherringham's cousin. Don't you know an American accent when you hear one?" His voice faded as they moved away, but Jason had heard enough for his suspicions to be confirmed.

He strode back upstairs to find the girl scrubbing at herself roughly, as though she were begrimed and stained for life. He stopped dead at the sight of her, amazed that she looked even more beautiful to him this morning. His gaze raked her body hungrily, lingering on the firm breasts and slender legs. She grabbed a towel to cover herself and stared at him with hatred.

He schooled his expression to silence and strode up to catch her arms. "You'd better be who you say you are," he swore. "If you're a partner to Sir Gavin's scheme, you'll rue the day you met me, girl."

"I already rue that day, I assure you, sir," she snapped hatefully. For the first time she realized he had an American accent. She jibed, "If you're American that in part explains the boorishness of your conduct."

Jason stiffened in rage. He yanked her closer to hiss, "You'll get another taste of my boorish behavior if you don't keep a civil tongue in your mouth, my girl." He crushed her against him to punctuate his warning. The towel slipped and her full breasts pressed against his chest, a contact that had immediate impact on them both. She struggled wildly, the pain of last night a vivid memory, and he thrust her away in disgust, her softness tempting him to repeat the pleasurable experience that still haunted him in the cold light of day.

He moved abruptly away and snarled, "Get dressed and we'll see if you're lying or not." He jerked up the rest of his scattered clothes and began to dress hastily. She retrieved the slipped towel, but remained where she was.

He snapped, "Well?"

"I don't know where my clothes are and I will not dress in your presence," she said with finality.

He stalked over to the armoire to fling open the door, clad only in boots and breeches. Despite herself, she admired the muscular width of his back, his firm legs, and almost animal energy.

He threw her clothes at her and sneered, "It's a pity you caught the wrong game in your little trap. Sir Gavin will not be complacent even if the earl doesn't press charges."

"If you're referring to the man who was just here, I've never seen him before," she said through her teeth. "I was the one trapped. Apparently you were too drunk or too stupid to realize I was locked in. And I didn't get this bruise by myself." She flung her chin at him defiantly, and for the first time he noticed the small blue mark on her jaw.

"That remains to be seen," he replied coldly. He combed a hand through his hair and ordered, "Get dressed and we'll let the earl decide this. If you're lying..." He left the sentence unfinished, but the threat glistened as clearly as an unsheathed sword between them. She couldn't stifle the tingle of fear that went up her spine as she met his hard gaze.

Then her chin came up as she seethed inwardly. After all, she was the one wronged. He had the audacity to accuse her of duplicity when he should be apologizing to her on bended knee. She vowed then and there that she would make him very sorry for what he had done to her if it was the last thing she ever did.

She glared at him for a moment, then wrapped the towel around herself more securely, grabbed her clothes, and walked with a queenly dignity to the wardrobe screen in the corner.

As they dressed, each dreaded the coming meeting with the earl for different reasons. Inwardly, Jason was hoping feverishly that the girl was not who she claimed. If she was, he had a cold feeling in the pit of his gut that he couldn't extricate himself without marrying her. Leanna was disgusted at the explanations made by the man she considered her nemesis, and she was deathly afraid of her future.

Chapter
Four

JASON HELD THE door with a mocking bow when they had
finished dressing. She ignored him and drew her skirts aside
as she passed, as though contact with him would contaminate
her. His mouth tightened as he slammed the door behind them,
but he let the insult pass. They were halted in their march to
the stairs by an agonized moan. Both looked around, startled.
They saw a trembling hand grasp the doorknob at the end of
the hall.

The hand was followed by a husky body, bent in pain. The
apparition's knees wobbled as though at any moment it would
fall to the floor. Jason and Leanna recognized the figure si-
multaneously.

"Harry! You look like you've been keel-hauled. Quite a
party, eh?" Jason teased unmercifully.

Leanna exclaimed in concern, "Mr. Jeffries! Are you ill?"

They looked with equal suspicion at one another when they

realized both were familiar with the gentleman. Harry's head jerked when he heard his name called and he groaned as pain shot up his neck. His bleary eyes focused with difficulty on Jason, then he blinked groggily at Leanna.

He blinked again, and when she didn't disappear, he croaked, "What are you doing here, my lady?"

Leanna flushed to the roots of her hair, too embarrassed to reply. Jason answered easily, "She was my partner for the evening, of course. And most talented she was, too."

Harry's eyes bulged, and he looked askance at Leanna, waiting for her to deny the statement. She shot daggers at Jason, hesitated as though debating a reply, then looked contemptuously at them both before she turned away to march down the stairs. Men! They were all alike. Even the nice Mr. Jeffries had a typical male appetite, judging from his appearance this morning.

Harry followed slowly, his aching brain too tired to try and solve the riddle of her presence. Jason halted him at the top of the stairs to demand, "Where did you meet her, Harry?"

Harry mumbled, "She's the girl I told you about. Can't understand why she's here, though. Would have sworn she was a lady." He looked so downcast that Jason was tempted to laugh.

Jason moved down the stairs again to catch up with Leanna, but he froze when he saw the sallow-faced woman rush into the hall in a threatening matter. "Not so fast, my dear. You won't escape so easily. I have to have some compensation for the trouble you've caused me...." She cried out Beekins's name.

Harry tensed to move to Leanna's aid, but Jason held his arm. He wanted to see if the woman would unknowingly confirm the girl's story. Beekins lumbered into the hall and gripped Leanna's shoulder. Her spirit finally broke as she felt the chains of bondage closing around her again. She kicked and screamed hysterically, "No, not again! Please, please, let me go!" As she flailed, Jason knew what would come next. He catapulted down the stairs before Beekins's raised fist could fall.

Harry followed and planted himself firmly by Jason, standing as straight as his aching body would allow. The servant lowered his head on his brawny neck as he prepared to charge like an enraged bull.

"Stop, you fool," Mrs. Horton hissed. She turned to Harry and reprimanded mildly, "Now, your lordship, you know it's not done to interfere with my girls. You've paid your shot and I'm grateful, but you really must leave now. This little minx will calm down after she's been here longer. We'll take good care of her." She tried to pull the sobbing girl out of Jason's arms, but he cradled Leanna closer.

He replied softly, "Yes, I've seen the care you've taken of her." He stroked Leanna's bruised jaw. "I don't believe she's one of your girls or that she's here by choice. Now, you'd do well to let us go without further trouble." His voice was mild, but the threat was clear.

She moved from the door in helpless rage. "You've not heard the last of this," she spat. "Sir Gavin does not take kindly to people who meddle in his affairs."

Jason bowed mockingly. "Nor does he take kindly to bunglers. And you can tell him from me and the Earl of Sherringham that *he* hasn't heard the last of this." His voice sent a shiver down Mrs. Horton's spine. For a moment fear showed in her eyes, then she pushed them out the door and slammed it behind them.

A weak Leanna sagged against Jason as he carried her to Harry's carriage. Inside, he cradled her tenderly in his arms. He was still not certain if she was genuine, but her fear was real enough and instinctively he tried to comfort her. She huddled against him, too dazed to notice that the rough stranger of last night had become a tender protector, if momentarily.

Harry sat opposite them as the carriage swayed through the streets. He asked in bewilderment, "What was that all about? What has Sir Gavin to do with this?"

Jason responded tersely, "Later." He massaged Leanna's neck with gentle fingers as he tried to soothe some of the tension away.

When they halted at the earl's townhouse, Jason gently lifted Leanna down from the carriage. She peered around with vague eyes, seeing huge, immaculate grounds surrounding a massive, imposing edifice of yellow brick that rose three austere stories above the ground. Black ironwork laced around the balconies and windows, saving the townhouse from total severity.

Leanna's shock gradually dissipated as she absorbed her regal surroundings. Her trembling slowed and stopped as she realized she had at last escaped. As her spirit bounded, her eyes narrowed in rage and her ire toward her guardian returned.

Harry grasped Leanna's arm to escort her up the semicircular steps, saying, "I'm sure you're longing for refreshment. Our host is one of the most gracious in London, and I know he'll be delighted to assist you in any way he can."

Harry rambled on, extolling Sherry's virtues, unaware of the fire growing in Leanna's eyes or the tight set of her soft mouth. Hastings opened the vast mahogany door before they reached it and greeted Harry and Jason sedately.

Harry asked as he took their hats, "Is his lordship in, Hastings?"

The butler replied, "Indeed, sir, he just returned from the War Office. He will be down directly." He looked inquiringly at Leanna.

"Leanna Hardwicke," she said curtly, aware that neither Jason nor Harry knew her name. Harry looked startled and would have spoken, but Jason grabbed him by the arm and pulled him toward the study.

"Please see that Miss Hardwicke has refreshment, Hastings. And notify the earl that we're back." He pushed Harry into the study and closed the door behind them.

Hastings felt the anger blaze in Leanna. He requested warily, "Please follow me, my lady." She stepped in behind him, relishing the picture in her mind of Jason and the earl bound and at her mercy. She was unsure of what she wanted to do with them, but she knew harsh punishment would be too lenient.

In the study, Harry expostulated, "My God, Jason, do you know who that girl is?"

Jason replied dryly, "I know who she says she is. I must admit that so far the evidence confirms her story. Will Sherry recognize her?"

Harry was as terse as Jason had been earlier. "Don't know. Hasn't seen her since she was a babe. Devil take it, man, do you know what you've done?"

Jason slumped into a chair without answering, but the moody look on his face was reply enough. Harry sat down also, still stunned.

"What was all that about Sir Gavin?"

"It seems he's the one behind this comedy of errors," Jason responded glumly. "I believe Sherry was the intended prey, probably to prevent him from marrying. However, proving it will be difficult unless we can get that old crone to give witness against him."

Harry nodded, unsurprised. As soon as he heard Sir Gavin's name, he had been sure Sherry was involved. His round face was wry when he looked at Jason. "You know you'll have to marry the girl, don't you?"

Jason replied grimly, "We'll see. Perhaps I can find a home for her somewhere. She certainly will have no desire to come back to America with me. We're too *boorish* for her ladyship's taste."

Harry could see he was still smarting from the remark. He found it difficult to feel sorry for Jason, however, when he recalled Leanna's beauty and smothered a sigh of envy.

The door opened and a jubilant Sherry entered. He appeared so gleeful that Harry and Jason were almost affronted.

Sherry laughed as he looked at them both. "I've never seen two such glum fellows. You should be contented as cats after last night. What's amiss?" Before either of them could answer, he bubbled on, "But let me give you my good news first."

He sat down next to Jason on the sofa, smiling briskly. "You may have suspected, Harry, that Boney was going to attempt again to invade?" Harry nodded and listened eagerly. Sherry continued, "We'd heard the French fleet combined with the Spanish to give them a far superior advantage. But by God, that didn't stop Nelson. He engaged them off the Spanish coast at a cape called Trafalgar. He was brilliant, Harry! He cut across the Villeneuve battle line and destroyed over half their fleet! And it's hard to believe, but we didn't lose a single ship!"

Even Jason was struck with admiration for a naval battle that was to be remembered as one of the most decisive and brilliant in history.

Sherry's face saddened as he continued in a subdued tone, "But we lost Nelson. He was wounded and died during the battle. England has lost a great admiral." He bowed his head for a moment and Jason saw moisture come to his eyes. Harry also bent his head.

All silent a moment, Sherry suddenly became animated. "What happened last night to cause those long faces I saw when I came in?"

Harry waited for Jason to respond, and when he remained wooden, Harry answered. "Sherry, how long has it been since you saw your ward?"

His brow creased in puzzlement, then he replied slowly, "I haven't seen her since she was a babe. Why?"

"Would you know her if you saw her?" Jason asked.

"I imagine so. She has an identifying mole, as I recall."

Jason stiffened. "Where?" he asked with foreboding.

"On her left shoulder." He watched as Jason groaned and sank his head in his hands.

Beginning to feel uneasy, Sherry asked, "What is this all about? Do you mean to tell me Leanna is here?"

Harry nodded when Jason didn't answer. He went over to the brandy decanter, poured a stiff drink, and handed it to Sherry.

Sherry looked from the brandy to Harry's grim expression, to Jason's bent head, and back to the glass. Without a word he took a large gulp, despite the early hour. He suspected he was going to need it. He coughed as the brandy burned a trail down his throat, then he croaked, "Now for God's sake, tell me what's going on!"

He sat quietly as Harry told him the story as briefly as possible. His face flushed with anger as he listened. "By God, I'll get that bastard this time. How dare he? An innocent girl! Will he stop at nothing?"

Harry let him rant on, then suggested, "Jason believes we might be able to persuade the madam to testify against him."

Sherry pursed his mouth, then nodded. "I'll get on it right away." He turned to Jason and said slowly, "You know you'll have to marry her, don't you, cousin?"

Jason looked away for a moment, then grated, "I doubt she'll have me, cousin. I confess I have no desire for a wife, especially not a society girl." A girl like my mother, he said to himself.

"Nevertheless, you must marry her, Cousin. She's ruined unless you do." Sherry sighed regretfully. "I'm more sorry than I can say that the trap meant for me closed around you instead. I wish I could do something to change that, but I can't. Only you can make restitution. I will, of course, settle a large dowry on her."

He became brisk as Jason didn't respond. "Come, Cousin, if she's anything like her mother, she's a real jewel."

Harry piped in, "One of the most beautiful women I've ever seen, Sherry. She's the girl I met by accident yesterday. The old hag with her was the madam. I wish I'd known—perhaps I could have prevented this. I wonder how they came to be together? I'd swear Leanna didn't know who the woman was."

"I'm afraid Leanna has not been out in the world much since her parents died. The woman probably told her some credible tale."

The earl turned toward the door. "I'd best speak to her and get it over with. I'll be back directly, Jason. Please wait here. We have arrangements to make."

Jason nodded reluctantly. He tried to ignore the queasiness in his stomach as he contemplated his future. It wasn't just that he had no desire to be encumbered with a wife. Instinctively, he recognized in Leanna a threat to his peace of mind. Still, her distaste for him should make it easier to stay aloof. He'd use her as housekeeper and mistress, but never as a soul mate. He relaxed somewhat as he savored the thought of that beautiful body that would soon belong to him, and only to him. This marriage was not of his choosing, but it had its compensations.

Leanna prowled up and down the morning room, waiting. She would derive great pleasure from telling the great Earl of Sherringham what she thought of him, then she would escape his house as fast as her legs could carry her. She hoped she'd never have to see either the earl or Jason again. She smothered the practical side of her nature when it tried to frighten her with remembrances of the dangers that awaited unprotected girls in London. There were societies that helped girls in her position, and she could probably find employment soon, she comforted herself.

The door opened and she whirled to confront the handsome man who entered. For a moment her anger fled in astonishment. This man nearly mirrored the appearance of Jason. He stared at her in equal amazement, startled by her beauty. She was even more lovely than her mother.

Leanna recovered first and watched with cold contempt as he advanced toward her, arms outstretched. "My dear, you are very like your lovely mother. I have rarely seen such beauty. I know your parents would be proud of you, as I am."

Leanna stepped away when he would have embraced her. He felt like a loathsome insect she wanted to squash as she sneered, "Indeed, sir, your pride in me in the past has been evident. Your concern is much appreciated."

He had the grace to flush, and for a moment the confident earl looked abashed. Then he said kindly, "I felt you would be happier at your cousin's until I could find the time to present you into society. I know you would have been very lonely here because I am rarely home. I intended to send for you soon."

As she looked skeptical, he insisted, "My concern for you has been great. Surely you don't think I would neglect the daughter of my best friend?" The hostility of her gaze was her only reply.

Sherringham sighed and escorted her gently to a sofa. He sat down beside her to take her cold hand and soothe it tenderly despite her efforts to pull away. "I see I can't convince you," he sighed. "I am sorry for any trouble I may have caused you and I will do everything in my power to see that the wrong done you is righted."

Leanna knew he was referring to Jason. "Your concern is much too late, sir," she said coldly. She jerked away to stand at the window that faced the drive, battling tears and despair. Her anger evaporated in the face of his earnestness. She admitted to herself that he probably *had* thought it best for her to stay with her cousin. She set her forehead against the cold windowpane and longed only to sleep and never wake up.

She started as Sherry gently spun her around to gaze into her moistened eyes. "Don't despair, my dear, everything will work out," he comforted. She didn't reply as he led her again to the sofa and poured her some brandy. She accepted the glass with a listless hand and took a tiny sip. She coughed hoarsely, leaned back, and shut her eyes.

He let her rest for a moment. "I have a sketchy idea of what happened from Harry," he said. "But if we are to catch the scoundrel responsible, we must have evidence. I know you're weary, but the sooner we act, the better. Please tell me how you came to be at, er, such an unsuitable place, and what conversation you might have heard that would shed light on the matter."

Leanna sat up and braced herself for the worst. She would dearly love to see Mrs. Horton brought to justice. She told Sherry everything she could remember from the time Mrs. Horton fetched her, to the time the woman had mentioned Sir Gavin and the plan they had hatched. Sherry listened intently, his still body belying the growing anger in his eyes.

He gently grazed the bruise on her jaw with a finger. "And this? How did you get this bruise?" She told him of her attempt to escape, deleting the crude threats made by Mrs. Horton. She finished with her hazy remembrance of her escape that morning.

Sherry steepled his fingers and arched them thoughtfully. "From what I have heard, I would hazard a guess that the woman could present damaging evidence against Sir Gavin. I'm sure we can persuade her, one way or another." Leanna looked up curiously at the sound of his grim voice.

"What has this Sir Gavin against me?" she asked in bewilderment.

"Nothing, my dear. You were merely to be the instrument of my destruction." Sherry's smile was rueful. "I'm shortly to marry his last hope of avoiding debtor's jail. He hoped to have me compromise you so severely that I would have no choice but to marry you. His plan might have worked if I had not been called away unexpectedly and my cousin had not looked so much like me."

Comprehension at last dawned on Leanna. She finally understood why Jason had been so suspicious of her. She creased her brow. "But you needn't have married me, sir. I've never been out in society and would be just as happy living in the country."

Sherry looked thunderstruck. He protested, "But my dear, you'd have had no choice. A man cannot dishonor you and leave you to face disgrace alone. We would have had to marry." He looked at her sidelong as he spoke and Leanna suspected he was no longer referring to himself.

She threw him a haughty look. "If you mean to insinuate, sir, that I have no choice but to marry your cousin, you are much mistaken. I will not be forced to marry any man, particularly one that has no more love for me than I do for him."

She sounded so final that for a moment Sherry was at a loss. A way to convince her came to mind, but he was reluctant to use it. He looked at her searchingly, noting the rigidity in her figure and the determined slant to her delicate jaw.

With reluctance, he said gently, "Leanna, it's possible you do not have only yourself to consider." When she looked confused, he almost whispered, "What if you carry a brat?"

She paled and swayed. He grabbed her for fear she would fall to the floor. She leaned back limply as her world darkened for a moment. She had been so glad to escape that the possibility of pregnancy had not occurred to her. She shuddered as she remembered the virility of the American, a man of such potency that even her innocence could recognize it.

She tried to master her whirling thoughts as the blackness slowly receded, but she was far too tired. "Your lordship, I must think before I can give you an answer. I take it your cousin is willing to marry me?" He nodded a silent confirmation.

"Not gladly, I'll wager." He looked away, embarrassed. Her lip curled as she rose.

Sherry escorted her to the door. "You must rest, my dear. We'll talk later." He led her himself to a cheery red chamber on the second floor, pulled the covers back on the delicate, feminine bed, and helped her lie down. "Ring if you need anything," he said quietly before he left her alone.

Exhausted, Leanna tried to sleep, but her thoughts scurried around one another, making rest impossible. She searched for a solution, but could see none. Finally, her frazzled mind succumbed to her tired body and she slept deeply.

When she awoke hours later, she felt much refreshed. She flopped over and cupped her chin to watch the hypnotic flames in the fireplace. The idea of marrying the American was not attractive in the least, but neither was the idea of seeking employment or bearing an unwanted child in her womb. She bit her lip as she realized she would be an embarrassment to the earl if she stayed with him. He was to marry soon, and his new wife would certainly not welcome a strange female in her home.

Leanna kicked her foot moodily as she considered all her options. The most attractive idea was getting her own cottage in the country, but she suspected the earl would have none of that. And truth to tell, she didn't exactly want to spend her days in bucolic boredom. Her eyes sparked to life as she thought of seeing America. She had always wanted to visit that country. Her father had been a great admirer of the plucky Americans who had won their independence. He had followed the course of the new country eagerly. Despite Leanna's aversion to Jason, she shared her father's desire to see that vast land.

Leanna jumped up and walked over to the fire. She leaned on the mantel reflectively. What better way to see America than as an American's wife? Judging from Jason's dress and manner, he was a man of some property. At least she would lack no material comforts.

Her mouth tightened as she remembered his threats this morning. She recalled her resolve to punish him and decided he deserved to pay for the pleasure he had stolen from her. She suspected he was just as unwilling to marry her as she was to wed him. She relished the thought of his discomfort.

Her mood no longer somber, Leanna smiled with satisfaction as she considered all the delightful ways she could torment him as his wife. Then she sobered as she remembered her revenge would not be exacted without a price. She would have to play the wife in his marriage bed.

She drummed her fingers thoughtfully on the mantel, trying to think of a way to avoid that distasteful prospect. Her eyes suddenly narrowed. Her face was all cat as she almost purred.

She poured some water into the bowl by the bed, washed the last traces of despair away, and combed her hair, repinning it into a neat, high knot that emphasized the determination in her delicate features. She exited the room with a bounce in her step that indicated her eagerness to join the fray.

Chapter
Five

WHEN SHERRY FINALLY went back to the study to tell Jason what transpired with Leanna, he found his cousin mellower. He laughed when he saw the brandy decanter at Jason's elbow. "I trust you're more resigned, Cousin?"

Jason smiled back, by no means drunk, but pleasantly at ease. "How did the girl take the news?" he inquired with latent sarcasm.

Sherry took a deep breath. "Not well, Jason. She's upstairs resting and pondering the matter. It seems she is also reluctant to wed." He hesitated a moment, uncertain whether to voice his next question, then he decided that Leanna's welfare must take precedence over Jason's resentment.

"What did you do to make her dislike you so?" Sherry asked with wonder in his voice.

Jason choked on the brandy he was drinking, sputtered, and finally snorted, "Nothing you or any other man wouldn't have done. Dash it, Sherry, I thought the girl was a whore! How did you expect me to treat her? Like Dresden china?"

He looked disgusted, but Sherry read the guilt his bluster tried to hide. The earl sighed and shook his head at the match he was promoting. Their current dislike of one another did not bode well for their future.

"Dinner will be at six. Harry has gone to his rooms to change but will be here to sup. We'll discuss arrangements over the port. I have sent for a runner to advise us on the best way to deal with the madam. I feel certain we can persuade her to talk."

Sherry watched with concern as Jason poured himself another drink. He picked up the crystal decanter, bracing himself for an angry tirade as he replaced it in the cabinet out of harm's way. Jason watched the movement, narrow-eyed, but said nothing. He knew getting drunk would offer only temporary respite from his dilemma. He straightened abruptly.

"I, too, need to wash. I'll see you at dinner," Jason said curtly, striding from the study.

Sherry sighed and sat down at his desk to peruse some papers from the War Office, but he was too worried to concentrate. Suddenly, he stiffened as his face lit up. There was a way to calm the stormy waters threatening his normally peaceful household. He pulled a piece of crested stationery toward him and penned a note to Abby, requesting her presence at dinner.

As he rang for a messenger to dispatch it, he smiled, pleased with himself. He had never seen a man his betrothed was unable to charm or a woman who wouldn't confide in her. She was the perfect person to help him bring Leanna and Jason together.

The white, delicate hand drew aside the curtain of the elegant coach as a small blond gentleman descended languidly, helped by the coachman who held the door. His nose wrinkled with distaste as he surveyed the squalor around him. Children vied with mangy dogs for scraps in the gutter as filthy, supine bodies lined the crumbling walls of the stinking alley. A drunken whore staggered up to him, the panacea and the doom of the lower classes clutched in her hand—gin, more popularly referred to as blue ruin.

"'Ow's about a little fun, guvnor?" The pitiable creature tried to smile ingratiatingly as she shuffled closer to him. Without hesitation, Sir Gavin struck her in the jaw with his goldheaded cane before she could touch him. He turned away before she hit the ground.

He entered the back door of a low, filthy building known inappropriately as the King's Tavern. The sullen bear of a man sitting at the blackened table staggered to his feet when he entered.

"Sor! What you be here fer?" he asked in amazement.

"I need some scoundrels for hire and where better to find them than from a scoundrel like yourself?" Sir Gavin inquired sweetly.

The huge man looked away, but Gavin caught the anger in his eyes. "A wise decision, Blackie," he mocked, "else you'll never get your daughter out of Newgate."

When his taunting brought no response, Sir Gavin grew bored and tersely commanded, "Send two of your bully boys to me immediately. I have a job for them." His eyes gleamed with anticipation as he added to himself, "Possibly several jobs for them."

Blackie hastened to do his bidding, like a dog eager to avoid another kick. An observer might have thought it incongruous for such a brawny man to be so afraid of the delicate Sir Gavin. The truth was that Blackie would rather take on a gang of drunken bullies than cross Sir Gavin. He didn't just fear for his daughter; looking into those celestial blue eyes made him shudder as though the devil himself had touched him. Aye, a mean one he was. He'd known many ugly characters born of the filth and hardship of London's lower quarters, but none as evil as this exquisite gentleman.

As Sir Gavin waited, he drew a shawl over his face and pulled his beaver hat down over his eyes. There must be no one able to connect him with this night's work. His coachman would die rather than betray him and Blackie knew his daughter would be in danger. Sir Gavin smiled slowly as he relished the thought of Sherringham's dismay when he found his star witness had disappeared.

Then his mouth tightened as he thought of the arrogant American. He, too, would pay. Coins had already exchanged hands to get a full history drawn up on Sherry's unsuspecting cousin.

It was a spirited Leanna who came down early for dinner and requested an audience with Sherry in an imperious tone. Still poring over papers, he looked up somewhat absently when she entered the study, but he smiled and rose to greet her as she seated herself near his desk.

"My dear, you look much better," he approved as he sat down again. "Have you reached a decision?"

She nodded. "I have decided I will marry him," she said coolly. Sherry heaved a sigh of relief, but before he could congratulate her she continued. "There is a condition, however."

He tensed and watched warily as she made her bid. "Mr. Blaine must promise not to touch me. My first taste of such intimacy has left me with no desire to repeat the experience."

Sherry groaned and closed his eyes as he thought of relating this turn of events to Jason. He opened his eyes, ready to coax. "But my dear, you must understand that Jason considered you, er, rather loose. His behavior a second time would certainly not be so rough." His voice softened as he explained. "A girl's initiation is always the worst. Your second experience could very well be as pleasurable for you as for him."

Her teeth clenched and her jaw looked even more unyielding as she repudiated, "There is no pleasure in being taken by a man you hate. If he does not agree to this condition, I will not marry him." The matter closed, in her opinion, she rose to stare into the fire.

Sherry rubbed his aching head and wished for a strong brandy. He rose slowly, reluctant to face Jason, but he knew that nothing would come of delaying the matter. "Dinner will be ready soon. Hastings will escort you to the dining room," he said curtly. "I will speak with Jason and we'll discuss this more after dinner." His bow was short and conveyed his displeasure succinctly.

Leanna shrugged her shoulders as the door shut behind him. He was quite put out with her, but she was tired of being manipulated. She would have her way in this, or there would be no marriage. She turned back to gaze into the fire, wishing she could see Jason's reaction to the news. She smiled to squelch the thought that as her husband, he could punish her in other ways.

Sherry found Jason dressing and admired his blue superfine coat. "Weston?" he inquired.

Jason nodded. "Have you seen the girl?" he asked reluctantly as he tied his cravat.

Sherry didn't answer for a moment, then he sighed and took the bull by the horns. "Yes, I've seen her, and yes, she's agreed to the marriage." He shifted from foot to foot. Jason turned to face him, sensing he would not like what he was about to hear.

"She agreed only on the condition that you promise not to touch her," Sherry said baldly.

Jason's eyes caught fire and Sherry felt blasted as he roared, "How dare the chit! She thinks to take my money and my name and leave me with nothing to make this marriage easier to stomach. Well, by God, she's mistaken if she believes me so malleable! I will not accept the condition. She can rot in hell for all I care!" He smashed his fist on the dresser. He was so enraged he didn't feel the impact.

Sherry waited a moment for his wrath to cool, then he chided with humor, "Damn me, I'm not sure which of you is more reluctant. It will certainly be a stormy union." He held up his hand as Jason whirled on him again.

"Now listen to me, Cousin," he said sharply. "You cannot blame the girl for being reluctant to share your bed. From what I understand, you were hardly gentle with her the first time." Jason looked away, his cheeks reddened. Sherry smiled and cajoled, "Come, dear boy, I'm sure such a handsome fellow as yourself can woo her into your bed. When she gets to know you better she'll doubtless be as charmed with you as are the rest of her sex."

Jason looked unconvinced and leaned morosely against the bedpost. Sherry's voice became brisk again as he finished. "It's all decided, then. I can tell Leanna you promise?" Jason gnashed his teeth, but he finally nodded curtly.

"You can tell her I agree. There are women aplenty willing to give me whatever I want. I have no need or desire for her. You can also tell her *that*." He didn't wait for Sherry's reply, but turned and hurried to the door.

Sherry strode beside him. "I think it best to go ahead with the wedding. There is no reason to delay." Jason's jaw seemed cast in bronze, but he said nothing. "Right, then." Sherry's inward relief did not show. "I'll obtain a special license and you can wed in a few days."

"I will be busy until that time," Jason stated unequivocally. "I have neglected my ship long enough. I still intend to sail within the next few weeks."

Sherry agreed smoothly, "Certainly, Cousin. Is there anything I can do to help?" Jason shook his head and entered the study. He stopped so short that Sherry careened into him.

Leanna was stretched out on the thick Aubusson carpet before the fire, reading a book. As she read she kicked her legs, sending her skirts whirling around her ankles. She was so intent she didn't hear the door and Jason watched her slender calves with pleasure for a moment. Sherry entered also and cleared his throat to catch her attention.

She looked around, startled, then bolted up when she saw them. She pulled her skirts down and got to her feet, rather flushed, whether from the fire or from embarrassment, Jason wasn't sure.

"Sirs," she greeted stiffly. Jason bowed mockingly, still angry. She turned away with a haughty tilt to her chin, which only angered him further.

Sherry hastened to intervene. "Jason has agreed to your condition, Leanna, and the wedding will be within the next few days." Leanna nodded, but didn't turn. Jason continued to stare at her, a red glow in the depths of his stormy blue eyes. She could feel his gaze impaling her back. She bit her lip and forced herself not to squirm. Sherry was seeking desperately for a way to smooth the situation when Hastings knocked and ushered in Abby.

"Abby!" he greeted with delight. Leanna turned and watched curiously as Sherry kissed the slim white hand of a petite, beautiful brunette. She had the gentlest, kindest blue eyes Leanna had ever seen and a mouth that seemed designed for smiling.

"This is Abby Reynolds, my fiancée. Abby, this is Leanna, my ward, and my cousin, Jason Blaine from America." Sherry ushered Abby forward, his pride apparent. Leanna smiled shyly and Jason bowed with curt courtesy before he returned to his perusal of Leanna.

Abby's smile at Leanna was sweet and sincere. "I've heard Sherry speak of you often. I'm very glad to meet you." She turned to Jason and laughed, a sound that tinkled in the room like bells, "I never thought I'd see a man as handsome as Sherry, certainly not one that looks so much like him." Jason cracked a smile, a mere movement of his mouth, but made no reply.

Sherry's lips tightened. He was becoming heartily sick of the whole affair. Jason had no reason to be rude to Abby.

"Come into the salon, my dear, and I will explain," he whispered. Then, louder, "Please excuse us. We have matters to discuss. We'll see you at dinner shortly." Sherry smothered the hesitancy he felt at leaving Jason and Leanna alone. They had to learn to live with one another sometime. He led Abby firmly from the study. The abigail accompanying her followed.

A forbidding silence descended on the room after they left. Leanna once more picked up her book and attempted to read. She tried desperately to ignore Jason's wandering gaze, but she could finally stand it no longer. She slammed her book shut and laid it on the sofa beside her. She looked at Jason, intending to give as good as she got, but she recoiled before his searing gaze. His eyes raked her body, enjoying her discomfiture as he feasted on her full bosom, her slender waist, and her legs, finally journeying back to linger on her mouth.

He continued to watch her lips as she snapped, "Why don't you rape me and be done with it?"

"Tsk, tsk, such language from a . . . *lady*," he mocked. "When you know me better, girl, you'll realize that I never break my word." His gaze finally lifted and locked on her blazing emerald eyes. He sneered, "You'll have to beg me before I touch you again. There are plenty of women willing to satisfy my every whim. I have no need or desire for a scrawny chit like you."

"That suits me just fine because I'll never ask you for anything." They glared at one another like gladiators wrestling to the death. Into this hostile atmosphere came the forever cheerful Harry. He stopped and stared in dismay at the deadlocked pair.

"Didn't mean to interrupt," he mumbled, starting to back from the room.

"Please don't go, Mr. Jeffries," Leanna pleaded. He looked at Jason's forbidding expression and hesitated, but Leanna's entreating eyes held him to the spot.

He advanced toward Leanna and kissed her hand, then met Jason's icy gaze. "Sherry informed me of your impending marriage when I came in. May I congratulate you both," he offered. As neither Leanna nor Jason looked particularly happy, he continued hastily, "I hope you can stay in London long enough to enjoy meeting some of our friends. We give some dashed great parties."

Leanna opened her mouth to accept, but Jason countermanded, "We will not have time. I plan to set sail as soon as possible."

Leanna blazed, "And my wishes are of no concern in the matter, I collect."

"That's exactly right, my dear intended," Jason replied with enjoyment.

Harry gasped at the rudeness, every chivalrous instinct he possessed horrified. He opened his mouth to chastise Jason, but Hastings entered and announced dinner before he could speak. He stiffly presented his arm to Leanna, who took it without a glance at Jason. They walked from the room, ignoring Jason. He followed, fuming at the deliberate snub.

The atmosphere at the elegant cherry dinner table was not conducive to good digestion. The only person in the room who was not angry at someone was Abby. Sherry had explained the situation between Leanna and Jason, but she was at a loss to understand the tension she felt coming from Harry. She sighed and began the Herculean task of easing hostilities.

"My dear, I understand you are new to London," she said

with an easy smile. When she received nothing but a polite nod from Leanna, she continued gamely. "We must waste no time in selecting your trousseau. I hope you will let me advise you. I would enjoy it very much." Leanna's cold facade began to melt in the face of such friendliness.

"I confess I am much in need of new clothes, ma'am. I would appreciate your assistance," she said.

Abby turned to Jason and cajoled, "I understand you're a ship's captain, sir. I have ever wished I could sail the seas, but these skirts would be rather awkward in the topgallants." She looked so wry that Jason was forced to laugh.

Abby continued her chatter, speaking to each diner in turn until everyone gradually relaxed. The wine served with the many courses helped her in this endeavor. By the time the gentlemen retired for their port, Leanna felt totally at ease for the first time since entering the earl's townhouse. Jason was still rather quiet, but his tenseness had disappeared. Harry was his usual cheerful self and the earl was delighted at the results of Abby's diplomacy.

He assisted her from her chair and kissed her cheek. "Bless you, my dear. You are a treasure," he said for her ears alone before he followed the other men from the room.

Alone with Leanna, Abby settled back on a settee in the parlor and patted the seat beside her invitingly. "Come, my dear, now we can have a comfortable coze." Leanna sat down beside her, but some of her wariness returned. She was in no mood for girlish confidences. Her pride rankled at the position of having to wed the infuriating man who had dishonored her. So Abby's gentle overtures met with a polite, but firm, refusal to be drawn into her schemes.

Abby sighed and encouraged, "I hope you will let me assist you in any way that I may. If you ever feel the need to talk, I am told I am a good listener. Anything you might care to say will, of course, be held in strict confidence."

Leanna thanked her crisply but became more animated when Abby switched the conversation to fashion. They'd made arrangements to go on a shopping spree tomorrow just as the gentlemen entered the room. Jason caught the subject of their conversation and looked contemptuous. She was probably as empty-headed as the rest of her sex, interested only in fashion and parties. He pushed aside the thought of the book of Shakespearean sonnets he had seen her reading earlier. It was far more comfortable to think of her as shallow than as the passionate, feminine creature his deepest instincts told him she was.

Sherry poured ratafia for the ladies and brandy for the gentlemen, then he lifted his glass. "To a happy marriage," he said with heartfelt sincerity to Jason and Leanna. He drank deeply. The others did likewise, and if the engaged couple refused to meet one another's eyes, no one remarked on it.

Leanna rose and smiled stiffly. "I will retire now, if I may. I am quite tired." The gentlemen rose and Abby stroked her cheek with such tenderness that Leanna's wary heart was touched.

"Sleep well, my child," she smiled. "Our day will be busy tomorrow." Leanna hurried out before the others could see the sudden moisture in her eyes. No one had showed her such concern since her parents died.

Jason bowed and was about to excuse himself when Hastings knocked and entered. The butler looked flustered, and Sherry fired quickly, "Yes, Hastings?"

"A Bow Street runner is here requesting an audience immediately, your lordship."

He looked disapproving, but Sherry waved him away and commanded, "Send him in immediately."

The disreputable-looking individual who entered looked more like one of the criminals he brought before the magistrates than the runner he was. Grimy hands clutched an equally dirty hat as he looked at them through greasy tufts of hair. When Abby met his eyes, however, she found them unusually alert and piercing. He made an elegant bow that was at ludicrous odds with his appearance.

"Which of you be Lord Sherringham?" he inquired.

"I am Lord Sherringham. What news have you?"

"The worst, I'm afraid, yer lordship. The woman calling herself La Bianca is dead." Sherry groaned and collapsed into a chair. "Looked like footpads. They did her up proper." He looked at Abby, cleared his throat and continued hastily, "Me superiors suspect t'was more to't and I agree. Don't have no evidence, I'm sorry to say, but we be still looking."

"I appreciate your efforts," Sherry said. "Please keep me informed of all developments." The man nodded and exited on silent feet.

The room was somber for a moment, then Sherry exploded, "Blast it, I know that bastard is behind this! He thinks he's covered his tracks, but I'll find a way to catch him yet." He stared grimly ahead, then his eyes gleamed and his teeth showed in a wicked smile.

He turned to Abby. "Thank you for coming, my dear. I will see you again tomorrow." He led her to the door despite her protests. Her abigail looked discreetly away as Abby argued with her betrothed.

"Really, Sherry, I'm involved also. If he hadn't been my suitor, none of this would have happened. I have a right to know what you're planning," she insisted even as he was helping her into her carriage.

"You are very precious to me, my dear, and I will not endanger you in any way. You will find out soon enough." He saluted her mouth and smiled as she sat back huffily when the carriage pulled away.

He turned to go back inside, hoping he had at last found a way to deal with Sir Gavin. In prison the man's malignancy would be contained, if not destroyed. Sherry entered the parlor to acquaint an impatient Jason and Harry with his idea.

They both nodded in approval, but Harry was still uneasy. He was afraid Sir Gavin would be a threat to Sherry and possibly Jason as long as he drew breath. If he found a way to escape, he would be a greater danger than ever.

PART TWO

"So musical a discord, such sweet thunder."
—*A Midsummer Night's Dream*, Act II, Scene II

Chapter Six

THE NEXT MORNING, when Leanna came downstairs for breakfast, she found the table unoccupied. Hastings informed her that Sherry and Jason were both involved in business affairs elsewhere. The lady Abby would arrive shortly.

Leanna nodded and enjoyed a hearty breakfast of kidneys, eggs, and muffins. When she sat back, replete, her spirits were almost buoyant. She determinedly pushed the thought of her marriage to the back of her mind and concentrated instead on the wardrobe she would need. Sherry had told her to spare no expense. Her new home was in a place called Georgia and would require both cool and warm clothing.

As she went upstairs to collect her pelisse and reticule, she thought how ridiculous it was that she must hear about her future home from her guardian rather than from her betrothed. She firmly silenced her conscience which told her she had made no attempt to mend matters between them. Like Jason, she preferred to remain as aloof as possible, an endeavor she grimly admitted might be difficult.

When Abby arrived, she found her protégée in command of herself and eager to begin their shopping. Throughout that long day, as they went from shop to shop ordering a wardrobe for Leanna more extensive than any she had ever dreamed of, Abby made no mention of Jason or any subject that could upset her.

Leanna threw herself with vigor into the selection of velvet pelisses, muslin morning and day dresses and satin, gauze, and velvet evening gowns. She fell in love with a brilliant emerald-green riding habit that looked almost mannish until she tried it on. The frock coat was cut along severe lines in deliberate imitation of a man's jacket, but the wide lapels and cuffs edged with black jet emphasized Leanna's delicate femininity. The curly beaver hat was swathed with a green, trailing scarf that added the crowning touch.

When she had selected her hats, slippers, and underclothing, Leanna reluctantly began looking for a wedding gown. She was determined to look as unattractive as possible. The modiste was horrified when Leanna smiled with satisfaction at her reflection in the glass. The dress was so loaded with ruffles, frills, and furbelows that her small figure seemed smothered and childish under the weight. She commanded that the gown be added to her purchases, against the proprietess's protests.

Engrossed, she didn't see Abby eying an exquisite gown of lush velvet that was trimmed in swansdown and small, pinkish pearls. The veil was of a spidery lace so delicate it seemed made of mist. Abby surreptitiously inserted the gown in their pile and smiled serenely when Leanna asked her opinion of the dress she was wearing.

"Why, I think it's perfectly awful, my dear, but I suspect that is your intention and I will not try to dissuade you." Leanna looked uncertain for a moment, then she shrugged and changed into one of her new day dresses. She didn't see Abby pick up the gown and hand it to the modiste or hear the words her friend whispered in the woman's ear. Nor did she notice the small package Abby secreted in the mountain of boxes.

When they arrived back at the townhouse, both were too tired to immediately notice the air of excitement as Hastings took their wraps. They collapsed in the salon and rested their aching feet on footstools as they sipped refreshing lemonade.

The door burst open and Sherry erupted into the room. Neither girl had ever seen him so pleased with himself. Harry followed and seemed equally jubilant.

"What's to do, my dear?" Abby smiled as she examined Sherry's exuberant face tenderly.

Sherry sat down beside her. He took her hand and beamed, "Sir Gavin Redfern will never bother anyone again. He is presently the newest resident of the Fleet. I doubt he will ever leave."

Abby jumped in shock and gasped, "But how?"

"I quite see why the War Office finds him so invaluable, Abby," Harry interjected. "Never have I seen a more persuasive fellow. He bought off Sir Gavin's creditors and holds all his notes. What he couldn't buy with money he purchased with guile." Harry shook his head in admiration.

Sherry flushed, but continued the story. "Most of his creditors had long ago lost patience. It was quite easy to obtain the notes. I wasted no time in foreclosing, either. He was at his lodgings this afternoon when we closed the trap."

He didn't tell them of Sir Gavin's venomous invectives or his final curse as they dragged him away: "You've not heard the last of this, Sherringham! Know this: as God is my witness, you and your cursed cousin will die for this deed!" The blue eyes had been so incandescent with hatred that Sherry was momentarily uneasy. Then he shrugged. What harm could he do them in prison?

Dismissing the thought of him, he said, "Leanna, my dear, your betrayers have been brought to justice and will never bother you again."

"Thank you, my lord. That is some comfort, at least," Leanna replied softly.

Abby broke the sudden silence by regaling the group with an amusing account of their day. Harry and Sherry laughed as she admitted, "I never believed I could ever say this, but I am sated with shopping. I don't want to look at another dress for some time to come."

Sherry teased, "Certainly, my dear. At least not until the next party, when you'll discover you don't have a thing to wear."

Abby tried to look insulted and failed miserably as she dissolved into delightful giggles. It was thus a pleasant scene that met Jason as he entered the room. Abby warmly drew him into the conversation, ignoring Leanna's sudden tenseness beside her.

"I hope your day was as productive as our own, Captain Blaine," Abby encouraged him.

"Quite productive, thank you, ma'am," Jason replied tiredly. Leanna glanced into his unfathomable blue eyes. She looked away hurriedly, but she could still feel his gaze examining her from head to foot. She decided her new dress was much too low and felt a compulsion to pull up the bodice. She sighed with relief when Harry repeated the story of Sir Gavin's imprisonment to Jason, dragging her betrothed's gaze away from her.

Making her excuses, she went to her room to refresh herself before dinner. Despite himself, Jason's gaze followed her from the salon. She was even more beautiful than he remembered in the thin, clinging muslin dress. He had spent a busy day at the docks, supervising the loading of cargo into his ship, but he had not been totally successful in relegating Leanna to the back of his mind. As he watched her walk away now, he wondered with despair how he was to survive the long voyage without enjoying the lovely body that seemed more desirable to him by the day. He bit his lip and forced himself to concentrate on what Harry was saying.

As Leanna walked to her chamber, she wondered why the man she hated seemed the personification of masculinity to her. Dressed in the rough trousers and heavy jacket, he looked too disturbingly handsome for her peace of mind. She shook herself and threw liberal splashes of water on her hot cheeks from a pitcher by the bed. She was merely tired and a short rest would do wonders for her morale. She would be more herself when she was not so exhausted.

Leanna lay down and cleared her mind of everything but

excitement over her new wardrobe. She decided dreamily that she would wear the new gold silk for dinner and try a new hairstyle. She didn't question why she wanted to look her best as she drifted off to sleep.

In the short time left before the wedding, Leanna and Jason saw little of one another, a circumstance that suited them both. Jason was busy getting his ship caparisoned for the long voyage home and Leanna was involved in wedding preparations. Abby had coaxed, cajoled, and bullied her into agreeing to a small but elegant wedding, complete with flowers and wedding breakfast.

"It's an opportunity for you to meet Sherry's friends," she told her practically. And as a final persuasion, "We are both very proud of you, my dear. It will likely be quite some time before we see you again and we would both treasure the memory of a lovely wedding. Do it for us if not for yourself." What could Leanna do but acquiesce in the face of such charming coercion?

When she had finally agreed, she found herself enjoying the preparations, if not looking forward to the actual event. Abby kept her so busy she had little time for her latent fears to resurface, so when the actual day arrived she was shocked at her calm.

She pushed the thought of Jason firmly away the morning of her wedding. Now, as she prepared to dress, she wistfully regretted she had selected such an unattractive wedding gown. She opened the wardrobe to search for the dress, but could not find it among the many gowns. Puzzled, she searched again. When Abby knocked and entered, she greeted her with a harried smile.

Abby stood silent for a moment, then she shifted uneasily. Leanna sensed her discomfort and turned toward her, mystified. Abby opened the drawer at the bottom of the wardrobe and pulled out the loveliest gown Leanna had ever seen. She stroked the soft velvet with pleasure and raised questioning eyes to Abby.

Her friend looked embarrassed as she admitted guiltily, "I

had the woman put the other dress back and substitute this one instead. I hope I haven't angered you, Leanna."

Leanna waved away her apology and kissed Abby's cheek. "I'm so glad you did, Abby. I confess I was not looking forward to wearing that awful gown. Will you help me dress? The maid was too fussy, but I would enjoy your assistance." With a pleased smile, Abby agreed.

When she stood before the glass, gowned and veiled, even Leanna was startled at her beauty. The velvet flowed softly from a high waistline to the hem which was caught at intervals with roses fashioned of pale pink seed pearls. Exquisite lace peeped from the gown's hem, and swansdown lined the low neckline. The sleeves were long, tight-fitting, and swansdown and seed pearls encircled the pointed ends. The veil reached just past her hips and was haloed with a small tiara of pale pink peares and diamonds. Her newly washed hair seemed to glow through the lace.

Abby nodded in approval. "Never have I seen a more beautiful bride, my dear. I'm sure you will be very happy if you'll just give yourself the chance." Despite Leanna's paling face, Abby continued doggedly, "Captain Blaine is a most handsome man and will make a good husband, given time and patience."

She hesitated a moment, then continued, "I know you are not feeling charitable toward him at the moment, but please try and understand. There are reasons why he is the way he is. He had a most unhappy childhood. It is not my story to tell, but perhaps, if you ask, he'll explain it to you one day."

She gave Leanna a fleeting hug and left the room to get Sherry. Leanna could no longer deny the fear she had so far banished. She remembered Jason's hostility and remoteness the last few days and wondered what there was in his past to make him dislike her so. She remembered his fiery passion and shuddered at the memory of those roaming hands. He had promised not to touch her, true, but when she was legally his wife, no one would say him nay if he should change his mind. She collapsed on the bed, a prey to every fear that had troubled brides since marriage began, and with far more reason.

In his room, a no less troubled Jason also readied himself

for the day that most bridegrooms looked forward to. His lip curled cynically as he reflected that most men were not about to wed hellcats who hated them. In the scant time he had spent with her the last few days, she had been remote but icily polite. He sighed and wondered how he was to break down her wall of reserve, since she had forbidden him the easiest way to win her.

He caught himself up sharply. Win her? By God, he didn't want anything from her but to be left in peace. The last thing he needed was a clinging, possessive wife. He should be thankful she was willing to let him go his way. His brow darkened as he wondered grimly if she expected the same freedom. For a moment a red mist clouded his vision as he imagined another man being offered the tempting lips and beautiful body denied him. His fists clenched, and as his vision cleared, he resolved to set her straight on that notion without delay.

Thus, when Harry escorted Jason to the chapel to act as his best man, he found him tight-lipped, silent, and far from happy. When Sherry led Leanna down the stairs to the waiting carriage, he found her white with fear, but controlled. His blandishments and compliments fell on deaf ears. She gnawed her lip and watched the city travel by all too quickly as she tried to keep from screaming in fear and rage. Only self-control and the realization she had no other choice gave her the strength to grasp Sherry's arm and allow herself to be led down the aisle.

Was there ever more reluctant bride or bridegroom? As Leanna met Jason's hard gaze, she swayed, and for a moment, Sherry thought she would faint. But then Leanna saw Jason's lip curl in disdain and she pulled herself erect. She walked with firmness the few remaining steps to the altar, gazing coldly ahead. As the minister commanded them to clasp hands, Leanna placed her hand in his with only a shudder. She said her vows in a soft but steady voice, trying not to gag at the mockery when she promised to love, cherish, and obey.

Jason repeated the words easily, hardly aware what he was saying. His nose twitched at her gentle perfume. The softness of her hand in his was an irritation. He longed to thrust her veil aside and kiss her until she melted under the heat of his passion and kissed him back. Her fairy-like beauty in the white gown merely increased his desire to whip her skirts above her head and take her until she begged for mercy. His emotions at that moment were a tormenting mixture of admiration, desire, and hatred. He crushed her hand cruelly, delighting in her gasp of pain. She jerked her hand away, but as it was time for the ring, the action went unnoticed.

Harry handed Jason a plain gold band, and as he slipped it on her finger, she reluctantly met the fiery possessiveness in his glance. When the minister pronounced them man and wife, Jason whipped her veil back and pulled her to him in a bruising embrace. He kissed her brutally, his tongue probing her soft recesses. She struggled in rage, and finally kicked him in the shin with her pointed shoe when he would not release her. He gasped in pain and slackened his hold. She wrenched away to stand trembling in revulsion. She met his furious glance with a glacier one of her own and wiped her mouth meaningfully. They were beginning to attract attention and a concerned Harry pushed Jason toward her. He presented his arm stiffly. She barely rested her fingertips on it and walked with regal grace down the aisle, a false smile painted on her face.

The byplay had not escaped Sherry or Abby and they exchanged a concerned glance. Sherry shrugged, looked wry, and offered his arm. They followed the newlyweds from the church. The only other guests, Jason's first mate and bo'sun, brought up the rear. They were dazed at Leanna's beauty and puzzled at the hostility they sensed between the captain and his bride.

The wedding breakfast was an event that was ever after hazy in Leanna's mind. All her worst fears seemed confirmed at Jason's actions during the wedding. At the breakfast he seemed more interested in the punch bowl than in his bride. Leanna pasted a firm smile on her face throughout that interminable event, holding tears at bay by pure will-power. She was grateful for Harry's support as he led her around the room introducing her to the guests.

Sherry stalked over to Jason and hissed angrily, "Don't make a bigger fool of yourself than you have already, man. Harry is much attracted to Leanna. He's only too glad to act in your stead."

Jason's head jerked up from his gloomy contemplation of his drink, and as luck would have it, Leanna was laughing at something Harry had said. He slammed his glass down and decided it was time to put aside his self-pity and assert his rights. He straightened his shoulders and strode arrogantly to her side.

Shouldering them neatly apart, he purred, "I'm sorry, my dear, I was detained. Shall we begin the dancing?"

Leanna longed to refuse, but as she looked at the smiling faces around her, she realized she could not humiliate Sherry by confirming the gossip she sensed circulating the room that all was not well between the newlyweds. She bared her teeth in a false smile and allowed him to lead her onto the dance floor.

The orchestra struck up a waltz, considered a daring dance in England, but one quite deliberately requested by Abby. At first, Leanna held herself stiffly away, but Jason pulled her closer until they were touching from shoulder to thigh, their graceful movements adding to the intimacy. A smile still on her face, she snarled, "You clod, this is a ballroom, not a bedroom. Don't hold me so vulgarly."

Jason squeezed her roughly for a moment, then loosened his hold somewhat. He could see they were exciting comment, and he had no desire to provide more food for the gossips. "You're quite right, my dear," he agreed pleasantly. "Your punishment must be in private." To punctuate the warning he squeezed her hand.

Her eyes reminded him of a furious cat's, and he imagined he could see her tail switch when she hissed, *"My* punishment? After your behavior today? If there was ever any doubt that ours is a normal marriage, you have laid it to rest."

She wanted to kick herself for her careless choice of words when she leered, "Indeed, my precious, ours is *not* a normal marriage. The lovely bride will not admit the handsome groom to her oh-so-virtuous bed." Leanna looked away and frantically wondered when this interminable dance would end.

The leer disappeared to be replaced by a frown so fierce that Leanna was alarmed. She eyed him warily as he grated, "But no one else will taste of the fruit you withhold from me, including the gallant Harry. Is that understood, wife?"

Leanna was tempted to laugh at the ridiculous notion, but she sensed a chink in his armor and didn't hesitate for an instant to drive her lance through it. "If you have the right to stray, sir, then so do I," she informed him loftily, then she gasped in pain as he brought her to a crushing halt, despite the fact that the music still played on.

"If I *once* have reason to believe you have cuckolded me, I will make you regret you were ever born," he enunciated clearly, with such cold menace that Leanna faltered. She met his flinty eyes and quivered, but she remained proudly erect.

Sherry grabbed Jason's arm and separated them. He led Leanna gently away and didn't leave her side for the rest of the breakfast. Abby coaxed Jason into a chair next to her and endeavored to erase the white look about his mouth. Gradually, he relaxed and responded to her conversation. Though Jason and Leanna sat side by side, they said not another word to each other for the rest of the breakfast. This fact was of course remarked on, and before the day was out, a good deal of London's ton knew that Sherringham's ward had wed hastily and not well.

Leanna roughly pulled off the beautiful wedding gown and threw it in the corner with loathing. She felt an almost irresistible compulsion to fling it in the crackling fireplace, but she resisted the temptation. The mess of her life was no fault of the lovely gown. She threw herself on the bed and burst into a storm of tears, incited more by rage than sorrow. Her marriage was a disgusting mockery of all that was decent. Her cad of a husband was interested in only one thing: her body. Her thoughts, hopes, and the dreams that he had shattered were a matter of supreme unimportance to him.

She cried until her chaotic emotions had calmed somewhat, then lay with a slim arm over her eyes. Gradually, her rage faded and was replaced with a cold calculation. He had made her life a hell of misery, and by God, he was going to share purgatory with her.

She flopped onto her side and bit her lip. His one vulnerability seemed to be his desire for her and his determination that no other man should have what he considered his. Eyes narrowed, she determined she would flirt like a light-skirt; she would fan his lust until he was half insane with wanting her, then reject him coldly. Satisfied, she set about repairing the ravages to her face. As she dressed in a warm blue velvet gown, she tried to ignore the uneasy thought that she might be precipitating the very thing she wanted to avoid—inciting him too far. Her face became fierce as she pushed the thought aside. He would never touch her again; no, she would kill him first.

She had intended to be civil and to try and be a dutiful wife, but it seemed he wanted only a mistress. Very well, she would play the whore, but he would find her favors ever out of reach.

She examined the daring gown thoughtfully. It was by far the lowest cut dress she had ever worn. She had been hesitant about selecting it, but Abby had pointed out that married women had more freedom of dress than young girls. And it did look lovely on her. The slashing V-neck revealed most of her breasts. It was lined with creamy, flowing lace that seemed to pull the bodice even farther down. The same lace circled the long sleeves and peeped from the hem of the gown. Leanna rearranged her hairstyle, leaving a number of soft curls loose around her forehead and the nape of her neck.

She admired the overall effect. She looked like a woman ready for love. She wet her lips and half closed her eyes. The effect increased twofold. With a gentle swaying of her hips, Leanna started downstairs.

When she entered the dining room, there was a startled silence. Harry's eyes widened as she deliberately ignored her usual place and sat down next to him. His eyes seemed glued to her bodice. She caressed his shoulder and confided huskily, just loud enough for Jason to hear, "I'm so glad you're here, Mr. Jeffries. Congenial company is so important to the enjoyment of one's dinner, wouldn't you agree? May I call you Harry?" At his bemused nod, she continued, "'Mr. Jeffries' seems so formal for such good friends as we have become." She smiled seductively at him, watching Jason's ominous stillness from the corner of her eye.

Sherry cleared his throat loudly. "Leanna, my dear, please sit next to me," he suggested. "I would like to tell you some stories about my days at Oxford. Your father and I were in some merry scrapes." He watched in suspense as she turned toward him. The seductive mask she was wearing slipped for a moment and the hurt anger peeped through. She hesitated momentarily, but the temptation was too great. She smiled with regret at Harry and moved into her usual chair at Sherry's elbow.

Abby sat next to Jason and breathed a sigh of relief as some of the fire faded from his eyes. He nevertheless answered her conversational gambits in monosyllables and rarely took his gaze off Leanna. Exasperated, she rapped his hand with her fan.

"Captain, please look at me when I speak to you!" she commanded. Jason looked at her, startled, then laughed at the exaggerated dignity on her face.

Her charming features relaxed into a smile. "You should know she's only trying to get her own back for your behavior earlier today."

He looked unrepentant as he replied, "The chit must learn who's master. I'll have none of her tantrums."

Abby shook her head pityingly, appalled at his naiveté. "Dear sir, haven't you made her measure yet? The surest way to make Leanna use every weapon she has against you is to try and coerce her into your idea of a proper wife." He looked impatient, but she tapped his hand again and insisted, "You'd do well to listen, Jason, else I'm afraid you're in for a very stormy relationship."

Jason shrugged and replied indifferently, "That may well be, ma'am. It might be best that way." Her gaze narrowed, then she mentally threw up her hands. She had done her best. They would have to work out their problems on their own, it seemed.

Sherry was having no better luck. He had relaxed Leanna with a couple of amusing stories about her father, so she was unprepared when he changed the subject.

"Leanna, my dear," he warned softly, "Jason is not the man to try these tricks on. His pride is already pricked at your rejection of him and I fear that if you incite him too far, you may not be able to appease him."

Leanna sipped her wine, unconcerned. "I can handle myself, my lord. He must learn that I will not be bullied." Sherry met Abby's rueful gaze. He shrugged and she nodded.

They had tried to help these two strong personalities set aside their differences and come to an understanding, but both were determined to fight for supremacy. As Leanna returned to her shameless flirtation with Harry, it was obvious to Sherry and Abby that the battle lines were clearly drawn. The only question was, What were the spoils of victory? Since both gladiators claimed to be indifferent to the other, what were they fighting about? Sherry decided he would enjoy the contest as he sat back to watch the first bout with reluctant amusement.

Chapter
Seven

LEANNA URGED HER steed to a faster canter, bubbling with mirth as she left Harry far behind. She pulled to an abrupt halt and stroked the quivering withers of her bay gelding as she waited for Harry to catch up.

The gleam in his eye expressed admiration and frustration equally as he reined in his gray beside her. It was the fourth time she had beaten him that week.

"Dash it, Leanna, where did you learn to ride like a centaur?" he asked sulkily, his face chagrined.

"My father taught me," she laughed. "I'm a country girl, remember. I had to be a bruising rider to keep up with him." Her eyes sparkled as she remembered the many happy rides she had experienced with her father on the Duke of Chester's estate. She sighed, longing for those happy times once more, then she wheeled around to leave Hyde Park, determined not to let sadness spoil the lovely morning. It was an unseasonably warm day for early November. The cloudless sky promised a mild day as the sun touched them with gentle warmth.

There were few riders out at this early hour. It was the only time Harry's rigid sense of propriety allowed them to have a refreshing gallop. Ladies of the ton were not encouraged to romp through the park, particularly at any hour but early morning.

Leanna's nose wrinkled as she considered all the restrictions that bound women. The only bright spot in her cursed marriage was the relative freedom it had given her to gad about London with Harry.

Unwillingly, her thoughts returned to Jason. She saw him only at dinner, in the company of the others. At her request, Harry usually dined with them. Leanna genuinely enjoyed his company. She treated him more like a playmate than a suitor—except in the presence of Jason. Still, her persistent flirtation had borne little fruit. Sometimes Leanna thought she spied a rabid gleam in Jason's eye as he watched her stroke Harry's arm or giggle mischievously at one of his sallies. But when Jason caught her furtive glance, his face would become wooden as he applied his attention to his food, rarely speaking.

Leanna was dissatisfied with her ploy, but so far she had envisioned no more effective way of putting Jason in his place. She shrugged and put her reluctant husband out of her mind.

"Harry, my friend," she began sweetly as they traveled down St. James Street. He stiffened at her tone of voice. He knew Leanna well enough by now to be certain she was up to something when she spoke in that demure voice. "We really *must* attend a masquerade night at Vauxhall Gardens before I leave." Of all London's pleasures, a Vauxhall masquerade most caught her fancy. The idea of wearing a domino and mask and dancing gaily with unknown gentlemen seemed vastly exciting to Leanna's romantic nature.

Her pleadings with Harry had so far been ineffectual and her sailing date drew ever nearer. Denied the opportunity to attend any of Harry's enticing parties, she was determined to have at least one gay dance to remember in the dreary life ahead.

"Now Leanna, I've told you over and over again that masquerade night is not a proper time for you to attend," he blustered.

"But you'd be with me, so what could happen?" she asked reasonably.

"And what if we should become separated? Roues and cads of the worst sort lurk in the Dark Walk, just waiting to take advantage of some innocent young lady," he discouraged.

"I am hardly an innocent any longer, as you well know, Harry." Leanna's sarcasm found its mark as Harry blushed a fiery red. He had never mentioned that ill-fated night at La Bianca's and he cursed himself for reminding her of it now.

Leanna's voice became brisk. "I am determined to go, Harry. If you won't accompany me, I shall attend by myself."

Harry looked at her uncertainly, then he sighed in defeat. When she tilted her little chin at that angle, arguing with her was useless.

"Very well," he agreed at last. At her shout of glee, he admonished, "But we'll arrive early and not stay late, mind."

"Of course." Her reply was demure, but he would have been disquieted if he'd seen the glint in her eye. "They have a masquerade night tonight," she cooed, looking at him sidelong.

"I suppose tonight is as good a night as any. I will obtain dominoes and masks for us and collect you around eight. No word to Sherry or Jason, now." Harry shuddered as he imagined both men's reaction should they hear of the outing.

"I wouldn't dream of mentioning it," Leanna said sincerely.

Leanna's air of excitement was almost tangible that night at dinner. Sherry bestowed an indulgent smile on her.

"What are your plans for this evening, my dear?" he queried.

"Oh, I'm just going to read in my room," Leanna sighed. Sherry looked skeptical, but after a glance at Jason's taut face, he said nothing.

He was becoming increasingly concerned at their chilly behavior. He knew his cousin was working feverishly at the docks, trying to get his ship ready for sea in a few days. Every time he tried to probe Jason's feelings or explain Leanna's actions, he was repudiated with a cool shrug and a hooded look. Sherry was not fooled, however. He sensed a torrent of emotions behind that wooden facade, and he feared the consequences of Jason expressing them. But the earl's warnings to Leanna were met with blithe unconcern.

As he watched her calmly sipping her wine now, he decided to try again after dinner. He would not be there to protect her on the long voyage home, and she must be made to understand that this continual dallying with Jason's emotions was dangerous.

As soon as the last dish was removed, Leanna excused herself to Sherry, not even looking at Jason. She walked sedately from the room, but when she reached the vacant hall, she rushed up the stairs.

She must hurry, or she would be late! She locked her door and fumbled through the many gowns in her wardrobe, finally finding the one she was seeking. She pulled it out and held it up against herself with satisfaction. It was a gorgeous, but daring, gown. Her face was a picture of mischief when she imagined Harry's reaction when he saw her in it.

Thirty minutes later, she examined herself in the glass uncertainly. Abby had thought the dress improper when she bought it, but had finally conceded it would be suitable for a special evening at home. Leanna pivoted slowly, uneasy at the way the gown clung to the curves of her body. The whisper-thin green gauze was laced with gold and seemed to float when she moved, then cling even tighter when she stood still. The bodice was precariously low cut, so much so that it seemed her breasts would tumble free at the slightest nudge. She was wearing only one thin petticoat beneath it as all of her chemises showed at the neckline.

Leanna hesitated, biting her lip uncertainly, then she shrugged as she reasoned she would be wearing an enveloping domino. She covered the gown with a long velvet pelisse and gasped when she saw the time on the clock by the bed.

She peeked out her door, locked it behind her when she saw no one in the hall, and sped down the stairs on silent feet. She stopped abruptly when she saw Hastings speaking to one of the footmen in the foyer. She tapped her foot impatiently, then decided to use the servants' entrance. By the time she reached the drive she was breathless, but jubilant. She felt like a little girl playing hooky as she waited for Harry under the branches of a huge elm. She halted his carriage at the gates, anxious that no one should see them.

She was unaware of the brown face that watched her furtive ascent into Harry's carriage from the upstairs window. She didn't see the man's hand clench the heavy velvet drape so fiercely that the seam tore as he watched the carriage pull away. Abruptly, the curtain fell back into place and all was still.

Inside the carriage, Harry was lecturing Leanna on waiting for him in the drive like a common servant girl.

She listened calmly, unrepentant. "I told Sherry I'd be in my room, reading. We'd have been in a pretty mess when you arrived to collect me, wouldn't we?"

Harry looked at her balefully for a moment, then he sighed and handed her a sedate black domino and mask. She pouted, disappointed, but tried the mask on. It covered her from hair line to lips and was anything but romantic. She removed her pelisse and looked up when she heard Harry release a strangled gasp.

"Do you like my gown?" she asked impudently.

He sputtered for a moment, then rasped, "What are you trying to do? That gown makes you look like . . . a . . ." He choked on the word.

"Oh, surely not that bad, Harry," she laughed. "I've heard the gowns are more daring at masquerades."

Harry didn't reply. He wondered morosely how he had let her talk him into this. That gown tempted him to make improper advances to her. He worried how on earth he was to protect Leanna from others when he wasn't sure he could control himself. He debated ordering the coachman to turn the coach around, but as he watched her happy face, he didn't have the heart to disappoint her. Leanna didn't see him drop a heavy pistol in the deep pocket of his domino.

When Leanna drew the heavy cloak over her sparkling gown, he relaxed somewhat, but he fastened it for her firmly. Her smile went to his head like heady wine, and he would have reached out to touch her if the carriage hadn't stopped at Vauxhall.

Leanna looked around, enchanted. Vauxhall Pleasure Gardens were brightly illuminated by thousands of colored lamps placed strategically among the trees. Fountains and cascades were nestled along stately avenues, while an orchestra added its voice to the festive atmosphere. Small, intimate supper boxes were barely visible among leafy arbors.

Leanna skipped lightly beside Harry, for the moment content to watch the people and sights around her. She no longer felt uncomfortable in her daring gown, for some of the women around her seemed almost indecently exposed. She was unfamiliar with the practice of dampening one's muslins. She blushed and looked away when she saw one of the lady's escorts caress her in a distinctly improper place.

Leanna didn't object when Harry pulled her protectively closer. "I warned you," he whispered. "I believe I see a vacant box. They make a tolerable syllabub here. Would you like one?"

Leanna nodded as Harry seated her. They waited a considerable time before a waiter finally came to take their order. Leanna shifted restlessly, uneasy. She felt a gaze boring into her from somewhere, but try as she might, she could discern no one watching them.

She finally whispered to Harry, "Do you see anyone you know, Harry? I feel like we're being watched."

He looked around the gay throng, but he could see no one that looked familiar. "I don't see anyone," he replied.

She shrugged and dismissed the feeling, concentrating with relish on the dessert that had just arrived. "Now may we dance, Harry?" she pleaded when they had finished the dish.

He looked around the boisterous crowd, uncertain. The Pleasure Gardens seemed unusually gay and rowdy tonight. A refusal trembled on his lips, but Leanna's coaxing smile settled him once again. It would be marvelous to hold her in his arms.

"Very well," he agreed. She jumped up and led him impatiently to the dance floor. They whirled in rhythm to the gay tune, neither of them aware of the tall scarlet domino that watched their every move from a dark corner. When Leanna smiled and brushed a speck of lint from Harry's shoulder, the man's jaw tensed and a tic appeared in the lean brown cheek beneath his scarlet mask.

Harry grasped Leanna's arm preparatory to leading her off the floor between numbers, but he found himself rudely shouldered aside. A tall blue domino snatched her away as another tune began. Leanna threw a reassuring smile at Harry, seeming quite at ease, and sending him to reluctantly weave through the dancing couples to wait on the sidelines. For a moment he stiffened in panic when he lost sight of her, then he relaxed when he saw a small black domino dancing gaily with a tall blue one.

Outside, Leanna was not at first alarmed when her partner waltzed her down a less crowded walk. She much preferred the cool evening air to the stuffy ballroom and she had enjoyed her partner's relaxed conversation. He finished telling her the history of Vauxhall, then halted when a tall scarlet domino tapped his shoulder.

With a regretful smile and deep bow, he relinquished her to her new partner. Leanna thought she saw the red domino hand him something, but she was uncertain in the dim light. Her partner danced them further down the walk as she attempted to make conversation with him.

"Most lovely evening for dancing, it is not, sir?" she inquired politely. He nodded without speaking.

"Do you come to Vauxhall often?" she tried again.

For a moment she thought he had not heard, then he shook his head. Leanna's mouth tightened, and she became impatient for the dance to end so she could return to Harry. Really, Vauxhall was nothing out of the common, after all. The music finally stopped and Leanna waited for her partner to release her. When he made no move to do so, she looked up to protest indignantly and froze in horror when she saw his eyes glittering at her lasciviously from behind his mask.

They had halted under a towering oak. It was illuminated dimly by one red lantern that reflected off the surface of a nearby fountain. The unsteady red light lent a surrealistic glow to her partner's tall figure until he seemed to be nothing but a demon conjured by her fears from the nether regions. Leanna opened her mouth to scream, only to find her lips muffled by his hand as he used the other to pull her, kicking and scratching, further into the brush.

Then he roughly jerked her mask off and seemed to savor her fear as she struggled wildly. His eyes glowed like coals as they roved her face, probing her face from her frightened eyes to her flushed cheeks to the mouth he still held covered. Unable to make any impression on his sinewy legs with her soft slippers and with her hands held behind her, Leanna took the only course left. She bit his hand with sharp white teeth until he let her go with a muffled curse. She managed one short scream before he jerked her to his broad chest and fastened his lips to hers.

Leanna gagged as she felt his hot tongue probing to enter beyond. Her struggles subsided and she went limp, opening her clamped jaws. He licked her teeth greedily then filled her mouth with his tongue. She once more bit down as hard as she could, delighted when he yelped in pain. He flung her roughly to the ground and stuffed a handkerchief in her mouth before she could scream again.

He chuckled as he pulled her arms above her head and stilled her thrashing legs with his own iron-muscled thigh. Impotent, she could only tremble in fury and terror when he sneered in a coarse, rough voice, "Been wantin' ta get me dabs on a gentry mort like yersel' fer a long time. If you wants h'it rough, don't matter none ta me."

Without further ado, he wrenched her domino off. He gasped in pleasure when he pulled open her bodice and let tumble free her lovely, trembling orbs. His eyes feasted greedily for a moment, then he fastened his lips to one of her breasts and began sucking until the pink tip became swollen. She gasped and struggled anew. He merely laughed and turned his torment to her other breast. Leanna stiffened when she heard that laugh. It sounded devilishly familiar.

She noted other things she had been too terrified to observe before. His hair released a familiar scent of lime soap and salty ocean breezes, and surely no other man had the same boldly-defined mouth and determined cheekbones? Leanna made strangling noises behind her gag, then went limp as a wet rag.

Jason stiffened and moved cautiously away so that he could see her face. It seemed uncommonly still and white. "Gal," he said harshly. And when there was no reply, "Leanna!" He shook her urgently. With quicksilver grace, she bolted from under him to her feet.

"You fiend!" she spat. When he stood warily beside her she flung off his mask and slapped his face, then turned to flee. Once more she found herself caught and held. His face was dark with rage and the imprint of her hand stood out whitely as he crushed her to him.

"How long did you think you could play me for the fool?" he snarled back. "Harry dear, Harry darling, and Jason always the cad. I'll not have it, do you hear?" He shook her with unknowing violence, then, as he realized her breasts were still uncovered, he groaned and pressed his mouth over hers. Leanna stood stiff in his arms, a pillar of icy hostility. She didn't dare bite him again, but she was determined to give him no pleasure.

Then one warm hand covered her breast and the cruel pressure of his mouth eased into a gentle persuasion. Leanna found her determination wavering as he nibbled gently at her lips and his hand rubbed the tip of her breast in a movement that was both rough and pleasurable. When his soft lips traveled down her neck, licked the warm hollow of her throat, and finally teased the breast he had coaxed to hardness, Leanna sighed and sagged against him weakly. At that moment she was aware of nothing but the heat in her body that had melted her hostility into a nectar that ran soothingly through her veins.

Jason felt her response and redoubled his efforts, conscious only of her softness against him and the need that throbbed within him to take and give her pleasure in ever greater portions. Thus, neither of them heard Harry's anxious voice calling Leanna's name, or even sensed his presence when he gasped in horror at the sight of Leanna being bent over backward in an intimate embrace. He jerked the pistol from his pocket and stealthily stepped behind the figure to bring the weapon down with crushing force on Jason's unsuspecting head.

Jason slumped to the ground. Leanna swayed weakly, at

first too stunned by her rioting emotions to realize what had happened. Harry grabbed her in his arms and asked anxiously, "Leanna? Leanna, are you all right?" He pulled his cloak around her, averting his gaze from her exposed breasts.

She shuddered and gasped in horror as she realized that Jason lay unconscious on the ground. Harry was bewildered and insulted when, far from thanking her gallant rescuer, she hissed at him angrily, "Did you have to hit him so hard? I can take care of myself!" She bent to stroke her attacker's brow with a tender hand.

Harry teetered in shock for a moment, then understanding dawned when he saw the attacker's face for the first time. He groaned, clenched his fists, and cursed the fates for embroiling him in this situation.

"I'll get some water and brandy," he muttered. As he walked away, he prayed he could revive Jason and get him away with no one the wiser. All this farce needed now was some old biddy coming upon the scene and making sure the entire ton heard of this incident. He could imagine with what relish the city would savor the scandal of Sherringham's cousin attempting to rape his own wife.

Jason's first sensation when consciousness returned was the softness of his pillow, not suspecting it was Leanna's lap he awoke in. His second was the blazing pain in his head when he moved it. His third, and most gratifying, was the sight of Leanna's concerned face as it swam before him. He slumped against her and moaned in agony as he pressed his face into her soft lap.

She stroked his hair with a gentleness that belied her curt voice as she spoke to Harry. "We must get him to a doctor immediately. If he doesn't recover, Harry, I'll never forgive you." Jason listened, delighted at the unexpectedly spectacular success of his scheme. Not only had he tasted the delicious response of her body before Harry so rudely interrupted, but he had at last succeeded in driving a wedge between Leanna and her reluctant suitor. He groaned again for good measure, then sipped his drink.

"Devil take it, how was I to know it was your husband?"

Harry sputterred, indignant at her cavalier dismissal of his gallantry. He grasped Jason and pulled him none too gently to his feet. The injured attacker groaned, genuinely this time, and rested his head on the other's broad shoulders. He swayed for a moment, then stood firm, staring into their anxious eyes.

"What the devil did you hit me with, Harry? The wrath of God?" The joke was weak, but it was evident he was recovering already.

"Just my pistol, old fellow. Could have been worse, you know," Harry pointed out. "If you hadn't held Leanna in such an, er, intimate embrace, I might have shot you instead." He shuddered at the thought.

The concern faded from Leanna's face as memory of their intimacy returned. She removed her arm from its support of Jason and stepped away from him.

Jason cursed under his breath and grabbed her arm. "Leanna, let me . . . ." He hurried beside her as she strode inelegantly to the coach in Harry's oversized cloak, which she held to her to protect her freed breasts.

"You've done quite enough for one evening, thank you, sir," she snapped. "So much for promises!" she concluded triumphantly, ignoring the coachman as he held the door for her. She stepped into the carriage.

Jason moved to follow, but Harry grabbed his arm. "Sorry, old chap, I didn't mean to set her off again." Jason said nothing, hostility evident in every line of his wooden features.

"I'll take a hack to my lodgings so you can be alone with her and explain. Things will be right as rain when you admit you just meant to frighten her because you were jealous."

"Jealous? Why, have I reason to be?" Jason's voice was soft, but the menace in it sent chills up Harry's spine.

"No, no, not at all. You know she was just flirting with me. Why, she treats me more like a brother when you're not around," Harry hastened to reassure him. He urged Jason into the carriage, sighing with relief when the door shut behind him. Harry flushed under the somber gaze of the coachman.

"To the Earl of Sherringham's, Henry," he commanded loftily, then he turned to hail a carriage.

Henry clucked to his team, but shook his head disapprovingly at the leader. "T'weren't right o' the marster, leavin' the gent ta face the missy's rage alone. Don't know wot 'appened, but h'it's plain she's in a proper taken'." His brief acquaintance with Leanna had led him to a hearty respect for the lady's spirit and determination.

His fears for Jason were unfounded. Leanna didn't scream, reproach, or cry. She merely stared through him as though he were not there, the most intolerable punishment of all to a man of Jason's temperament.

Finally, he grasped her limp hand firmly. "Leanna," he said with decision. "I had no intention of being . . . intimate with you. I merely wanted to impress upon you the dangers inherent in such situations. You need the protection that only a husband can give in places of that sort."

She was taken aback. "Protection? I agree heartily, sir. I need protection *from* you, not by you," she said, turning a scornful cheek to him.

Jason reddened in anger, but clamped his jaw. "We can deal together better than this, my dear," he said. "I have shown as much restraint as I am able. I know you have a distaste for me, and I own I can't blame you, considering the start to our marriage. Can we not set aside this eternal enmity and at least be friends?" His voice was as close to pleading as he could make it. His pride growled in rage, but he ruthlessly stifled it, forcing himself to remember her all-important response to his kisses.

Leanna bit her lip nervously. She was torn. She wanted to accept his olive branch, but the other side of her feared she would be used and cast aside. Her emotions were further confused by the memory of that shattering embrace. She had never dreamed it possible to experience such pleasure in the arms of a man, certainly not the arms of the man she professed to hate. If he stirred her so now, surely she would be lost if she allowed him any closer?

"No," she said softly, instinctively. "You have no interest in a scrawny chit like me, remember?" she reminded him haughtily. "Our relationship suits me as it is." She sounded the death knell to his hopes.

He looked on the verge of strangling with rage for a moment, then he expelled his breath slowly through his teeth. "Very well, wench," he gritted, "if its war you want, it's war you shall have. But no more flirtations with Harry or any other man, or by God, I'll consider myself relieved of any promise I gave and will enjoy the favors you allow others. Do I make myself clear?" The hardness of his voice rang out like clashing swords.

Leanna nodded, biting her lip at the humiliation, but she was afraid to push him further. Both sat back in their respective corners, preserving a silence fraught with smoldering emotions for the remainder of the drive.

Sherringham paced the study until Abby was certain she could see a path forming in the lush carpet. She stifled her own fears for Leanna as she encouraged, "I'm certain Jason would never harm her, no matter how angry he was, my dear."

"I wish I could be so certain," the earl muttered to his pacing feet. "He's a possessive and passionate man, and I'm afraid Leanna might have gone too far this time."

He had gone to Leanna's chamber to have a talk with her and found the door locked. He became concerned when she did not answer his calls, so he obtained the master key from Mrs. Jory and entered a vacant room.

Hastings and the servants could provide no clues as to her whereabouts, but one of the under footmen had seen Jason exit hurriedly. He carried a red domino over his arm, and, as the servant put it, "A look o' murder h'in 'is peepers."

Sherry knew Leanna wanted to visit Vauxhall Gardens, and he was preparing to set out after them when Abby arrived. She was also worried at the tense situation between Leanna and Jason, but she felt the pair had reached a stalemate and needed something to bring matters to a head between them. In addition, she believed their long voyage home would help them reconcile their differences. Two people as attracted as they were to one another could not long remain hostile when forced into such close proximity for an extended period of time, she soothed Sherry.

He tenderly considered his betrothed's earnest, sweet face

and felt a great rush of love for her fill his heart. He had guarded his passions assiduously whenever he held her in his arms, a task made no easier by her own fervent response. She was a deeply sensual woman who had no conception of the lengths to which unfulfilled desire could drive a man. Sherry wondered how he would react if, after enjoying the bliss of her arms, she should suddenly deny herself to him. He shuddered at the thought and feared for Leanna even as he sympathized with Jason. He resumed his pacing.

Muffled voices in the hall penetrated his preoccupied thoughts and the earl rushed to the door to stand aghast at the sight of the two bedraggled figures that met his eyes. Leanna stood proudly beside Jason, anxiety marring her lovely face. Her hair tumbled in wild disorder about her shoulders and flushed cheeks as she held a man's cloak tightly to her breast. Jason was no less disheveled. His domino was ripped and dirty, his hair mussed, but most disquieting of all was the rage in his eyes.

Sherry clasped Leanna in his arms as he implored, "My dear, are you all right?"

The concern in his blue gaze was her undoing. Her painfully constructed facade of composure crumbled and she pulled away to flee, sobbing, up the stairs. Abby, with a worried glance at Jason, followed.

Sherry stood to his full, imposing height to look Jason squarely in the eye. "Have you harmed her in any way, cousin?" he asked directly.

Jason burst into bitter laughter. "Only her dignity. All else is unchanged," he rasped, then strode into the study to pour himself a hefty shot of brandy. He gulped it down, coughing as his throat protested the brutal treatment. He poured another and moved to stare moodily into the fire.

"Would you like to tell me what happened, Jason?" Sherry sank into his favorite chair near the fire and awaited a response with foreboding.

For a moment it seemed Jason wouldn't reply, then he rasped in a voice so low that Sherry had to strain to hear, "She hates me so that she'll not accept me even as a friend. She prefers witless fops like Harry." His hand gripped the stem of his snifter so tightly Sherry feared the glass would crack.

The earl rose, took the glass from Jason's hand, and escorted him firmly to a comfortable chair beside his own. "I'm certain Leanna doesn't hate you, Jason," he disagreed calmly, reseating himself.

"You see," he continued, "Leanna rarely had companionship of her own age, male or female, because of her secluded childhood. She knows little of men. I suspect you arouse strong emotions in her that she's never felt before and consequently has not learned to deal with." Jason looked up, some of the bleakness leaving his face as he listened.

Sherry smiled bracingly. "Be patient. Women are stronger creatures than men believe. Leanna has been prodding you to see how much she can get away with. If she now knows the limits of your patience, she'll be a less abrasive companion on your voyage home."

Jason digested this advice in silence, still hurt at her rejection. He rose to pace the floor where Sherry had paced earlier. Never in his life had he tendered an offer of friendship to a woman. He had been interested only in the momentary gratification provided his body; a woman's thoughts, feelings, or comfort were matters of total indifference to him.

He pulled aside the heavy drape and stared into the darkness of the night, occupied in a soul-searching he found as painful as it was atypical. Aye, he had wronged her. He ravished her innocence, then expected her to accept him with open arms when he gave her the reluctant protection of his name.

His lips tightened. But she had been as difficult as possible, defying him at every turn. If he had made no effort to mend matters between them, neither had she. Most rankling of all, she had thrown his belated offer of friendship back in his face, blithely rejecting the truce it took every ounce of his will to extend.

Sherry said nothing, watching the battle rage within Jason. The two opponents, pride and desire, were equally matched, and he hoped Jason's innate sense of justice would tip the balance in favor of his desire for Leanna. Once his cousin admitted she was more important to him than the sterile comfort of pride, they could begin building a relationship that Sherry suspected could be as fulfilling as his own with Abby. He waited, a slight smile on his face.

Jason opened his clenched fist and rested his elbow on the sill as his inner turmoil began to subside. One thought was crystal clear in his mind: he fervently desired Leanna, and short of rape, the only way he could ever win her was if he wooed her into his bed. For a moment he faltered, remembering her hatred. Then his memory of her burgeoning response to his embrace before Harry cut it short surfaced and his old arrogance returned.

Had he ever met a woman who denied him what he set out to win? Leanna was a mere girl, after all, and should fall easy prey to his practiced seduction. He stood straight, then turned to face Sherry, resolve plain in his expression.

"I've been a fool, Cousin," he admitted with a smile. "I still desire Leanna and if I'm to win her, I must display more patience than I have displayed heretofore." His smile faded as he confessed, "Still, it will not be easy. Her haughtiness drives me near madness at times. But the voyage home will allow me ample opportunity to learn the benefits of patience and teach her the potency of desire."

"Bravo!" Sherry congratulated. "You've made a wise decision, Jason, and I'm sure you will succeed. Is there anything I can do to help?"

"You've helped more than you know," Jason replied hesitantly. He cleared his throat in embarrassment. "I want to thank you for your consideration toward Leanna and myself. Let me assure you that I will do everything in my power to mend things between us and give her the happiness she deserves." The two cousins shook hands, in perfect accord, certain in their male arrogance that Jason could seduce the inexperienced Leanna into his arms.

They wished one another a cordial goodnight. Jason's mind was once more at ease, but that night he dreamed uncomfortably of a gorgeous, golden-haired enchantress who eased his loins but tormented his mind.

* * *

When Abby knocked on Leanna's door, the sounds of muffled sobbing were choked off abruptly. Leanna's voice, cold and hostile, commanded, "Go away! I don't wish to speak with anyone."

"Leanna, it's Abby! Please let me speak with you," she pleaded.

Silence reigned for a moment, then the key turned in the lock and Leanna, red-eyed and pale, reluctantly opened the door. Abby shut the door behind her and watched compassionately as Leanna turned away, refusing to meet her eyes.

Both stood silent for a moment, then Abby put a gentle hand on the younger girl's shoulder and murmured, "My dear, it would probably make you feel better to talk about what happened. I feel as though a dear sister is in despair but refuses my help. It's most distressing for me to see you so upset." The tenderness in Abby's voice loosed another flood of tears from Leanna's eyes.

She stammered, "H-he b-broke his promise not to t-touch me. A-at the masquerade." She released her grip on the cloak and Abby gasped when she saw her exposed breasts.

"Did he harm you?" she asked sharply.

Leanna laughed, teetering on the verge of hysteria. "Not in the way you mean. H-he said he only meant to s-scare me. He succeeded b-beautifully." She choked on another sob, then buried her face in her hands. Abby cradled her close, rubbing her back soothingly until the storm of emotion subsided.

She made her lie down, then poured some eau de cologne on a handkerchief and stroked her brow and temples. Leanna sighed as the tenseness in her body slowly dissolved under Abby's ministrations. She told her the whole story, ending with Jason's offer of friendship.

Abby stopped when Leanna admitted she had rejected the offer. "Oh, my dear, was that wise?" Her soft blue eyes were concerned.

Leanna sat up and propped the pillows behind her. She twisted the bed cover and admitted, "I had to. You see, I found out something about myself tonight that disturbs me greatly." She bit her lip, hesitated, then blurted, "When I realized who he was and he kissed me again, I began to, to..." Leanna looked away, flushed.

Abby inserted gently, "You enjoyed it?" Leanna nodded without speaking. Abby hid a smile as she sighed in relief. Perhaps things would work out between them after all.

"Jason is a handsome, virile man, Leanna. It's natural for you to find him attractive," she soothed.

Leanna looked up, a protest dying on her lips as she met Abby's steady gaze. She sighed instead and confessed, "But I thought I hated him. How is it possible to enjoy being embraced by someone you hate?"

Abby rinsed her hands in the bowl beside the bed, considering her reply carefully. "Have you considered the possibility that you don't hate him as much as you thought?" she inquired lightly.

Leanna frowned, her lips tightening as she recalled Jason's arrogant assumption that she would become a compliant wife and mistress. Then she remembered the almost boyish eagerness on his face as he offered her his friendship. She shook her head, unable to make sense of her own jumbled emotions.

"I would suggest you sleep on it," Abby advised. "But remember, my dear, Jason is now your husband. You will be leaving soon and he will be the only familiar figure in your new life. Wouldn't it be much better to have a warm, dependable relationship with your husband rather than this constant bickering?" Abby refused to feel remorse when Leanna whitened at the reminder of her imminent departure. It she would sheathe her claws and accept Jason's offer, Abby was sure the attraction between them would bring them together.

She kissed her lightly on the cheek, then took her hand and smiled. "Sherry and I love you very much, Leanna, and we want you to be happy. If you accept Jason's offer, I think you'll enjoy your life much more. Please at least consider it." She gave Leanna a brief hug, then quit the room with the light, graceful step that was so much a part of her.

As Leanna dressed for bed, Abby's words echoed in her ears. Truth to tell, she was tired of the continual battle with Jason. She dreaded the long voyage to America and was forced to admit continued hostilities would be unbearable.

She climbed into bed, blew out the taper on the nightstand, and pulled the covers up to her chin. She shuddered as she recalled the strength in Jason's hands and the passion in his kiss that had awakened some unknown, wanton creature within her breast. The notion of losing her independence to his sexual dominance was a dangerous one. Yet surely they could at least be friends? The idea was strangely appealing as she visualized Jason's long-lashed blue eyes soft and gentle instead of stormy or cold.

She yawned. After all, he was her husband now. They had to reach some accord to make their marriage bearable. Leanna drifted off to sleep, determined to hold her temper and accept Jason's offer. She pushed the memory of that disturbing embrace firmly to the back of her mind, only to dream of a dim figure that took her time and time again, washing away her fears in waves of agonizing pleasure. She couldn't see his face, but the pleasant scent of lime and ocean breezes drifted off his hair.

Chapter
Eight

WHEN LEANNA WENT downstairs for breakfast the next morning, she was surprised to find the morning room deserted except for Jason. She was even more surprised when he rose courteously and seated her, bestowing a warm smile on her all the while. She sat frozen for a moment. She was amazed at his amiability. She had expected icy indifference from him on their next meeting. She looked at him sidelong as she folded her napkin in her lap, uneasy as she noted the slight smile at his lips.

"The last of the *Savannah*'s cargo has been loaded and we'll be ready to sail on the morrow, my dear," Jason informed her smoothly. He buttered a scone, ignoring her suspended fork and white face. "Is there anything you would like to purchase before we leave?"

Leanna shook her head mutely. The long-dreaded day was almost upon her and she wasn't sure she was brave enough to go through with it, after all. If England had brought her sorrow, it had also brought her happiness. She was afraid America would bring her only sorrow.

She shoved her plate back and rose on unsteady legs. "Please excuse me, sir."

As she turned to flee, she found her way blocked by a large, muscular figure who pulled her close. A steady heart beat under her ear, soothing hands stroked her back, and a calm voice above her comforted, "Don't fret, my dear. My country is a beautiful land. You'll grow to love it as I do. You have nothing to fear. I protect what is mine."

The calm possessiveness in his tone grated on Leanna's nerves, but also, incongruously, quieted her down. An unacknowledged corner of her mind admitted it would be nice to belong to someone again. She relaxed against his shoulder, letting his gentleness soothe her.

Jason held her away, his thumbs caressing her delicate collarbones as he coaxed, "It would be so much nicer to enjoy our voyage as comrades rather than endure it as enemies, wouldn't you say, my dear?" His smile mesmerized her. The white teeth shone in his bronzed face, while the creases in his cheeks lent a playful look to his handsome features.

Unable to tear her gaze away, Leanna admitted shyly, "Indeed it would." She flushed, then blurted, "If your offer still stands, sir, I most gratefully accept."

It was Jason's turn to be enchanted by her smile. The dimple playing at one corner of her mouth tempted him, but he stifled his desire to kiss her. It was too soon yet for that. He contented himself with a brief hand squeeze and led her back to her chair.

"Now that's settled, are you sure there's nothing you wish to purchase? Luxuries in Georgia as yet are few. Do you have all the clothes you need?" At her nod, he continued decisively, "Very well. Please have your maid pack your belongings. You'll need to dress warmly in the morning. The early breezes are quite cold."

They finished breakfast and left the table in a cheerful mood, both satisfied with their newly established rapport. Jason felt he had begun a relationship that would surely deepen to better things, and Leanna was pleased at his friendly and unthreatening behavior.

He excused himself to see to some last-minute preparations and Leanna went upstairs to begin packing. As she helped the maid organize her gowns for their trunks, she couldn't entirely stifle her unease. Jason's sudden temperance was surprising, the more so because of her recent rejection of him. She was reluctant to let her guard down entirely. She'd best maintain a friendly, but distant, manner.

A knock on the door was a welcome diversion. Abby entered at her command, a small package held gingerly between nervous hands, a hesitant smile on her face.

Leanna watched with curiosity as Abby dismissed the maid, seated herself on the bed, and toyed with the string on the package. "May I ask how things went with Jason this morning? I understand from Sherry that you had breakfast with him." Abby looked inquiringly at her.

"He seems very friendly. I decided last night to try and mend matters between us, but this morning I found there was no need for any effort on my part." She frowned, her confusion obvious. "I expected him to be hostile at first, but he was quite charming and considerate."

"And you're a little suspicious as to why," Abby interpolated.

When Leanna nodded, Abby sighed and wrinkled her brow in thought. Sherry had not confided in her about his talk with Jason. In fact, he had been deliberately evasive. Abby also wondered at Jason's restraint and worried at his motivation. If his sole aim was to seduce Leanna into his bed to slake his male hunger and pride, she feared the situation between the two would worsen. While the physical attraction between them could act as a magnet to draw them together, it could also push them farther apart if intimacy was initiated for the wrong reasons.

There was no doubt that Jason desired Leanna, but Abby doubted he loved her. Without at least a degree of mutual respect and fondness, she was certain Leanna would never accept a physical relationship with him. Desire alone, no matter how strong, is not enough for a woman. She either feels cherished, or used. Abby doubted that Jason, and possibly not even Sherry, understood this peculiarly feminine need. She looked at the package in her lap and wondered if she should give it to Leanna now.

Leanna watched Abby in puzzlement, wondering what problem was causing her such concern. When Abby twisted the parcel in her lap, she used it as an excuse to break the heavy silence. Abby jumped when Leanna asked, "What have you in the parcel?" Abby hesitated, then handed the package to Leanna almost reluctantly.

"A gift for you, my dear," she explained. She waited, tense, as Leanna tore off the wrapping with eager hands. Leanna gasped when she pulled out what was inside: a flesh-colored silk nightgown with lace inserts of the same color. The minuscule, low-necked bodice was banded with lace and thin silk. The long sleeves were entirely lace. From the high waist to the flounced hem, thin strips of lace were set at intervals opposite those in the bodice. The sheer, unique gown was designed for only one purpose: seduction.

Leanna raised a flushed, puzzled face to meet Abby's gaze. "Why have you given me this, Abby?" she asked in confusion.

Abby rose from the bed to finger the ornately carved bedpost. Leanna had the strangest feeling that the other woman was afraid to answer. She waited, becoming more concerned the longer Abby delayed.

Finally, the older woman turned back to sit beside Leanna and take her hand. "Leanna," she began, "I've never told you how Sherry and I met, have I?" Leanna shook her head.

"We were at a ball given by a mutual friend. He requested a dance with me, but my card was full. When I explained that to him, he asked who was next on my list. I told him, he bowed and disappeared, only to return a few moments later to take my hand and lead me onto the floor. When I protested, he gave me a charming smile and said, 'Don't worry your pretty head, my dear. Your former suitor doesn't object. When I told him I intended to marry you, he most nobly withdrew his suit.' And he whirled me around the floor as calmly as though we were discussing the weather."

Abby smiled as she reminisced, her eyes misty. "Needless to say, I thought him quite mad and impossibly arrogant. He left shortly thereafter, but not a day passed that he didn't call on me, send me flowers or some other triviality, or follow me on my drives in the park. At first I refused to even see him, but he was so persistent that finally I gave in out of sheer exhaustion. It took him all of a week to convince me that he was the man I wanted to marry." She looked at Leanna's bemused face and laughed shakily.

"I have never had cause to regret my acceptance. I am eager to become Sherry's wife, companion, and mother of his children." Her voice was husky as she continued. "And I am eager to share his bed." When Leanna looked shocked, Abby reddened but continued with determination, "Desire is a strong emotion, Leanna. It is also nothing to be ashamed of. I gave you that gown in hopes that someday you will be able to wear it with the same joy that I will take to Sherry on our wedding night."

Leanna seemed ready to protest, but Abby put a gentle, silencing finger on her lips before she could speak. "Please, let me finish." Abby withdrew her finger to run it tenderly down Leanna's cheek. "The Blaine men are strong, but honest and reliable. I see much of Sherry in Jason. If you can win his love, I am certain he will make you as happy as Sherry has made me." Abby waited for Leanna's response, hoping that she had not done more harm than good.

Leanna's brows drew together and her forehead wrinkled as she tried to understand Abby's hint. She asked slowly, fingering the gossamer gown, "Are you suggesting that I use this gown to seduce Jason? That I try to win his love thusly?"

Abby blanched. "Certainly not!" She sighed and explained, "I wanted you to realize that desire is not a shameful emotion. Quite to the contrary, it is the body's natural response to love. I realize you don't love Jason yet, but should you find that you do, one day perhaps you'll want to wear this gown." She hesitated, then shifted her position and took a deep breath. She found this last piece of advice difficult to voice.

"One other thing, my dear. While men can much enjoy intimacy without love, sometimes love can come upon them unawares. Should you find yourself precipitated into such a relationship, don't despair. Jason *is* your husband, and your union is blessed in the eyes of both man and God. Love could well develop, on both your parts."

Abby rose, her voice brisk. "Now, let me help with your packing. Do these gowns belong in this trunk?" She began folding some muslin day dresses carefully away. Ignoring Leanna's silence, she chatted happily, quelling her own inner fears at her interference.

Abby soon departed, leaving an agitated Leanna sitting on the edge of the bed, deep in thought. Despite Abby's assertion that a physical union with her husband was blessed, Leanna felt with every nerve in her body that such a relationship was wrong unless they grew to love one another. It had been hard enough for her to smother her distrust and accept his offer of friendship; anything closer was impossible. The pain and humiliation she had suffered on that dreadful night was still an all too vivid memory.

She looked at the shimmering gown on the coverlet. It seemed to beckon her, tempting her to forbidden thoughts and emotions. A vision appeared before her eyes of a curly-headed figure, with hair as black as night and eyes as deep blue as dusk. He was smiling tenderly at her, with strong brown hands that gently caressed her.

Unaware, she reached out to stroke the smooth silk, returning to the here and now with a guilty start when she touched the fabric. She met her flushed reflection defiantly in the glass. After all, where was the harm in just trying on the gown? She quickly pulled off her simple morning dress, stripped off her petticoats, hesitated, then pulled the chemise over her head and added it to the pile of clothing on the divan.

She donned the nightgown, smoothing it over her hips, and turned to confront herself. She gasped when she saw the temptress staring at her. The glimmering silk was almost exactly the color of her peachy skin, and it clung intimately to every curve of her lissome body. The effect was to make her seem almost, but not totally, naked.

She was so startled by her appearance that she didn't hear the soft knock on the door or notice the male figure that entered until a low gasp pierced her absorption. She whirled to face Jason's heated, startled gaze. For a timeless moment, his blue eyes locked with her green ones, one gaze intent and passionate, the other frightened and embarrassed. Then he pulled away, lowering his eyes to sweep her body hungrily. Leanna's paralysis erupted into a flurry of agitation. She scuttled to the bed, pulled the covers to her chin, and hid like a reluctant peahen confronted by a lustful, strutting peacock. Her face was so uncharacteristically timid that Jason almost smiled, despite the pounding of his heart.

"I've finished preparing my ship for sea. I came to offer my services in any, er, endeavor you may desire." The double entendre was wasted on Leanna. His words sailed over her mortified head.

Jason forced himself to calmness and walked to the end of the bed to lean against the post with seeming indolence. A close observer would have seen through the coolness, but Leanna was too embroiled in her own embarrassment to notice the bulge in his breeches. He cursed the tight pantaloons.

Leanna tucked the covers securely under her arms and folded her hands together on top of them. She calmed somewhat under his level gaze, unaware of the effort it cost him not to leap under the covers with her. Dash it, he wasn't made of stone! Why was she trying on such a seductive gown, anyway? She surely wasn't considering wearing it for him? His heart beat even faster at the thought.

"What did you say you wanted, sir?" Leanna met his shuttered gaze demurely.

"I merely wanted to see if I could assist you in any way. Have you any trunks ready to send to the docks?" He dragged his gaze from her with difficulty as he looked about the room.

"Yes, the two in the corner are ready."

"I'll order their removal immediately," he stated, backing slowly to the door. "I'll see you at luncheon." He left the room, but not before casting her one lingering glance to absorb her slim, shielded form.

Leanna sighed, relieved that he had gone. She rose and dressed, her thoughts scurrying around like squirrels chasing their tails. Humiliation, embarrassment, and a strange warmth suffused her mind. She remembered the gleam in Jason's eye when he first saw her and almost panicked when she thought of the months she would have to spend with him alone. She cursed the impulse that had made her try on the gown in the first place and resolved to be more circumspect. She knew Jason desired her and she had no intention of encouraging him.

She bathed her flushed face in the bowl beside the bed and pinned her hair up tighter. She refused to wonder at the rush of warmth that filled her when she met his ardent eyes for that brief moment. She buttoned her demure bodice all the way to her throat and avoided her gaze in the mirror. She would not admit, even to herself, that for an instant the heat in his gaze had ignited an answering flare in her own body. She walked slowly to the door, determined to be courteously aloof when she saw him at luncheon.

Three pairs of eyes were riveted on Leanna the moment she walked into the dining room. She smiled impartially at all and took her seat. Abby and Sherry were relieved at her calmness, but Jason was disappointed. He had wondered how she would receive him after their encounter in her chamber. He had expected embarrassment, possibly anger, but not the calm, collected behavior she now displayed.

Mystified, Jason eyed her quietly as he ate heartily of the delicious luncheon. He watched her push the leg of lamb and Scottish salmon around her plate and wondered about her mood. He wiped his mouth and suggested, "You'd best enjoy the meal, Leanna. We'll not see this freshness and variety again until we reach home."

Leanna forced herself to eat a few bites, but she was glad when Sherry diverted attention from her. "What's the tonnage of your vessel, Jason?"

"She's a little more than one hundred fifty. She has sharp lines, though, so she carries less than, say, a brig of comparable size." Leanna watched as Jason's face lit up proudly. "But it's a small price to pay because of her swiftness. I'll match her speed against any vessel her size afloat."

Interested, Sherry asked, "How is she rigged?"

"She's two masted, fore and aft, with square topsails. She maneuvers especially well in coastal winds. The chief advantage of a schooner is that her canvas is divided into a number of sails that are easily handled and require fewer hands aloft."

When Sherry opened his mouth to ask another question, Abby hastily interrupted. "She sounds a beauty, Jason, but are you sure you can't stay until our wedding a month hence? It would mean a lot to us both to have you and Leanna present."

Regretfully, Jason shook his head. "We'd love to stay, Abby, but I've already delayed too long. The weather will be bad enough as it is and I've cargo badly needed in Savannah."

Abby acquiesced gracefully and kept the talk light for the remainder of the meal. She could see that Leanna was still upset at the thought of leaving, but she didn't know how to reassure her.

Leanna excused herself as early as possible, but Jason caught up with her before she could escape to her room. She halted a few steps up the staircase and turned reluctantly to face him.

He mounted one step until their eyes met. "I would be proud to be your escort to the theater this evening, if you care to attend. *Hamlet* is on the bill at Drury Lane. Sherry has a box there. It will be a goodly time before we have such an opportunity again. I fear Savannah boasts little in the way of a theater as of yet." His intent eyes searched her face as he waited for her response.

Though Leanna was surprised at the invitation, she hid any expression on her face. She forced herself to meet his deep, probing glance. "I would most enjoy such an outing, sir. What time should I be ready?"

Jason was disappointed at her lack of excitement. Her attitude only heightened his distress. He hoped their accidental meeting in her chamber had not aborted their truce.

"We'll depart straight after we dine. Sherry and Abby attend with us." He watched her for a moment longer, then, as though compelled, he reached out to touch her. "Leanna," he began, his voice almost pleading. He broke off abruptly when she shied away as though alarmed. His hand dropped and he turned away, muttering, "Until this evening, then."

Lenna watched as he strode into the study and shut the door gently behind him. Her heart slowed as she finished her climb up the stairs. His closeness alarmed her and she did not yet trust his sudden concern for her welfare. Worse, she did not trust her response to his touch. She wondered what he had started to say before she pulled back. A fleeting look had crossed his face; almost a look of pain. Surely he had not been hurt by her flinch?

It was a gay, glittering party that climbed into the earl's most elegant carriage that evening. Sherry looked dignified and handsome in a claret coat and satin knee breeches, while Abby complemented him in a wine velvet gown trimmed in gold lace. Rubies glittered at her throat, wrists, and ears.

Jason was dashing in a dark blue, wide-lapeled satin coat that matched his eyes. The snowy lace at his throat emphasized his bronzed coloring. But it was Leanna who drew eyes and excited whispers among the packed crowd when they emerged from their vehicle, the driver holding open the door.

She was wearing a pink gown of Chinese silk so luminescent that the lanterns reflected off the shiny fabric. Sherry's gift of pink pearls circled her throat and wrists. Except for small seed pearls banding the puffed sleeves and ruffled hem, her gown was completely free of ornamentation. The low decolletage made a fitting frame for Leanna's silky shoulders and beautiful bosom.

She was relaxed and gay due to Abby's lively chatter and Sherry's excellent dinner wines. She didn't even shrink away when Jason helped her off with her cloak as they took their seats in Sherry's box. Sherry and Abby nodded to friends in adjacent boxes while Leanna and Jason looked around, intrigued.

The theater was large and ornately decorated. Filigree adorned the tiered boxes and the domed ceiling was intricately molded. The stage was immense and so brilliantly illuminated it almost hurt the eyes.

"Have you seen *Hamlet,* Jason?" Sherry asked as he settled back in his plush chair.

"I regret to say I have not. The nearest theater of any consequence is in Charleston, and even that doesn't compare, of course." Jason looked around with admiration once again.

"And you, Leanna? Have you seen this most tragic of tragedies?" Abby inquired sweetly.

Leanna shook her head. "I can recite a good deal of the lines, but I've never seen it performed. It is one of my favorites. But I particularly wanted to see Mrs. Siddons perform as Lady Macbeth. I've heard so much about her. I take it she doesn't perform this evening?"

"Mrs. Siddons went to Covent Garden in oh-three," Sherry answered. "We could have gone there this evening, but she doesn't perform again until next month. Possibly on your next trip we can take you to see her. She is indeed magnificent. Such resonance! Such diction!"

The light was dimmed and the buzz of voices faded as the play began. Jason watched the play only desultorily, for Leanna drew his gaze from the stage like a magnet.

He was grateful to Sherry and Abby for putting her at ease, but he was impatient for their departure so they could be alone. He was eager to woo her, gently if possible, roughly if need be. He was determined to make her his before the voyage ended. Confident that his powers of persuasion were adequate to the challenge, he looked forward to the pleasurable task.

Leanna lost herself for several marvelous hours in the suffering of one whose plight was worse than her own. She sat enthralled until Jason's gentle arm about her shoulder broke the spell. Like Hamlet, she felt torn between two warring impulses: fear and attraction. She reluctantly admitted it was pleasant to be the recipient of Jason's warm smiles. Part of her was reluctant to disrupt their newfound accord, but another part was afraid of her own susceptibility to his intoxicating presence. A harsh, angry Jason she could deal with; the charming protector of late was all too menacing to her peace of mind. Leanna was uncertain at this juncture whether she feared herself or him the most. She doubted she could keep him at arm's length for the entire duration of the voyage unless she resumed hostilities between them.

As the curtain closed after Hamlet's death, Leanna met

Jason's smiling eyes and wryly wondered if madness would also be her fate. It sometimes seemed that she indeed did not know her own mind. She admitted some wanton part of her responded to this arrogant man's embrace and fiery glance, but she still feared his passion. Nor could she dismiss her girlhood dream of a tender, considerate lover who put her needs before his own. As Jason possessively took her arm to escort her from the box, Leanna knew that while he probably passionately desired her, there was little tenderness in him.

Leanna was startled from her somber thoughts by a familiar voice calling her name. A smile lit her face as she looked up into Harry's merry eyes. He had been conspicuously absent all day.

"Harry! I'm so glad to see you! I was afraid I wouldn't be able to wish you goodbye." Harry's face fell at the news and he ignored Jason's glare as he hugged Leanna.

"I'll miss you greatly, my dear. I hope you'll write me from your new home? You know that I will always be at your service should you ever need anything." His voice quavered for a moment, then he turned to Jason and held out his hand.

Jason met his steady gaze icily, then relented and grasped his hand. "Take the best of care of her, Jason. You don't know what a treasure you have here." Harry stepped back. His eyes swept Leanna from head to toe, as though imprinting her on his memory. He bowed low, kissed her hand, and turned away to melt into the crowd.

Leanna's eyes sparkled with tears as she met Jason's stony glance. She lifted her chin defiantly and opened her mouth to speak, but she was interrupted by the return of Sherry and Abby, who had been visiting with friends.

Abby noticed Leanna's distraught face. She grasped Leanna's arm and walked a little ahead of the two men as they exited the theater. "What has brought the tears to those lovely eyes, Leanna?"

Leanna sniffed into her handkerchief, then she wiped her eyes and lifted her chin. "We met Harry and I suddenly realized how much I will miss him and what a strange new place I'm going to. I only wish it could have been him that night instead of Jason."

Wisely, Abby ignored the bitterness in her voice. "Harry would not make a stable husband, Leanna. He is far from dependable in many respects." Her tone brightened as she added, "As for America, why, I vow I am quite envious of the adventure awaiting you. I have a cousin who emigrated to Virginia many years ago. We keep in touch by post, and the land he writes of sounds vibrant and exciting. Wild, but lovely, is the way he describes it. I'm sure it will be exciting helping Jason build his plantation and participating in Savannah's growth." Abby watched Leanna from the corner of her eye as she spoke. She was relieved to see a thoughtful look replace her bleak expression.

When they reached the carriage, she drew Sherry and Jason into the conversation. On the return drive to the townhouse, they discussed the pleasurable topic of America. The pride in Jason's voice as he spoke of his country excited Leanna's curiosity, renewing her passion to see the land that boasted vast forests, mountains, swamps, and beaches, as well as large cities and thriving ports.

Thus, when Leanna went down to a very early breakfast the next morning, she was more reconciled to the journey. She still dreaded being confined with Jason, but at least now she could look forward to something at the end of the voyage.

Jason eyed her warm woolen gown and fur-lined boots approvingly. He had not referred to their meeting with Harry last night, and he was relieved to see that she seemed to have forgotten the incident. He swallowed his last appreciative bite of egg and finished his coffee.

When Leanna pushed back her plate, he asked, "Ready, my dear?"

She took a deep breath and nodded, following him from the room. They had said their goodbyes to Abby and Sherry the evening before. The parting from Harry had caused Leanna little grief when she compared it to the anguish of saying goodbye to those two. Sherry had held her close to kiss her brow.

"I am very proud of you, my ward, as I am sure your parents would have been." He held her away to search her sad eyes. "If there was one piece of advice I had to give you, it would be that happiness is always within your grasp, no matter what your name or station. I believe you and Jason can have a rewarding relationship if you don't allow recriminations or pride to stand in your way." He cupped her cheek tenderly and smiled, "Be happy, Leanna. And always remember that my prayers and love go with you."

Sherry left her room to say his goodbye to Jason. Abby met her eyes, tears in her own. Leanna sobbed and rushed into her arms where Abby held her close, sniffing, "I'll miss you terribly, my dear. You've become vastly important to Sherry and me. Please take care of yourself and that loutish husband of yours. He's not as insensitive as he seems. I feel sure that one day your marriage will be a joyous one, with deep love and respect on both sides."

Abby hugged Leanna tightly, then released her and admonished, "See that you write often, mind. And maybe when this horrible war is over and Sherry has more time, we can come to visit you. I would love to see your new homeland." Abby kissed her cheek and quit the room quickly, leaving Leanna crying on the bed.

As she now entered the carriage with Jason, Leanna wondered why she always lost the ones she loved. She watched the streets of London travel by in the early morning darkness and hoped she could find her much yearned-for happiness in the American wilderness. She turned to look at Jason's handsome profile and doubted that Sherry's prediction would come to pass. A happy marriage was possible only between two people who cared for one another. Jason's passion and her own fear formed a meager base on which to build a marriage. Leanna contemplated Jason's wooden profile and wondered what he was thinking.

Sherry's advice to Jason had been brief and succinct. "Be patient with her, Jason, but above all, be gentle. She has borne a lot in recent years. You'll answer to me if you cause her more grief." After this initial harshness, they had parted amicably enough, with a good deal of regret on both sides.

Jason frowned as he wondered if he had strength enough to follow Sherry's advice. His heart beat faster at the very thought of the weeks he would spend with Leanna cramped together in his small cabin. It had but one bed, and surely she didn't expect him to long tolerate lying next to her beautiful body with only sleep to look forward to?

As they neared the harbor, Leanna and Jason were thus troubled with vastly different, yet similar, concerns. Both were worried that the proximity necessitated by the long voyage might resolve their conflict unpalatably, or worsen it irretrievably. Jason was afraid of losing control and pushing her into further retreat from him; Leanna was concerned that her responsive senses might precipitate her into an unwanted relationship. It would be a trying, dangerous time for them both.

Chapter
Nine

———⌐———

THE FILTHY INDIVIDUAL in dirty rags ambled up the noisome
alley behind the King's Tavern. His gait was incongruously
arrogant for such an obvious plebeian. The soft hand that pushed
open the cracked, rusted door was also jarringly different from
his appearance. He slipped inside the back room of the smoky,
noisy tavern and took a seat in a shadowy corner. The room
was lit only by two candles. The man set a large bundle on
the floor beside him, then took a knife from his sack and hid
it in his ragged sleeve, for insurance.

Blackie strode wearily into the room and sat down at a large
table to take a tired sip of ale. He never touched gin. Owning
a tavern in this poorest district of London had taught him well
what the foul brew did to a person's mind and body. And now
that he'd finally seen his only child, Peg, released from Newgate,
he had no need of a tonic.

Blackie briefly thought of Sir Gavin Redfern and wondered
how he did in the Fleet. It would be unbearable for a man so

used to the benefits of rank to spend the remainder of his days in that rotting debtor's prison. Blackie shrugged, deeming the devil had finally gotten his due for the ruination he had meted out to others so uncaringly over the years.

Blackie looked up warily when a soft scraping sound from the corner reached his ears. He saw a shadowy figure sitting motionless in a chair. He leaped up and grabbed a pistol from a crooked cabinet on the wall nearby. Holding it at the ready, he growled, "'Oo be ye and wot be yer business?"

The figure rose and strode into the light. Blackie gasped and almost dropped his weapon when he recognized Sir Gavin. His arm fell to his side as he wondered with a shiver if his very thoughts had conjured the devil up.

"Hello, Blackie," Sir Gavin said softly. "Surprised to see me?"

Blackie collected his scattered thoughts and reseated himself, resting the pistol in his lap. "That I be, sor," he answered drily. "'Ow did yer h'escape?"

Sir Gavin fingered his cuff tenderly before answering. "It was not difficult. The turnkeys are always open to a little, er, persuasion." In fact, his escape had been ridiculously easy. He had waited impatiently for one unbearable month as his valet pawned his jewels and clothing to bring him the bribe money. When he received no word, he finally admitted that the servant must have betrayed him. During that time, his hatred for Sherringham and the American only increased a hundredfold. Without them, he would never have arrived at this unconscionable position.

So, in desperation, he lured the jailer to his cell in the quiet of the night, promising to share his last few swigs of French brandy if the man would grant him a game of cards to woo his sleeplessness. The bored guard accepted with few questions, for Gavin had taken pains to convince his jailers of his foppish harmlessness.

When the man was relaxed and enjoying the last swig of the carefully hoarded flask, Gavin slit his throat with the dagger guards had failed to find in the sole of his custom-made boot. He quickly wrapped the man's neckerchief around his throat to stem the spurting flow of blood until he could get him to the cot. Blood would alert the merest glance, but a figure lying face down in a stupor would be considered nothing out of the ordinary.

Yanking off the fellow's trousers, boots, and jacket, Gavin exchanged them with his own. He covered the corpse with the cell's blanket, pulled the man's cap low over his face, and tied his own filthy neckerchief over his lower face. He called hoarsely for the turnkey, using the guard's scarf to muffle his voice. He waited, nerves on edge, for what seemed years before the shuffling steps of the old man neared. Peering into the cell with his bloodshot, near-sighted eyes, the man saw his underling waiting to be released. Scolding him for the late night work, he opened the door.

Stifling the urge to hurry, Gavin forced himself to the clumsy, slow gait of the dead man. He couldn't kill the turnkey because the man would soon be missed. Luckily the old man was too involved in relieving his own grievances to expect any response.

When Gavin stopped to urinate in the corner, the turnkey went back to his station with a final disapproving glance. Gavin waited a moment, then slipped by the turnkey's doorway. He had two more stations to pass before he reached the gate, but his own luck held. The drowsy guards recognized the clothing and shuffling step and offered a muttered greeting as he passed. He encountered no resistance at the gate.

As he examined Blackie now, he was perturbed at the man's changed attitude. He still seemed slightly afraid of him, but the former respect had fled. And he didn't like the way Blackie kept the pistol handy in his lap.

"Now that I'm out of prison, I want to help release your daughter." When Blackie seemed unmoved by this offer, Gavin continued, "I was most grieved when I was taken before I could win her release. I would like to correct that oversight now."

Blackie was no fool. He realized that Sir Gavin was in no position to promise anything. Blackie relished the thought that he, for once, had the upper hand. Why, he could have the slimy bastard arrested on his whim, and he had half a mind to do so.

"Thanks fer the h'offer, but the law found new h'evidence that proved me Peg h'innocent and released 'er."

Blackie waited gleefully for Sir Gavin's reaction. He was disappointed when the haughty lord merely narrowed his eyes and took a quick turn about the room.

"Why, I'm delighted to hear that, Blackie." Gavin stopped to smile charmingly into Blackie's hooded face. "I wonder if you, in your joy, could afford to make me a small loan?" Blackie's raucous laughter was the wordless reply he expected. It was to be the hard way, after all.

He took another apparently aimless turn about the room, circling unobtrusively nearer with each step. Blackie's laughter finally stopped and he wiped his streaming eyes to look at Sir Gavin. When Blackie's neck prickled with danger, he grabbed for the pistol and whirled, but he was a second too late. His last sight was the smiling blue gaze of Sir Gavin Redfern as he was stabbed in the heart.

Gavin kicked Blackie's body contemptuously as he searched under the battered table for the loose board he knew was in the floor. He had arrived early for a meeting with Blackie one night. Unaware that he was being observed, Blackie had tossed his evening take in a box beneath the floor.

Gavin found the box and pulled it out with trembling eagerness. He was amazed at the amount of money inside. This would be plenty to finance his disappearance from England after he had repaid his debt to the arrogant Earl of Sherringham and his officious cousin. There might even be a way to use the information he'd paid dearly for about the American—and already Gavin was calculating a sweeping, more unscrupulous plan. He knew the American had a mother in Boston, as his greasy informant had told him. Why not cut out the Sherringham clan from the roots up?

A gleam of evil danced in Gavin's eyes. He removed the knife and wiped it on the dead man's coat, then he peeked out the door at the vacant alley and dragged the body out to prop it in a dark, mouldering corner. He poured gin over the corpse and dropped the bottle by the limp hand.

He retrieved his bundle, the old but still serviceable pistol,

and the heavy purse of money. He shut the door behind him
and ambled casually away. What little sky he could see above
the soot-blackened roofs was streaked with dawn. He should
have just enough time to savor the sweetness of vengeance
before the hounds baying on his trail made departure imperative.

Sir Gavin wrung his hands in anticipation. Killing Sherringham would bring him more pleasure than any wager he
had ever won or any wench he had ever bedded. It was a pity
he couldn't see the bastard's face when he did it, but his plan
must be enacted from a distance.

He hired a hack and gave the driver his old address. As
expected, he found the townhouse stripped bare when he jim-
mied the lock. Mouth tight, he resolved to settle *that* score
with his traitor of a servant if ever he saw him again. Angrily,
he opened his bundle and donned yellow pantaloons and a
broadloom jacket in bottle green. He stepped into gleaming
shoes and cocked his hat at a rakish angle over his face. Wrapping the guard's clothes tightly in the bundle with a wrinkle of
distaste, he listened at the door, then exited quietly when he
heard no sound. Sherringham's munificence in allowing him a
change of clothing would cost him his life.

He made his way to the harbor. Inquiring after Captain Jason
Blaine, he was disappointed to learn that his quarry had sailed
that very morning. Biting his lip thoughtfully, Gavin made an
abrupt decision. It was possible that England might win the
war, leading to his capture and hanging, if he should be connected with Sherringham's death despite all his precautions. It
would be wiser to try his luck in America. Dole out his sweeping punishment, then stay. There should be plenty of raw
Colonials with pockets to fleece at the gaming tables. Yes, now
was the time to do all he had dreamed about in prison. Decisively, he purchased a ticket to Boston on a Charleston brig,
then sauntered into the tap room of a nearby inn.

He ordered port despite the early hour and surveyed the
room leisurely. He waited thirty minutes, tapping his fingers
on the table. He swallowed the last of his drink and rose to go
to a less respectable inn when a ragged adolescent entered the

room. The boy trudged wearily to a corner table, searched his
pocket, and pulled out a few coins. He counted them carefully,
sighed, returned the meager hoard to his pocket, and bowed
his head in his hands. Gavin smiled, gathered up his bundle,
and approached the youth. Yes, he would do nicely. For a start.

That evening, as Sherry dressed for the theater, he wondered
how his stubborn cousin and no less stubborn ward were faring.
It was a pity they had to leave; Abby's gentle influence had
soothed their fractious tempers. Sherry smiled tenderly as he
thought of his beloved. Her charms were ever new to him and
more appealing every day. Aye, she would make a marvelous
countess. Praise God, his waiting was almost at an end. Only
one more month!

Eager to hold her in his arms once more, he hurried down
the stairs. "Has she arrived yet, Hastings?" he asked. She was
to meet him for dinner, their first alone in many weeks, and
he was looking forward to it immensely.

Hastings ran a white-gloved finger over the hallway escritoire before replying. Frowning at the tiny speck of lint on the
material, he answered, "Indeed, your lordship. She awaits in
the salon." From the disapproving note in his voice, Sherry
deduced that she had left her abigail at home.

Sherry tiptoed to the closed door and pushed it ajar to peek
inside. Abby stood with her back to him, staring into the fire.
He devoured her slender form with his hungry gaze, then entered and shut the door noiselessly behind him. He crept up
and grabbed her from behind, cupping both of her breasts
impudently.

She shrieked, then relaxed as she recognized the feel and
scent of him. She rested her head on his chest and clasped her
hands over his, pressing them into her flesh. Startled, Sherry
released her and watched as she turned to caress him with soft
eyes. He had never touched her in such a manner. He had
expected her to be indignant. Instead, she looked at him with
a hunger that almost matched his own. "Abby," he groaned her
name like a prayer, then fastened his mouth over hers.

She kissed him back eagerly, her lips soft, warm, and yielding beneath his. When he nibbled her lower lip with his teeth, she shuddered and pressed closer to him. She had never kissed him with such passion and he forgot himself as his own desires were fanned to a roaring blaze. Undoing the back of her gown with trembling fingers, he drew her down before the fire and impatiently lowered her underclothing to release her taut breasts. Groaning deep in his throat, he smothered each globe with famished kisses, caressing the turgid tips with his warm tongue until she groaned in her turn.

A loud knocking on the door startled them both. Their eyes met, Sherry's dark and passionate, Abby's shyly receptive. He kissed each breast tenderly, saluted her mouth with one last hard kiss, then helped her fasten her clothing. "Yes, Hastings, we'll be out directly," he called. Footsteps withdrew and Sherry helped Abby to her feet, his gaze still heated but amused as he watched a rosy flush spread across her cheeks.

"It's fortunate Hastings interrupted, else I might have had to make an honest woman out of you immediately," Sherry teased, laughter shining in his voice.

Abby blushed brighter, holding her hands to her heated cheeks. "I don't know what came over me. I feel so ashamed."

Sherry raised her chin, caressing it gently until she met his gaze. His voice serious now, he said, "I am the one at fault, my dear. You have naught to be ashamed of. Your response was all a man could wish and perfectly proper in a prospective wife."

Kissing her brow, he pleaded, "Forgive me? I had resolved to restrain myself until we are married, but your delightful response made me lose my head. It won't happen again until we are wed."

Abby smiled into his eyes saucily. "What a pity."

Sherry gasped. "You minx! You're making it devilishly difficult for me," he scolded, but his quivering mouth told her she had succeeded in relieving the tension between them.

Buoyed with happiness, they linked arms and went to the door, Sherry ignoring Hastings's disapproving gaze as he ushered them into the dining room, Abby flushing slightly. "How can he know?" she whispered to Sherry when they were seated next to one another.

Sherry watched Hastings's stiff back retreat from the room

before replying. "A woman who's been making love has a certain look about her that you now have in abundance, my darling," he smiled. Abby looked mortified, her hands going to her coiffure.

"You look delightful. You can freshen up after we dine," he choked, taking a hasty sip of wine to disguise his laughter. Abby stiffened, affronted, then she relaxed and laughed with him.

Their joyous mirth brightened the room with a greater radiance than the aura cast by the candles. They tasted their first course with enjoyment, unaware that their happiness was to spill like blood on the dirty streets that very night as Abby watched Sherry fall, victim of a festering hatred so twisted that only death would assuage it.

Sir Gavin, again dressed in the guard's rags, stood beside the boy in the shadow of the tall shrubs that bordered the earl's grounds. He savored the knowledge that his long stay in that stinking hole was soon to be avenged. A bribed footman had earlier informed him of the earl's planned outing, so the stage was set. It required only the entrance and the final exit of the major character. Gavin looked up at the cloudy sky and decided he couldn't have wished for a better night. He peered down the street and noted with satisfaction the night watchman making his rounds.

The boy was trustful as a lamb at his side. The poor lad had been overjoyed to accept a meal from the only person who had shown him kindness since his arrival in the cruel world of London. Dazed with admiration of Sir Gavin's finery and obvious nobility, the boy was eager to return his benefactor's largesse in any way he could.

He eagerly agreed to help Gavin safeguard his sister from the unsavory nobleman who planned to abduct her that very evening. His youthful soul fired with visions of chivalry, the boy didn't question why the rescue necessitated a change of clothing for Gavin. Yet as he waited outside the palatial townhouse, he began to feel uneasy when he glanced at Gavin. His mentor's aristocratic aura was even stronger in the filthy rags, but there was a new element of cruelty that had not been apparent earlier. Hatred seemed to vibrate from the man in a palpable wave. Gavin felt the boy's eyes and flashed him a charming smile. The lad relaxed and smiled back.

They both stiffened when the townhouse door opened and Harry stepped out. The lad started to ask if he was the man, but Gavin waved him to silence. Out of curiosity the boy watched the door intently, unaware when Gavin turned aside to draw the pistol from his coat, his hand steady but his soul trembling in hatred as he pointed his weapon.

Sherry exited next, but his arm was around Abby and Gavin couldn't get a clear shot. For a moment, he was tempted to shoot anyway, then Abby and Harry descended the steps to the carriage and the earl paused to speak to a servant, his body a perfect silhouette against the light.

The boy heard the pistol cock; he turned, startled. His eyes bulged in disbelief as he watched Gavin pull the trigger. The look on his mentor's face froze the scream in the boy's throat. Gavin's teeth were clenched in a snarl of rage, his eyes were pools of liquid fire that watched Sherry jerk once with the impact, then roll limply down the steps. The wounded man landed in a heap on the driveway, his handsome blue jacket stained with a dark red spreading circle.

The boy's limbs were still frozen with horror when Gavin pressed the pistol into his limp hand and ran toward the watchman, crying, "Murder! A bloke's been shot! The man wot did it is in them bushes!"

The watchman ran to the scene in time to see a dim figure drop a pistol, cry out in terror, and start to run. The portly man gave a last, unaccustomed leap and tackled the boy.

Meanwhile, pandemonium broke out on the driveway. Harry was assisting Abby into the waiting carriage when they heard the shot. Both whirled, Abby falling clumsily into Harry's arms as she lost her balance. They watched with equal horror and disbelief as Sherry fell down the steps, leaving a trail of blood in his wake.

Abby screamed, the anguish in the sound satisfying to the man who listened, crouching at the side of the house, unseen by anyone. Abby gathered her betrothed's head into her lap and sobbed, "Oh my God! No!" Her tears fell onto his face, but he didn't stir. She buried her face in his bloodied jacket, trembling in shock.

Servants rushed outside when they heard the shot, Hastings in the lead. He sent a footman for the doctor, his face for once without its usual wooden impassivity. Harry drew Abby away, then he opened Sherry's jacket to feel for a pulse. His countenance, already white, turned gray as he said numbly, "There's no pulse." Abby looked at him with dazed blue eyes, teetered, then fainted, unable to contemplate existence in a world without Sherry.

Gavin waited only long enough to catch Harry's words and ascertain that the watchman was, as yet, paying no heed to the boy's hysterical explanation. He walked away, a lightness in his step and pure exhilaration in his black heart. He was unable to stifle a laugh as he left anguish behind him. Only one victim yet remained.

Over the babble of voices as several footmen carried first the lifeless figure of the earl, and then Abby, into the house, a faint but chillingly familiar laugh reached Harry's ears on a gust of wind. His head bobbed up to search for the source. The clouds parted and moonlight bathed the street briefly in a silver glow that revealed the guinea-gold hair of a graceful figure walking casually away. Then darkness descended once more.

Harry listened closely, then frowned and turned aside. It must have been some evening reveler, for Sir Gavin was safely in jail. The earl's assailant was still struggling in the watchman's arms. Harry dismissed the fancy, then he reluctantly entered the townhouse, sorrow and dread spreading in his heart as he wondered how he was to comfort Abby.

Chapter
Ten

LEANNA'S FIRST GLIMPSE of the *Savannah* was a sight she would never forget. As dawn shadowed the cargo ship in the first hues of pink and gold, she seemed more a graceful bird than a mere, mundane merchantman anchored in the bay.

Two-masted, with fore and aft square sails that the tiny, busy seamen unfurled, the ship seemed to tremble with eagerness, ready to spread her wings before the breeze and head out for the open sea. Her slender, lean hull was studded ominously with several gunports yawning in her sides.

Leanna was unaware of Jason's intent gaze as he watched her reaction to his vessel; she was enthralled at the unexpected beauty of the scene. As they were rowed closer, the bird-like impression dissolved when they were under the towering hull. Leanna had never been so close to a vessel, and she was awed by the sheer size of the *Savannah* as they stopped under the ladder.

Her gaze was admiring when she finally turned to Jason.

127

"She's a beauty, sir. You are justified in being proud of her."

Jason was gratified, but he disguised his pleasure with a shrug. He gestured for the sailor who had rowed them out to climb aboard first, then suggested, "I can carry you on my back if you feel unequal to the climb, Leanna."

Leanna craned her neck to peer up at the ladder and surveyed the distance thoughtfully, but she had climbed many a tree in her girlhood without such a sturdy ladder to cling to.

"I am equal to the task, Jason," she replied simply. She put one tiny foot on the first rung and tried to ignore Jason's fingers around her waist as he supported her slight weight. He watched her graceful, swaying skirts for a moment, then climbed behind her. The rhythmic swing of her hips dried his throat, and he had to force himself to look away.

When she reached the deck, Leanna was assisted aboard by eager, but courteous, hands. While she examined the ship, Jason's crew examined her. To a man, they were avid to see the girl who had finally caught their wary captain in the matrimonial trap. Their natural curiosity had been whetted by the description of her beauty given by the two officers who had attended the wedding.

Leanna vaguely sensed the surreptitious stares, but she was too involved in her appraisal of the ship to mind. The deck was planked with solid, polished oak, and a small poop deck in the stern was flanked by steps nearby leading into the hold and the crew's quarters. Leanna had to crane her neck until it hurt to find the top of the mountainous masts. Most interesting of all was the enormous wheel amidships that she knew steered the vessel. She walked over to the helm and touched the smooth, varnished wood with interested fingers.

When Jason came on deck, the men quickly turned back to their separate tasks. He oversaw the winching of the shore boat aboard, then he moved to stand by the helm. Leanna turned away to the railing to catch her last glimpse of England.

Jason watched her back warily. He decided it would be best to leave her be. Anything he said would only make her leave-taking more difficult.

He began bawling his commands, "Weigh anchor! Hoist the tops'ls!"

Leanna bit her lip as she watched the harbor slowly recede into the distance. She didn't mind leaving England as much as she feared what life held for her in America. With no one but an indifferent husband to help her adapt to the new country, Leanna was afraid she was in for a difficult time indeed.

Ever receptive to new experiences, Leanna could not long remain somber under the restorative freshness of the ocean air. She inhaled deeply, enjoying the feel of the ship trembling beneath her feet as it ran before the stiff morning breeze. The crying gulls and creaking sails were novel sounds that also invigorated her spirits.

Jason spoke at her side, startling her from her absorption in the new sights, smells, and sounds bombarding her senses. "Would you like to see our cabin, my dear?"

Leanna turned to him reluctantly. Here was the moment she had dreaded. For an instant she was tempted to say no, then she sighed and decided she'd best get it over with. She nodded and allowed him to escort her to the poop deck.

He led the way up the steps to a heavy door in the bulkhead, which he opened, then he bowed with a flourish for her to pass him. Taking a deep breath, she dragged her steps into the small cabin. As she had feared, it contained but one bed, a small bunk built into the starboard bulkhead, with storage beneath. A round table with heavy chairs was bolted to the floor and a tiny desk stood beneath the larboard windows. A tall armoire stood on one side of the bed, with a cabinet full of nautical equipment and weapons on the other.

She spied a small door set unobtrusively in the stern and walked over to investigate. She opened the door and gasped in delight. A tiny sternwalk with an ornately latticed railing jutted out over the churning wake of the vessel. She leaned her elbows on the brass railing, savoring the view.

Jason stood beside her in silence, enjoying the delicacy of her features against the elemental background of sky and sea. When a silky strand of hair whipped his face, he held it captive against his cheek, rubbing it back and forth to relish its texture.

Leanna felt a tug on her hair and turned to protest, but before she could speak, she felt Jason's fingers in her hair, pulling the pins away. She tried to escape, appealing, "Please,

Jason, the wind will tangle it dreadfully."

He ignored her and released the final tress from its bondage, his heartbeat quickening when the shining waves flooded her shoulders with molten gold. He grasped a handful and coiled it around his hand, studying its fairness against his brown fingers. Slowly he pulled, bringing her inexorably nearer, his blue gaze as compelling as the grip on her hair.

Leanna, her heart reeling, tried to break the grip of his eyes. Unconsciously, she wet her dry lips, and when his gaze dropped to her mouth, her frightened heart galloped faster. She opened her lips to plead for release and gave him the opportunity he was waiting for.

He swooped down, pressing his lips to hers. Leanna struggled, but since his fingers were coiled in her hair, she only managed to hurt herself. His warm mouth possessed hers urgently, the teasing torment crumbling her eroding defenses. She kissed him back, her lips as eager as his.

Exultantly, Jason crushed her closer, running his hands up and down her back. But he lost his advantage when he cupped her buttocks and pulled her against his aroused body. The hardness against her belly shocked Leanna into realizing the danger she was in. She struggled again, and when he only held her closer, she kicked him sharply in the shin. He gasped and his grip loosened long enough for her to pull away. Fleeing back into the cabin and outside to the main deck, she was frantic to escape from his passion and her own vulnerability.

Jason stood where she left him, rubbing his aching shin with a rueful hand. He berated himself for letting his passions get out of control. He had meant to kiss her tenderly, proving that he could be gentle as well as passionate, but her response had so aroused him that if she hadn't kicked him he would have gone beyond the point of no return. He leaned against the rail moodily, wondering what it was about this slip of a girl that made him lose his head. He had taken other women as beautiful, and all were far more experienced in the art of pleasing a man than his own reluctant wife. Yet she had only to kiss him, her lips innocent but eager, for his ardor to soar to heights unknown before.

Grimly, he decided he had best keep physical contact between them minimal and instead use his much-vaunted charm to woo her. He also resolved to have a hammock brought in, for it was certain he couldn't trust himself next to that tempting body night after night.

Leanna clutched the railing with trembling fingers, her heartbeat gradually slowing. Oh God, she had melted like butter in his arms despite what had passed between them. She closed her eyes and called up the memory of their first meeting, but somehow the rough stranger of that night was superseded by the passionate suitor of five minutes past. The embraces that had been so distasteful the first time were now tempting her to mindless surrender. Her eyes flew open and she took several deep breaths, forcing herself to calm down.

She must avoid a repetition of such a scene at all costs. She would occupy herself with reading, sewing, and exercise, avoiding his company as much as possible. When Jason came on deck, she went to their cabin to unpack, giving him a remote nod as she passed.

As Jason was already upset by his lack of control, her disdain was the last straw. He moved to take the helm, glaring at her retreating back and resolving to put her out of his mind. She was but a female, after all. Despite milady's disdain, her response proved she'd soon come to him like all the rest. He stared arrogantly ahead, confident once more. Nevertheless, he ordered a seaman to set up a hammock in his cabin, ignoring the man's look of astonishment. Shaking his head, he did his captain's bidding, but he knew if the beautiful missy were *his* wife, *he*'d not be sleepin' in no hammock.

Leanna ate a solitary lunch, relieved that she didn't yet have to meet Jason. The plain meal was served to her by a young red-headed lad who couldn't have been more than fifteen. He had a thin, freckled face with an engaging, gap-toothed grin and bright blue eyes that reminded her of Harry. He seemed painfully shy until she asked him his name and how long he'd been to sea. Then he startled her with a flood of words.

"I's Benjamin Collier, ma'rm, 'n I been with the cap'n 'fer nigh on seven years now. He found me in Nantucket, sleepin' on the dock. Lost me mum, I did, and t'was nigh to starvin' when he took me in as his cabin boy. None of t'other cap'ns 'ud give me a chance, said I's too young. But not Cap'n Blaine, no sir. Worked me like a dog, he did. Tough, but kind, he were. Give me life for him, I would." The boy's face was glowing with devotion as he spoke of his captain. Leanna was to find that he was but one of Jason's crew who admired him to the point of adulation. Thoughtfully, she finished her lunch, wondering yet again what it was in her husband's past that made him so sympathetic to members of his own sex, yet so hostile to hers.

Leanna had finished unpacking and was admiring the fine dueling pistols in the cabinet when Jason entered. She slowly turned to meet his indifferent eyes, her own demeanor calm. They started to speak at once. Leanna gestured for Jason to begin.

He sat down at the table. "Leanna, there are certain difficulties caused when a woman is aboard ship. My crew is no longer at liberty to dress and speak as they normally do when you are about. I must consequently request that you remain in our cabin until noon every day to allow them time to attend to their, er, personal needs. Understood?"

Jason's brisk, businesslike manner raised her hackles, but she realized the sense of what he was saying and nodded in agreement. However, she couldn't resist the thrust: "And when am I to attend to my, er, personal needs?" Nose in the air, she met his hard gaze defiantly.

His jaw tight and his voice dangerously soft, Jason said, "At any time, of course. And naturally I, as your loving husband, will be glad to offer my assistance."

Leanna faltered before his meaningful look and turned away to fiddle with the hammock suspended between two beams. "And this? Do you intend to sleep here?"

"I do," he ground harshly. "Why, dear wife, do you object?"

Leanna whirled to meet his look, a retort on her lips, but the tic in his cheek gave her pause. "No, I am most grateful," she said instead.

Her attempt to placate him had the opposite effect. Jason

jammed his fist down on the table and leaped to his feet. He found it ludicrous that his own wife refused to appear before him undressed. Worse, she was even grateful that she didn't have to sleep at his side. Afraid of what he might do, he stomped out of the cabin without another word.

Leanna stood where she was, stunned at his reaction. What had she said to anger him so? Sighing heavily, she took out her embroidery, sat down on the bunk, and began to stitch. Sewing had never been a favorite pastime, nor was she very good at it, but the activity soothed her nerves. She had the premonition that she would need a lot of sewing on this voyage.

It was a scrupulously polite couple who met for dinner that evening. Jason held Leanna's chair for her, smiling benignly. She narrowed her eyes at him, for his innocent gaze was a little too at variance with his earlier anger. Nevertheless, she was grateful for his unexpected forbearance and gladly accepted the tacit truce with a nod, then she began her dinner of potatoes, biscuits, and dried beef. Jason eyed her covertly, his reason now returned. Deciding it was time to begin his offense, he began to tell her of America, using the opportunity to put her at ease.

Leanna gradually relaxed, entering into the discussion with spirit. When Benjamin came to remove their plates, he found them involved in a lively debate over slavery.

Leanna was insistent. "Slavery is an abomination that should be abolished from the earth. No amount of profit or convenience can excuse the misery caused by this traffic in human lives."

Jason said mildly, "You'll find no misery at Whispering Oaks, my dear. Indeed, our darkies are a great deal happier and certainly much better fed and housed than the rabble of London." His voice harder, he derided, "It's always amazed me that the gentry in England—whose profits do not depend on the institution they malign so loudly—are so outraged over our 'cruelty,' yet they work children of their own country to death in mines and factories with conditions not fit for dogs, much less people."

Leanna looked away, unable to dispute the point. She no

more approved of the child labor laws in England than she did of slavery, but she feared any attempt to change the laws would meet with massive resistance. England's great industrial machine *was* dependent on the cheap labor provided by her indigent children.

She met Jason's eyes. Her voice was clear as she concurred, "I totally agree with you, sir. I only hope that a Wilberforce will soon take up the banner against this atrocious inequity as he has against slavery."

Jason knew she spoke of the great statesman William Wilberforce, who had eloquently attacked the slave trade in Parliament, supported by Pitt himself. A bill to end the trade in England passed the House of Commons in '92, but failed in the House of Lords. However, Sherry had informed him that sentiment was growing in support of Wilberforce, and the bill was expected to become law before many more years.

He was reluctant to admit that he had often abhorred slavery himself. While darkies on his plantation were treated with kindness, he knew several other landowners who were not so forbearing.

Changing the subject, he described Savannah to her as favorably as possible, explaining that many of its buildings were new since the '96 fire destroyed most of the town. "It's not what you're used to, of course, but we're improving continually, as our profits have been good of late." He was silent for a moment, then added as if goaded, "There's social life aplenty, if you've a taste for it. Certainly we have nothing of the magnitude of Almack's or Vauxhall, but we contrive to keep amused in our own crude way."

Leanna sensed a defensiveness in his manner that surprised her. Evidently he was afraid she would be bored. Wondering why he thought all females cared for nothing but clothes and balls, she admitted with an enchanting smile, "You forget I was raised in the country. I enjoy a good gallop far more than dancing through the night."

Jason searched her clear gaze, measuring the truth of her words. He relaxed as though a weight had been lifted from his chest as she held his eyes steadily. Here's a woman a man could depend on, the thought crept slyly through his mind, but he stopped it short. She might be different from most females, but she would probably prove just as flighty as all the rest.

Clearing his throat, he shoved back his chair and came to his feet. "I'll take a quick stroll before retiring. You'll find extra blankets beneath the bed." He strode quickly out the door, leaving Leanna surprised and touched at his unexpected thoughtfulness in allowing her privacy to prepare her for bed. More at charity with him than ever before, she quickly removed her clothing and donned her warmest flannel gown, standing close to the stove in a futile effort to keep warm as she brushed out her hair.

She was still standing there when Jason returned. The prim cut of the nightgown did little to conceal her lush figure. Jason stood stock still for a moment, the breath caught in his throat. The flames of the fire illuminated her full breasts, and the cold made her nipples stand tauntingly erect as she drew the brush through her rippling locks. He raked his eyes over her shapely waist, hips, and legs, his hands and lips hungry for the feel of her. Unaware, he took a step toward her, and she stopped her ministrations.

Unable to see his torment because he stood in shadow, she smiled at him in welcome, straining his control even further. She set the brush aside, drew back the covers to the bunk, and slipped between them. "Good night, Jason," she said serenely. She stifled a yawn with a dainty hand, then added drowsily, "I've left covers in the hammock for you. Sleep well." She turned on her side away from him, burrowed deeper into the covers, and drifted off to sleep.

Jason clenched and unclenched his hands, trying to control the burning in his loins. Damn the girl, didn't she know what she did to a man? He undressed in disgust, reluctantly admitting that she did not. He crawled, naked, into the hammock, and turned away from the bunk. After much tossing and turning, he finally fell into a fitful sleep, but his dreams were bedeviled by visions of a laughing, seductive temptress who enticed him into her bed, only to turn into mist and dissolve in his arms when he reached for her.

He awoke with a foul taste in his mouth and in a fouler mood. The sight of Leanna sleeping peacefully with a slight smile on her face did little to improve his humor. He dressed and gulped down a scalding cup of coffee, almost welcoming the pain when the hot liquid burned his tongue. His crew eyed him warily when he went on deck, stepping lightly around him. He snapped at the helmsman, "Bring her up a point!" The man nervously complied, his anxiety heightened by the restless pacing of his captain.

It was a trying day for all aboard. Jason found fault with everything, from the recently mended canvas to the cleaned cannon that gleamed with oil, inside and out. He avoided the cabin entirely, and when Leanna came on deck for fresh air, he went below, ostensibly to inspect the hold.

Leanna watched him retreat with puzzled eyes, more than a little hurt. She had believed they were at last becoming friends, but for some inexplicable reason he was ignoring her. Confused at his moods, she stalked off to read, spending the remainder of the day seated in a chair on the sternwalk, determined not to let his behavior affect her.

Yet when she met him at dinner, he was the same genial, witty companion of the previous night. Exasperated, she ignored his conversational sallies at first. She gradually lost her resentment when he discussed the merits of Shakespeare's plays.

As they argued over the ending of *The Taming of the Shrew*, Jason reflected wryly that he had never used his intellect to seduce a woman before, but so far it seemed to be his most effective weapon yet.

"I still think Petruchio was not as clever as he thought. What man would want a woman who is but a meek reflection of his mildest whim?" Leanna wondered. Jason forbore to tell her that most men of his acquaintance wanted, and expected, exactly such a wife.

"It has always been my feeling," he returned, "that Petruchio ended as much tamed as the tamer. He was so enamored of Kate that he would thenceforth grant *her* mildest whim, I don't doubt."

Leanna ruminated on the point for a moment, then conceded,

"That may well be, but isn't that the way of two people in love? Surely pleasing the person one loves is as enjoyable for the giver as the receiver?"

Jason looked at her with arrested eyes, his hand clenched around his wine glass as he searched her face for irony. He had always found women far more interested in the baubles and sexual satisfaction he could give them than in anything else. They had always expected something in return for their favors. He doubted Leanna was different. After all, she had agreed to marry him, but withheld her body, despite the high price he had paid for that one brief night, enjoyable as it might have been.

Leanna wondered at the sour look around his mouth, but she shrugged mentally as she took a calm sip of wine. She was becoming accustomed to his moods and merely retreated into her own thoughts when he looked at her with that hostile glower.

He left for his customary walk about the deck and she prepared for bed, reflecting that their proximity had not led to the intimacy she had so feared. She was almost put out at his total avoidance of any physical contact with her. She wondered what she had done to kill his desire. She told herself she was glad, but she ached when she wondered if she would ever again be cherished and loved by anyone.

Their first two days aboard set the tone for the voyage's first half. Jason stayed busy about the ship; Leanna occupied herself in the cabin. They met only for meals when they spent time discussing neutral subjects. When Leanna evinced an interest in the operation of the vessel, Jason gave her a tour of the ship, offering to let her take the helm. She was alarmed at first of the awesome responsibility and the power she could feel vibrating in her hands, but under Jason's guidance she lost her fear and enjoyed the pull of the enormous wheel.

When a capricious gust of wind knocked it from her grasp, she didn't protest Jason's encircling her waist to help her steer. Jason wondered at her pliancy when she leaned back against him. He was vastly tempted to see if her docility extended to other areas. He was loath to risk the growing amity between them, however, so he decided to bide his time a while longer.

Jason took great care to inflate his evening walk to give her time to get in bed. It was agony enough watching her trim figure walk about the ship without constantly seeing her *en déshabille* to add to his discomfort. On one memorable occasion, however, he went to the cabin in the morning, startling Leanna at her ablutions. She had taken to bathing shortly after breakfast, for she seldom saw him again before lunchtime.

On this particular morning he came to fetch a chart he had forgotten to take with him earlier. Leanna was standing, stark naked, in the middle of the cabin, bathing herself from a small bowl. They gasped together at the sight of each other, Leanna in embarrassment, Jason in shock. Their eyes locked for a startled moment, but when Jason's gaze dropped, Leanna hastily grabbed a towel and wrapped it about herself. The salient parts of her anatomy were covered, but her graceful shoulders and shapely legs were still exposed. In Jason's present mood, they were temptation enough for his starved passions.

He took a quick step toward her, determined to end the ache in his loins, be damned to the consequences, when a knock at the door brought him back to his senses. Leanna dashed to the bed to put on a heavy robe and called for entrance. Ben came in with an armful of clean linens, smiling a knowing grin that indicated he had spotted the aroused state of his captain and the embarrassment of the mistress. Giving a perky little salute, he went back out, leaving a heavy silence behind him.

Leanna held her breath, poised to jump away if he should make a move toward her. She felt like a lone tree helplessly exposed to an ominous, building storm that was about to burst in a deluge of fury.

Jason clenched his jaw at the fear in her face and forced himself to back away. He stood with his hand on the doorknob and gave her one last burning look before retreating without another word. He slammed the door so loudly behind him that the bang reverberated through the small cabin. He had left without his chart.

Leanna slumped in relief and hastily dressed, trying to put that last look out of her mind. No one had ever glared at her in such a way before. There had been a fury of passion in his eyes—almost a look of hatred. She wondered despairingly if she was ever to understand him.

Jason was impossible for a good two days after this incident. Even after he had reverted to being her charming instructor, Leanna sometimes encountered by surprise a hard gleam of resentment in his eyes before he could mask it under a surface of urbanity. They had still not completely recovered their former comfortable relationship when the accident occurred.

They were nearing the Azores when the storm hit. They had ample warning. The clouds darkened to pitch, blocking out the sun, and the wind increased in velocity until the schooner bucked like a wild horse before the waves. Jason dressed in a heavy slicker and went to take the helm, curtly ordering Leanna to remain in the cabin.

For the first hour of the storm, she was obedient, but the humidity in the air combined with the constant rolling of the vessel built to make her stomach reel. She felt suffocated in the still air of the cabin and, not pausing to consider, she donned her heaviest cloak and went on deck.

The shrieking wind knocked the door from her hand, and the noise of the gale was so loud she didn't hear the portal bang against the bulkhead. Buffeted by the wind, she staggered outside, welcoming the salt spray against her face. She held on to a spar for support. Her cloak flapped around her, more of a hindrance than a protection. She rubbed the stinging moisture from her eyes and peered down into the gloom on the main deck, trying to find Jason.

She could dimly discern members of the crew scurrying about, tying down canvas and fastening down the guns. Seamen dreaded nothing more than a loose gun during a storm, for, unbolted, it could become a battering ram that could kill a man and even sink a ship.

Leanna finally found Jason standing, legs spread for balance, at the helm. She could see his shoulders straining with effort as he forced the pitching *Savannah* to follow the safest course before the storm. Water inundated the lower deck as the ship plunged through the trough and crest of the waves. Jason bowed his head as waves splashed over and drenched him, but he allowed nothing to distract him from his task.

With the crew so occupied, Leanna was the only one who heard the ominous creak overhead. From her vantage point on the higher deck, she looked around frantically, trying to find the source of the noise. She finally spied a sail flapping erratically above Jason's head and watched as the added strain on the mast snapped it with a loud *thwack!* She screamed a warning as it hurtled straight for Jason's unprotected head, but she knew he would never hear her above the shrieking wind.

She felt frozen in some awful nightmare as she watched it glance his head with a fearful blow, snapping his neck back under the force. He collapsed to the deck. Leanna leaped down the stairs as nimbly as she could, reaching his side at the same time as several seamen. She knelt, cradling his head in her lap, searching gently for the wound, her heart thumping in terror at his stillness. Her fingers discovered a growing lump on the side of his skull, oozing with blood. She felt for his pulse and sagged in relief when she found that it throbbed quickly but strongly.

The first mate took the wheel and barked the command to carry Jason to his cabin. The willing hands of several seamen gently lifted him, carrying him as steadily as the pitching of the deck and the wind would allow. Leanna followed, tears brimming in her eyes and a prayer in her heart for the safety of the man she had vowed to hate.

Chapter
Eleven

IN THE STRESS and confusion that followed, Leanna didn't at first have time to consider her reaction when Jason was struck down. She was too busy ordering hot water, bathing his wound, and trying to make him comfortable to listen to the little voice that mocked her shaken composure.

Benjamin assisted her, his face as white as her own, his lips trembling in fear. Leanna wrapped Jason's head with clean strips of linen, attempting to stanch the flow of blood. They watched tensely as the flow slowed to a trickle and finally halted.

Sighing with relief, Leanna directed Benjamin to strip him and wrap him in every blanket that could be found to warm his quivering body. When he still shook, Leanna dressed in a warm gown, and climbed beneath the covers, holding Jason's large, quaking frame tightly to her own warm body. He gradually quit shaking as his shock receded. He fell into a deep, but apparently, natural, sleep.

Leanna savored the feel of his muscular warmth against her and enjoyed his dormant and unthreatening body. She brushed his damp hair away from his forehead and searched the handsome angles of his face with a curious hunger, wondering at the great tenderness that swelled her heart as she watched him sleep.

In the peace of the moment she could no longer stifle the voice that had been clamoring in her. If she still hated him, why did her heart ache in such terror as she watched him fall? Ever straightforward and honest with herself, Leanna knew that there was but one explanation—far from hating him, she loved him so that she would have gladly exchanged places with him to receive the mast's blow.

Stroking his cheek tenderly, Leanna wondered almost with detachment how she, a girl who was starved for love, could foolishly give her heart to a man who was incapable of returning it. Biting her lip to stifle a sob, she kissed him, her tears falling on his face as her lips moved on his. She would allow herself this one caress since he seemed so vulnerable and helpless. If he ever recovered, she would have to guard her emotions with an impregnable wall.

At least now she understood why she responded to his kisses so passionately. She had shied from his embraces because she was ashamed of her wanton response to a man she believed she detested. Now she had even more reason to avoid intimacy between them. If he recovered now and made love to her, she would helplessly respond with all the passion in her unruly heart, leaving her bereft of even pride's cold comfort.

As her heart beat faster at his nearness, Leanna dreamed of lying in his arms, returning his kisses and caresses with an abandon that only a woman in love can experience. Half pain, half pleasure in her liquid green eyes at the thought, Leanna searched the imagined face above her for some small measure of affection. All she could find was burning desire as he made her his.

Jason stirred beside her, relieving her of the agonizing vision. He moaned, then subsided once more. She searched his unconscious features, resolved he must never know she loved

him, for he would not hesitate to take advantage of her. The
ecstasy of sharing his bed would turn to bitterness when he'd
had his fill of her and turned to another. Lust is a heady but
poisonous draught to offer a woman starved for love.

Leanna's wrenching emotions so exhausted her that she fell
into a heavy sleep, unaware when Jason again stirred beside
her. Jason's first thought on waking was riveted on his ship.
He tried to sit up, only to sink back in agony before his head
had left the pillow an inch. When the pain receded, he realized
that the *Savannah* was smoothly plunging through the seas.
The storm had died and the day was clear. He sighed in relief,
then reached a hand up to search for the source of the stakes
being driven through his head. His elbow brushed against something soft and warm. Startled, he jerked away and drove the
stakes in deeper.

The agony receded for a moment as it was superseded by
amazement when he saw Leanna slumbering beside him, her
hair a cloud of gold over the pillow. He vaguely recalled standing at the helm, steering the ship through the storm, then . . .
nothing. He again felt his head and swore when he felt the
lump on his scalp near his ear. He was naked, wrapped in an
inordinate amount of blankets. Obviously he had received a
hefty blow on the head.

Curiosity satisfied, Jason eased closer to Leanna under the
blankets. Gently, he slid his arm under her, ignoring his throbbing head as he pulled her to him until they lay front to front.
Her soft breasts were flat against his chest, setting his heart to
pounding in a way that had nothing to do with his injury.

He studied her face at his leisure, searching the flawless
skin, delicate nose, and lush lashes until the familiar ache
settled in his loins again. Finally, he dropped his eyes to her
mouth. Her soft pink lips, parted softly with her breathing,
tempted him unbearably. Unable to help himself, he placed his
lips over hers, savoring their soft warmth. He was surprised
when, far from pushing him away as he had expected, she
began to kiss him back hungrily, her lips parting under his. He
ignored the pounding in his head as he pushed her beneath
him, placing himself strategically above her as his hand pushed

up her bed gown to stroke her silken thigh.

Leanna fought her way up from sleep, reluctant to waken from her dream. Jason's hands and lips were so real, she could almost feel them devouring her. Opening her eyes, she was shocked to see the blue orbs of his eyes watching her from their dangerous position above. He pushed his knee between her thighs, leaving her in no doubt of his response as he rubbed against her.

Leanna forced her lethargic limbs into movement. She pushed at his chest, squirming frantically to close her legs and ease her hips from under his. He resisted, still drugged by her nearness. When he pulled the bodice of her nightgown from her shoulder and began to kiss her breasts, Leanna moaned and grasped his head between her hands. She intended to pull him away, but his sucking mouth drained her willpower. Instead of pushing him away, she threaded her fingers through his thick, silky hair and pulled him closer, her head thrown back as she helplessly submitted to the waves of pleasure coursing through her.

Jason sensed her weakness and quickly moved his other leg between her own, pushing her thighs farther apart as his distended hardness began to probe. A growl in his throat, he raised his head to seek her lips again, his hips poised for that first vital thrust.

Leanna's pleasurable trance snapped. In that critical instant, she opened her dazed eyes and met his urgent gleaming ones, so reminiscent of her dream last night that the last mists of pleasure receded.

"No!" she half shrieked, half sobbed, pushing his head away near the injury, forgetful of it. Leanna barely noticed when he groaned in agony, clutching his head between his hands. She scooted from under him and fled to the sternwalk, her instinct for escape so primitive that she scarcely felt the cold slicing through her thin gown when she slammed the door shut behind her.

Leanna slumped against the rail, searching the sea with unseeing eyes. She had come dangerously close to betraying herself, if she had not actually done so. Rubbing her numb arms with her hands, she took deep breaths and tried to stop sobbing. Her hysteria slowly receded, leaving her more anguished than she had been since the night she met Jason. She watched the waves pitch under the stern, and, for an instant, she was tempted to jump. The cold grip of the sea was surely preferable to the clutch of the rapacious, greedy arms of her husband. He desired only her body, with no care for the anguish his lust caused her vulnerable heart.

As her shock receded, Leanna's depression gradually gave way to wrath that sent life tingling through her limbs once more. Use her at his leisure, would he? Two could play that game. Before she was finished with him, he'd be half crazy with desire. She would then inform him exactly what he could do with his arrogant male pride. A lust of a different sort turning her eyes into molten emeralds, Leanna opened the door and entered the cabin.

Jason was lying weakly against the pillow, one hand still held to his throbbing head. He was in too much pain to even mind his unsatisfied desire, though he vaguely resolved that Leanna would pay for the tricks she kept playing. To rouse him beyond control, then reject him, was the dirtiest trick a woman could play on a man. He'd not stand for her hot-cold ardor any longer. He moved his head restlessly as he remembered the feel of her against him. Fresh pain shot through his skull and he reluctantly lay still. Her comeuppance would have to wait until he was in a better condition to deal with the hellion.

When Leanna entered, Jason ignored her, even when he felt her standing beside the bed looking down at him. Leanna gritted her teeth, then forced her voice to sweetness as she cooed, "How is your head, Jason?" She placed a cool hand on his brow, startling him so that he jumped. He swore as pain again lanced him.

"I'll survive despite your *tender* concern," he snarled. Leanna stifled a smile of satisfaction at his obvious discomfort. Her last fear over his safety had been laid to rest at his response to her in bed. No man at death's door could be so passionate!

She tut-tutted in false commiseration, meeting his gaze innocently when he narrowed his eyes at her in suspicion. She wetted a cloth with cool water and placed it gently against his brow. Jason relaxed a bit, closing his eyes as the coolness soothed his aching head. Had he seen the glare Leanna gave him, he would not have felt so relaxed. She looked at the bump in his hair with narrowed, glittering eyes, vaguely wondering how he would look with a matching lump on the other side of his head.

She smiled in absent pleasure at the thought, but merely removed the cloth to rewet it. When a knock sounded at the door, she donned her robe and called for entrance.

Benjamin poked his head around the portal, anxiety in his gaze. He saw Jason very much awake and very much disgruntled. He smiled in relief. Whistling, he pushed the door open and carried in a tray loaded with several steaming dishes.

Leanna lifted the lids and sniffed appreciatively. Plain the food might be, but it was always appetizing. She took the tray and opened her lips to dismiss Benjamin, when an idea came to her. A slow smile spread over her face. Her back was to Jason, so he didn't see it, but Ben did, and he almost backed away in alarm.

"Ben, where is the captain's dinner?" Leanna asked, as though puzzled.

Ben and Jason frowned in unison, their eyes meeting. Ben looked back at Leanna, replying slowly, "There must be plenty fer two, ma'rm. The cap'n's favorite, the stew be. Cook made it up special, just fer him."

Leanna's eyes widened in horror. "He can't eat this! Why, everyone knows that those afflicted with head injuries must eat sparingly of bland food, else nausea will set in."

"Nonsense," Jason snorted. "Bring the tray here. I'm fair starved."

Leanna shook her head resolutely, a tender concern in her eyes. "No, dearest, you must eat little in your, er, *weakened* condition." The implication was obvious to Jason, but when he searched her face sharply, she met his gaze with sweet serenity.

She felt him dissecting her back when she turned to Ben. "Tell cook to prepare a weak gruel for the captain. That will suffice for now," she ordered. Ben looked uncertainly at Jason, but when his captain said nothing and merely glared at his wife's back with stormy eyes, he nodded and retreated. He was glad to escape the undercurrents running rampant in the small cabin. Scratching his head, he went below to pass along the order, wondering at the female mind. He would have sworn the missy was afeared o' the cap'n dyin', yet just now she looked as though she'd gladly run him through, savoring the thrust.

Leanna sat down to serve herself some stew, ignoring Jason's furious look. She was unable to avoid a small start at his roar, "Leanna! you'll not starve me to death to be rid of me. Bring me a bowl of stew, *now!*"

Leanna met his gaze calmly, careful to keep her smile in place. "Why, certainly, dearest, come to the table and I'll know you've plenty of strength and your stomach can stand the rich food." She had a shrewd idea of how his head still ached. She couldn't quite smother her smile of triumph when he groaned as he tried to sit up.

He caught that little smile and fixed her with a glare. "You win for now, my dear. But I'll remember this. It will be my turn to play the pipes next."

Leanna shrugged and made enjoyable noises as she began dinner, made even more satisfying by Jason's quivering jaw as he watched her eat. When Ben next made his wary entrance, he found an empty tray, a well-satisfied mistress, and a smoldering captain. He switched trays and exited hastily.

Leanna took the tray to Jason, propping him up with pillows behind his back. He fell back dizzily for a moment, and Leanna's vengeful heart almost softened. Then he sat up, meeting her gaze with forced indifference, and her mouth tightened again. She sat next to him on the bunk with the tray on her lap and fed him the gruel, her breast brushing against his shoulder each time she leaned toward him. Jason gulped the repulsive stuff quickly, eager to end the torment. He couldn't decide which bothered him more, the ache in his head or the ache in his loins as he felt the warmth of her and inhaled her tantalizing scents.

Leanna's smile wavered when she fed him the last few sips. Her vengeance was a double-headed monster, it seemed. If she wasn't careful, it would gobble her up instead of Jason, for his nearness was a torment to her as well. She tried to avoid looking at his broad, muscled torso, resolutely denying her fingers the treat they begged for—to feel those rippling muscles covered with a smattering of fine, dark hairs.

They both sighed in relief when Jason drank the last sip. Leanna retreated, breathing easier with half the space of the cabin between them. She avoided his intense stare, and without a word she began to arrange blankets in the hammock.

She started when Jason barked, "What are you doing?"

She glanced at him in surprise. "I'm getting ready for bed, of course." She fluffed up a pillow and removed her robe, preparatory to getting in the hammock.

"I thought you might sleep with me," Jason objected, almost peevishly.

Leanna almost laughed at the little-boy disappointment in his face. "You'll be adequately warm, I think. If you need anything, you've but to ask."

Jason grunted in disgust and lay on his side watching her as she tried to get in the hammock, shoulders first. Jason opened his mouth to correct her, then stopped and smiled wickedly. He settled back to watch, enjoyment gleaming in his eyes.

Leanna fell to her knees on the first attempt, unable to swing either leg into the hammock as it seemed to shy away from her. Perplexed, she got to her feet and tried again. This time she succeeded in getting a leg inside, only to have it sway so wildly that she lost her balance and fell to the floor with a loud thump. She heard snickers from the bunk, but when she looked at Jason suspiciously, he gazed blandly back, his mouth straight.

She gave him a haughty glare and came to her feet to try again. Bracing her weight, one hand on each side of the hammock, she set down a wary knee and gradually moved her other foot off the floor, only to have it rock from under her when she tried to bring her other leg inside. She fell to the floor again, landing once more on an already aching posterior.

Jason couldn't smother his laughter this time, and his deep, rich chuckles filled the room. Leanna stared at him with smoldering green eyes, clenching her teeth in frustration. She shut her eyes, trying to remember how Jason had entered the hammock which seemed to have ideas of its own.

Eying it warily, Leanna approached again. Backside first, she eased her weight into it, leaning back with her shoulders, then bringing her feet up. The hammock quivered, but subsided, almost with reluctance. Leanna shot Jason a triumphant glance. She turned a disdainful shoulder to him and settled down in her hard-earned perch, drawing the covers snugly up.

Jason sighed, settling himself into the mattress after blowing out the lantern. Looking broodingly out the porthole at the moon-washed sea, he wondered if they were ever to reach an understanding. He doubted they could make peace with one another until the sexual tension between them was released. But remembering her response to him that evening, he felt it was just a matter of time before she accepted him in her bed, if not in her heart.

Wondering why the latter caused him pain, he yawned and drifted off to sleep, determined to renew his pursuit of her as patiently as his temper and his eager body would allow.

The moon bathed the two figures in a silver glow, their proud, passionate natures dormant in sleep as they fortified themselves for the battle resumed in the morning. Their conflict was as old as time, as old as lovers: man wanting an eager, responsive body, using all his strength and cunning to receive it; woman wanting love and tenderness, using her charm and beauty to earn the devotion she craved.

Despite Leanna's vigorous protests, Jason took the deck in the morning. He could not rest until he'd viewed the wreckage from the storm himself. Aside from some snapped lines and ripped canvas, the only damage was to the mast that had fallen on Jason. Losing one of their tops'ls would slow them down, but as the storm had blown them in a westerly direction, they were approximately on course anyway. He would have liked to progress under full sail, but repairs would cost them too much time. It was certain they'd not make it home by New Year's as he had hoped.

Jason was fully recovered within a few days. However, the

accident caused a subtle change in Leanna that Jason could not explain. Oddly, she seemed to enjoy his company more, responding to his gallantries with flirtatious smiles. She even seemed to welcome his touch, returning the clasp of his hand when he assisted her about the ship, or letting her knee brush his under the table during meals. But when he tried to take her in his arms one evening after dinner, she slipped gracefully away, trilling a gay laugh as she reminded him of his promise.

But most puzzling of all was the expression on her face he sometimes glimpsed when she thought he was not looking. Some strong emotion darkened her eyes until she noticed him, then she would smile and distract him with some light remark.

Jason became exasperated at her evasiveness. It was like flirting with a will-o'-the-wisp. So he resolved to press his suit in a more direct manner, beginning on Christmas Eve. He had ordered an extravagant gift for Leanna in London that he had intended presenting to her after their first night of love. Instead, he would use it to cull her favor, since his other tactics had failed. He had yet to meet a woman who didn't melt when given an expensive gift.

Leanna, for once, had listened to her instincts rather than her pride. Her desire for vengeance melted when he flashed that devilish grin at her, creasing his cheeks and making his eyes sparkle. Perhaps if she responded to his flirtation, she could warm his interest into affection. However, she knew it was a delicate game she played because she was still determined to allow no intimacy between them.

Christmas was almost upon them. An air of merriment pervaded the ship. Cook made shepherd's pie in honor of the occasion, and Benjamin decorated a yule log for Leanna, using dried berries and ribbon around driftwood. Although not an elaborate offering, Leanna could not remember being so touched by a gift. She was so delighted that she hugged Ben fiercely and kissed him soundly on the mouth.

Jason watched sourly as the lad turned beet red, shifted his feet, and backed out of the cabin with a mumbled, "Glad you like it." Jason knew it was ridiculous being jealous of his own cabin boy, but he'd labored long and hard to win Leanna's affections and had yet to see any results. For Ben to so easily earn her attentions seemed unfair to him.

Leanna and Jason ate dinner with the crew on Christmas Eve. The boisterous crowd of men fell silent in homage to her beauty when she appeared with Jason. She was wearing a red velvet gown inset with white lace at the sleeves and hem. The rich color reflected off her white skin, setting her shoulders and face aglow with a pink radiance.

She smiled warmly at them all, then led the prayer, her blond hair flowing around her shoulders as she bent in reverence. The table was silent during the first part of the meal as the crew thought of family and home. Most had children and wives they heartily missed.

Jason broke the solemnity. "Come, lads, we'll be home soon and with a tidy profit to savor. You've been long away, but your homecoming will be all the sweeter for it, eh?" Jason winked suggestively and the men laughed as Leanna blushed.

The rest of the meal was merry once the grog and unusually rich food took hold. When Jason and Leanna left, good-natured whistles and catcalls followed after them. Jason ignored the lapse in ship's etiquette. Christmas only came once a year, and they were a good bunch of men. He smiled wryly as he escorted Leanna out on deck. If they only knew, they had little to be envious of.

When they reached the cabin, Jason was astonished when Leanna pulled his head down to plant a soft kiss on his cheek. "Merry Christmas, Jason," she said softly, her eyes glowing a brilliant green. Jason tried to pull her closer, but she slipped out of his arms to fetch a small package from beneath the bunk. She offered it to him with a shy look from under her lowered lashes. He pulled her down to sit beside him on the bunk and opened the gaily wrapped package. He was surprised and touched at the contents.

Inside was an exquisite paperweight in the shape of a ship. He touched the delicate Venetian glass, astonished at the resemblance to the *Savannah*.

Leanna felt warmed at his obvious pleasure. "The proprietor assured me that it was modeled after a sharp-lined schooner.

Do you think it looks like your ship?"

Jason was moved at her thoughtfulness. She had bought this while they were in London, despite the hostility between them. He had to clear his throat before he could answer. "Yes, indeed, it looks exactly like the *Savannah*. It's beautiful, Leanna. I'll treasure it always." Their eyes locked and for once there was no bitterness or passion between them, only a spirit of togetherness as husband and wife on this most important day of celebration.

Finally, Jason went to his small desk and pulled out a green velvet case elaborately tooled in gold. She looked at the case in her lap, at Jason, and back to the box. She wanted to fling it away from her at the cynicism in his eyes, but she forced her numb fingers to release the delicate latch.

It was as she had feared. On a bed of white satin lay a twinkling ensemble of emeralds and diamonds: necklace, bracelet, earrings, and ring. Her gaze clouded as she dimly realized that the workmanship was masterful. The jewels were set in a delicate filigree pattern of leaves and flowers. She shut the lid and stood up to turn away from Jason. "Thank you, Jason, they are most lovely," she said colorlessly.

Jason was stupefied at her reaction. Far from the sparkling pleasure he had expected, she seemed almost hurt. Frowning in puzzlement, he asked, "Don't you like emeralds, Leanna? They are very flattering to your coloring, and they complement your lovely eyes."

"The emeralds are beautiful, but I'm wondering why you have made me such an expensive gift," she replied, turning to watch his face. She was not surprised when his cheeks flushed, his chagrin confirming her suspicions.

"Why, there's no better time to present my wife with such a gift than on our first Christmas together," he replied, as though bewildered.

Her lip curled. "That's the *only* reason?" She met his gaze directly, and when his eyes dropped, she gave a mirthless laugh. "It's as I thought. You hoped to buy me like some doxy. Well, sir, my affections and my body are not for sale. God knows they are the one thing I have left to give freely, and I will not squander them on a man who holds me and my entire sex in such contempt." She wheeled toward the sternwalk, but his iron hands brutally gripped her shoulders and he brought her to a painful halt.

"You are a fine one to speak of contempt," he said. "I am daily dosed with your freezing disdain though I have done all in my power to set things right between us." He whirled her around to meet his granite eyes.

"Very well, girl, I admit that I had hoped you would look more favorably upon me after my gift, but I also genuinely wanted to please you. Well, no more. You have made it abundantly clear that you'll have none of me, but you are my wife and no one before God or man would fault me if I chose to throw you upon that bed and take my rights." Leanna trembled in his grasp, terrified when his voice sank to a menacing whisper. His eyes glowed like blue diamonds that made goose bumps stand out on her skin.

"I do not choose to do so. Understand me well, wench. I will take you when and if I please. To hell with your sensibilities. I've been patient with you far too long. Now, you will wear the ring I purchased for you and be glad of it, or by God your first lesson will be now, despite the fact that it makes my stomach sick to look at you."

Leanna churned with fury, fear, and anguish, but she looked at his quivering jaw and decided she had better extend her hand for the ring. He slipped it on her finger, an indefinable pain in his own stomach enveloping him because her hand trembled in his own crushing grip. Then he flung it away as though disgusted and stomped out of the cabin without another word.

Leanna sank into a chair, looking at the sparkling jewel weighing down her hand and staring back at her with menace, a symbol of this travesty marriage. She stifled the urge to yank it off and throw it overboard, for she was too afraid that Jason might make good his threat. She doubted she could ever forgive him if he possessed her in anger. She had been taken by him once without love. She would not allow it to happen again. Her pride reared at having to accept his dominance, but if meekness was the only way to nullify the danger, then she would have to be conciliatory.

She prepared for bed, too tired to hang up her dress with

her customary neatness. She flung it carelessly on a chair, donned a warm gown, and released her hair. She was too weary to give the tresses their usual one hundred strokes. She balled up in the hammock, shivering within and without as she looked at the jewel case lying on the bunk. Vaguely she wondered why it wasn't red instead of green, for her bleeding heart colored everything.

Chapter
Twelve

LEANNA SAW LITTLE of Jason for the remainder of the voyage. He avoided the cabin when he could, eating his meals with the crew. When he came to bed at night, Leanna lay still, pretending to be asleep, though she stayed wide awake with unexplainable yearning. Her eyes became shadowed with sleeplessness, and their haunting green depths took on a sad but proud look. As he had no need of her, she could do naught but display a like indifference.

On those occasions when a meeting could not be avoided, Jason was polite but withdrawn. He, too, became haggard, and a frown permanently creased his brow. His crew took his surly temper with equanimity, aware that all was not right between their captain and his wife. Benjamin did what he could to comfort them both, cheerily discussing his adventures at sea with Leanna and pampering Jason with his favorite foods or distracting him with games of chess.

A brooding tension pervaded the ship, a tension that intensified whenever Jason and Leanna met. Ben saw the feral gleam in his captain's eye when he looked at Leanna and he feared for her safety. He had seen his captain jubilant, he had seen him furious, and he had seen him sad. But he'd never seen him boiling with an inner rage that was all the more dangerous for being stifled. He tried to keep them apart, steering Leanna about portions of the ship to avoid Jason and encouraging his captain to eat with the crew.

Jason's rage resulted from mixed emotions: frustrated desire, hurt, shame, outraged pride, and a reluctant admiration for Leanna's spirit. He vacillated between a desire to strangle her, rape her, or smother her with kisses.

Leanna sensed the turbulent emotions raging within him. She was distressed at the tension between them. She longed to clasp him to her bosom and kiss away the frown between his brows; to shower him with the love and devotion he needed more than he knew. Instead, she avoided him when possible and shielded her own pain from his view. Her tossing and turning in the hammock at night had finally convinced her it was best to let the break between them remain. She doubted Jason would make another attempt to mend fences. When they reached land it would be easier for them to avoid one another. He would doubtless take up again with one of his old mistresses.

Her heart wrenched at the thought of Jason making love to another woman. But common sense told her it would be easier to bear that pain than the torment of being used by him as a convenience. No, it was best to suffer a lesser pain now than to be rejected and possibly even scorned when he had had his fill of her body.

So she bore the rift between them as bravely as she could and stemmed the tears by reassuring herself that if the situation became too unbearable, she could flee and build a new life. She refused to think of what it would do to her to leave and never see Jason again.

It was a relief to everyone aboard when they heard the longed-for cry, "Land ho!" Leanna rushed out on deck, her heart pounding with a mixture of eagerness and fear. She clutched the railing with damp hands, peering into the distance intently.

At first she could discern little but a blur on the horizon. But gradually the blur became red bluffs and wooden buildings hugging the slopes. As they neared, Leanna saw ships in the harbor and more buildings by the wharf.

Leanna jumped when Jason spoke at her side. "Savannah at last, thank God." There was relief in his voice. He seemed to gather himself up with an effort. "The buildings you see on the bluff are the countinghouses and warehouses of the harbor. The steeple in the distance is the City Exchange."

Leanna asked hesitantly, "How far to your plantation?"

"About an hour's drive. I have a carriage and team stabled at the wharf. We'll go after I leave instructions with my mate."

He turned abruptly away. Leanna watched him wistfully for a moment as the breeze combed his handsome black locks. She sighed and went below to make a last check of their baggage.

When Leanna returned, they had docked and the jubilant crew was unloading the cargo. Leanna soothed her gold velvet cloak lined with fur and pulled the hood up to protect her neatly coiffed hair from the wind. She was wearing a long-sleeved gown of brown taffeta with gold frogging at the bosom and sleeves. Her dark half boots were fur-lined and laced with gold frogs.

Leanna watched the activity for a moment, apprehension moistening her palms. She knew very little of Jason's grandfather; only what Sherry had told her. "Uncle Thomas is a brusque but kindly man, from what I hear. If you gain his approval, you'll find him a strong ally, but I believe he would make a formidable enemy. I would suggest you curry his favor, Leanna. It should smooth your marriage considerably if you can call him friend."

Leanna felt strong fingers grip her arm and slowly turned to meet Jason's grim stare. She wondered how his grandfather could possibly approve of her when she had so obviously made his beloved grandson unhappy.

Jason sensed her tension and couldn't resist a taunt. "Ready to beard the lion, Leanna? You'll not find my grandfather as malleable as I have been," he mocked.

Leanna looked at him haughtily, her confidence restored in

a rush of anger. "Indeed, sir, I only hope he is more of a gentleman. I would enjoy some amiable company as a refreshing change from your surliness."

Jason ground his teeth together, snarling, "You'll see more of me than surliness unless you take care, girl." She paled and turned away. He wondered why he felt no satisfaction at distressing her.

With a muffled oath, he picked her up and flung her over his shoulder, tired of bandying about words. She gasped and struggled, crying, "Let me walk, you bully!" He slapped her hard across the rear, then began to climb down the ladder. She quit writhing as she realized she could tip them both. Tears of rage in her eyes, she looked at him with hatred when he set her down in the shore boat.

Jason met her angry gaze indifferently, then turned away to survey the approaching quay. When the boat nudged against the wharf, he tied it up, stepped out and reached out a hand to assist Leanna. She ignored him and gathered her skirts to negotiate the steep step herself. When she stood with both feet firmly planted on the wooden planking, she was puzzled. The boards swayed disconcertingly under her feet. She tried to take a step, only to have her knees fold.

Jason roared with laughter and again lifted her over his shoulder. Leanna made no protest this time, though she was mightily embarrassed at the passing backs of the men she saw. Jason answered their greetings cheerfully, laughing at their teasing. "Quite a cargo you brought back, Jason. Must have had a pleasant voyage." A deep, booming voice joked, "Your share of the booty, Jason?" Leanna tried to peer at the man walking beside them but could only see massive, muscled legs clad in crude buckskins.

She was relieved when they reached the stable. Jason set her down on a bale of hay and bowed mockingly. "Leanna, this ruffian is my dear friend Rian O'Hara, trapper, trader, and hunter extraordinaire. Rian, this is my wife, Leanna." Jason watched with amusement when the blond giant's mouth dropped open. His dazed eyes looked at Leanna, then back to Jason.

His lips worked helplessly for a moment, then he gasped,

"Mighty pleased to meet you, ma'am. It's about time someone took this fellow in hand. His grandfather will be pleased to see you." His deep, melodious voice had a slight Irish lilt.

He smiled at Leanna with genuine warmth radiating from his velvety brown eyes. She smiled back, the dimples indenting her cheeks. "Thank you, Mr. O'Hara. It's a pleasure meeting you, also."

Jason looked at the happy smile on her face and the grim look returned to his mouth. She never smiled at him like that! He strode angrily away to an end stall, brought out two bay horses, and harnessed them to a buggy on the side of the stable. All the while, he was conscious of the banter between his best friend and his wife.

"So this is your first trip to America, eh? This land has a beauty that puts the Old World to shame, and I would enjoy showing you part of it." Raising his voice, Rian teased, "So if you can get rid of that husband of yours, we can start with my cabin." He winked roguishly at her, gesturing at Jason's averted back.

Leanna giggled in delight at his devilment, her heart lighter than it had been in many a day. "I'll look forward to it, Mr. O'Hara."

"None of that, none of that. As close as we're to be, you must call me Rian," he scolded.

"Certainly, Rian. Please call me Leanna."

"Leanna? I thought I'd call you me darlin'." He deliberately emphasized his brogue, looking at her with a mocking leer.

Jason stopped their banter ruthlessly. "If you're through flirting with my wife, Rian, it's time we left. I'm sure Grandfather must be anxious, for I was longer than I expected."

Rian sobered. "That he is, Jason, that he is. We were becoming feared you'd been taken by privateers."

He looked at Leanna's downcast eyes and Jason's taut mouth and groaned inwardly. His mule-headed friend had stumbled onto a jewel of a lass, yet he failed to appreciate her, from all signs. Typical of him.

"Do you mind if I ride with you, Jason? I was to visit Thomas this morning anyway. He wants me to see a 'gator he shot.

Says it's the biggest he's ever come across. And I'll point out where my cabin is located, missy," he winked. He then assisted Leanna into the buggy while Jason loaded their luggage. Leanna, sandwiched between the two men, was disconcerted to feel Jason's hard thigh pressing hers. She moved closer to Rian, breathing freer when the contact ceased.

Jason was angered when she shrank away and his mouth tightened. He flicked the whip at the horses and they were off after a momentary jolt. As they began driving through Savannah, Rian waited for Jason to tell his bride about the town. When he made no effort to do so, Rian sighed heavily and began pointedly, "As Jason probably told you, Savannah was founded in 1733 as the first settlement of Georgia. King George intended it to be a defense for Carolina from the Spanish in Florida. James Oglethorpe proposed the settlement and was one of the original twenty-one trustees. The first settlers were poor Europeans. They were burdened with intolerable restrictions: They could not drink rum, they had to plant mulberry trees on every ten acres of their land, and, most hindering, they could not own slaves."

Leanna had been listening only desultorily, more involved in the quickly passing town than in Rian's history lesson, but here she pricked up her ears. She turned away from her contemplation of the frame homes and buildings clustered around muddy but neat town squares.

"But I thought slavery is accepted here as elsewhere in America," Leanna said, confused.

"The colonists complained so bitterly about the disadvantage that the prohibition was relaxed around 1750."

"What a pity," Leanna murmured.

Rian eyed her with a half-smile. Thomas will approve, he thought. He always admired a lass with spirit, but she'll set the town down by the ears with her liberal ideas. He grinned in anticipation.

They left Savannah and traveled down a rough track that meandered under some towering pine, hickory, and oak. Leanna shivered under the cool shade cast by the pine trees. She huddled deeper into her cloak. When Jason ignored her trembling,

Rian glared at him and drew Leanna under the warmth of his own arm.

Jason turned to examine the brawny, protective arm around his wife but Rian met his menacing gaze with a cool, level stare that said plainly, "Dolt, if you've not sense enough to protect the bonnie colleen, I'll do your duty for you."

Jason reddened under the condemning brown eyes and turned abruptly away, urging the horses to a faster pace over the trail which, because it was rutted, jolted the buggy and its occupants.

As they came out of the forest onto the bluff of the river, the track smoothed out. Leanna gasped when she saw the lovely sight of lucid water churning over riverbed rocks. The river widened around a bend, slowing down as it turned, but still rippling in a brisk current.

"We've had a lot of rain recently and the water is up. Luckily most if it came after picking, so the crop is good this year, Jason. That newfangled idea of yours to rotate the acreage has paid off. Your grandfather has never yielded so much, even with the fallow land."

Jason smiled. "Excellent. Does Grandfather have the new gin running smoothly?"

"Aye, at last. He found a man to train Silas and there have been few problems since," Rian answered cheerfully. He was relieved that Jason had at last broken his sullen silence.

Suddenly, Leanna choked a scream, startling both men. They looked wildly about for the danger. "What is it, Leanna?" Jason asked sharply, his body coiling into readiness.

Her beautiful face pale, Leanna pointed at a huge, scaly lizard basking on the muddy bank of the river. Jason roared with laughter, Rian joining in heartily. "It's but an alligator, Leanna," Jason finally explained. "Ugly critters, but they're of little danger as long as you stay out of the water. They're ungainly on land."

Leanna turned back to look at the repulsive reptile again, both fascinated and repelled. The leathery head turned and its slitted eyes seemed to look straight at her. The creature yawned, showing sharp, yellow teeth. Leanna turned quickly away, shivering.

They were climbing a rise now, with eagerness apparent in Jason as he urged the horses forward. Leanna's instincts told her that her new home lay beyond the slope.

She craned her neck as they crested the hill and got a panoramic view of the plantation sprawled below. Jason pulled the team to a halt, breathing deeply and savoring the sight of the only home he had ever known or wanted.

Leanna was shocked at the size and beauty of the plantation. Small outbuildings, neatly fenced, clustered together at the foot of the slope. Most had small gardens and chickens busily clucking in the yards. Large barns and buildings occupied a site even further from the river.

But the view most spellbinding was Whispering Oaks itself. Set back from the other buildings and closest to the river, the manor was built of white stone, with four massive columns supporting the roof. It gleamed among the other structures like a benevolent father beaming with pride among his children. Verandas on the first and second floors ran the length of the home. Two of the largest oaks Leanna had ever seen, both gnarled with age, stood like sentinels between the house and the river.

"The trees gave Grandfather the idea for the name," Jason said softly. "When he stood under them they seemed to whisper with the breeze." Suddenly, Jason came alive and with a loud whoop, he urged the team into a dangerous gallop down the hill.

Leanna saw hands in the field pause to watch their descent, and as they neared the figures, she was astonished to see so many welcoming smiles. Many of the field hands waved, and one giant of a man danced for joy before breaking into a run to meet them.

Jason pulled the team to a halt and leaped down to be enfolded in a crushing bear hug, his feet dangling free of the ground.

The black man gently set him back on his feet, emotion apparent in the bright, dark eyes. He was dressed in coarse woolen trousers that stretched tautly over his thighs, a warm woolen coat, and brown laced boots. He seemed to be about Jason's age.

"Mistuh Jason, we'd feared fo' yo' life. Plumb worried, the mastah is. Git yoself into the house and ease his mind." The man gave Jason what was meant to be a gentle push, but Jason stumbled before the force of that enormous, calloused hand, before racing into the house.

The man then turned to Leanna, examining her from head to foot as Rian helped her down. Approval and curiosity gleamed in the soft brown eyes, but he waited respectfully for Rian to introduce her.

Mischievously, Rian drawled, "Gus, this is Leanna, from England." He left it at that for a moment, meeting Gus's exasperated eyes calmly.

Gus nodded. "Mighty pleased to meet yo', Miz Leanna," Gus said politely, then waited.

Laughing heartily, Rian finished, "She's Jason's wife." He watched with a satisfied grin as Gus's mouth dropped open, then stretched into a huge, white smile.

"*Right* pleased to meet yo', ma'am. Now mebbe we'll have laughter in this ol' house agin." He gave Leanna another warm smile, then touched his brow respectfully and returned to his duties.

Leanna looked so bemused that Rian laughed. "Gus is more part of the family than a slave. He and Jason were raised together as boys and they're almost like brothers," he explained.

Rian led Leanna up the stone steps, then pushed open the great carved oak door. The sight she beheld was overwhelming.

Jason was clutched tightly in the arms of an old man about his size. The craggy face, turned in her direction, trumpeted much love and joy. His eyes opened and caught sight of Leanna and Rian. He gently pushed Jason aside and stepped closer to Leanna, studying her with sharp, dark blue eyes that were exactly the color of his grandson's.

Rian watched gleefully, and Jason with foreboding, as the two figures, so dissimilar, faced one another. Leanna saw a tall man, slightly stooped with age, framed by a thick shock of white hair and brown skin that denoted a vigorous, healthy way of life. His sharp nose was longer than Jason's, his lips thinner, but the dark blue eyes mirrored his grandson's. Leanna read strength tempered with kindness in every proud line of him, and some of the tension dissipated in her body. She felt she would indeed be able to call him a friend.

Thomas turned from his dissection of Leanna to eye Jason with his sharp gaze. "I apprehend this is the cause of your delay?" he questioned drily, his voice deep and booming.

Flushing, Jason nodded. "Grandfather, this is my wife, Leanna." Thomas looked at Leanna noncommittally, reserving judgment.

"Well, missy, what think you of Whispering Oaks?" he probed.

Leanna paused to examine the foyer before replying. It was a graceful, lofty entryway, with a gleaming hardwood floor and a domed ceiling lined with intricate molding. A lovely staircase curved to the upper floors, the waxed bannister indicating age. A large inlaid secretary flanked by two Sheraton chairs was the only furnishing in the hall.

"It's lovely, from what I've seen, sir," Leanna replied sincerely.

"Let me show you around, my dear," Thomas offered. He greeted Rian, then suggested, "Jason, why don't you take Rian to the stable to see that alligator I was telling him about? I want to get better acquainted with this young lady."

Jason hesitated, loath to leave them alone. Despite his earlier taunting, he wanted his wife and grandfather to get along, and he felt it would be best if he explained his marriage to his sometimes cantankerous relative.

"Go, lad," Thomas insisted. His eyes gleaming perspicaciously, he added, "I'll not question the girl until you get back."

So Leanna found herself being escorted about the large house by her new grandfather-in-law. She said little, but she approved of the spacious rooms and elegant furniture. The dining room was particularly impressive. Oval in shape, with leaded windows that looked out over the lawn, it had a long mahogany table in the middle and a sideboard on each side. Leanna judged that at least thirty people could be seated comfortably. An exquisite crystal chandelier cast enchanting rainbows on the walls and ceiling as the morning sun caught its prisms.

When they came to the study, Leanna paused before the great portrait over the massive stone fireplace. A lovely brunette, her green eyes sparkling with vitality and mischief, was holding the reins of a beautiful black horse. She was wearing a simple calico dress and stood against the backdrop of the two oak trees.

Thomas cleared his throat. "My wife," he said simply, but there was a wealth of emotion in the two words. "She died of yellow fever before Jason was born. We met when I was a struggling farmer with one slave and a bare fifty acres. Her father was one of the largest landholders around and objected bitterly when we married. He never spoke to her again."

The acute blue eyes dimmed a moment with memories. "She never complained at the hardships she endured to help me build my holdings into a profitable farm," he continued. "We slowly saved enough money to add to our acreage, then plowed the profits back into the land. We lived in a two-room cabin for most of our marriage. She possessed three dresses. The one you see there was her best. That horse was the only luxury she ever let me purchase for her. She loved animals. We finally became profitable enough to build this house. It was under construction when she died."

He blinked rapidly, then led her out of the study and up the stairs. He, at least, seemed no woman-hater. Leanna resolved to ask him when she knew him better why Jason held her sex in such contempt.

There were eight bedrooms upstairs, each with doors opening onto a veranda. Most were sparely decorated, with white walls and simple furniture. Thomas explained, "These rooms still need redecorating. Perhaps you can help me with that, my child. I asked Jason to bring home some period furniture, so we should be able to brighten these old rooms considerably."

Thomas opened the door at the end of the hall. "This will be your room. I'll have Jason's things moved immediately." Leanna stiffened at the words and backed away from the enormous four-poster bed. The room was larger than the others, with a handsome chiffonier and armoire that matched the carved bed. A tapestry sofa stood before the fireplace, and a lovely dressing table sat against the wall.

Thomas sensed her unease and wondered at it, but said nothing. Leanna seemed weary, so he suggested gently, "Why don't you rest until dinner, my child. I will send a girl to attend you. You can wait until after dinner to meet the house servants."

Leanna was too tired to refuse. She stood on tiptoe to softly kiss his wrinkled cheek in thanks. "I appreciate the tour. The house is lovely. I am most impressed."

Thomas harrumphed, then smiled at her for the first time. "I'm glad you like it, child. I hope you will be happy here." He shut the door behind him, and Leanna undressed and climbed under the cool linen sheets. She dropped off immediately, and the little maid who came to assist her found her dead to the world. She slipped back out.

Downstairs, Jason was occupied in the unpleasant task of explaining his marriage to his grandfather. They sat in the study, drinking black coffee. When he finished, Thomas was silent for a moment, then he asked, "Am I correct in assuming you've not had relations with her since your meeting?" It would explain the girl's tenseness when he showed her their bedchamber.

"Aye." Jason dropped the word like a stone, and there was bitterness in the sound.

Thomas almost smiled, but caught himself in time. He was not so old that he couldn't remember passion in his own youth. And from the way Jason looked at the girl, he believed his grandson was not as indifferent as he would like to pretend. Aye, she must be quite a lass if she had held off this hot-headed lad for so long. It would be interesting to watch things develop between them. Thomas nearly rubbed his hands in anticipation. His grandson had at last met his match. His prayers had been answered. Surely a girl as beautiful and strong as Leanna could break down that wall of contempt Jason had held inviolable for so long.

All he said, however, was, "Be gentle with the lass and she'll come around, I'll wager. She seems a wife a man can be proud of, so your patience will be well rewarded."

Jason snorted but did not reply. His patience had been stretched thin and he was considering pressing his suit more forcibly. He had come to the conclusion that the sexual tension between them must be released before they could relax around one another. He would give her another week. If she still avoided him, he would take her willing or no.

Thomas saw the dark look on Jason's face and sighed. It seemed a shame that wisdom only came with age, for it was obvious his grandson had need of large measures. He changed the subject, telling Jason how the plantation had been faring.

Leanna timidly descended the stairs after her long rest. She felt fortified and much more able to face Jason and his formidable grandfather. She was attired in a simple blue velvet gown, plain except for an embroidered panel running down the front.

Jason and Thomas came out of the study as she passed the door. "Well, my dear, I hope you feel better after your nap?" Thomas asked.

"Yes, I do, thank you," Leanna replied shyly.

Jason raked her from head to foot with glowing eyes, lingering on the smooth expanse of skin exposed at her bodice. She flushed and hurried on to the dining room.

When they entered, Leanna was startled to see the room crowded with servants, all of whom looked at her with curious eyes. They ranged in age from a lad of about fourteen to the housekeeper, who looked to be in her sixties. She came forward, curtsied, and greeted Leanna in a soft, musical, and surprisingly educated voice. "My name is Sarah, ma'am. On behalf of all the servants I want to welcome you to Whispering Oaks." She pushed the boy forward gently and Leanna was touched when the lad scuffed his feet in embarrassment, then presented her with a lovely bouquet of dried flowers. He was a handsome fellow, his skin tone paler than the others. He peeped at her out of melting brown eyes, then looked away hurriedly.

"Thank you all," Leanna said huskily. Sarah clapped her hands and the servants scattered in different directions to continue with their duties. Sarah smiled warmly at Leanna again.

"I will be pleased to consult with you about the running of the house, ma'am. Perhaps we could begin tomorrow?"

She was a plump woman, small of stature and with a delicate bone structure. She was still handsome, and Leanna imagined that in her youth, she must have been stunning. "I would enjoy that, Sarah. Thank you. Perhaps in the afternoon?" Sarah nodded acceptance, then walked briskly toward the kitchens.

Leanna sat next to Thomas at the head of the table, Jason across from her. For the first part of the meal, she and Jason concentrated on the delicious food. The fresh pork and peas and carrots were a marvelous change from the shipboard fare. The candied yams were a new, exotic experience for Leanna, but she found them much to her taste. A fresh, hot roll steamed as she opened it to coat it liberally with rich, creamy butter.

Her hunger abated, Leanna asked, "Is the lad a child of someone on the plantation? He seemed so different from my expectation of servants in America."

Thomas smiled. "Quincy is Sarah's son. Both are free. Sarah was educated by my wife, over her father's protests. I'm sure she would have wanted the same for Quincy. He may help Jason in the shipping end of our business someday, so he needs to be able to read and write," Thomas explained.

Leanna was startled. "Do you mean you educate all of them?"

Thomas shook his head. "That's not possible, I'm afraid, though I have allowed a few of the brighter workers to take reading lessons. That will improve their chances to advance and earn money of their own. In fact, Jason studied with Gus at one time, before finishing his education in Charleston. Isn't that right, Jason?"

Jason nodded, a gleam of pride in his eyes. "A better man there never was."

Leanna looked stunned and bit her lip. "I should have known a man of your kindness would pay particular attention to his slaves. It's just that in England, we hear such tales . . ."

"Certainly, I understand. But I fear some of the tales are undoubtedly true. Many slaveholders *do* mistreat their help. But I am not one of them, nor is Jason." He glanced at his grandson and teased, "To the contrary, I've the suspicion that a number of the maids—dark or no—wish he were not so conscientious." Jason's dark blush broadened Thomas's smile and stiffened Leanna's back.

"I would like to give you a tour of the plantation tomorrow, Leanna. I believe I can set your doubts at rest," Thomas said, his mannerisms reminding Leanna irresistibly of Jason at his most mischievous. "Even such a radical as yourself will be reassured, I'll wager. Tell me, child, from whom do you get your beliefs? Was your father a Whig?"

Leanna laughed musically. The happy sound made Jason's jaw quiver. "Indeed, sir, he was. I confess we spent many hours discussing England's social ills and the need for Parliamentary reform."

When her eyes clouded a moment, Thomas distracted her hastily. "I can sympathize with your beliefs, but I hope you will not speak against Savannah society. My fellow Georgians are sensitive on the issue of slavery, and I do not want my new granddaughter accused of fomenting rebellion."

He patted Leanna's hand and rose to escort her to the door. "You must be tired, child. Get a good night's rest, for you have a busy day scheduled tomorrow." When they reached the end of the staircase, he kissed her and suggested gruffly, "It would give me great pleasure if you would call me Grandfather, Leanna."

She impulsively kissed him back, rising on tiptoe to reach his cheek. "I would be delighted, Grandfather. You have made me feel most welcome. I look forward to tomorrow." She drew back and smiled. When she glanced at Jason, however, her face became expressionless, as though a shutter had been closed. "Good night, Jason," she nodded.

He bowed mockingly and sneered, "Good night, sweet wife. Sleep well in your chaste bed."

She turned away haughtily, but not before Thomas saw her trembling lip. He watched her climb the steps, her back straightened with pride, then turned to his rakish grandson. "You've a deal to learn about women, Jason. If you want to win a place in her bed, you're certainly going about it in an odd sort of way," he said.

Jason paced the hallway restlessly, as though he couldn't bear inactivity another moment. "I have tried everything I know, Grandfather. She recoils from my touch, ignores my compliments and spurns my gifts. What am I to do but take her and end this tension between us?"

Jason kicked the edge of the rug. "Her first time was quite

painful, but when she experiences the pleasure I can give as well as take, perhaps she will be more receptive." The desperation in his voice disturbed Thomas.

"No, lad, don't be so hasty," he said, gripping Jason's shoulder to emphasize his words. He ached at the anguish he could see in his lad's eyes, but patience was the best strategy to use. "Leanna does not strike me as a woman amenable to coercion, Jason. Be gentle and patient a little longer, and all will come right, you'll see. She is not indifferent to you, I'm certain of it."

Jason sighed and resumed pacing. He finally halted at the window next to the front door. The serenity of the silvery night only added to his torment. "I will think on it, Grandfather," he agreed finally.

They climbed the stairs together, both men thinking of the woman above. She tossed from side to side in her comfortable bed, hoping that Jason slept no better than she.

Her wish was granted. Near dawn, Jason gave up his useless attempt at sleep and walked, naked, to the window. Despite Thomas's counsel, Jason sensed Leanna would never accept him willingly, no matter how long he waited. Briefly Jason wondered why she was so adamant. They were married, he was reasonably handsome and intelligent, and he would swear that she desired him. So why? His weary brain worried over the question but could not find the answer. Defeated, he gave up. What man could know a woman's mind?

Jason touched his warm forehead to the icy windowpane, trying to ignore the familiar tightness in his loins as he thought of his wife. For a moment, he considered riding into Savannah to seek relief with one of his old consorts. A buxom, sensuous redhead came to mind. She had led him through new and exquisite delights. But when he tried to recall those pleasurable moments, somehow her image faded into a slender, gilt-haired girl who tilted her long white throat and groaned in pleasure when he took her.

Jason cursed and smashed his hand against the window frame. Damn the girl for tormenting him so! His mouth tightened with rage and his blue eyes became stormy; he straightened with resolution. Only Leanna could feed this hunger. He would not be made the laughingstock of Savannah by seeking out its whores after bringing home a young and lovely bride. He would have her if she hated him ever after. His mind made up, he resolved to have his things moved into her room the next day. If she was presented with a fait accompli, perhaps they could yet learn to love one another.

It wasn't until he climbed back into bed that he realized he had used that word. Love? He pushed the thought away violently. He would love no woman, wife or no. When he was sated with that silky body, her image would fade from his mind and he would at last find peace. Reassured, he yawned and dropped off to sleep. But when he dreamed, he saw himself not as the confident seducer, but as the eager lover offering his heart after an explosive union.

PART THREE

*"O you gods! Why do you make us love your goodly gifts
and snatch them straight away?"*
—*Pericles*, Act III, Scene I

Chapter
Thirteen

—————

LEANNA DRESSED IN a warm, woolen gown, folded her fur-
lined cloak over an arm, and went down to breakfast. Her heart
pounded as she braced herself for a meeting with Jason. However, she found only Thomas seated at the long table, an empty
plate in front of him and a full cup of coffee in his hand.

He grinned a warm hello. "Good morning, child. I hope
you slept well?"

Leanna nodded and went to the sideboard to select eggs,
ham, and biscuits. While she ate, Thomas explained, "Jason
will be out all day. He's in Savannah disposing of his cargo
and dividing the shares among his crew." Thomas mentally
clicked his tongue over the look of relief that swept her face.
Ah, the follies of youth! Leanna's haggard eyes contradicted
her claim that she had had a restful night and Jason's surly
mood and drawn face had attested to his equally sleepless
evening.

When Leanna pushed back her half-finished plate, Thomas

scolded, "We've a long day ahead, Leanna. Finish your breakfast, child."

Leanna couldn't force another bite into her churning stomach. "I've had sufficient, thank you, Grandfather. I am ready whenever you are." She stood up and waited.

Thomas looked at her with disapproval, then he sighed and held her cloak. "We'll begin with the outbuildings, then I'll take you over the acreage."

In a carriage they drove by the small, neat cottages, and Leanna was surprised to see several women sitting on the steps, sewing or even talking idly. One held an infant in her arms, cooing to him happily, maternal pride lighting her face.

Thomas smiled at her puzzlement. "We do not drive our slaves continually, Leanna, despite what you may have heard. These women came out of confinement recently and will not be assigned tasks for a month to give them a chance to recover. Even then, they will be given light duties in the dairy house or nursery. Only the strongest hands, mostly men, work in the fields or gin house."

Thomas halted the carriage next to a large cluster of buildings. He gestured with the whip toward a low, blackened brick structure. "The smokehouse. We raise our own meat year 'round. We have about eighty head of cattle and forty hogs at the moment."

Pointing to a larger building, he offered, "You can see the gin house, if you like, though of course it's not in operation at present. We don't plant again until the end of April. Right now the hands are working on squash and potatoes."

"I'd love to see the stable, Grandfather," she said with eagerness.

Thomas smiled in approval. "Ah, you like to ride, my dear?"

"I love it," Leanna returned simply. Thomas assisted her from the carriage, then led her into a lofty barn. Leanna's nose twitched appreciatively at the familiar scent of hay and horses. She was amazed at the number of stalls. At least twenty stretched the length of the barn on both sides. Thomas introduced her to the men and boys tending the animals. They smiled broadly when she praised the condition of the horses.

Indeed, they were beautiful animals. Even the work horses glistened with good health as they ate their meal of hay. Thomas led her down the aisle to several stalls separate from the rest. Leanna peeked in a roomy cubicle and gasped in delight at the beautiful gray mare suckling an adorable coal-black foal.

"These are the descendents of the stallion in the portrait of Jenny. The foal's sire, Night Wind, is Jason's favorite mount. He's a handsome beast, full of temper and fire. The gray is a lovely lady named Morning Mist. She's yours, my dear. It's the best wedding present I can manage on such short notice."

Leanna's radiant smile warmed Thomas's heart. "Thank you, Grandfather. You couldn't give me a gift I'd more cherish." She kissed his cheek.

He cleared his throat. "Come, child, we've a deal left to see," he rumbled.

They drove away from the outbuildings toward the fields. As they neared the laboring workers, Thomas explained, "Whispering Oaks is run on the task system of labor. The hands work from sunrise until eight, when breakfast is brought to them in the fields. At twelve they stop for dinner, and most tasks are completed by three. Tasks are assigned by Gus, who is the driver. When their work is complete, they spend the remainder of the day as they wish. They can raise and sell poultry, keeping the proceeds for themselves."

As they neared, Leanna watched the workers closely. They wielded their hoes with rapid efficiency. When Thomas stopped the carriage, Gus signaled the field hands to stop and he removed his hat. "This here's Miz Leanna, Mistuh Jason's missus," he told the group of workers. Leanna smiled and received wide, friendly smiles in return. She searched the faces intently. Most were open and content, but a few seemed sullen and wary.

Leanna sighed and was glad when Thomas clicked to the team after speaking with Gus for a few moments. While the slaves at Whispering Oaks were apparently treated kindly, they were still slaves; pampered chattels, but chattels nonetheless.

Thomas said nothing, though he suspected the reason for her silence. She would have to come to terms with her conscience, as he had, over the years. Slavery was as essential to Georgia's economy as shipping was to England, and if Whispering Oaks was to remain profitable, he had no option but to employ it.

When they returned to the house, they ate lunch, then Leanna met with Sarah to familiarize herself with the running of the household. This occupation engulfed the rest of the afternoon, so it wasn't until she went to change for dinner that Leanna discovered Jason's things had been moved to her room. When she opened the wardrobe door to select a gown, Leanna was startled to find it bulging with jackets and trousers. She fell back a step, her consternation shifting to anger. She grabbed the first gown her hand fell upon, so enraged that she didn't notice it was of light, summer muslin, a fabric entirely inappropriate for the cold weather.

Her little maid, Sukey, a lovely child of no more than sixteen, watched Leanna warily as she helped her into the pretty yellow gown. Leanna stared with unseeing eyes into the mirror as the maid buttoned the dress. She scarcely noticed as Sukey dressed her hair in a fussy style she disliked. When the girl accidentally stabbed her with a hair pin, Leanna whirled around to reprimand her.

Poor Sukey was wondering frantically what she had done to so displease her mistress. She stood with downcast eyes and nervous, wrenching hands as she waited for a scolding. When Leanna saw her scared face in the mirror, some of the tension drained from her body. She took a deep breath and vowed not to let her boorish husband so upset her that she unjustly fixed her anger on the servants. So she smiled at Sukey and thanked her for her help. The girl relaxed and returned a shy, pretty smile of her own.

The door opened and startled both women. Sukey watched in alarm as Leanna's smile changed into a narrow-eyed glare. The object of her condemnation stomped into the room. Jason was tired, hungry, and disheveled, and in no mood for a confrontation with Leanna. When he saw the look on her face he groaned inwardly and almost backed out the door again. Only pride forced his steps forward. Be damned if he was afraid of the chit. Now was as good as any time for her to learn her place.

Sukey scurried from the room when Jason gestured for her to leave. The gentle closing of the door left an ominous quiet in the chamber as Leanna aimed flaming eyes at Jason. Both refused to look away. The silent battle ended when Jason snapped, "I apprehend you do not approve of the new sleeping arrangements?"

He winced as his words unleashed a torrent from her. "No! Nor will I agree to them. The *gentleman* needs reminding of the sacred oath he made me . . ."

"Hell's teeth, woman, that's a promise I should never have made and one you should never have asked for! I have tried everything I know to win favor in your eyes, yet you still show me naught but scorn." Jason stalked up to the dressing table and put a heavy hand on her shoulder. Leanna stiffened, alert to danger like a wary gazelle confronted by a leopard. She met his hard eyes in the mirror bravely, her chin high.

"You will be mine, and soon," he said flatly. "I will not seek relief elsewhere when I have a lovely bride under my own roof."

She pulled away, stood, and whirled to face him, determination in every feminine curve. "No, Jason, I will not," she said, scornful. "I am not one of your whores to lay down at your command. I will have nothing of a man who has no respect for me or my sex. The matter is closed."

She sauntered to the door, apparently unconcerned, but her neck was prickling with danger as she felt his gaze stabbing her back. The door seemed miles away, but she forced her feet to walk in her normal steps despite the fact that they itched to run. She sighed with relief when she reached it. She turned with her hand on the knob. Her face paled at the look on his face. It was totally calm, void of anger, hurt, or passion; void of everything but implacable purpose. "We shall see, my dear, we shall see," was his only response. Leanna retreated hastily, the quiet sureness in his manner unnerving her far more than rage would have.

She waylaid Sarah in the kitchen and requested that her

things be moved to another chamber. Sarah looked confused. "Does the one you're in displease you?"

"Er, yes, it does, Sarah." She recouped. "Please see that it's done before dinner is finished."

"Very well, Miss Leanna," Sarah agreed, and called one of the housemen to relay the command.

Jason's manner at the table was disconcerting. He conversed pleasantly with his grandfather, including her in the discussion about the moderate return he made on his cargo.

"Profits would have been better if I hadn't been delayed so long. The linens and woolens brought scarcely enough for me to break even, for Billings brought similar stuff a week earlier. However, the luxury items—the silver, furniture, mirrors, china, and the like—brought a goodly amount."

"How many more voyages before the *Savannah* has recovered our investment?" asked Thomas.

Jason took a sip of wine before answering. "Unless I make a higher profit, probably four more," he said.

"Never mind, lad, it could have been much worse. Why, I remember back in eighty-three . . ."

Leanna listened sleepily as Thomas reminisced about the years following the War for Independence. When she couldn't stifle a yawn, Thomas broke off and smiled ruefully. "Sorry, child, I didn't mean to bore you."

"I'm not bored, Grandfather," Leanna protested, "merely tired. If you gentlemen will excuse me, I believe I'll retire for the evening." She smiled at them both and made her way slowly to the stairs. Jason watched her slim form climb the stairs, a flame burning in him until he turned back to his grandfather, when he became serene once more.

This seeming forbearance on his part set the tempo of his meetings with Leanna for the next several days. At first, she was guarded in his presence, shying away if he came too close and keeping the conversation impartial. When he made no threatening moves, she slowly relaxed. Perhaps he had accepted her refusal, after all.

Even the fact that Rian made every excuse to visit the plantation and flirt with Leanna failed to undermine Jason's composure. Leanna flirted gaily back, glad to have Rian's cheerful nonsense lighten the heaviness in the house. Jason watched with apparent unconcern as they laughed together, puzzling Leanna and astonishing Rian.

Thomas observed Jason's relaxed manner with suspicion. Sarah had told him of Leanna's change of room, and he would have expected Jason to be furious instead of conciliatory at her refusal. When Jason disappeared for a time each day, Thomas was sure his hot-headed lad was up to something, so he followed him one day. Jason drove the buggy to the old homestead, now unused and rather isolated, and unloaded what seemed to be supplies into the cabin.

Jason was disconcerted to find his grandfather blocking his path with his big bay gelding when he began the return trip. Thomas's eyes held a withering glare, but Jason refused to be reprimanded. "I see you've decided not to heed my advice, eh, Grandson?"

Jason flushed. Thomas only called him Grandson when he was extremely angry. "I cannot, Grandfather. I'm so crazy with frustration I hardly know what I'm doing any longer. This marriage is not natural and it is rapidly becoming unbearable. Besides, Leanna will enjoy it, I swear it."

The pleading in his voice softened Thomas's severe countenance. "Lad, lad, don't you understand that her enjoyment could only make her hate herself and you the more?"

Jason contemplated this silently. "I have to take the chance," he replied grimly. "We cannot go on like this."

"Very well, Jason. I still council patience, but if you can wait no longer, I will not interfere. She is your wife." Thomas leaned forward to emphasize his words, his eyes more piercing and direct than Jason had ever seen them. "But I expect you both back, unharmed, within two days. And Jason, if Leanna is so unhappy that she wants to leave you, I will help her do so. Understood?"

Jason nodded, his expression sterner than his grandfather's. If this was to be his last chance, then so be it. "I understand, Grandfather," he said.

* * *

When Jason invited Leanna for a ride the next day, she hesitated only briefly. Aside from one short outing with Thomas, she had not had a chance to ride the gray mare, and she was anxious to try her again. So she smiled sunnily. "I would love to, Jason. I will change and join you soon." She flew up the stairs and dressed in her new habit. She pulled the black hat cockily over one eye and curtsied to her handsome reflection. Her face became wistful as she hoped he would find her attractive. She crushed the desire ruthlessly. She had promised herself to take each day as it came and enjoy what life offered her.

Jason had changed into a handsome brown riding jacket and comfortable buckskin breeches. His high-topped brown boots emphasized his lean, muscular thighs. Leanna's heart beat faster when she saw him, and his smile almost made her burst with gladness. Perhaps he was growing fond of her at last.

"You look lovely, and anything but masculine in that mannish habit, Leanna," Jason said, his eyes roguish as they rested on the bodice of her wide-lapeled jacket.

His burning eyes brought her back to her senses. She must always be on her guard. "Thank you, Jason. Shall we go?"

Jason cursed himself mentally, but he smiled when he held the door for her. A groom helped her mount. Jason leaped into the saddle of the fractious black gracefully. He slowed the high-strung beast to the smaller stride of the delicate gray.

They rode in silence at first, swinging into a canter when they passed the great oaks. Jason led the way along the river, slowing so Leanna could enjoy the sights and sounds around her. He followed a maverick tributary that rushed over some rocks, leading them ever deeper into the forest.

She urged Morning Mist to catch up with Jason. "Where are we going?"

"I thought you might want to see the old homestead." His manner was offhand, almost nonchalant. "Of course, if you'd rather go back . . ."

Leanna demurred hastily. "No, I am much enjoying the ride, but I would like to gallop."

"There's a field near the cabin. We'll be there soon." Leanna sat back in contentment, enjoying the scent of pine, the noisy stream, and the crackling leaves underfoot.

They soon turned away from the stream, and as the trees thinned, Leanna was glad to see the promised clearing up ahead. She quickly gave Morning Mist the command and the graceful gray surged forward. Jason laughed and finally gave his own impatient stallion his head.

Leanna took advantage of her surprise lead and urged Morning Mist faster, for some reason determined to beat Jason in this unplanned race. But graceful as she was, the lovely gray was no match for Night Wind. His mighty hooves pounded the rough terrain to close the gap, and before long the two horses galloped neck and neck until the powerful black pulled away. Jason reined Night Wind to a rearing halt at the cabin and turned to watch Leanna.

She was too happy from the gallop to be overly upset at her defeat, so she ignored Jason's mocking look. When he clasped her waist lightly to lift her down, she stiffened and pulled away when her feet touched the ground. She went inside the cabin, curious to see the home where Jenny and Thomas had been so happy. Jason quickly unsaddled the horses and stabled them in the shed behind the cabin, serving each a large bucket of oats.

Leanna was surprised to find the two-roomed cabin clean and tidy. A log fireplace, flanked by a wood stack, dominated the small living and eating area. A plank table with two plain, straight-backed chairs stood near a tiny window. An ancient stove and small cupboard completed the kitchen arrangements. Idly, Leanna opened the cupboard and was disconcerted to find an ample stock of bread, fruit, wine, ham, and cheese. Her eyes widened with suspicion. When the door opened, she spun like a top to meet Jason's eyes.

His heart pounding, Jason firmly shut and locked the door behind him. Leanna's eyes widened still further at his slow deliberation and she backed away, looking frantically about for some avenue of escape. When Jason walked toward her, Leanna gave a little moan of terror and fled to the only other door. She slammed it behind her, scrabbling desperately for a lock, but there was none.

She scrambled over the bed toward the shuttered window, dismayed to find it nailed shut. She was biting her knuckles, her heart hammering at her ribs, when the door opened, then closed. Taking a deep breath, she squared her shoulders and turned to face her husband.

Jason was disconcerted at the fear in her face. What had he done to put such terror in her? "Leanna," he pleaded softly, "please don't be afraid. Surely you know I will not harm you. I want to give you pleasure even more than I want to take it. Don't you see that it's the only way to end this battle between us?"

Leanna took heart from his gentle, almost entreating, words. "I will hate myself and you, ever after, if you take me with no words of love between us. Can we not be friends? Mayhap one day love will come to both of us if we can respect and trust one another first." Her eyes were misty with pleading.

Leanna's heart sank as Jason shook his head. "We can never be friends. I want you too much and, if you're honest, you'll admit you want me, too. I respect you now, and I trust you as much as a woman can be trusted." He edged closer to her as he spoke, catching her in his arms when she tried to climb across the bed.

She struggled wildly, desperately afraid she would be unable to control her response. He held her wrists behind her back with one hand and used the other to unbutton her jacket, ignoring her cries of rage. He covered one full breast with a large palm, watching her face as he stroked the quivering flesh until it grew taut. Her head was thrown back, her face tight with emotion, whether rapture or rage, he wasn't sure.

He could contain his starved need no longer. Groaning, he pulled her against him and fastened his mouth over hers. Leanna resisted valiantly, trying to ignore the movements of his warm, mobile lips as he passionately devoured hers, as though famished for her taste and feel.

Her passivity drove him wild. She gave a faint moan against him, her terror now of him rather than herself. She feared she was once more to be the victim of rape.

His senses, soaked by her sweetly scented hair, her softness, and the potent seduction of her struggling body, became so heightened that the raging desire he had stifled for so long became an acute pain that he must assuage at all costs. Consideration for Leanna, honor, respect, pride—all were engulfed by the irresistible flood of his desire. He came perilously close to throwing her onto the bed and relieving his masculine hunger without thought for Leanna or their future. Then he felt moisture on his cheeks, and when he released her mouth, he saw tears streaming down her terrified face.

The sight was as effective as a face slap. He drew back, disgusted at his own lack of control. His crushing grip loosened into a tender embrace. He stroked her trembling back with shaking fingers, horrified at their narrow escape. His mouth, gentle now, kissed the tears from her face and grazed her sore lips with a butterfly's touch.

When her trembling subsided, he apologized softly, "Forgive me, my love. I have hungered for you for so long that I lost my head. You are too beautiful."

Leanna opened her mouth to plead for release, only to once more have it taken by his hungry lips. But the former cruel pressure was now gone, startling Jason as much as it did Leanna. He wooed her with soft caresses, his lips so persuasive that, against her will, Leanna began to return his kiss.

Jason exulted at her response and carefully eased her over to the bed, never taking his mouth from hers. When she felt the mattress under her, she stiffened in alarm and tried to push him away. He gently held her, pinning her hands at her sides while his mouth nibbled the sensitive lobe of her ear, then forayed down to the warm, pounding hollow of her throat.

Leanna shuddered and tossed her head from side to side, willing herself to blank out this renewed seduction, tender as it now was. When he began to unbutton her shirt, her mind forced her reluctant hands to his shoulders with the intention of pushing him away. Instead, they pushed the jacket off his shoulders and searched under his shirt for the warmth of his broad chest. Jason eagerly assisted her, flinging off his warm coat and shirt.

He loosened her blouse, and when he reached to lower her

chemise, Leanna knew it was her last chance to resist. She grasped his wrists to stop him, fighting a bitter battle with her own arousal. He stopped, reluctant to use force. Their eyes locked fiercely for a moment. Leanna's eyes were the dark green of the pine that scented the air, slumbrous with desire, but still shy and afraid.

Jason's eyes were the midnight blue they became only when his deepest emotions were stirred. The pleading in them moved Leanna, but it was the vulnerability and need she read that decided her. Surely if he wanted her so, he must have some small measure of love for her, whether he would admit it or not? She could deny him and herself no longer. Somehow, at this moment, it was suddenly unimportant whether he loved her; she needed desperately to please him, and for now, that was enough.

Jason scarcely breathed as he waited. He yearned for her willingness with every muscle in his body. It was important to him not because of masculine vanity or pride, but because he wanted the essence and spirit of Leanna to reciprocate his desire. Her fulfillment was as important to him as his own.

When Leanna closed her lids in assent, she unleashed a storm of pent-up desire. Jason yanked off her skirt, petticoats, chemise, boots, and stockings. Leanna shut her eyes in embarrassment when she lay naked before him: She didn't see his look of awe at the beauty that had haunted him day and night. He took off his boots and socks with furious haste, then joined her on the bed.

He traced a gentle path from her delicate collarbone, down the side of her tiny waist, over the fullness of her hip, and along her leg all the way to the ankle. He traced another path up the other side of her body until he came to her breasts. He covered them with both hands, willing her to look at him.

When Leanna felt his hands cup her, her eyes flew open and caught his passionate gaze. His fingers teased the sensitive, rosy tips with light, circular motions that fed the fire within her. He leant down with his even more tormenting lips and licking each erect nipple, sent waves of sensation through her body. He grasped her with one arm behind her waist to hold her against him, while his other hand teased the back of her knee, higher to the top of her thigh, and down again.

Leanna pressed the back of her hand against her mouth to stifle a moan of pleasure, shocked by her own sensuality. When he left her breasts to cover her mouth again, she kissed him back passionately, letting him probe her soft places eagerly. He rubbed his furred chest against her soft breasts, and a moan escaped her lips.

Leanna ran her hands over his shoulders as they kissed, treasuring the feel of his hard body against her, solid as oak. Jason's hands were also busy, gripping her buttocks and, finally, parting her thighs to search out her most sensitive self, swollen now with passion. Leanna gasped when he stroked her there, stunned at the pleasure that throbbing flesh gave under his persuasive fingers. She moaned and squirmed under him until he blanketed her body.

He laughed softly at her sounds and eager, clutching hands. He peeled off his trousers and underwear, at last releasing his rampant, eager flesh. He lay down at her side, and as his hand explored, his lips once more devoured her mouth while his other hand teased her aroused nipples.

Leanna stroked his flat nipples, eager to return the pleasure he was giving her. He shuddered and grasped one of her hands to place it on him. Leanna flinched and almost pulled away when she touched his urgent manhood. But his hoarse plea, "Please, Leanna," brought her hand back, at first reluctantly, then eagerly. She was spellbound by the size, hardness, and length of his velvety strength, passion clouding all feeling but need.

Jason removed her hand, aware that he could not wait much longer. He rolled on top of Leanna, kissing her, as his knees spread her thighs widely apart. Leanna was so hungry for him that she gladly moved her legs, as eager for his entrance as he.

To enflame her ardor more, he teased her sensitive vaginal lips with light brushes of his organ, the contact an intoxication. At the same time he rubbed his chest in a circular motion over her breasts, until her body seemed one aching nerve, throbbing with need, from head to toe. Panting, she begged, "Please don't torment me more, Jason, I need you."

"Yes, my darling, it's time," he groaned. Holding her hot face in his shaking hands, he ordered huskily, "Look at me, Leanna." She opened her heavy lids, staring into his blazing eyes, desperate to satiate the ache deep in her loins. Jason's gaze seemed to consume her as he slowly sheathed himself into her so he could savor the intimacy of the moment. Pushed within her to the hilt, he remained still for a moment, enjoying the passion on Leanna's face as she moaned and clutched him to her. She pushed upward to meet him, eager for fulfillment. Jason subdued his own need and forced himself to a slow pace, to match her rhythms.

Leanna gasped when he filled her, amazed at the sensations flooding her body. He belonged in her as though God created him specifically for her. When he began his first gentle thrusts, she arched against him to receive him more fully.

Her response loosed Jason's control. He thrust within her wildly, plunging onward until both soared.

Jason drove powerfully, no longer worried about Leanna's response. She was as eager for completion as he. At his urging, she lifted her legs around him further, opening her more to his ever-deeper lunges. The tension built in her until at last it burst into a thousand stars, her every nerve tingling with spasms of pleasure.

Jason felt her contractions grip him tightly and could restrain himself no longer. He plunged as far as he could reach and burst within her, his soul carried to the heights of ecstasy and fulfillment.

Gasping for breath, Leanna and Jason both relaxed, Jason still pulsating inside her. He was reluctant to leave her blissful warmth. Leanna didn't complain of his weight. She held him sweetly to her breast so he wouldn't see her tears of joy. She hadn't known it was possible to experience such pleasure, and she would always be thankful that he had ignored her wishes and brought things to this pass. This radiance they could give one another was surely an unbreakable bond that would forge stronger claims on one another.

Jason kissed her breast softly, almost worshipfully. His own eyes were suspiciously moist. He finally, reluctantly, withdrew and lay down beside her to hold her tight. "Thank you, my darling. I didn't know it was possible to feel such pleasure."

Leanna laid her cheek on his chest, admitting shyly, "Neither did I, Jason. Is it always thus between a man and a woman?"

Jason laughed, his voice and eyes more tender than he knew. "No, dearest, seldom do a man and a woman find as much joy as we discovered today." He kissed her brow, then lay back with his eyes closed, his body totally relaxed for the first time in months.

They remained thus for several moments, not speaking, both content to relish this unusual peaceful accord. Jason stirred first, running his hands over Leanna's shoulders, arms, and back. "Your skin is like satin," he murmured, bending his head to nibble her neck and shoulder.

Leanna began her own exploration, curious about the differences between them. She stretched out a slim, shapely leg next to his own hairy one and giggled at the contrast. Jason raised his head to see what she was laughing at and a slow smile creased his cheeks to form Leanna's favorite expression.

"Laugh at me at your peril, wench," he mocked. "We can't all be perfect specimens like you."

Leanna's smile faded as she examined him minutely from head to toe, running her hand down a path on his side, her face intent. She raised dark green eyes to meet his. "But you are a perfect specimen of manhood, Jason, far more beautiful than I." The look in her eyes, the full beauty of her breasts hanging so temptingly near, and the scent of their lovemaking still clinging to the sheets aroused him again.

Smiling wolfishly, he grasped her gently and smothered her breasts with kisses until her nipples were hard points of sensation.

Between kisses he teased, "Since you admire my attributes so, my dear wife, it's time you took advantage of them." Leanna felt him hardening against her and sat up abruptly. Jason would have pulled her back, but he saw what she was looking at and laughed with tender joy. Leanna's face flushed, but her eyes remained open in amazement as she watched his organ grow under her eyes, stiffening as it became engorged with blood until it stood up proudly, as though preening under her admiring gaze.

Leanna stroked him, delighting in the throbbing softness that filled her palm. She finally met Jason's darkened eyes, wonder in her own. "Amazing," she said simply.

They made love again, this time their fusion even more tender than before, since their previous tension was gone.

Finally, exhausted, they slept. When they woke it was dark and both were ravenous. Leanna felt a lusty slap on her buttocks. Jason roared, "Woman, I want my dinner!" Giggling, she fumbled for the candle by the bed, lit it, and donned his shirt in the flickering light.

Jason lay abed, absorbing the enticing picture she made in his shirt. The fine cambric clung to her slim curvaceous form, and when she bent down, revealed the dimpled cheeks of her buttocks. Jason was amazed to feel himself harden again just looking at her. She left the door open while she found the lantern in the other room and lit it.

He listened to her cheerful humming as she banged pots in the kitchen, a frown creasing his brows as he recalled the last few hours. He had thought once his passions were spent he would be able to put her from his mind. Instead, he felt as eager for her as ever. Even worse, he felt a tender need to protect, cherish, and please her. Uneasy, he rose and pulled on his breeches. Telling himself he had not yet made love to her enough, he went into the kitchen.

Leanna threw him a sunny smile and set two loaded plates on the table. She held a chair for him, her lips forming an inviting grin that dimpled her cheeks. Shaking off his mood, he insisted on seating her first.

They ate hungrily, speaking of inconsequential things. Jason seemed more relaxed than she had ever known him, so she decided to ask him about his hatred of women. No propitious opportunity to ask Thomas had presented itself. Taking a gulp of wine for courage, Leanna asked steadily, "What happened in your life to give you such a distrust of women, Jason?"

Jason stiffened in the act of raising his glass to his lips. His mouth tightened and his eyes clouded as he brought the glass to his lips and took a large draught. Setting the glass down, he toyed with the stem before answering. "What makes you think I don't trust women?" he asked finally.

Leanna nearly choked on a piece of ham. "You jest!" she exclaimed. "Your distrust is apparent in your every comment and look at women." She stared at him until he lifted his eyes to meet hers with an angry look.

"Very well, I admit it!" he snapped. He pushed his plate back, his appetite gone, and began to pace the floor, muttering as he walked. "Of all the women I have ever known, you are only the third I have ever respected. Women are usually grasping, greedy creatures more concerned with their own comforts than the welfare of the family they supposedly love." He stopped in front of her to sneer, "Love! I saw that much-vaunted emotion take the father I adored and turn him into a weak caricature of the man he was before my mother deserted him. And why did she leave us? She missed the society of Boston! She couldn't bear the savage wilderness of the plantation even though she had a comfortable home and a husband and son who adored her."

Tears came into Leanna's eyes at the pain in his voice. She rose to take him in her arms, but he whirled away. Her cheeks were burning with humiliation. He was incapable of love, it seemed, as she had feared all along. But she had to know for certain. "Am I right in assuming that you bear no love for me, then? Despite what has passed between us?"

Jason strained to hear her, so low was her voice. He hesitated, wondering how to reply. He didn't want to jeopardize their new accord, but he could not lie to her. He turned to face her. "Leanna, I have more regard for you than I have ever had for a woman. Your smile, your scent, your laughter fill my heart with happiness. I want nothing so much as I want you by my side and in my bed. Please don't let this change anything between us. We have too much joy to give one another."

She met his eyes with shuttered ones of her own. "Do you love me?" she asked steadily.

His heart tight with pain, Jason looked away and whispered, "No."

She flinched, then donned a wooden mask. Without another word, she returned to the bedroom and began dressing. Jason followed her, grabbing her by the shoulders when she picked up her chemise.

"Don't destroy what we have, Leanna. Our bodies were made for each other . . ."

She cut him off with an hysterical laugh. "And what of our hearts, Jason?" She cupped his chest. "You have a heart; I can feel it beating. I've seen the look in your eyes when you look at your grandfather. You're kind to your crew and your horses. So much love scattered everywhere but where it most belongs: me, your wife." She jerked away and pulled the shift over her head, then stepped into her petticoat.

When Jason tried to stop her she slapped his hands away. "Do not touch me," she said, her voice cold and deadly. "You don't want to soil your hands with a woman unworthy of the love you hoard so greedily," she sneered, pulling on her stockings and boots.

Jason grasped her to him desperately, trying the last persuasion he knew of. He pulled her to him and lowered his mouth over hers, demanding she respond. She didn't struggle. She stood immobile, inanimate, and totally unresponsive. Defeated, he finally looked up. He was shocked at the look of contempt in her eyes. He didn't try to stop her when she finished dressing.

His mouth dry with fear, he pulled on his own clothes, trying to ignore the warmth of his shirt and her scent that clung to it tenaciously. He followed her out of the cabin and pushed her aside to saddle the horses. Silently, they rode back to the house, Jason dreading the meeting with his grandfather and Leanna mercifully numbed.

Thomas was in the study when they returned, but he came out at the sound of their voices in the hall. He searched their faces, then slumped a little at their expressions.

"I must speak with you, Grandfather," Leanna entreated huskily.

Jason knew what she was going to say and his heart raced in panic. Under no circumstances must she be allowed to leave. He would have touched Leanna on the shoulder, but she pulled away with a scornful look. His face whiter still, he cast a pleading look at his grandfather.

Shaking his head slightly at Jason, Thomas led Leanna into his study and closed the door behind them. Jason slumped into a hall chair and rubbed his sweaty hands over his creased breeches, waiting tensely.

Thomas poured Leanna a tot of brandy and insisted that she drink it. Too weary to argue, she sipped it. He sat down on the divan next to her and waited for her to speak. He watched her struggling to compose herself and for a moment he was angry at Jason for causing this anguish.

Finally, she muttered, "I want to leave, Grandfather. I can no longer bear living with a man who despises me merely because I'm a woman."

Thomas turned her with a gentle but insistent hand. "I know it seems that way, Leanna, but please let me assure you that Jason does *not* hate you, no matter what he has said. Has he told you of his mother?"

At her nod, he sighed. "He adored her. He was such a happy, well-adjusted child before she left. It tore him apart, losing his mother, then watching his father crumble before his eyes. The scars run deep, Leanna, but I swear to you since you've been here, I've had hope that he could put the past behind him at last."

He lifted Leanna's downcast chin and forced her to meet his eyes. "He cares for you more than he knows, child. He hasn't yet learned to cope with the emotion, but if you can be patient a little longer, he will make a husband and lover that most women only dream of."

Thomas smiled at the flush in her cheeks. Apparently, in that regard, they had no problems! "If you insist, I will buy you a house in Savannah or Charleston." His voice became gravelly with emotion. "But you'd condemn an old, lonely man, and a young, lonely one to lifelong despair. If you leave Jason now, the progress he has made since knowing you will be aborted and he'll grow into a bitter man, like his father."

Leanna leaned against him, easing some of the weight she felt on her shoulders. Thomas stroked her back as she cried, his heart heavy but hopeful. Finally, Leanna regained her composure and sat up.

Drawing a deep breath, she agreed, "Very well, Grandfather, I will stay a while longer." Looking away, she admitted almost inaudibly, "I think you know that I love him. If I cannot soften his heart, I must leave. It's unbearable to ache for someone who can't return your love."

"Thank you, child. I think you'll be glad you stayed." Thomas escorted Leanna to the door, his arm bolstering her weight.

Jason leaped to his feet when the door opened, his heart in his throat. Leanna looked at him expressionlessly, but she wished him goodnight and climbed the stairs.

Jason looked at his grandfather, straightening as if for a blow as he waited for him to speak. "Grandfather, please! Is she leaving?" he insisted, anguished.

Sighing heavily, Thomas replied, "No."

Jason sagged with relief. He met his grandfather's eyes with heartfelt gratitude. "Thank you, Grandfather."

"You are welcome, Grandson. But I suggest you search your heart and divine *why* you are so relieved she isn't going." His voice became tart. "For a man of such intelligence, you are amazingly obtuse," Thomas said in disgust, then returned to his study.

Jason remained in the hall, a stunned look on his face. He had food for thought, indeed. But he refused to think tonight. He told himself he was too weary, but deep down, he sensed he was not going to like what he discovered.

Chapter
Fourteen

ABBY SAT BY the bed, sewing. Her trembling fingers drew the thread in and out of the embroidery hoop with jerky, abstracted motions. The only sound in the room came from the logs in the fire and the porcelain clock on the mantel.

She dropped her hands in her lap, no longer able to concentrate even halfheartedly on the task. She leaned forward in her chair and stared at the figure on the bed. So white, so still. All the vibrancy and energy gone from the man she loved.

Abby rose and knelt beside Sherry with little of her usual grace. She took his hot, limp hand to her cool cheek, her eyes squeezed shut as she tried to transmit some of her own vitality to Sherry.

Not long before, she had recovered from her stunned state, for she dreaded a world without her beloved. Sherry had been carried to his townhouse and deposited. When she awoke, her first sight was the old family doctor preparing to bleed Sherry. At first, her joy at the doctor's finding him alive transcended all else. Then her heart started pounding heavily as she watched the doctor draw out his knife to make an incision.

Sherry had been contemptuous of the medical aptitude of his family doctor. Like most ton doctors, the man seemed more concerned with exotic, ineffectual remedies than with the health of his patients. Sherry's own father had died shortly after being bled by this same physician, now silver-haired, though still slight of build. The sight of that knife about to cut into Sherry's vulnerable flesh startled Abby out of her stupor.

"No!" she shouted, wrestling the doctor's arm away.

"Really, madam, if you don't want his lordship to die, you must let me bleed him. He's full of poisons," the doctor protested, looking at her reprovingly.

Trembling with shock and fear, Abby cried, "I know little of medicine, but mere common sense tells me he's lost enough blood. You shall not kill Sherry as you did his father. Now get out!"

The man looked outraged and flung his instruments in his bag before quitting the room, slamming the door behind him.

Harry entered soon after, protesting, "Abby, Sherry must have care or he will assuredly die." He watched her distracted, anguished face. Concern clouded his normally merry blue eyes.

Abby bit her lip, trying frantically to remember the name of a doctor Sherry thought brilliant. The young physician had studied under the innovative Scottish surgeon John Hunter. John . . . John Weber!

"Have Jenkins send for John Weber immediately, Harry," she commanded sharply. Then he reached for a towel, dampened it in the bowl by the bed, and pressed it to Sherry's feverish forehead.

Aghast, Harry exclaimed, "That crackpot! Why, his own peers spurn him!"

"Yes, probably because he repudiates their outlandish practices. That merely recommends him to me more highly. Now do as I say." Abby's voice rang with authority as she fixed him with a determined gaze. She was very much the aristocrat at that moment.

Harry looked vaguely insulted, but he reluctantly did as he

was bid. It seemed an age before the doctor appeared. He was a young man with restless, brilliant dark eyes that were startling in his gaunt face.

He greeted Abby brusquely, then walked to the bed to examine Sherry. He removed the blood-soaked bandage and gingerly fingered the area around the chest wound. Turning his patient slightly to the side, he explored Sherry's back, straightening like a hound on the scent at something he felt under his fingers.

Washing his hands, he said curtly, "The bullet must be removed. It has lodged between his ribs. I believe it missed his vital organs, but I am not certain. It is imperative that the bleeding stop. I must operate immediately before he recovers consciousness. If you are squeamish, you had best leave, madam."

Abby stayed rooted to the spot. He cast her an approving look before he went briskly about his preparations. He set out a scalpel, a large pair of tweezers, a long, curved needle, and some thick thread on a clean towel. Abby and Harry watched, disconcerted, when he first ran his instruments through the fire, then poured brandy over them and his fingers.

Abby moved to the bed to hold Sherry's hands, her face averted as the doctor cut deeply into Sherry's flesh. Thirty agonizing minutes later, the doctor tonged the bullet, pulled it from its bleeding fissure, then stanched the copiously flowing incision after probing for any foreign substances that might remain and pouring more brandy into the incision. He sewed up his handiwork with an efficiency that astounded Abby, who was convinced she could not make stitches so neat. Finally, he bandaged both wounds, then felt Sherry's pulse. Appearing satisfied that the operation had not been too traumatic for his unconscious patient, he tucked the white wrist back under the covers and gathered up his instruments.

"The bleeding should stop soon. The greatest danger now is infection. See that someone stays with him at all times, and if the wound becomes inflamed, send for me." He brushed aside Abby's thanks, accepted his fee and left as abruptly as he came.

                           *   *   *

Sherry indeed developed a slight infection, but three days later,
his fever broke. Dr. Weber assured Abby he would recover
over time. At that moment she felt a faint movement in her
balled hand which clutched Sherry's. Abby tensed and turned
to stare at Sherry's face.

His eyelids fluttered, then opened. He looked at her groggily, as though he had trouble focusing. "Sherry," Abby whispered. His gaze sharpened and his lips formed a weak smile,
then he groaned with pain as full consciousness returned.

Giddy with relief, Abby prepared him a dose of laudanum
in water. She supported his head while he gulped greedily.
Clenching his teeth against the pain, he asked, "What the devil
happened? Was I shot?"

Abby debated briefly before replying. It had not taken long
for them to discover the true perpetrator of the attempt on
Sherry's life. The authorities grudgingly checked out the boy's
claim when it became apparent he had no motive. They told
Harry and Abby his story. Both were horrified, but certain even
without verification, that Gavin was the culprit and must have
escaped.

Indeed, their suspicions were confirmed. The jailers had
that very day discovered the guard's body. They became suspicious when the cell's occupant did not eat his meals.

Following the boy's story, they searched the docks, only to
discover that Gavin had sailed that morning for Boston. On
hearing the news, Harry and Abby met one another's eyes
soberly. Gavin's venom had not yet been spent. Abby penned
a hasty letter to Jason, warning him that Redfern was loose
and dangerous.

Even drugged and weak as he was, Sherry sensed that Abby
was upset. His voice as commanding as he could make it, he
said, "I have a right to know who wishes me dead. I can think
of but one man, and surely he is safe in prison?"

Abby turned to meet his eyes. "No, he escaped, my darling.
It's only by the grace of God and the skill of John Weber that
you are alive. I believe Gavin intends to try for Jason next. He
has sailed for America."

Abby smiled when Sherry cursed fluently. Yes, he would recover. She knew the question hovering on his lips when his anger was vented. She assured him, "I have written to inform Jason that Gavin has escaped. There is naught else we can do."

Gloomily, Sherry had to acknowledge she was right. They could do nothing, at least until he recovered. He'd a mind to go to America himself and get rid of that bastard once and for all. However, to Abby he only said, "I am deuced hungry, my dear. Please order me something to eat." Abby eagerly complied, feeding him the bowl of soup that she fetched herself.

Sherry searched her face, concerned at the tired lines under her eyes. He reached up to touch her cheek. "You look exhausted, my dear. Please go home and rest. I will be fine now. Your tender care has done the trick."

Abby wiped his mouth, then kissed him gently. He kissed her back, trying to enfold her in his arms, but he winced as the movement sent stabs of pain through his body. He slumped back against his pillows, the food and drug making him drowsy. "This will not delay our wedding, you know," he yawned. "I will not wait longer to make you mine if I have to be carried to the church."

Abby kissed his brow noncommittally. "I will be here when you wake, dearest." She tucked the covers under his chin and smiled at him with love shining in her eyes.

Sherry made rapid progress. His determination to be well enough for the wedding spurred his recovery. Of his resolution to confront Gavin, he told no one. As soon as he was well enough to leave the house, he went to the War Office to seek passage to America on one of His Majesty's finest war ships. His superiors could do nothing but grant his request, though they hated losing his sorely-needed services for such an extended time. Sherry decided to go straight to Savannah.

When their wedding day arrived, Sherry was almost recovered. His wound still ached if he over-exerted himself, but he could walk normally and he had resumed most of his old activities.

The wedding of Lady Abby Reynolds and Jason Arthur

Blaine, sixth Earl of Sherringham, was to be one of the most talked about and attended weddings of the year, despite the fact it was held in December. They were married in Westminster with all the pomp Sherry could contrive. He was proud to make Abby his wife, and he wanted the whole world to share in his joy.

He thought Abby the most beautiful bride he had ever seen. He smiled proudly as she walked down the long aisle attired in cobwebbed Irish lace. Her gown was high-necked, ruffled at the collar, and hemmed with ruche. The mutton sleeves were of transparent lace. At her throat she wore a diamond brooch that was a Reynolds family heirloom. It was set with an enormous yellow diamond that was the envy of the ton. The gown was sprinkled with topazes that flashed as they caught the morning sunlight until Abby seemed the living embodiment of all that was beautiful and radiant in Sherry's world.

They said their vows softly, so moved with love that the priest, the enormous crowd, and their many attendants faded away until they were aware of nothing but each other. Encapsulated in the warmth of their adoration, blue eyes met blue in a loving embrace that gave new meaning to the age-old vows they uttered. When they kissed to seal their union, it was done chastely. Passion would come later, but for now, overwhelming love and joy swelled their hearts until there was room for nothing else.

During the festivities that followed, Sherry and Abby laughed and danced with their customary ease. But when their eyes met, the air was charged with pent-up tension. Desire, stifled for so long, was becoming unbearable.

When they left their breakfast early, they ignored the knowing looks exchanged by the men and the titters of the women. They set out for the earl's country estate, talking desultorily of safe subjects to quiet the pounding of their hearts.

It was near dark when they at last arrived. Sherry bore the customary introduction of his new countess to the servants with ill-concealed impatience. They sighed in unison when the butler informed them proudly that the French chef had been cooking for a week so they would have a wedding dinner they would long remember. They picked at the delicious food, forcing down several bites of each rich course before waving the plates away.

The French cook was so enraged at this cavalier treatment of his masterpieces that he waved a butcher knife dangerously, threatening in a vituperative flow of French to quit throwing pearls before these English swine and return to France where good food is appreciated.

He calmed down when he overheard one disgruntled footman talking to another. "Ain't proper, the way they eye each other. The earl's barmy in 'is noodle, if you arsk me. Always thought 'e was a sensible bloke, but 'is missus 'as set 'im on 'is beam's end, all right." The brawny young man shook his head pityingly. "Aye, 'e'll ne'er be the same again. A real shaime it is. A real shaime."

The chef smiled philosophically when he heard this conversation. If there was one thing a Frenchman relished more than good food, it was love. Happily, the chef decided only that glorious emotion could make even the iron-stomached English so insensitive to great food. His pride assuaged, he returned to his duties.

Abby and Sherry climbed the great staircase with relief, unaware of the turmoil they had caused in the servants' quarters. When they at last reached the sumptuous master suite, they exchanged a long, tender kiss which turned into passion. They began to undress one another with eager, trembling fingers.

Abby stood before him with a shy, bent head, a wild flush on her cheeks as Sherry examined her minutely from head to foot with wandering eyes and hands. The touch of his fingers so excited her that passion soon banished shyness. She examined him in her turn, her fingers timid at first, then bolder as the pleasurable look on his face encouraged her.

"I have long dreamed of this moment, my darling. You are even more beautiful than I imagined." Sherry's voice was husky with ardor. His breath caught in his throat as Abby's shy smile turned bold and she touched him with ever more daring fingers.

"Vixen!" he exclaimed, his smile shaky. Lifting her in his arms, he carried her to the bed and lay her down tenderly. For a moment he remained standing, drinking in her loveliness as she lay in the abandoned disorder of her rippling dark hair, her breath rasping between parted lips and her eyes a deep, smoky blue.

Groaning, he covered her body with his and excited her with burning caresses and eager kisses. Her passionate response so excited him that he was hard pressed to control himself.

The night that followed was the culmination of Sherry's and Abby's love life. When dawn came, their bonds were forged into an immutable chain that would hold them happy prisoners always.

They spent one entrancing week riding, talking, dining, dancing, and loving. This time together was the happiest they had ever known; it was a time of enchantment that was all too brief. When they reluctantly forced themselves to face the world again, this magical fulfillment of the heart and body fortified them for the unpleasantness that was to come.

In a quiet moment, Sherry had at last confided to Abby his intention of going to America. She vehemently opposed the idea, but when Sherry reminded her that Jason was in danger and should not have to fight Sherry's battles for him, Abby reluctantly agreed. To Sherry's consternation, however, she insisted on accompanying him.

"I have just discovered the joy I can find with you. I will let nothing jeopardize it, least of all a snake like Gavin Redfern." The asperity in her voice softened. "Besides, I want to see Leanna and discover if your stubborn cousin—who much reminds me of you, incidentally—has made a total botch of his marriage." She looked at him saucily.

Sherry slapped her on the rear, leering at her when she pretended to be affronted. "Very well, wench. I have good use I can make of that lush body on the cold, long voyage." He whispered to her exactly what he would do until she blushed and pushed his wandering hands away. Their argument ended, as all their talks had of late, in a finale that was very acceptable to both of them.

* * *

Gavin fanned himself with a languid hand, then stifled a yawn as he waited for his opponent to throw. Edward Forrester was a tall, handsome man with brown hair and warm brown eyes. His hand shook as he picked up the throwing box. He had lost several hundred pounds to Redfern on this night alone, and he was determined to recoup his losses. He shook the dice violently, then flung them on the table. He smiled broadly. "It seems the luck is mine for a change, Redfern." He raked in the pot.

"Congratulations, dear fellow. Shall we see if it holds?" It did seem that Lady Luck no longer smiled on Gavin, that evening at least. Normally, he would have ceased playing, but as he eyed the hostile faces around the table, he deemed it prudent to let Forrester win back some of his money. He was not yet ready to leave Boston, and he had no desire to be forced out, so he'd best let the fool win. In the long run, it would probably be more profitable, anyway, for those who had refused to play with him would be drawn back when they heard he had at last hit a losing streak. So he smiled negligently and played until Forrester won back his losses of the evening, then he excused himself with smooth charm and went to his lodgings.

He halted at the door as his wary ears heard a noise inside his chamber. Soundlessly drawing the knife from his boot, he eased the door open. A pretty young girl lay on the bed clad only in a sheer nightdress. She started at the sound of the door, then smiled at him shyly.

Amused, Gavin set his knife aside and asked, "To what do I owe the honor of this visit?" He walked leisurely to the bed and reached out to play with a blond strand of hair.

Swallowing hard, she answered, "You told me how lonely a stranger in a foreign country can feel, and I want to make you happy." Looking away, she whispered, "I love you, Gavin. Please don't send me away."

He raked her body with his eyes. She was a lovely little thing, fresh as a peach and ready for plucking. He reached down to one breast and began kneading the soft flesh with his hand, almost absent-mindedly. She was the daughter of the innkeeper and couldn't be a day above fifteen. He had teased and flirted with her more out of boredom than an intent to seduce.

The innkeeper had been at great pains to protect his daughter, and he had no mind to anger the burly man. "I am touched at your offer, but I hesitate to dishonor such a lovely young girl. Your father would be most upset." Gavin faked a tender smile.

As he had expected, his pretend forbearance made her more eager than ever. "It's not dishonorable when I have come to you. Besides, Father need not know. I certainly won't tell him." Her little face looked mulish. Gavin suspected she had come to him as much out of rebellion as infatuation.

Smiling conspiratorially at her, he began to remove his clothing. "Very well, little Lilith. But no one must know, mind." She nodded eagerly, but her eyes widened in fear when she saw his engorged manhood.

Quickly, before she could change her mind, he peeled off her sheer gown, pried open her thighs with his knees, and began kissing her in practiced passion. Soon she was panting, and as he prepared to impale her body to the mattress, she suddenly reminded him of another blonde even more beautiful. Smiling in pleasure at the vengeance forming in his mind, he took the girl, and the vision made his conquest all the sweeter.

Chapter
Fifteen

———⌇———

LEANNA WAS PALE with fatigue when she went down to breakfast the next morning. She had spent the night wrestling with her instinctive need to please Jason and her even more instinctive need to preserve herself. She was still struggling with her two alter egos when she entered the dining room and saw the object of her inner debate. He smiled at her hesitantly.

"Good morning," she said curtly, in no mood to be pleasant. Jason sighed at the stubborn look of her face as he seated her. He was tempted to touch the soft blond locks that fell around her shoulders, but he forced himself to pull away and retake his seat.

"You haven't been into Savannah since your arrival, and I was wondering if you might like to visit some of the shops this morning? We have nothing to compare with Bond Street or Picadilly, of course, but we import some lovely muslins and silks that could be made up to suit your taste."

Leanna forced herself to meet his inquiring look. An inflexible attitude would not help them solve their problems, so she coolly assented. "Very well, Jason. I have no need of new clothes, but I confess I would like to see more of Savannah."

"Excellent! I'll have the team hitched up immediately and we'll leave as soon as you eat." He had a boyish grin on his face when he went outside to give the order.

Leanna forced down a few mouthfuls of the succulent ham, then pushed the plate away in defeat. She wondered if she would ever be hungry again. Thomas entered and made a welcome distraction from her dreary thoughts.

He searched her face with those disturbing, keen eyes, then he gave her an approving smile. "I understand you and Jason are going into Savannah. I'm glad. The fresh air will do you good. Be sure to dress warmly, for the wind is quite nippy this morning." He kissed her cheek, then served himself a full plate of ham, grits, and eggs and sat across from her.

"My dear," he proposed after swallowing an appreciative bite, "I would like to hold a ball to present you officially as Jason's wife." He sighed at her frozen expression and continued doggedly, "It's been too many years since we entertained, and I want to show you off. What think you of the idea?" He knew her response even before she answered.

"No," she cried. "It's not possible with things the way they are between us. It's difficult enough staying. I can't go through such a farce. Please don't ask it of me." Her voice shook and she looked quickly away to disguise her tears.

"Of course I won't, child. Think no more about it. It was just a suggestion," Thomas hastened to reassure her. He patted her hand and returned to his food.

Leanna dismissed herself and went upstairs to collect her cloak, leaving Thomas grimly wondering if he hadn't made a mistake in asking her to stay. He had no desire to put the child through such anguish as she seemed to be experiencing.

When Jason returned he was astonished at the hostile stare his grandfather gave him without so much as a "good morning." "I expect to see that child in a happier mood when you return, Grandson, else I might yet help her leave." His eyes were the chilliest Jason had ever seen them.

Flushing, Jason protested, "I have done naught to upset her this morning." He met that icy look with indignant eyes.

"But you are nevertheless responsible, are you not?" Thomas smiled in grim satisfaction when Jason looked away. Leanna entered at that moment, and she looked curious as she sensed the room's charged atmosphere. However, both men smiled at her easily, so she said nothing.

Outside, Leanna tensed when Jason lifted her into the carriage. He wrapped a fur lap robe around her and smiled at her so warmly she flushed and looked away. For once their eyes were on a level as he stood at her side, and when he still stared at her, she squirmed uncomfortably. He lifted her chin to force her to meet his eyes.

"Good morning, wife. I haven't had a chance to greet you properly yet." His lips inched nearer, allowing her plenty of time to draw back, but she was mesmerized by the little flame in his eyes. He kissed her gently, his lips tender rather than ardent. When her lips trembled and opened, he quickly drew away.

"Now we've started the day off right, we can leave." He gave her the roguish grin that never failed to move her, then he climbed up beside her and clucked to the team.

Leanna fidgeted under the lap robe and wrung her hands. She was far too vulnerable to his charm. When he smiled at her so, she wanted to throw her common sense to the winds, fling herself into his arms, and confess her love. Swallowing hard, she forced herself to put his nearness out of her mind.

Jason wondered at her unease. Determined to make the day an enjoyable one, he decided to play on her love of history. "Georgia was one of the original thirteen colonies. Savannah was the original capital of Georgia, but Atlanta is more central to our population, so she was given the honor after the war."

"Did Georgia play an important part in the War for Independence, Jason?"

Jason threw her a wry look. "Actually, Georgia was slow to catch the fever of independence. Savannah, for example, traded mostly with England. I was born in the same year Savannah really became involved in the effort, 1775. My father was among the militia that occupied the courthouse and ousted Governor Wright."

Jason looked shame-faced as he admitted, "Our moment of glory didn't last long, unfortunately. Savannah was easily taken in December of seventy-eight. A slave showed the British a secret passage behind our lines." His face was grim as he recounted the tale he had been regaled with many times. Thomas was one of the first to urge independence from his former homeland, and outrage still filled him when he remembered Savannah's humiliating defeat.

"It wasn't until the end of the war in eighty-two that the troops were driven out. One of my keenest memories is Grandfather's jubilation at their defeat." Jason half-smiled, but that happy memory was crowded out by another, disturbing one. It was only a few years later that the trouble began between his mother and father.

It was Leanna's turn to distract Jason. Her heart ached at the melancholy look in his eyes. "Rian said General Washington stayed in Savannah after the war. Is it true?"

She was relieved to see the tautness recede from his finely chiseled lips. "Indeed it is. He stayed at Stephen Miller's house on State Street. I'll show you when we arrive."

They soon entered the town, and once more Leanna was struck by the orderly nature of the city. Neat squares were enclosed by low fences. Most houses were simple frame affairs with gabled roofs.

Jason nodded in greeting to people as they passed, doffing his hat to the ladies. Leanna felt the curious looks directed at her from the men and women alike. She smiled at most of them and generally received warm smiles in return.

Jason halted in front of a fenced, frame house with a simple front veranda. He pointed with the whip. "Stephen Miller's house."

Leanna was startled from her contemplation of the building by a gale of laughter coming from a large crowd of people nearby. She and Jason both peered curiously in that direction, but their distance prevented them from seeing what stirred the excitement.

Jason smiled at her. "Shall we investigate?" At her nod, he clasped her waist lightly and swung her down, holding her hand a warm captive. They walked in the direction of the crowd and could soon make out a garish sign that hailed, "Mr. Salenka and his Learned Dog." A small, bow-legged, bizarrely dressed man stood beside a little dog on a raised platform.

Children giggled as the scruffy, spotted mongrel pawed the stage. The crowd chanted in time with the movement until they had counted eleven times. On the eleventh count the dog stopped and panted engagingly while his master proudly proclaimed, "What did I tell you, ladies and gents? Is that the correct time or isn't it?"

A bluff man in the crowd peered at his watch and shook his head in wonder. "Eleven exactly." The crowd cheered and flung coins on the stage. Leanna laughed with the children as the dog seemed to give the man a triumphant look.

Jason eyed his wife hungrily. She so seldom laughed. When she did, the happy sound seemed to light up her face and everything around her. Leanna felt his gaze and turned to smile at him. Her cheeks were rosy from the chill wind. His eyes dropped to her parted lips.

Leanna's smile faded at the look on his face. She tried to force herself to avert her eyes, but she was fascinated by the unabashed hunger he radiated. The crowd slowly receded until the only reality was the need they felt for one another. Forgetful of their audience, their lips met in a kiss so intense they were almost frightened at the emotions it aroused.

Desperately, Jason pulled her closer, his hands encircling her slim waist under the concealing cloak. Gasping under his marauding lips, Leanna trembled as though with a fever when he explored the moist interior of her mouth.

The laughter and clapping around them eventually reached them. Jason's lashes fluttered as he drew away. He was stunned at the fire Leanna lit in him with a mere kiss. The man strutting about the stage had also noticed.

"The Learned Dog has once again proved his superior canine abilities. This couple has very obligingly proved his contention that they are the ones most in love." Jason flushed at the words and his bright eyes darkened. He gave the man a haughty look.

Leanna was mortified. Dear God, to let him make a display of her in this way! Was she so weak he had merely to touch her before all her fine-honed resolutions melted? Humiliated, Leanna almost ran back to the carriage.

Jason followed more slowly, his ears still ringing with the man's words, "They are the ones most in love." His grandfather's words came back to haunt him, "I suggest you divine *why* you are so glad she isn't leaving!" Jason shook his head to drown out the tormenting jeers, sweat beading his forehead despite the cold.

No, it was impossible. Leanna was beautiful beyond description and he desired her above all else, but love her he did not. He would not! Mouth set stubbornly, he climbed up beside Leanna.

His eyes were remote. "Would you care to stop anywhere else? Perhaps the docks to see the newest goods?"

She replied with equal distance, folding her cloak about her. "No, thank you, Jason. I am ready to go home."

Jason concentrated fiercely on his driving. His agitation receded as he reassured himself that his explosive reaction to Leanna was the result of his desire. Their afternoon in the cabin had whetted his passion. When she finally came to him willingly, he would sate himself until she no longer intrigued him, no longer stirred him.

He looked at her set chin and admitted with inward mockery that coaxing her was easier said than done. Frowning, he remembered her almost helpless response to his kiss. She was far more susceptible to him than she would admit; a wanton woman lived in that small, feminine frame. Perhaps he could find a way to prove it to her. She had tormented and tempted him long enough. It was time to turn the tables.

With gleaming eyes, he tried to break the uncomfortable grip holding them, but this time she was not to be distracted. She huddled to her cape, castigating herself roundly. Fool! You came perilously close to giving yourself away. Will you never learn to keep him at a distance?

Leanna was so involved in her self-immolation she didn't

notice when Jason pulled away from the main road and drove the carriage to a sunny spot beside the peaceful river. When the buggy jolted to a halt, she looked around in confusion.

Jason leaped down and offered her a hand. She clamped her soft lips in a mutinous way. "Why have we stopped?"

Jason disguised his irritation with an effort. "It's time we talked, Leanna. We will not be interrupted here."

A refusal trembled on her lips, but it turned into indignation when he hauled her down none too gently. Casually, he spread the lap robe on the ground and pushed her down. He sat next to her, propping an elbow on his upraised knee in an indolent pose, but his eyes restlessly searched the brush for danger.

Leanna fulminated, her anger at herself now directed at him. "Well?" she snapped. Satisfied they were in no immediate danger, he calmly met her angry eyes.

"If milady will come down off her high horse, perhaps we can make something of this mockery of a marriage that was forced upon us." He placed a brown finger against her mouth when she would have retorted. "Your turn will be next." He looked away, but honesty compelled him to confess, "I admit I have not been the most understanding of husbands. Your refusal to take your rightful place beside me in bed ground in my craw until I could scarce think sanely." He turned his head to pierce her with disbelieving eyes.

"It seems incredible to me that you aren't aware what you do to a man. Don't you know how beautiful you are? You could corrupt a saint, and God knows I am no saint." He laughed at the tart agreement on her face, easing some of the tension between them.

He moved closer to her, ignoring her little start of fear. His voice was rough with feeling. "The attraction between us is a rare and lovely thing, Leanna. I have never known such pleasure as you have given me. Surely this is a good basis on which to build a marriage? If you would only stop fighting me, I'm certain we can make one another happy."

Leanna held his earnest eyes as long as she could, but she was forced to look away to keep herself from giving what her heart longed to give. She bit her lip in indecision. She was afraid to refuse him again lest she ruin any chance for them, but she was just as afraid to accept. Would his respect and desire be enough when she ached for his love? What happened when the flame of desire died? Without love to warm them, they would be left with only the cold, dead ashes of defeat and their marriage would wither, as had his father's.

In the midst of her turmoil, she suddenly remembered Abby's advice: "While men can much enjoy intimacy without love, sometimes love can come upon them unawares."

Sighing, she bowed her head in her hands and said softly, "I will think on it, Jason. That is all I will promise."

He was disappointed but still hopeful. At least she hadn't refused him outright. He pressed his luck a little further. "I want to have my things moved to your room, Leanna." When she looked at him sharply, he hastened to reassure her. "I only want to be near you at night. My bed is cold and lonely—I will attempt nothing else unless you wish it, I promise."

Her heart in her mouth at the tantalizing vision of his hard body beside her in the huge bed, she almost nodded. However, this time common sense reigned. She would never be able to resist him. She shook her head.

Jason looked away to hide his disappointment, then he shrugged as he helped her into the carriage. She would change her tune. He would see to it. Leanna would have been alarmed at the predatory gleam in his eye, but he looked straight ahead, his mouth quirked with satisfaction at the strategy developing in his mind.

When they arrived back at the plantation, Thomas was relieved to see Leanna more composed. He looked sardonically at Jason's secretive, but satisfied, smile. "Productive outing, was it, Grandson?"

Jason smiled at Leanna, his eyes intent. "I believe it will prove so, Grandfather." She looked adorably confused and embarrassed. She excused herself to change her rumpled clothing and hurried to her room.

Jason pursed his lips in a happy whistle as he followed her up the stairs. His eyes narrowed on her swaying hips. Her reluctance would make her surrender more delectable than before. And come it would, he promised himself as he changed. Soon.

The game of cat and mouse that followed was nerve-wracking to Leanna. No matter how hard she tried to avoid Jason, it seemed he was always at her side, teasing, flirting, and threatening until she thought she'd go mad. And somehow, during the course of his conversation, he always managed to brush against her, a lean hip pressing her soft one or a brown cheek grazing her skin as he bent down to whisper in her ear.

If Leanna tried to avoid him by staying in her room, he appeared, bringing a book to read while lying beside her on the huge bed. He would gradually inch closer until the length of his body touched hers. If she moved over, he followed, until she was in danger of falling off the bed. If she demanded he relent, he'd look at her with wounded eyes but obey, only to inch back again moments later.

If she tried to escape by riding, he would track her down, even though she had disguised her trail by trotting in and out of the river. One day, when he didn't appear out of the woods behind her like the large, persistent shadow she had come to expect, she removed her boots and stockings, tied her habit around her waist, and plunged her legs in the icy river. She gasped at the sharp sting of the water, but she soon found the tingle invigorating. She gasped when a shadow blocked out the sun, and she leaped to her feet in alarm. Her mouth tightened when she saw her husband smiling wolfishly at the sight of her curvaceous legs exposed well above the knee. Flushing, she untied her skirts.

Jason grinned at her unrepentantly. "Don't stop dabbling on my account. I quite enjoyed the display of your, er, enjoyment of the water."

Leanna gritted her teeth, but choked back a retort. Sparring with him would only be an admission he was irritating her. Without a word, she pulled on her stockings, defiantly refusing to turn her back as she secured them at her thighs. Jason watched with appreciation until she unrolled her skirts to pull on her boots, then he took off his jacket and began to undo his shirt.

Leanna's fingers stilled and her eyes rounded. "What are you doing?" she said.

"I'm going to take a swim. Care to join me?" He asked, peeling off his pants and underwear to stand stark naked in front of her. He was totally unabashed at his nudity. She gulped at the sight of his magnificent body. Muscular arms and legs mirrored the beauty of his powerful shoulders and chest, tapering down to a flat stomach. He watched her eyes lower and her face flush, and felt himself harden. Leanna was alarmed at her instantaneous response. She jerked on her boots, mounted the gray, and galloped away as though the demons of hell nipped at her heels.

Jason slammed a fist into his hand. In exasperation, he jumped into the river to still the persistent ache in his loins. He swam with vigorous strokes against the current, welcoming the icy bite of the water as he wondered which of them would be the first to break.

Leanna felt like a hunted creature. Jason reminded her of a hungry, sly cat, watching in amusement as she frantically attempted to escape. He would wait until she was exhausted, then pounce. If she had never known the ecstasy his beautiful body could give her, perhaps she could resist his blatant attempts to seduce her. But the lean, starved look in his eyes inflamed her own desire. Many times she almost went to his room during her lonely nights. Only pride kept her from submitting to his unspoken but potent demands; pride and fear he would tire of her and turn to another. So the battle continued.

Jason came to her room in the mornings while she dressed and in the evenings when she disrobed. He would lounge against the door or in a chair, never touching her with anything but his starved eyes. Leanna longed to order him from her room, but she bit back her fury because Sukey was always nearby. She was unwilling to give the servants more cause for gossip.

He made no attempt to hide his desire for her. His possessive eyes branded her as she sat before her dressing table while Sukey fixed her hair. Her sheer chemise provided scant cover and, all too often, Leanna's susceptible breasts would tighten in involuntary response to the virile look he cast her.

By the time she was safely clothed, her face was flushed and her breasts heaved with emotion, but her discomposure only emphasized the contempt in the fierce glance she gave him. He would bow a mocking acceptance of her opinion of him before quitting her chamber. Her anger only grew when, paradoxically, instead of feeling relief at his absence, the room seemed strangely empty to her.

Jason dreaded these times in her chamber. Seeing her delectable body so temptingly near, yet so frustratingly unattainable, strained him alarmingly. After experiencing her wanton response, he found it increasingly difficult to restrain his aching desire.

But he was determined to make none of his past errors. He had not pressed for an answer to his proposal made that day in the glade. He would wait until she came to him. And he was convinced her resistance was weakening. Her quickened breath when he was near, her avoidance of his eyes; all signs pointed to the fact that his patience would win out. He decided grimly she would pay dearly for her stubbornness. He would tease her until she was wild before he finally satisfied their mutual, gnawing hunger. But for now, his nights were so restless he took to pacing on the veranda.

One such evening Jason was startled to find Leanna leaning against the rail near him. Despite the chill in the air, she was wearing no night robe. His heart pounded as her beauty enticed him. Her hair streamed down her back like a waterfall of molten gold, gleaming in the moonlight while the wind tossed the strands about with invisible fingers. Her flannel gown clung to her breasts as she leaned forward. He longed to grasp those high, firm mounds in his hands as he buried himself within her warmth. Instead, he walked up to lean at her side on the railing.

Leanna started when she saw him out of the corner of her eye. She fought the desire to go to him and let him give her momentary respite from the torment he had deliberately inflicted. She had come outside without a wrap, hoping the cold would douse the fire in her body. But to see the cause of her discomfort lean nonchalantly at her side only enraged her. When he crooned, "Having problems sleeping, my dear?" a red mist of fury clouded her vision. If an ax had been in hand, she would have used it on him.

But a fitting revenge formed in her mind. She smiled.

Jason was watching the shimmering river, so he didn't see the menacing look she hid behind half-closed eyes. "Jason," she cooed, "I have decided you're right. I can fight my desire for you no longer." She ran her finger inside the lapel of his robe, barely brushing his chest with a provoking trail of fire.

Jason was stunned but jubilant. His heart pounded harder as he wheeled her into his arms. He frowned when she danced gracefully away. With her long flowing hair, gleaming cat's eyes, and snug-fitting gown, she seemed a beautiful but dangerous witch. Her mouth curved into a seductive smile.

"Not here. I so long to make love by the river. What about that enchanting spot we visited so recently? You remember, when you bared yourself before me so charmingly." She drifted back into her chamber as she spoke, the long gown hiding her feet so she appeared to glide instead of walk. She dressed rapidly, calling out to Jason, who stood rooted on the veranda, "Please, my darling, it would mean so much to me. The sound of the river rushing makes me feel so *passionate!*"

Jason's desire had been struggling with a voice that warned him she had capitulated too suddenly and too easily. However, her sultry emphasis on the word "passionate" sent the blood rushing to his head in a deluge. He hurried to his room and tossed on the first clothes he came to.

Jason grabbed a down comforter from a closet and met Leanna at her door. Again, he tried to pull her into his arms, but she sidestepped and raced down the stairs, holding a conspiratorial finger to her lips.

She tapped her foot impatiently while Jason saddled the horses. When he saw the motion, his caution returned. His eyes narrowed in sudden wariness. "Leanna, are you sure this is what you want?"

Leanna's foot stilled instantly. She smiled at him, her eyes slitted so he could only see incandescent green. "Yes," she assured him, her voice deep and husky.

He helped her mount, then led the way to the river. It didn't take long to reach the spot of their earlier turbulent encounter. Jason leaped down and helped Leanna off her mount with eager hands. His mouth closed over hers before her feet touched the ground. She responded with passion, her lips open and inviting as her hands stroked the back of his neck.

Shuddering, he went to remove her cloak, but she halted him. "You first," she pleaded. At that moment, he could deny her nothing. He disrobed impatiently, his eagerness obvious. Leanna gathered up his clothes and folded them into the saddlebags, then she handed Jason the comforter to spread on the ground. He reached for her, but once more she evaded him.

"Not so fast, dearest. We have all the time in the world." She reached as though to unfasten her cloak, but when Jason turned his back to spread out the comforter, she jumped on Morning Mist, grabbed the stallion's reins, and dug her heels into the mare's flanks.

Jason wheeled but could only watch with impotent rage as she galloped off, her triumphant laughter floating back to him. "This should cool your lust, my dear husband," she cried. She rode away still laughing.

Jason gnashed his teeth in fury. He clenched his fists, almost strangling with rage. Then, unexpectedly, the appropriateness of her act struck him and he barked a rueful laugh. To leave him mother naked on a cold night, aching with unfulfilled desire, on the very spot where he had used his body to tempt her on another occasion, was fitting revenge indeed.

His anger abated, he smiled grimly as he gathered up the comforter and wrapped it around him. This round to you, my sweet he thought, but the bout is far from over. Cursing as a twig punctured his sensitive foot, he began the long, cold trek home and prayed he could reach his room without being seen.

Chapter
Sixteen

JASON BREATHED A sigh of relief as the plantation outbuildings at last appeared. He hurried down the hill, ignoring the rocks and twigs that got in his way. The sky was the midnight blue of very early dawn, and he knew the workers would be stirring. If he was discovered, he'd tan Leanna's hide. His thoughts naturally progressed to other parts of her anatomy and the exquisite torment he would inflict on her. He was so involved with his planning he almost collided with the man who silently materialized out of the trees lining the river.

Having been startled himself, Rian held his gun at the ready, a brace of possum dangling from his belt. He peered warily at the enormous shrouded figure, unable to distinguish the face in the dark. His neck prickled as he wondered if the tales he had often scoffed at of ghosts and witches were true. When the figure almost ran him down, however, he was close enough to get a good look at the face. His mouth dropped open as he recognized Jason who, having recognized him, groaned in frustration.

Consternation dissolved into laughter. It shook Rian's huge frame as he took in the comical picture Jason made. When the wind caught an edge of the pink comforter, a lean thigh was dimly visible.

Tears in his eyes, Rian finally gasped, "Is this the newest style you bring back from London, Jason? Somehow I don't think it will become popular here." He broke into gales of laughter at the furious look on Jason's face.

Jason stalked down the hill without a reply. Rian followed, concerned now as his mirth died. "Are you all right, Jason? What on earth are you doing out like that?"

Jason sighed with relief as he opened the front door and saw an empty hallway. "I suggest you ask my vixen of a wife!" He slammed the door in Rian's face.

Rian hurried in after him. "Jason, you haven't left her in the woods alone, have you?"

Jason laughed harshly, then choked so hard Rian had to pound him on the back to help him breathe. "Try the other way about," he finally gasped, opening the door to his room. At Rian's fresh burst of laughter, he wheeled angrily to face him.

"If I hear this tale bandied about anywhere, I'll have you shanghaied after I've drawn and quartered you."

Rian swallowed his mirth and kept a straight face with difficulty. "You have my solemn word that the story will not pass my lips." When Jason turned to enter his room, he couldn't resist thinking of the woman with soft blond hair. "You've got enough problems. What a lass!" Shaking his head admiringly, Rian descended the steps to return to his traps.

Leanna dozed off as soon as she returned, a small, self-satisfied smile curling her lips. Whoever said vengeance was a sour victory was never married to an arrogant beast like Jason, she thought with drowsy satisfaction before sleep claimed her.

The next morning, however, she was not so sanguine when she opened her eyes to face him. His forehead was creased as if an ominous thundercloud hung overhead. She was at first bewildered at his anger, but then recollection occurred and she sank against her pillows in alarm.

Casually, arrogantly, he pulled the covers off her huddled body as though peeling a succulent fruit his white teeth longed to taste. He leered at her slim, quivering form, reaching out to touch her throat, his eyes veiled. When he cupped his other hand around her throat and squeezed very lightly, she whitened. Surely he wouldn't strangle her?

Jason's teeth bared in a satisfied smile at the look on her face. Roughly, he pulled her up. "No, you don't get off that easily, my lovely." He pulled her against him, grasping her buttocks as he arched her body into his. "Do you know how painful it is to be left as you left me, last night?" He pressed his hips into her for emphasis. A hot flush swept through her as she felt his hardness pressing urgently into her belly.

He stepped back. "Undress," he commanded, arms folded and legs planted wide apart.

She backed away, still frightened, but defiant. "No! And if you come near me, I'll scream," she warned in a shaking voice as he walked toward her, his menacing face cast in iron.

"Scream away," he sneered. "The servants have been ordered to stay out of this room, no matter what they hear."

"And what about Grandfather?" she flung back. "He will break the door down, if he has to."

Her blood chilled at the malicious look in his eyes. He had her cornered against the wall and now leaned so close she could feel his breath at her temples. Her eyes were glued to his sensual lower lip as he said, "That he would, if he were here." Her gaze leaped to his face.

He leaned both palms negligently against the wall, trapping her in a seductive but menacing stance. "You see," he whispered in her ear, "Grandfather made his rounds early this morning and, purely coincidentally, you understand, he had to examine our fallow fields on the far side of the plantation." He drew back to smile at her gently.

"Thus, my sweet vixen, no one will come to your aid." His voice hardened again. "Now, undress, or, by God, I'll do it for you and I will *not* be gentle."

Leanna's eyes spat with green fury as she wondered what to do. She balled her hands into claws. He clicked his tongue.

"I wouldn't," he said with a mocking smile. "If you do, I'll retaliate with my belt to your backside. It's not too late to teach you some manners."

She stood indecisively, her teeth nibbling at her lower lip. Jason shrugged, reached with large, calloused hands and ripped the flannel gown from throat to hem with a tug. Leanna gasped and bent to retrieve the gown, but he kicked it away contemptuously. He hauled her to his whipcord length, smiling with enjoyment at her impotent struggles.

When she finally lay, gasping, against him, his hands roved her body from nape of neck to thigh. She was immobile, eyes closed and jaw tight as she tried to ignore him, but when he kissed her shoulder, then lowered his lips to suck a breast, she began to tremble. He laughed at her reaction and turned his attention to her other breast, while his hand stroked the soft flesh of her inner thigh. She moaned, then lifted her hands to wrap around his neck as he lowered his mouth over hers, his lips searing her with a heat that tingled her toes. She was vaguely aware of being carried. Her languorous dream state was rudely shattered when he dropped her into a large, steaming tub before the fire.

The bewildered, dazed look in her eyes touched him, but when she sat up and looked at him in fury, his mouth tightened. He knelt beside the tub, rubbed some scented soap on a cloth, and began to scrub her back. "What are you doing? I am perfectly capable of bathing myself," she snarled. She tied her long braid on top of her head and tried to grab the cloth.

He continued his unhurried, soothing movements. "The least I can do is play lady's maid after ordering Sukey away." She shifted uncomfortably under his hands, but she didn't try to escape. She was curious as to what he was up to.

When he massaged her shoulders, her tension eased and she began to enjoy his ministrations. Her eyes were half-closed with pleasure as she propped her head on the rim. He turned his attention to her breasts, bathing them leisurely until her breathing quickened again. He pulled the cloth over her abdomen, stroking lower and lower on her quivering belly. He fastened his mouth over the orbs of her breasts as they bobbed in seductive temptation above the water. The teasing cloth now washed between her legs, rubbing back and forth until the throbbing in Leanna heightened to an urgent pulsing.

She made no protest when he lifted her from the tub and carried her to the bed. He lay her down gently, gasping in breaths as he tried to quiet his own arousal.

Leanna moaned and reached up to him. "Jason," she pleaded huskily. He laughed harshly to steady his wavering determination. Her eyes flashed open at the unexpected sound. "Perhaps this will cool your lust, my dear wife," he sneered, turning away to stride to the door.

He paused before leaving, raking his eyes over her curvaceous body. "Now you know how it hurts to be left aching with desire. Not a nice feeling, is it?" He gave her a taunting, satisfied smile. "This round to me, my sweet." The door clicked shut behind him in contempt.

Leanna turned her flushed face into the pillow and sobbed, her body aching as her mind recollected her humiliation. When she slumped, spent on the bed, she stared unseeingly at the ceiling. Ever honest, she had to admit she had played an unpleasant trick upon him. Is this the way he had felt when she left him last night? This painful, throbbing emptiness and frustration? She now regretted the action. She rose and dressed tiredly, resolving to apologize to him despite the cost to her pride.

They must stop this continual torment of each other, or she must leave. If they discussed their differences rationally, perhaps they could come to terms. Her eyes bleak, she remembered his outburst in the cabin. She still doubted he would ever let a woman into his heart, but she couldn't quite smother a last glimmer of hope. Reluctantly, she thought again of Abby's advice. It seemed increasingly apparent that she had no other option.

It was anticlimactic to learn Jason was gone for the day. He had business in Savannah, Sarah informed her with a surreptitious look at Leanna's wan face. Sighing heavily, Leanna forced a smile. "Thank you, Sarah. I will be in the study, reading, when he returns. Please tell him I wish to see him."

Sarah nodded, hesitated, then softly inquired, "Can I get you anything, Leanna? Or would you like to talk?"

Leanna smiled more naturally, her eyes grateful. "Nothing, thank you. I have much to think about, it's true, but only I can make the decision."

Sarah's brow was wrinkled with concern as she watched Leanna walk into the study and close the door behind her. Leanna and Jason were tearing each other apart and something had to be done to help them. She resolved to speak to Thomas as soon as he returned.

Thomas was in a jovial mood when he stomped into the hallway. Sarah had been listening for his footsteps, so she met him before he had removed his coat. She looked reprovingly at his muddy boots. Thomas grinned at her expression.

"No lectures, Sarah. If a man can't muddy his own hallway, the world's a sorry place." He winked, then pulled back to beam, "The vegetables are big enough to feed an army of Goliaths this season. All the rain we've had has given us one of the best crops in years..." He tapered off when he realized she was inattentive. Concerned, for she normally listened eagerly to his progress reports on the crops, he lifted a brow. "Nothing's wrong with Quincy, is it?"

Sarah's frown deepened, but her look was one of anger now instead of concern. "No, not at the moment, but there will be when he returns. He's slipped out again, trying to avoid his lessons. I imagine he's gone into Savannah to see Benjamin." Sarah took his coat as she spoke and hung it in the hall closet. She beckoned to Thomas from the parlor door. When he entered, she shut the door quietly behind them.

His unease intensified at this unusual behavior. "What the devil is it, Sarah?" he demanded curtly.

She sat down opposite him. Twisting her apron, she asked slowly, "Thomas, are you aware that Jason ordered the servants to stay away from Leanna's room this morning, no matter what they heard?"

Mouth grim, he shook his head. "Has he harmed Leanna?" he asked sharply.

Sarah hesitated. "He didn't harm her physically, but I believe emotionally . . ." She looked away, uncertain how to continue. "Thomas, I don't wish to interfere, but I believe something must be done to help those two before Jason loses his head or Leanna flees."

Thomas eyed her downcast face tenderly. Raising her chin, he smiled into her soft brown eyes. "You are like part of the family, Sarah, you should know that. I would never accuse you of interfering. In fact, I greatly appreciate your concern," he said. "You have made my twilight years very happy. We would all be lost without you."

Sarah sat with sadness in her heart as she listened to his soothing voice. She turned her face into him to hide a maverick tear. Yes, you need me, she cried inwardly, but you will never love me as you did Jenny. Her unswerving devotion through the years was not the result of loyalty to him and Jenny, as he had always thought. She had fallen deeply, helplessly in love with him long before Jenny died. But she had reconciled herself to the fact he would always remain avuncular, and that in his own way, he loved her. But she also knew the barriers between them of station and color were too high to ever be scaled completely. Eventually, she became contented when she accepted the fact that their relationship must always be close yet paradoxically distant. She accepted the tenderness he offered, thanked God she and Quincy were free and cherished, and put her dreams of love firmly behind her.

Her failure made her all the more sensitive to Leanna's pain. She would do everything in her power to see that the man she loved like a son and the girl she admired found the happiness only the fulfillment of love could bring.

Thomas was also silent, debating whether to talk to Jason. He had not tried to speak to him about Bella in years. Thomas was certain the stumbling block in Jason's marriage was his distrust of women. If the lad could realize Bella still loved him and had good reasons for leaving the way she did, he could undam his love for Leanna. Thomas remembered Jason's furious reaction when he last tried to talk about Bella. "That bitch? How dare you defend her! No matter the provocation, she had no right to desert us and drive my father to his death.

I have no mother. If you speak her name to me again, I will leave this house and live in Savannah." And he slammed the door, his face so white with anguish that Thomas had never mentioned Bella again.

Watching Sarah, he reassured her tenderly, "Don't worry, dear companion, things will yet come right between them. Jason is stubborn, but this time he will listen if I have to tie him down. If he can forgive Bella, I'm certain he'll at last admit his love for Leanna." He kissed her cheek, then shooed her out of the room. A wistful smile stretched her lips as Sarah went to prepare him a light luncheon.

Jason walked along the docks, moodily recalling the events in Leanna's chamber that morning. Her punishment had not brought him satisfaction. To the contrary, not touching her had been one of the hardest things he had ever done, but he had been determined to have revenge. One day she would finally admit defeat and come to him. If she didn't acquiesce soon, one of his sleepless nights would end in her bed, whether she wished it or not. He wanted tenderness between them, but he would have her without it if she refused to submit. Uneasily, he again wondered why he still hungered for her, and only for her.

He had met Vivian, the gorgeous redhead he had once enjoyed so much, on the street that very morning. When she pouted at him charmingly for not visiting since his return, he looked at her full lips and wondered why they didn't excite him as they used to.

When she ran a graceful white hand across his chest, he stood still and calm under her formerly arousing touch. Bewildered, he had made his excuses and escaped. He frowned in perplexity. It was a new experience for him to want only one woman. Since taking Leanna again, his desire for her had increased instead of diminished as he had expected.

He shook his head vigorously as though to free himself from an unwanted restraint, then felt relief as he recognized two familiar figures ahead of him. Smiling, he folded his arms and waited for the boys to walk up to him.

Benjamin was saying eagerly, "I bet the cap'n would let you

come, if you can convince yer ma. I tell you there's nothing in the world so rewarding as a life at sea. I'll ask the cap'n fer you, if you like."

Quincy's downcast expression lightened but for an instant. "No, my mother would never let me come. Thomas says we'll probably be at war with England soon, and the seas are too dangerous. He doesn't even want Jason sailing again." The boys were so intent on their conversation they didn't see Jason until the last moment.

He grasped Quincy by the ear, rooting him to the spot. The lad started guiltily, then hung his head. "You know how it upsets your mother when you avoid your lessons," Jason scolded. "Now you get right home before I wear out your breeches, and if I catch you playing hooky again, I'll order the *Savannah* off limits to you." Quincy's eyes widened at this threat and with a hasty wave to Ben, he scampered to the frisky pony tied to a nearby shack, climbed into the saddle, and started for home.

Ben squirmed under Jason's condemning eyes. "Aw, Cap'n, it don't hurt to miss a lesson once in a coon's age," he protested.

Jason sighed. "Ben, despite your belief that a sailor only needs to know about tides, clouds, and knots, an education is an important asset to any man. Quincy's lot will be hard enough as an educated man. As an ignorant one, he will never win acceptance in Savannah society." Jason watched the boy's disappointed frown. "Do not encourage him to avoid his lessons again, or I'll have to find myself another cabin boy." Jason ignored the hurt look on the boy's face and clapped him on the shoulder.

"If you'd try 'book learnin', you might find it more interesting than you think." Ben looked so horrified that Jason couldn't smother a grin. He circled an arm around the boy's shoulders and walked him to the dock where the *Savannah* was berthed.

Even with bare masts, she was a lovely sight. For a moment Jason was tempted to leave his problems behind and sail for the Indies. He toyed with the idea as he went aboard his vessel to examine the new mast. He climbed aloft to get a better vantage point, feeling with exploratory fingers for the slightest

crack that could spell disaster in rough seas. Satisfied, he shim-
mied back down to the deck, then went below to find Ben.

The boy had repeatedly refused Jason's offer of a room at
Whispering Oaks. He preferred living aboard ship. He said he
always felt uncomfortable and stifled if he was away from the
sea air for long. Jason worried about the lad more than Ben
suspected. Tough the boy might be, but the docks were sometimes a dangerous place for the strongest of men, and Ben was
not noted for his calm temper.

Jason smiled when he found Ben whistling and whittling a
small piece of oak. The rough outlines of a ship were forming
under Ben's skillful knife. Jason sat down next to Ben and
poured himself a cup of ale from a nearby keg.

"Who is the ship for, Ben?" he asked idly, taking a sip.

Ben flushed to the roots of his hair, the two reds clashing
dreadfully. "Yer missus," he admitted in a low voice. "Her
birthday is comin' up soon, and I thought she might like a
model of the *Savannah*. She enjoyed the voyage."

Jason felt a stab of pain. He resented the fact that Leanna
had never mentioned her approaching birthday to her own husband, yet she confided in his cabin boy. He looked away to
disguise his tension. "When is the date?"

Ben looked surprised at Jason's ignorance, but he replied
easily enough. "March twenty-ninth." Jason filed the date away,
then finished his ale and rose.

"Come see us soon, Ben. The invitation to stay is always
open." Smiling a farewell, Jason went back out on deck. He
leaned against the rail for a moment, almost reluctant to return
home. He was weary of the battle with Leanna. Resting his
chin on his hand, again he played with the idea of sailing for
the Indies. Unwillingly, he remembered Leanna's face as he
had last seen it. He put the idea aside as he wryly admitted he
would never find peace until he satisfied the ache within him
for her. Sighing, girding himself for the return home, he left
the peace of the *Savannah*.

Thomas cornered Jason as soon as he walked in the door.
Groaning inwardly at the determined look on his grandfather's

face, Jason followed the older man into the salon. Sarah stopped him before he could close the door. "Leanna would like to speak with you, Jason. She's in the study." Her normally warm brown eyes were cold as she relayed the request.

Jason sighed. "Very well, Sarah, I will see her after I speak with Grandfather." He closed the door. Sarah walked back to the kitchen, praying Thomas could shake some sense into the boy.

Jason sat opposite Thomas, wondering what he had done to put such a sour look on his grandsire's face. Thomas steepled his fingers together, watching his grandson with penetrating eyes. "I can't help wondering why you suggested I examine the far pasture today, Jason. Could it have anything to do with the little contretemps with Leanna this morning?"

Jason flushed, his eyes hooded.

Thomas shook his head, his mouth grim. "When will you learn Leanna will not be coerced, Grandson?" Thomas lowered his hands to clench the arms of the wing-back chair. He looked at Jason with almost pitying eyes. "Tell me, lad, what exactly do you want of Leanna? You claim you don't need the love of any woman, and surely if you want merely a bed mate, Vivian would make a more compliant choice?"

Jason shifted uneasily. He had avoided answers to these same questions, but Thomas's were not as easy to ignore. He rose to pace the room impatiently. "I swear I don't know why I want her so, Grandfather," he said, pausing to gaze into the fireplace. "I only know I must make her surrender before my body and mind can find peace."

Thomas smiled at Jason's revealing statement. Indeed, the lad did love her deeply. Now, how to make him admit it? Setting his jaw, Thomas decided to broach the subject of Bella. "Jason," he said, "do you ever think of your mother, lad?"

It was like poking a stick at a wolverine. Jason bristled and clenched his teeth. "Not more than I can help."

"I need to go to Boston to attend to business. I am asking you to come with me. You can see your mother, and no matter what you may think—" He broke off as Jason leaped to his feet and headed for the door, his face red with rage.

"Grandson!" Thomas's voice reverberated with authority. Jason halted but didn't turn, his back stiff. Thomas rose and went to touch the rigid shoulder with a sympathetic hand. "Lad, lad, don't you see how you're destroying yourself with your hatred? All I ask is that you see her. If you still can't forgive her I will never mention her name again." Jason finally lifted his eyes to meet his grandfather's. Thomas gasped at the play of emotions in their blue depths.

His jaw quivered and his face was tight with the effort to reply. "I will say this only once. I don't want to see the bitch in this life. She disgusts me. Do not again try to bring us together, or I will take Leanna and leave." He slammed the door open against the inside wall, and strode toward the stairs just as Leanna appeared in the study door.

"Jason," she called. Sighing with exasperation, he turned. "May I speak with you?" she asked hesitantly.

He barked a laugh. "Why not? I've been badgered so much today that once more won't make any difference." He stomped into the study. Leanna leaned against the door, eying him warily.

"What is wrong, Jason? Have you and Grandfather had an argument?"

He poured himself a stiff drink and gulped it down. Somewhat steadier, he sat down wearily. "No, not about anything of import, anyway. Why did you want to speak to me?"

Leanna sat down and folded her hands in her lap, her gaze intent on her interlocked fingers. Jason laughed inwardly at the demure picture she made. Ah, deceptive bitches, every one of them.

"I wanted to see if we couldn't reach an understanding, but, more importantly, I wanted to apologize to you."

He straightened, his attention alert now. She lifted her gaze to his, her mouth set in resolution. "I didn't realize how cruel of me it was to leave you the way I did last night. Please accept my apology. You taught me a much-needed lesson this morning."

Jason searched her gaze for mockery, but she met his eyes steadily. He looked away, ashamed at his earlier thought. Leanna truly was different from most women; maybe that was why he wanted her so. "Apology accepted. I'm sorry if I was rough on you this morning, but Rian discovered me before I could reach my room, and my pride was ruffled." Leanna met his eyes and giggled at the picture he must have made, and he smiled in return. Suddenly the tension had dissipated like mist under sunlight.

Jason stopped laughing to ask, "What else did you want to talk to me about?"

Leanna's smile faded. "I want us to end this torment of one another, Jason. Can you not accept my friendship and let me be? An intimate relationship between us without love would make me feel unclean." Her eyes were entreating pools of green.

Jason took her hand to caress it as he framed his reply. "Leanna, I thought you understood we can never be mere friends. It's not natural for us to live as man and wife and not enjoy one another's bodies."

His eyes raked her downcast face with a tender look that would have surprised her, had she seen it. "I will confess something to you that I never intended to." Leanna's eyes shot to his face. "I want only you, my sweet. You can't imagine how it disconcerts me to find that only you can fulfill my desires. I need you, my love. Please come to me and let me give you the joy we were meant to find in one another." It was his turn to plead, his eyes so compelling she felt herself swaying toward him.

She swallowed. This was not what she wanted—a union of bodies, not of souls.

"I cannot!" she cried. Using every ounce of her will, she propelled herself out of the room instead of into his arms. Jason rested his head against the back of the couch, listening to the sound of her departing steps. He closed his eyes, trying to shut out the memory of her anguished face as she fled from him. At that moment he desperately wished he had never set eyes on Leanna. Cursing under his breath, he cast the entire female sex to perdition.

Chapter
Seventeen

LEANNA MADE A disconsolate, lonely figure as she leaned against the oak tree. She watched the rhythmic flow of the river, trying to concentrate on its soothing motions instead of her own unhappy thoughts. Two days had passed since her talk with Jason in the study. Two days of somber reflection that had brought her no closer to a decision. Her choices were limited. She could either accede to Jason's demands, or she could leave. It was certain the present tenseness between them could not continue longer.

Jason had halted his offensive maneuvers. He was extremely polite but remote the few times they met. He was gone most of the day, either in Savannah or helping about the plantation. Despite his denials, a rift seemed to have developed between him and Thomas. A distinct chill pervaded the air when the two were together. Leanna was aware that she was the probable cause of the conflict, and she regretted it most of all. It was all the more imperative she reach a decision, and soon, so the usually warm relationship between Jason and his grandfather could resume.

Leanna turned and put her arms around the gnarled tree, welcoming the rough bark against her skin. The wind whispered in the branches, acting as a sad, lyrical accompaniment to her misery. How could she bear to leave him? Yet how could she bear to accept his meager offer of physical satiety when her heart so thirsted for love? Round and round her thoughts went, faster and faster until she put her hands to her aching forehead and moaned.

Leanna was startled out of her dejection by a gentle touch on her shoulder. She lifted red-rimmed eyes to Sarah, whose face was lined with concern and sympathy. "Did you want something, Sarah?" Her eyes dared Sarah to comment on her tears.

"Yes, Leanna," Sarah responded calmly. "Gus is getting married this evening, and the workers would be delighted if you would attend. I think you would find the celebrations enjoyable."

Leanna was fond of the great driver, Gus. His deep voice leading the workers in song was as appealing to the ear as his magnificent physique was attractive to the eye. His kindness to his fellows made him the most popular slave, and his privileged position made him a good catch for any girl. Leanna could well understand his marriage was a cause for celebration among the workers.

"I wouldn't miss it for the world, Sarah," Leanna smiled, glad for the chance to escape her own problems. She walked back to the house with Sarah, wondering why Jason had not informed her of the wedding. "Who is he marrying, Sarah?" she asked.

"Monique, a girl who came as a child from San Domingo with her mother. She's a lovely little thing, all eyes and legs."

"Is there anything I can do to help in the preparations?"

Normally Sarah would have pooh-poohed the idea, but she sensed Leanna needed distractions. "I could use some help with the rice bags." The two women went to the kitchen and spent the entire morning tying colorful bags of rice with equally colorful ribbons. Sarah kept up a steady stream of chatter, reminiscing about her memories of Jenny and the fun they had together, until Leanna's wan face regained its healthy color.

"It's amazing the master didn't sell me off long before Jenny married. Some of the things she talked me into! But of course, he realized Jenny was the leader in our schemes." Sarah's eyes misted as she recalled the past and the childhood companion she still missed. "I remember one time when we put a snake in the parson's coat. It wasn't poisonous, of course, but it might as well have been for all the racket he made." Sarah smiled gleefully at the cherished memory.

"He was a sanctimonious old goat, but that didn't stop him from leering at me and trying to pinch me every time he went by. Jenny put a stop to that. We ducked around a corner to watch. He took out his gloves and put them on. The snake had curled up in one of them and it bit his finger. He yanked the glove off and shook it loose, cursing loud enough to wake the dead. We were giggling by this time and he heard us. He shook his fist and called us children of the devil, then stomped out. Of course, when Jenny's father found out, we both got a licking that left us bruised for a week, but it was worth it. The parson never bothered me again." Sarah winked playfully. Leanna laughed until her sides ached at the picture Sarah painted.

Neither Thomas nor Jason returned for lunch, so Leanna insisted she eat in the kitchen, despite Sarah's protests. The gay camaraderie between the cook and the kitchen maids warmed Leanna and for the first time in a long while, she gave herself up to laughter.

The house servants were agog with the preparations and excitement. Weddings were lively occasions for the slaves. A huge dinner was normally followed by music and dancing. Festivities were participated in by white and black alike.

Leanna listened with interest as Sarah explained how Gus had proposed to Monique. "It's the custom hereabouts for the man to go to the woman of his choice, roast peanuts in ashes, place a stool between them, and while eating, propose. Normally, this ceremony is accepted by all and the couple is regarded as man and wife. But Gus is a strict Methodist and he

wants to sanctify his union in the eyes of God as well. The
ceremony will be performed by a Methodist minister."

The women finished their light meal, tied the last of the
bags, then rewarded themselves with a cup of strong, black
coffee. The excitement around Leanna was contagious, and she
began to look forward to the evening. At Sarah's urging, she
finally went to her room in the late afternoon for a nap to fortify
herself for the long evening ahead. She undressed to her petticoat and clutched a soft down pillow to her body for comfort.
She didn't expect to sleep, but her weariness caught up with
her and she soon dozed off. She didn't hear the door open or
see the man who came in to stand beside the bed appraising
her with appreciative, but somber, eyes.

Jason had deliberately kept himself busy in an effort to
squelch his painful longing for Leanna. The talk with Thomas,
Leanna's behavior and his own tiredness had wearied him. He
was disgusted with what he viewed as the capriciousness of
the female mind. Despite the pleasure they had found in one
another, she still refused to admit her desire. So be it. He would
try to influence her no longer. She could rot in her pristine bed
until hell froze over.

He had come to escort her to the wedding, but he was
reluctant now to wake her. She looked too peaceful: Her sweetly
parted lips and sleep-flushed cheeks speared him with an indefinable pain. He too often forgot she was little more than a
girl. Her ignorance of her beauty made her attractions all the
more alluring. His heart tightened with dread as he loathed to
acknowledge her hold on his every thought. No matter where
he was or what he was doing, she always lurked in the back
of his mind like an impish sprite, ever ready to torment him.

Leaning over, he kissed her soft cheek very lightly. Sighing,
he walked out the door and shut it gently behind him. Leanna
awoke with a start. She stretched, yawning, then jumped out
of bed and rang for Sukey when she noticed it was dark outside.
Frowning, she looked at the wall sconces flickering in the room
and wondered who had lit them. Shrugging, she decided the
servants must have been in, then she went to the dressing table
and tied her hair on top of her head in preparation for her bath.

Sarah had informed her the servants would be wearing their finest, and Leanna wanted to contribute to the party atmosphere, so she chose one of her loveliest dresses. As Sukey laced her up, she wryly admitted her efforts were influenced by a desire to please Jason. Although he had stopped his forays, she wished some of his attention would return. Shaking her head at her own foolishness, she went to stand before the mirror. Even she was startled at the reflection gazing back at her.

Her gown was of lustrous aqua taffeta that rustled gently with every step. The short puffed sleeves were laced with black inserts. The round, low bodice was frilled with the same lace and the hem of the gown was deeply flounced, one side caught up to reveal a lacy black underskirt. The black-jetted lace seemed to twinkle wickedly as the light caught it. Her simple chignon was made alluring by damp curls that teased her temples and a black feather pinned by Sukey on the side of her head with a black jet ornament.

Leanna bit her lip, tempted to change. She did not want to look wanton. This dress gave her a mature sensuality she had not known she possessed. She tugged uneasily at the low bodice, alarmed at the expanse of snowy skin exposed. Sukey smiled at her mistress's obvious discomfort.

"Yo looks powerful lovely, Miz Leanna," she reassured her.

"Am I too, er, over-dressed, Sukey?"

Sukey shook her curly black head. "No'm, we's all like gettin' fancied up foh ouh weddin's."

She threw a heavy black velvet cloak over Leanna's shoulders and tied it closed. She smiled in mischief at her mistress's obvious relief and whispered audaciously, "Mistuh Jason will eat yo up."

Leanna flushed, then hugged Sukey tightly. Suddenly, she was exhilarated. Something marvelous would come of this evening, she felt it in her bones. She gaily tripped down the stairs, smiling at Thomas when he came out of the study. He smiled with pleasure at her obvious happiness. He was attired in a gray satin coat worn with a wine-red waistcoat and snowy neckcloth pinned with a large black pearl.

He drew her into the study, kissing her hand gallantly as he presented her to Jason. "The loveliest girl in all of Georgia will grace our celebration tonight. May we see your dress, Leanna?"

Leanna swallowed, then threw back her cloak with a flourish. Both men gasped. Jason stood frozen with his glass halfway to his lips and Thomas lowered his eyes to hide his glee. She was certainly ready for battle. It seemed she had finally decided to quit her brooding and fight back. He poured her a glass of sherry, smothering a smile at the stunned look on his grandson's face.

Jason cut an elegant figure, wearing a black velvet coat and black trousers. The dark color emphasized his height and muscular build, but at the same time it endowed his intelligent face with a sardonic, slightly satanic look.

Jason gulped down the liquid in his glass and slammed it down on the fireplace mantel, turning away to gaze into the flames. His nose twitched as Leanna's gentle perfume wafted into his flared nostrils. The little tease. How dare she deny him, then dress like a tart to torment him.

Leanna surreptitiously glanced at Jason, her heart dropping when she noted the angry look on his face. Nothing she did could please him, it seemed. She swallowed her sherry, then drew her cloak around her with trembling fingers. Thomas took her arm and led her from the study, leaving his angry grandson to follow.

Sarah was already at the chapel, as were most of the workers. She looked regal in deep blue velvet. Thomas sat next to her, leaving Leanna reluctantly sandwiched between him and Jason. Jason put his arm around her, playing with the curl on the nape of her neck, his eyes ostensibly absent, but his fingers quite deliberate.

Leanna tried to concentrate on Gus. He cut a fine figure in a simple but attractive tweed suit. His dark eyes glowed with pride as he watched his bride walk toward him. She was wearing a pretty, ruffled yellow dress and carried a bouquet of dried flowers. Her enormous dark eyes were solemn as she met her betrothed's glance.

They joined hands and knelt at the black preacher's command. The service was simple but moving. The couple spoke their vows with a sincerity obvious in the husky timbres of their voices. When they kissed, the reverent atmosphere in the simple little chapel was broken by shouts of joy and congratulations. Leanna blinked away tears, meeting Jason's look defiantly. The sardonic smile on his face infuriated her. She glared at his broad back when he went up to congratulate them.

"Well, old friend," he teased Gus, "you've been caught at last. She's a beauty and I wish you both every happiness." He slipped some money into Gus's pocket and smiled at the bride before striding out to the banquet tables. Leanna smiled tremulously at the couple, offering her congratulations in a husky voice. Gus's sympathetic look almost ruined her precarious composure, so she hurried outside. She took deep, reviving breaths of the night air, then walked to her place at the head table, her face calm.

An enormous bonfire so warmed the air Leanna felt stifled in her cloak. She removed it and laid it over the back of her chair. She felt Jason's glance raking her bodice, but she ignored him and concentrated on her plate, surprised at her hunger.

The pork had been roasting slowly all day, turned untiringly by one of the cook's sons. Candied yams, fluffy rice, corn fritters, and green beans accompanied the juicy pork and smoked brisket. Pies and cakes of every description rounded out the meal.

Thomas and Sarah sat opposite them. The bride and groom ate slowly at an adjacent table, never taking their eyes from one another. Gus took a bite of ham from his bride's fingers, licking the tips teasingly while he kept his eyes on her. Leanna looked quickly away, sickened by the stab of envy within her. Slaves they might be, but in that moment they possessed more happiness than she would probably ever know. Jason met her troubled eyes. He was acutely aware of her sorrow, but he was too furious with his own weakness and her obstinacy to sympathize. He ate quickly, then retreated to play a game of horseshoes with several others.

Leanna pushed her plate away, her appetite gone. She felt isolated amidst all the gaiety and laughter around her. Sukey was giggling flirtatiously at a nearby table with a husky field hand. Most of the slaves had paired off, either holding hands or smiling happily. Even Thomas and Sarah were intent on one another as they carried on a low-voiced conversation.

Leanna looked at Jason. The flames highlighted his handsome face, emphasizing the remoteness of his expression as he looked back at her with hooded eyes. Leanna's throat tightened when he raked his glance over her, then looked away as though he found her wanting. She clenched her hands to stem the tears welling in her eyes. Dear God, she would lose him forever if she didn't give in.

Sarah's voice made her jump. Gesturing to Monique, Sarah laughed, "Look, Leanna. Monique has been persuaded to dance the sioca for Gus. It's a dance she learned in San Domingo." Monique laughingly protested as she was carried to the ground in front of the tables. She was deposited gently, directly in front of Gus. A slave pounded a drum in a languorous beat made even more seductive by the soft melody from a flute-like instrument.

Monique at first merely moved her feet in time to the music. Then she undulated her arms and upper body, bending so far backward her head almost touched the ground. Soon her hips joined the dance, weaving back and forward in a graceful motion quickened in time with the drum beat. Her eyes on Gus's face, she writhed seductively closer and closer to him until she had worked her way around the table and danced directly in front of him. Her entire body swayed now as though the music had taken possession of it, arms and torso beckoning as her hips rotated erotically.

Gus's face was beaded with sweat. His nostrils flared as he leaped to his feet and began dancing with her. They swayed around one another, never touching, but with their eyes locked in a desire obvious to all present. Each dancer enticed the other with suggestive thrusting movements.

The blatant sexuality of the dance quickened Leanna's breathing as the drums assaulted her senses. Unwillingly, her eyes shifted to Jason. She was unaware of the hunger in their green depths, but they took Jason's breath away. His own hunger grew to a painful acuity.

His eyes darkened, then burst into flame as he responded to her unspoken message. His look raked her body, an invitation as succinct as it was seductive. Leanna quivered, her nipples tight and her body aching in unwilling response. When his eyes met hers again, she felt not only seared but mesmerized by the bright, flaming torch of blue. His eyes plunged deeply into hers, then he turned and strode off into the shadows, his meaning crystal clear. She would come to him now, or he would not ask again.

Leanna was unaware when the instruments crashed a triumphant crescendo as Gus swooped on Monique to carry her off amid a shower of rice. She didn't see Sarah's concerned look or Thomas's staying hand on Sarah's arm. She followed Jason into the darkness, leaving her cloak on the chair. She didn't even feel the cold biting into her exposed skin as she left the warmth of the bonfire.

The only reality, the only meaning, was the need pulsing ever more urgently through her body as her mind remembered nothing but the fire in Jason's blue eyes. She was almost in a trance as she walked slowly up the stairs to his room, her yearning growing painful now as she at last gave it free rein.

Jason stood tensely at his window, his ears straining for the sound of her footsteps. When he at last heard them, he exhaled in relief and excitement. He turned to watch her walk in, his heart thudding loudly. She closed the door and leaned back against it, her head slightly to one side and her eyes half-closed as she looked at him. She remained thus for a full minute, her eyes traveling up and down his tense, muscular body as though luxuriating in his obvious male desire. She finally raised her eyes to his face and smiled so seductively he gasped. "You win, my darling. I can fight you no longer."

The words were a vindication, a soothing balm, and, he hoped, a new beginning. When he pulled her into his arms, he thought he heard her whisper to herself, "Mayhap the victory will be mine, also."

He undressed her with eager fingers. When she stood before him naked, he undressed himself just as rapidly, his eyes roving over her body possessively. She made no attempt to cover herself. When he was nude she reached out and caressed his shoulders. He did likewise, his breath uneven as he at last felt the warm velvet of her skin once more. They explored one another with curious, eager hands, their faces intent as each rediscovered the beauty of the other; a beauty so different, yet so complementary.

The desire they had so long held at bay engulfed them and their light exploration became urgent. Jason caught her breasts and traced their contours with his large hands, then he bent down to translate his yearning with his tongue. Leanna clutched his shoulders, her nails digging into his biceps as she shuddered with longing.

Jason growled deep in his throat as he carried her to the bed. He lay her down and released the pins from her hair, spreading the silky waves over the pillow and her shoulders while she looked at him with enormous, hungry eyes. She grasped his arms impatiently and pulled him to her, her lips yearning for his.

He obliged, fastening his lips to hers as though famished. They explored each other in an erotic dance like the one they had witnessed earlier. Hands fondled, kneaded, and stroked until their lips at last broke apart and they moaned in joy.

Jason kissed her shoulder, his mouth working avidly. His lips traveled downward, circling each hard peak of her breasts with his tongue, never quite touching the nipple until she pushed her torso upward, her eyes closed in sweet torment. She groaned when he at last devoured the throbbing, hardened tip. His lips pressed harder as he continued over her belly, then probed her inner thigh. When his tongue explored her most secret core, she twitched almost in pain, then she tried to pull him back on top of her. He laughed throatily, the taunt fanning the blazes between them. He continued his delightful punishment until they were both breathless.

Leanna finally forced his head upward with fingers entangled in his hair, sighing with satisfaction as he at last fitted his body to hers. She reached down to caress his ravenous manhood, her fingers working until it was his turn to groan in anguish. Roughly, urgently, he pushed her legs apart with his knees and guided himself into her moist core with one hard, sure thrust.

They sighed in unison, their eyes closed as they savored the contact. Leanna found the sensation of his hard warmth so deep within her soothing, and Jason reveled in her soft constriction around him. Murmuring endearments, he kissed her brow, her cheeks, her closed eyelids, and her neck as he began pumping slowly, barely moving within her. Leanna swiveled her hips eagerly, urging him into harder thrusts.

His head filled with her scent, his senses exploding with the feel of her, he pressed her deeply into the mattress with primitive rhythmic lunges. Leanna moaned continually as she opened herself to receive him, her pride, her need for love momentarily held in check by her feminine need to give herself to her mate.

Their tempo increased until the bed groaned with their gasps of approaching fulfillment. Jason withdrew to the glistening tip of his masculinity, then filled her aching loins again. Leanna arched into him, her body tense from the tight pulsing within her, and when he felt her approaching climax, he held onto his control with an effort.

When he at last felt her convulsions grip him he lunged to the hilt and shook in an agony of pleasure. Pressing deep, he sucked one of her nipples as he filled her womb with eager spurts. Leanna's eyes opened wide in that final moment, and had he been looking into them, he would have seen the love she could not hide at the ecstasy rising in her. But Jason had buried his face in her breasts, and remained thus until the racing of their hearts slowed to a throb.

When he at last raised his head to smile at her, she smiled back shyly, veiling the love and sadness filling her heart behind lowered eyes. "Thank you, Leanna. You're every man's dream of the perfect lover." His voice was husky with emotion, but she still refused to look up. He withdrew, adding to her sense of loss.

He lifted her chin so he could gaze into her eyes. "I am not such a beast, am I? We have been given such a rare and wonderful gift. Please deny our bodies their natural need no longer."

What of the heart, Jason, she longed to cry, what of the heart? Her throat tight, Leanna finally met his pleading eyes. She had no other choice but to accept her slim chance of winning his stubborn heart thusly. She buried her face against his chest, clenching her teeth to stop the tears from coming. "Very well, Jason. I confess that since my body has learned the pleasure you can give it, I would find it extremely difficult to deny myself again."

He sighed in relief, then hugged her so tightly her breath was expelled from her lungs with a whoosh. He pulled her from the bed, then danced gaily around the room, dragging her along. His glee was infectious, and when he grasped her around the waist and spun her around, she laughed helplessly.

Her head whirling, she finally protested, "Jason, stop! You're making me dizzy." He pressed her close before lowering her slowly to the floor, deliberately rubbing her skin against his inch by inch until her feet at last touched the ground. She was amazed to feel his hardness pressing against her.

Half-laughing, she scolded, "You're insatiable. I would like to get *some* sleep this eve." Nevertheless, she made no protest when he carried her to the bed and pulled her into his arms. But later, much later, when he fell into a deep, dreamless slumber, Leanna cried herself silently to sleep.

Jason woke early, as he always did. He was momentarily surprised at the feel of her, soft and warm against him. When he saw her, the memory of the evening enveloped him in a warm embrace. He lay on his side facing her, savoring the beauty that at last belonged to him. He marveled that she could look so sweetly innocent in sleep, yet be so wanton in passion. For a moment, his brow wrinkled quizzically as he tried to piece together the enigma of his wife.

She was not the greedily sensual type of woman he was used to, yet her response surpassed any he had ever experienced. She had never known passion with anyone but him, of that he was certain. Was she a wanton who would ignite at any man's touch, or did her body react only to him? His every cell screamed a denial of the former, but the latter thought intoxicated him strangely. What if Leanna did indeed love him? His heart leaped at the idea, and he dissected her features, wishing desperately he could read the answer in her face.

Leanna stretched luxuriously, wondering why she felt so

relaxed. When Jason leaned close to possess her mouth, memory of the night returned. At first, she kissed him back sweetly, but when his hands began to wander, she jumped out of bed and belted his robe around her tiny waist with decision. Jason roared with laughter at the clown-like figure she made as the sleeves trailed past her knees and the hem formed a pool around her feet.

She gave him a mock haughty look. "Sir, you dare to laugh at me? We can't all be great hulking brutes like you." She shook her fist at him playfully, almost smiling herself at the oddity of the material flapping around her waving arm like the wing of a bird.

Jason leaped out of bed to pull her into his arms, still chuckling. He whispered in her ear, "I wouldn't change a single delectable inch of you. You're dangerous enough to mankind in a small package. Why, if you were tall, the world would not be safe." Leanna flushed when he looked at her meaningfully. She wrapped her arms—what she could find of them—around his neck. He lowered his mouth to her eager lips.

Neither of them heard the soft knock on the door or noticed when Thomas entered. He stood watching their passionate embrace, then he finally cleared his throat loudly, startling them apart.

He chuckled when he got a better look at Leanna. "I apprehend the two of you were too busy last night to think about such a minor item as clothing. I hope this means the jousting and dueling between you is at an end?" He looked from Jason's smiling face to Leanna's flushed one.

"On my part it is, Grandfather. Leanna?" She met his eyes and tilted her chin.

"We can but try, Jason," she replied softly. She uttered a silent prayer for strength, meeting Thomas's understanding eyes. He gave her an encouraging wink before offering his arm with a flourish.

"I would be honored to escort you to your boudoir, my lady."

Leanna nodded her head regally, curtsying as low as the yards of material engulfing her would allow. Jason chuckled when she had to hitch up the robe before she could walk. She gave him a saucy little look over her shoulder before Thomas shut the door behind them.

Jason whistled jovially as he dressed. He stood at the window, deciding it was a beautiful day despite the cloudy, sullen sky. Leaping down the stairs with boyish boisterousness, he snatched Sarah close and hugged her so hard she protested.

When he released her she straightened her apron and tried to look stern, but failed miserably. When Jason winked at her she relented and smiled slyly. "Your evening's rest appears to have agreed with you," she teased.

He nodded, unabashed, then went to the laden sideboard to fill his plate to the rim. Munching on a fluffy buttermilk biscuit, he requested, "Sarah, please have Leanna's things moved into my chamber." He seemed to relish his next words: "I no longer sleep alone."

Sarah watched him eat heartily with a rather sour look on her face before she retreated to relay the order. What typical masculine arrogance. He was pleased as a rutting stallion among a group of fillies, but what of Leanna?

Thomas remained in Leanna's room while she dressed behind a screen. "Are you all right this morning, my child? Jason didn't pressure you into anything against your will, did he?"

"No, Grandfather, not really. I want him as much as he wants me. Luckily, he's not yet wondered *why* I want him so." She came from behind the screen, dressed in a plain, warm yellow gown. Thomas smiled at the bemused look in her puzzled eyes as she sat before her mirror to brush her bountiful locks.

Thomas stroked the shining gold gently. "When a man desires a woman the way Jason desires you, my dear, he does not wait to examine her motives before taking her. Jason is no more dull than the rest of our sex." He kissed the top of her head, smiling.

"You have made both of the stubborn Blaines very happy men, Leanna. Thank you for the sacrifice you made for my lad." He turned her to face him, his eyes serious now. "I know how it must pain you to give your body and heart when Jason offers only his body in return. But your patience will earn its reward. Jason will admit his love for you when he realizes how vital you are to his existence. The intimacy between you will hasten that admission, if I'm any judge of my grandson." Thomas smiled almost with pity. "It will bewilder him indeed when he finds his desire for you increasing rather than diminishing."

She bit her lip uncertainly. "Do you really think he loves me, Grandfather?" She met his look with anxious, entreating pools of green that moved him deeply.

"Yes, my child, I do. One day, despite himself, he will admit it." He patted her cheek, then walked to the door. He turned to face her with Jason's roguish look. "I expect to hold my great-grandchild in my arms before too long, Leanna. I'm sure you and Jason will much enjoy the task, hmm?" He laughed tenderly at her flushed face, then shut the door behind him.

Leanna touched her abdomen with trembling fingers. Jason's child could already be growing within her. She met her troubled eyes in the mirror. If Jason did love her, the child would be born to the happy home she had always dreamed of. Inevitably, the darker side of the cloud invaded her thoughts. And if he would never love her?

Leanna couldn't bear the thought of birthing a child who couldn't grow up in the warm glow of his parents' happiness. He would grow up a miniature of Jason, afraid of love and commitment. No, at all costs, that must not happen. If she found herself pregnant and still without the love of her husband, she would leave. The child would have more of a chance with one loving parent than with two unhappy ones. But she would first do all in her power to see that any child she brought into the world had the happy home it deserved.

Leanna stared at her wistful reflection, then set her mouth resolutely. She would fight for the love of her husband in any way necessary. As long as he was not enamored of another woman, she had a chance. If he wanted a temptress, then a temptress she would be. Blushing at the memory of the previous night, she admitted her role would not be onerous.

Chapter
Eighteen

THE NEXT DAY Jason challenged Leanna to a race, adding with a wicked gleam, "The winner gets to claim the forfeit." His exaggerated leer left Leanna in no doubt as to what forfeit he would demand. She dropped her eyes demurely to hide her own impish designs. She had plans of her own, when she lost, as she most certainly would. Despite Leanna's skill and the mare's swiftness, Morning Mist simply could not match the power of the black.

In a flurry of hooves, they were off. Morning Mist was unusually frisky after having breakfasted on her full ration of oats, and the lighter weight she carried gave her the initial advantage. However, long before they were halfway to the agreed-upon finish line, Night Wind closed the gap. Briefly, both riders galloped neck and neck. Jason turned his head to smile at Leanna teasingly, and she realized in frustration that he was actually holding the stallion back. She grimaced at him and urged Morning Mist faster, but the mare was tiring.

Leanna heard Jason laugh triumphantly as he gave Night Wind his head and took the lead. Leanna's eyes blazed like wicked emeralds when she jerked Morning Mist to a rearing halt and urged her to move quickly in the opposite direction. By the time Jason reined in at the finish line and turned, she was almost out of sight among the trees. Grinning appreciatively at her trick, he dashed off in pursuit. The little minx knew what he had in mind for the loser's forfeit, and she was determined to make it as difficult as possible.

When he reached the trees where she had disappeared, he was alarmed to see Morning Mist hitched to a branch, her nose probing the leaves. There was no sign of Leanna. Concerned, he dismounted and tied Night Wind to another branch. "Leanna," he called anxiously. Silence met him. He stepped out of the trees and looked down into the river, briefly afraid she had fallen in. Nothing. Then a gleam of white amid some bushes caught his eye.

Sighing with relief, he strode toward the hollow between the bushes, sharply reproving, "You frightened the daylights out of me. I thought—" He broke off with a gasp at the sight that met his eyes when he rounded the vegetation.

Leanna lay on a blanket in the hollow, beautifully bare of adornment but for the rich luxury of her hair. She half-reclined with her head propped on her hand and one knee coyly bent. Her hair rippled in the slight breeze, shielding then exposing the silky orbs of her breasts. Her nipples stood erect with cold.

Leanna laughed gaily at the stunned look on his face when he dropped to his knees beside her. "It took you long enough. I'm frozen. Please hurry and warm me." Astonishment melted away under the warmth of desire. He needed no second urging. Almost ripping his clothes in his haste, he quickly lay down beside her and covered them with the blanket.

She lay quietly against him at first, content merely to luxuriate in his warmth and closeness. He whispered, "You never cease to amaze me. I'm not complaining, mind you, but why here?"

She looked surprised. "Don't you recognize this spot, Jason?" He surveyed the area carefully. And a wide grin split his face as memory returned. This was the very place where she had left him aching for her not so long ago, as fit punishment for his arrogance.

He kissed her cheek softly, his eyes dark with emotion. Leanna looked at him with bated breath, praying that the look in his eyes was at last the recognition of her love that she sought. When he merely said, "What a beautiful idea, my love. You are a genius," she almost winced with disappointment.

When his hands began their arousing journey over her body, she had to force herself to respond. Soon, however, disappointment floated away like dried leaves blown by the wind and her body responded with its usual enthusiasm to his intoxicating touch.

He rubbed his leg between her thighs, the rough hairs scraping with delightful friction on the tender skin of her upper legs. In retaliation, she rubbed her breasts against his chest, her eyes gleaming with satisfaction when he moaned at the erotic stroke of her soft, full breasts against his own sensitive nipples. He cupped a breast roughly in his hand and pressed it upward to his hungry lips. He feasted leisurely, smiling at the little panting sounds she made when he replaced his leg with his hand.

He stroked the softness between her legs gently, teasing rather than fulfilling her. She pushed up against him hungrily, catching his wrist to pull his hand closer. He caught both her wrists in one hand and held them high above her head, leaving her defenseless at the exquisite torture he performed on her body.

She writhed against him, exciting him unbearably. He resisted his body's urge to take her without delay, for he wanted to draw out the pleasure of this delightful encounter as long as possible. He settled between her thighs, burning her sensitive womanhood with delicate strokes of his loins, barely inserting himself, then withdrawing to heighten her excitement. His brow beaded with the effort it cost him to keep from thrusting deep within her.

He fastened his lips over one nipple to feast fervently. Her heart beat a wild, primitive rhythm that sent the blood rushing to each sensitized nerve ending. Leanna sobbed, "Don't, Jason,

I can't stand any more. Please, please end it."

He pushed her legs far apart and plunged full length within her, no longer able to deny himself or her. He lunged in and out, too aroused for gentleness. She met each movement, enraptured in the sensations rippling through her body. She clasped her legs around his waist, biting her lip to keep from shouting the joy he was giving her. The elemental sound of the river rushing close at hand whetted their passion so sharply he could only manage a few violent, hungry entries before the familiar spasms of pleasure overcame them.

Gasping, Jason buried himself within her soft warmth and erupted. His strong frame seemed vulnerable as he trembled and convulsed, a helpless victim of the pleasure engulfing him. Leanna clutched him to her tightly with arms and legs as the tension within her crested into fulfillment. She prayed, Give me his child, dear God, no matter what. I need his son growing within me, a part of him always with me.

Jason slumped, totally spent. Leanna stroked his sweaty back, tears escaping her lids to trail across her temples and into her hair. When Jason withdrew and lay by her side, she turned her head so he wouldn't see. They were quiet, listening to the slowing beats of their hearts and the loud, triumphant flowing of the river.

Relaxed and awed at the pleasure they had experienced, Jason turned her face to him and stroked her tears away from her delicate temples. "Why do you cry, my love?" he asked with concern.

She sniffed, then gave him a watery smile, her eyes appearing jade green under the sheen of tears. "I am moved at the bliss you gave me, Jason. Do I please you as much as you please me?"

He caressed her face with tender eyes. "Probably many times more, my darling. The luckiest day of my life was when La Bianca mistook me for Sherry."

Her heart beat faster. "Do you mean that, Jason?" she asked softly, almost fearfully.

He folded her close, as though he clutched something precious and fragile. "Indeed I do, my sweet." He grinned. "Though

I confess at the time I certainly didn't feel that way."

Leanna searched his face eagerly. Perhaps Thomas was right and he truly did love her. She had certainly never expected to hear such an admission from him.

Jason coiled a blond strand of hair, marveling anew at its silkiness. Meanwhile, he searched for words to frame his next question. "Leanna, " he said hesitantly. "Have you ever been in love?"

She froze. He felt her immediate tension and was afraid to press for an answer. She finally replied, "Why do you ask?" Her eyes were guarded as she looked at him.

He sighed and uncoiled the hair on his finger. "I am a little confused at your . . . passionate reaction to me. I merely wondered if you had ever responded to anyone else." When she looked wounded, he continued hastily, "I know you've never had such union with another man, but have you ever desired anyone but me?"

She swallowed and glanced away for time, searching frantically for a reasonable explanation. She tried to brazen it out. "No, I've never been in love. There were men I was attracted to, but whether I would respond to them I cannot tell you," she lied calmly. No one but Jason could ever melt her soul with a look or a touch, of that she was certain.

He grunted, unsatisfied, but he didn't insist on more explanation. They dressed quickly, some of the enchantment gone. They trotted back to the house, both preoccupied with their own thoughts.

Leanna was in a panic. What if he discovered she loved him? He would never let her go, especially if she carried his child. She must try to stifle her response in order to allay his suspicions. Sighing in depression at the complexity of her situation, she dismounted at the door, then silently handed the reins to Jason and went up to change.

He stood frowning where she left him in a swirl of skirts. So involved was he in his thoughts he didn't notice the stable boy who took the reins from his hand. She was hiding something from him, he could feel it. But what? He sat down in a porch rocker, rocking absent-mindedly.

She would probably not admit it even if she did love him. Yet what other explanation could there be for her behavior? He would bet his last ha'penny she was no wanton. Leanna was too strong a person to allow her body to rule her mind. He was so excited at the notion that she loved him that he jumped up and paced restlessly up and down, unable to keep still.

What bliss it would be to win the heart of a woman such as Leanna. He would gladly sacrifice his freedom and other women if she would live by his side, in his bed, mother of his children, wife, mistress, and lover. That would be the closest thing to heaven he could imagine. When the old wounds quivered and taunted him with a reminder that Andrew must have felt the same about Bella, he dismissed the jeering voice impatiently.

Leanna was not Bella. He knew instinctively when she gave her heart she would not do it by half measures. Nothing under God's heaven would pry her from the side of the man she loved. Heart beating wildly with hope, he wondered how he could discover the true state of her feelings.

He paused to lean against the porch railing, looking unseeingly toward the river. What would he do if he were Leanna, too proud to admit her love? He'd try to hide it by acting indifferent. Very well, he would watch her carefully. If she still responded to him as passionately as before, he would have to conclude their conversation did not concern her. However, if she tried to dampen her ardor, he would know she was alarmed at her vulnerability and was thus shielding herself from hurt.

He turned to go back in, then halted abruptly. He stood as rigid as a stone statue as a frightening thought struck him. Why was the thought of Leanna's devotion so intoxicating? If he was indifferent to her, surely the state of her emotions would be of no interest to him. He swallowed, still fighting a desperate, ancient battle. The old instincts died hard.

He walked into the study and poured himself a stiff brandy, hoping it would clear his head. Then he searched for Thomas as an excuse to escape his disturbing thoughts.

Since the night of Gus's wedding, he and Thomas had not

argued again. Jason shrewdly suspected Thomas was glad
Leanna and he were intimate because his grandfather yearned
to hold his great-grandchild. Jason's throat tightened as he
visualized the child who could be growing this very instant in
Leanna's womb. As he rode to the field where he thought
Thomas was working, he dreamed of a boy with Leanna's green
eyes and unquenchable spirit. What a son they would have!
The fruit of his seed, planted in ecstasy and nurtured in her
beautiful body.

Typically, he never even considered they might have a girl.
Frowning, he pondered why it was so important to him that
she have his child. Certainly it was time he had an heir, but
they had ample opportunity. They hadn't even been married
six months yet. No, he was forced to the reluctant conclusion
that a child would bind them together. She was becoming increasingly vital to his happiness, despite his every effort to
guard against her. Once more he shied away from the precipice
of doubts and fears he had about marital vows.

He spied Thomas with relief. His grandfather was examining
the weeded, clean field that had been readied for spring planting. Thomas bent down to scoop up a handful of rich, black
earth, examining the soil closely. When Jason dismounted and
walked over to him, he smiled in welcome.

"Your idea of leaving part of our acreage to rest for a season
certainly paid off last picking time. I decided to experiment
with a few acres by leaving them fallow for two seasons."
Thomas took Jason's hand to fill his palm with dirt. "Look at
the soil, Jason. I haven't seen it so rich in years. We should
yield an excellent average indeed from these acres, come har-
vest."

Jason played with the soil distractedly, sprinkling it from
one hand to the other. For the first time, Thomas noticed the
preoccupied look on his grandson's face. They walked side by
side over the bare field, the communion between the two men
as strong as their pride in the land they loved.

When Jason didn't speak, Thomas urged him, "All right,
lad. Out with it. What's troubling you?"

Jason looked down moodily, loath to admit his fears even

to himself. But the emotions raging within him were too strong for him to control, so he finally burst out, "Grandfather, do you think it's possible Leanna loves me?"

Thomas stopped to watch a hawk's graceful acrobatics before he framed a response. How to encourage Jason without betraying Leanna's confidence? Finally, he replied, "It's possible, lad." He pierced Jason with sharp eyes. "Though I certainly would not encourage her in such a fruitless emotion." When Jason looked angry, Thomas frowned.

"Come, come, Grandson, aren't you being just a wee bit unreasonable? You want Leanna's devotion, yet you remain unwilling to give her aught in return. Certainly I would do everything I could to spare the child such anguish." Thomas stood with both feet planted on the ground, his weathered face increasing his resemblance to an ancient, sturdy oak that had survived many a gale and icy winter.

Jason could not refute the truth of his statement. Why, indeed, should he expect Leanna's passionate devotion when he gave her nothing but admittedly enjoyable lovemaking in return?

Thomas sensed his wavering. There would be no better time. He grasped Jason's arm, looking into his grandson's troubled eyes. "Lad, don't you think you're making a mistake in expecting Leanna to pay for your mother's sins? Surely by now you realize Leanna is a strong girl capable of great devotion. The man who wins her love can call himself fortunate indeed." Thomas winked, then formed an impish grin so like Jason's. "Not to mention her beauty and, I suspect, her considerable passion."

He became serious again. He took a few staccato strides, then stopped and turned. Jason tensed at the sternness on Thomas's face. "You have no right to stifle such a lovely girl, Jason. This marriage was no more her wish than yours. If you're determined to hold yourself aloof from her, you should let her go back to England, if that's her desire." He hesitated, then struck. "Perhaps one day she will find a man worthy of her warm heart. She reminds me more of Jenny every day." And with this final accolade, Thomas mounted his steed and left

Jason standing in the middle of the field.

Pain ripped through his body. He clenched his fists at the thought of Leanna in the arms of another man. Leaping onto his horse, he shot toward the river, his brain awhirl. He rode until the stallion foamed at the mouth and his own breath was harsh with exertion. He finally reined the wheezing beast in at the spot where they had made love that morning. Jason slouched in the saddle, lost in thought as he remembered their tryst.

Finally he straightened. Thomas was right. If Leanna did love him, he must either put aside his bitterness and distrust of women to heal the old hurts, or he must let her go. Feeling somewhat better, he headed slowly back to the house.

Curiously, for the first time since he was a bewildered boy, he thought of Bella without his usal rage. He remembered his mother as he had last seen her, kissing him goodbye with tears in her striking gray eyes. A residue of bitterness lingered as he remembered his anguish when he discovered she would not be returning, but at least his hatred had diminished. Vaguely aware something momentous was occurring within him, Jason went in search of Leanna.

He found her sitting on the veranda outside her room, her face remote as she turned her head at his footsteps. The smile she gave him was perfunctory, and when he pulled her out of the chair into his arms, she was startled. He held her close, resting his chin on her sweetly scented hair, his eyes closed at the confusing mixture of pain and pleasure she always stirred in him.

Leanna didn't try to pull away. His need drew her like a magnet. He was her lodestone, the guiding force in her life, and without him she would be doomed to wander aimlessly through an arid desert without hope of succor or rest.

The moment did much to ease their mutual pain. Each sensed and welcomed the need of the other, but neither was yet willing to voice their feelings. What despair could have been avoided had courage conquered pride in that moment! But when Jason sighed and held Leanna at arm's length, his gentle smile belied his true roiling hopes and fears. When presented with such a smooth facade, what could Leanna do but present a similar barrier? So the two proud, stubborn souls smiled calmly while they ached inside.

Jason pulled Leanna onto his lap. "For shame, wife. Why didn't you tell me about your approaching birthday?"

Leanna started guiltily. She was reluctant to admit she had wanted to avoid another extravagant, soulless present, so she replied, "I didn't think of it, Jason. We haven't been on the best of terms until lately, and I didn't think it of consequence."

Jason caressed her forearm, watching in fascination as the waning light shone on the tiny, almost invisible, golden hairs. "Is there anything special you wish for your present?" he asked absent-mindedly, his thoughts now on other, more seductive, parts of her anatomy.

Something lodged in her throat as she wildly wondered what he would say if she replied, "Yes, I want your love, Jason. Without it nothing else has meaning." She cleared her throat and answered huskily, "No, nothing. You have been more than generous. What could I possibly need?"

Jason heard her emotion-clogged voice, but when he tried to guide her head around to face him, she jumped off his lap. She laughed in a high-pitched voice. "I have something I need to discuss with Sarah. Please excuse me." She almost ran from the veranda.

Jason leaned back thoughtfully. He was more convinced than ever she was hiding something from him. His mouth tightened grimly. He would worm her secret out of her no matter how long it took. There would be no secrets between them, in or out of bed.

Leanna had calmed by the time the family met for dinner. She smiled serenely when Jason gave her a probing glance, not flinching when he kissed the soft nape of her neck. She had swept up her hair into an elegant style.

During the course of the meal, Jason rarely took his eyes off Leanna. She avoided his glance as she discussed her redecorating plans with Thomas. "I thought perhaps the south bedroom would look pretty in cornflower blue. The new canopy Jason brought from London should look delightful with blue satin hangings. The wall covering I selected has tiny blue forget-me-nots on a cream background with yellow daisies scattered here and there." Her voice wavered under Jason's intense look, and she finally glanced angrily at him. His returning smile was bland and innocent.

Thomas almost despairingly buried his head in his hands at the sparks flying between the two. He hastily intervened. "Sounds lovely, child. Do whatever you please. Your delicate hand will do a much better job than I ever could."

He cast Jason a reproving look which went unnoticed by his intent grandson. He cleared his throat peremptorily, finally dragging Jason's eyes from Leanna. "I need your assistance tomorrow, Jason. We're overhauling the gins, and you know you're much better with the damn contraptions than I am."

Jason nodded and returned to staring at Leanna. Unable to stand any more, Leanna flung her napkin on her plate, gave a regal nod to both men, and left. Jason gulped down his wine and followed. Thomas opened his mouth to call him back, then clamped it shut. He had tried everything he knew to bring the two together. To be honest, he was impatient with the whole affair. He stomped angrily toward the kitchen in search of Sarah's soothing presence.

The scene in Leanna's bedchamber was anything but soothing. She was struggling angrily with the hooks on the back of her dress when she heard a deep, rich chuckle behind her. She whirled. Jason was leaning against the closed door, arms folded and a satisfied smile on his lips at her obvious confusion.

She gave a frustrated "Oooh!" and whirled back to yank harder on the recalcitrant hooks. She stiffened when slow footsteps sounded behind her, and she tried to shy away when he reached out to assist. He grasped her firmly around the waist, stopping her completely.

"Be still unless you want to go to bed in this blasted thing," he ordered loftily. She gritted her teeth but remained as still as her rising fury would allow.

Before he had reached the last hook she bolted away and stepped out of the gown, leaving it on the floor in an untidy heap. Ignoring him, she removed her petticoats, stockings, and chemise. Jason reached out to fondle her breasts, rising taunt-

ingly as she pulled her warm gown over her head. She slapped
his hands away and jerked the pins out of her hair, not bothering
to brush it. When she tried to climb into bed, Jason grabbed
her around the waist.

"Not so fast, my dear. I have something I want to discuss
with you." He smiled pleasantly into her dangerous eyes.

"Well?" she asked when he waited, deliberately drawing out
the tension.

He massaged her tight neck soothingly. "I am still puzzled
as to why a woman who has only contempt for me should
respond so . . . ardently to my love-making," he said.

He had been leading up to this all evening, so Leanna was
prepared. "Why, because you are such a marvelous lover, of
course. What girl could help but respond to your . . . excessive
masculinity?" she parried sweetly.

Jason eyed her askance, but persevered with the bravery of
a fool. "Would you respond to any skillful lover?" he riposted.

"Certainly. Would you like me to put it to the test?" She
lunged for the killing strike.

His face darkened ominously. "No, I would not," he said,
his mouth stern.

"Then shall we drop this inane conversation and retire?"
She flashed him a false smile and climbed into bed with a
triumphant look on her smug face.

She had out-smarted him this time, he admitted ruefully as
he undressed. However, she had an even more rigorous test to
pass.

Leanna lay on her side, taking deep breaths and trying to
relax. When Jason lay full length against her back she was
unable to control her instinct to retreat from his seductive warmth.
He snuffed the candle beside the bed and edged closer once
more, putting his arms around her for good measure. He smiled
when he felt her heart pulsing against him. He tried to turn her
to face him, but she resisted.

"Please, Jason, I am quite tired. Let me go to sleep." Her
voice trembled.

Jason gave up and turned onto his back. "Certainly, my
dear. Sleep well," he said blandly. He peered toward the shad-

owy ceiling, his mouth pursed in thought. Despite her brave efforts at evasion, she was having difficulty stifling her instinctive response to him. He smiled slowly, a delighted grin that would have disquieted Leanna, had she seen it. She loved him, surely? What other explanation could there be? He almost laughed joyously, but caught himself just in time. She would admit it soon, despite herself.

And when she does? the sly little voice said. His jubilation faded. The next move would definitely be his. He sighed tiredly. He was still not certain of his own feelings, nor could he control his instinctive revulsion at the thought of placing his heart in the hands of a woman, any woman. But one thing he knew beyond a shadow of a doubt: If she left him, the light would go out of his world. He must prevent that, at all costs.

Chapter
Nineteen

LEANNA WAS TOO upset during the next few days to notice the furtive excitement around the house. When her womanly flow was late, she at first believed her emotional state of mind had affected her cycle. But as the tell-tale spots still refused to appear and she became unusually hungry between meals yet had difficulty keeping the food down, she was forced to the obvious conclusion. She was pregnant.

She slumped down on the bed on the morning she admitted her condition. She gasped a bitter laugh, recalling the date. How ironic that she should acknowledge the new life growing within her on the date of her own birth.

Her eyes burned when she remembered how she had prayed for Jason's child during their passion. His baby had already been growing in her womb. The child must have been conceived that afternoon at the cabin. Her earlier eagerness to bear Jason's child was now buried under a heavy weight of dread. How could she bring an innocent life into a world shadowed by an unhappy marriage? Absently, she entwined her hands protectively over her abdomen.

Jason knew she loved him. She saw the knowledge in his eyes. If he returned her feelings in the smallest measure, surely he would not let her suffer so?

Incredibly, he seemed to expect a verbal admission from her, as though nothing mattered but her complete subjugation. She never would have believed him capable of such cruelty. He hovered over her like an avenging angel, a burning look in his eyes. She would have believed he needed her as much as she needed him, had he showed more interest in her than in her body.

Even his desire seemed to be waning. Nightly, she pushed him away when he reached for her, though she found her resistance increasingly weaker. When he accepted her refusal noncommittally, her despair heightened. She would die before she ever admitted her love for him. Her identity as Leanna would be stifled forever under her role as Jason's wife. She would become his puppet, his toy to play with at will until he tired of her, set her back on the shelf, and searched for a newer doll.

Leanna sat up abruptly, her delicate face almost pugnacious. She was no object to be cast aside. If Jason was tired of her, if he would never love her, she had no alternative but to leave. Leanna clamped her eyes shut at the thought of never seeing him again.

Her hands clutched her belly tighter. The pain she'd know on leaving him would be less than the agony all would feel if she stayed and tried to raise their child in a loveless marriage. The comforting portrait in her mind of a handsome, raven-haired son or daughter with dark blue eyes became a terrifying caricature as she visualized the child watching his quarreling parents with bitter, condemning eyes.

She rose wearily and straightened her hair before the mirror. She must make certain that Jason's unhappy childhood was not repeated in his child. She wondered if Jason's mother had felt as agonized on leaving her husband as she now felt. Her secret sympathy for the woman increased along with her admiration.

Leanna doubted she would have been courageous enough to leave her child where he would be happiest.

She smoothed her skirts with agitated hands, debating her best course of action. Perhaps she should go to Charleston? She could never return to England; life with Edith would be intolerable. Rian had told her if she ever needed respite from her stubborn husband, she could visit him. He had pointed out his cabin on one of their carriage trips. Should she avail herself of his aid?

Sighing, she dismissed the tempting idea. Rian had made his attraction to her obvious, and Jason would be ravenously jealous. She wanted to cause no further problems between Jason, his grandfather, and Rian. A heavy sack of gold was kept in the study for household needs, and it should more than cover her disappearance. She would take her emeralds, just in case. It was only fitting that the opulent gift given in lust rather than love should aid her escape from her indifferent husband. Miserable but resigned, Leanna rose and moved to the door. God help me get through this day, she prayed. Delaying her departure would only make it more painful, so the sooner she left, the better. She could probably complete preparations by the evening.

She took a deep breath and set her face in a calm mask, then descended the stairs at a measured pace. She even managed to nod serenely when she saw Thomas. But when he warmed her with a tender smile, she hurriedly looked away, her throat once more constricted with tears. Her shaky composure didn't fool Thomas for an instant. It was obvious the child realized that Jason suspected her feelings. He would have a long talk with her after the festivities and explain that Jason's awareness of her love was a positive thing. The lad's wariness was at last crumbling, and if she would forget her pride one last time, she would probably be surprised at Jason's response. However, the discussion would have to wait for a less busy time.

So he merely said, "I was just coming to fetch you, my dear. Jason has informed me you celebrate your birthday today. I would like to give you your present before this evening." He led her gently in the direction of the study as he spoke, then left her standing by the door while he fetched a huge, gaily wrapped box.

Leanna swallowed and did her best to appear delighted. "Why, thank you, Grandfather," she trilled brightly, but he didn't miss her trembling lips as she tried to smile. She ripped open the present quickly as some of her misery fled before genuine curiosity. She burrowed through layers of tissue, then gasped as she saw a gorgeous gown of iridescent green silk.

Leanna unfolded the dress and held it up against her, rushing with eager excitement to the mirror near the desk. The fabric was so cleverly dyed it shimmered between deep emerald and sea green as she turned in the light. A glittering golden cord criss-crossed the high bodice to meet in back and trail to the flounced hem. The minuscule cap sleeves were three golden cords looped together.

Thomas sighed with pleasure at the happy look on Leanna's face. It was the first such look he had seen in days. He cleared his throat. "I have invited a number of people to a celebration dinner and dance tonight, Leanna." When she stiffened, he pleaded, "Please, child, it's time you met our friends. Everyone has been asking about you."

Leanna could not refuse him. Surely she could hide her misery long enough to please this old man she loved so deeply, one last time? Perhaps she could leave with one fresh, happy memory of how it could have been. If she tried hard enough, maybe she could even pretend Jason loved her. The fantasy would help dull the pain of her departure from the house she had come to call home.

"Very well, Grandfather." She nodded quickly before courage deserted her. He kissed her brow, love glowing in his eyes, then led her into the dining room.

They had barely started breakfast before Jason entered. His eyes went immediately to Leanna. She met the intent blue gaze with a strange glitter in her own eyes. She didn't shrink away when he kissed her neck before taking his seat.

Thomas asked, "Are the gins in good working order, Jason?"

Jason nodded absent-mindedly, his eyes resting on Leanna as he ate. She seemed different, somehow. Her sulkiness of late was replaced with bright eyes and flushed cheeks. They made him uneasy. She was up to something.

Leanna sensed his perplexity and lowered her eyes to hide her satisfaction. She fiercely hoped she disturbed him. It was a small solace to her bruised emotions, but his reaction bolstered her determination. She would hold composure before her like a shield. When she was gone, Jason would never suspect her agony at leaving him.

Her tormented thoughts were rudely interrupted by her stomach now churning. She paled, but excused herself with as much grace as possible. Jason looked alarmed and leaped to his feet to follow, but Thomas waved him back down. Leanna barely reached her chamber pot before her stomach broke into violent spasms.

In her misery, she didn't hear the soft knock or the opening of the door. The first she knew of Thomas's presence was his gentle hand helping to support her heaving back. He wiped her face with a damp cloth when she finally stood, trembling and drained, then he led her to the bed where he made her lie down. He sat down next to her and took her hand.

The gleam in his eye was half-hopeful, half-sympathetic. Leanna wearily forestalled the question she could see forming. She turned her face away to hide the lie. "No, I am not with child, Grandfather. I have been feeling poorly of late, but I'll be fine soon. Please don't worry about me."

Thomas watched her averted face with a frown. The child was lying. Why? A sense of half-dread weighed him down. He probed, "Leanna, won't you please tell me what's troubling you?" When she shook her head, he insisted, "I can't bear seeing you so unhappy, dear child. How can I help if you won't tell me what's wrong?"

She forced herself to meet his gaze. The shuttered green eyes pained him. She had not been so withdrawn at their first meeting. "I'm merely feeling a mite homesick. I miss Sherry and Abby." The excuse sounded feeble to her own ears, so she rose to her feet and went to the window to avoid her eyes. His solicitation threatened the composure she had vowed to maintain.

Thomas hesitated as he watched her rigid back. Then he sighed and went to the door. She would probably be more relaxed and receptive after the party. He paused with his hand on the knob. Leanna would have broken down had she turned to see him, for the strong old planes and crags of his face were soft with tenderness. He comforted, "Please remember that I love you like my own, Leanna. I want only what will make you happy. If you need to talk, I'm ready to listen." And with a last smile, always gentle, he left her.

Leanna sagged against the wall, buried her head in her arms, and sobbed bitterly. She choked back the tears after a few minutes. She could not allow herself the luxury of tears if she was to get through this day without someone suspecting her plans. With clenched teeth, she washed her face and held the cloth to her reddened eyes. She had just decided she was presentable when a knock sounded at her door. At her assent, Sarah entered.

"You have a visitor, Leanna," Sarah informed her gently, her eyes searching the pale but composed face before her. "Ben has brought you a present."

Leanna smiled in genuine pleasure. "How thoughtful of him! I've been wondering how he was." She hurried down the stairs and entered the parlor.

Ben was twisting his cap nervously as he sat cautiously on a straight formal chair in the parlor. A large box on his lap dwarfed his slight figure.

He smiled when she burst into the room, and he stood hastily. "How you be, ma'rm?" Ben reddened with pleasure when Leanna kissed him on the cheek.

"It's so good to see you, Ben. Why didn't you come sooner?" she reproached him.

He shifted from one foot to the other. "I don't like bein' away from the port fer long, ma'rm. But I been wonderin' arfter you. I made you a little somethin' fer yer birthday." He offered the package with a proud gleam in his eyes.

Leanna tore the plain brown wrapping. Her eyes watered when she saw the contents of the box.

Ben had painstakingly carved a beautiful replica of the *Sa-*

vannah. Down to the carved sternwalk railing and the size of the wheel, the little craft was as accurate as Ben's loving hands could make it. She seemed eager to sail with canvas unfurled.

Leanna cleared her throat to thank him. "She's a beauty, Ben. It makes me want to take to sea again, just looking at her."

Ben beamed at this ultimate compliment. Leanna rang for refreshment, then watched indulgently as he wolfed down two of Sarah's apple tarts. He was regaling her with tales of the excitement of living at the wharf and a fight he had witnessed between several sailors when Jason walked in. He nodded at his captain, but continued with his story. "Built like bars, they was, both o' them. They fair beat the other two to a pulp. I never seen such big fists. Brothers, they be, Dan and Pete Duggan. Hear tell they hire out between voyages. I seen one man beat near to death by the two o' them."

Jason looked with amusement at Leanna's horrified face. He nodded at Ben, then walked up behind Leanna to put a caressing hand on her shoulder. She stiffened, then forced herself to relax and listen to Ben's words. But the lad had realized his tale was not appropriate drawing room conversation. He reddened, and when Jason jerked his head toward the door, Ben was only too glad to comply. He felt like a fish out of water in the subdued elegance of the drawing room.

Ben rose. "I'll be goin', ma'rm," he said laconically. When Leanna protested, Ben winked at Jason before answering, "I can see the cap'n has somethin' to discuss with yer." He bobbed his head and smiled. "Hope yer birthday is yer happiest, ma'rm."

Jason pulled Leanna into his arms after Ben had left. His eyes shone brilliantly into hers. "Indeed, I want to make it your happiest as well, Leanna." He lowered his mouth over hers, ignoring her instinctive move to escape.

Anger, pain, pride, and determination all fled under the persuasive warmth of his lips. Leanna's mouth opened like a bud before the sun to his hungry exploring. His gentle kiss deepened as passion flared between them, their hands beginning to wander. The opening of the door startled Leanna out of her pleasurable haze. When a houseman beamed at them in approval as he removed the tray, Leanna stepped safely out of Jason's reach.

"Have you seen the gown Grandfather gave me, Jason?" she asked with a too-bright smile as she put the sofa between them.

He nodded, but his eyes eloquently expressed his impatience with such mundane matters. Leanna toyed with a china figurine that sat on a low table. She searched frantically for something to distract him. "Was it your idea to have a party this evening?" she asked, her voice muffled.

"No, it was Grandfather's. The celebration I had in mind was a little more . . . intimate." His wandering gaze left her in no doubt of his meaning. She watched with wide, frightened eyes as he walked around the sofa. Her glance shied away. She could feel her sturdy shield buckling under the intensity of his look. When he lifted her chin, she still refused to look at him.

"Why have you pushed me away of late, Leanna?" he asked. His handsome face was alert now as he tried to will a truthful answer from her.

Leanna swallowed, then stated, "I have not been feeling well recently, Jason." Her lips curled into an ironic smile, and had he seen her eyes, he would have been upset at their ineffable sadness. "My malady is not fatal. The pain will fade soon."

Jason frowned at her broodingly. He knew she was not speaking of a sickness of the body. He longed to comfort her, but the only words that would soothe her were words he was not yet ready to speak.

Leanna took advantage of his silence to retreat. "If you'll excuse me, I have things to attend to if I'm to be ready for this evening." She gave him a polite, meaningless smile.

Jason's voice was imperative. "Wait, Leanna." When she reluctantly turned to face him, he smiled. "Aren't you curious to see what I've bought for your present?"

A shaft of pain and anger pierced Leanna. Dear God, couldn't she be spared another display of his possession? "No, not particularly, but I suppose I must see it anyway." Her eyes were icy.

Jason reddened at the insult, and his arm as he led her from the room was not gentle. Leanna bit her lip, wishing she could call back her angry words. She so wanted to have one last, happy memory to take with her when she left tonight, but she couldn't seem to avoid baiting him.

Jason dragged her through the front door. His order was harsh. "Wait here."

Leanna's mouth tightened, but she obeyed. Jason soon returned, leading Morning Mist, but the mare was transformed. Her always graceful lines were now accentuated by beautiful trappings. Her plain brown sidesaddle had been replaced by an ornate, tooled saddle of black leather and silver, inlaid with trees, flowers, and birds. The mare's bridle, reins, and stirrups mirrored the same pattern, but the silver was not used as lavishly.

Leanna's throat constricted and she clenched her hands so tightly her nails left red marks in her palms. No heartless attempt at seduction was this gift. The trappings were expensive, but Jason had made a genuine attempt to give her something that would please rather than entice her into his bed. His present was an expression of thoughtfulness and empathy rather than an attempt to further his own selfish ends, as the emeralds had been.

Leanna could barely make out the image of her husband through her swimming eyes, but she vaguely sensed his gentle concern. He whispered teasingly, "Females! You try to please them, and instead of thanking you, they turn into watering pots." When he kissed her cheek, she felt the contact with every fiber of her being. She slumped in weary surrender against him, oddly comforted by the arms of the man who had caused her such pain.

They stood quietly for a time, relishing the closeness and warmth. Inwardly, both acknowledged their need, but the curse of pride kept their lips silent. Jason patted her on the rear and led her into the house. Leanna managed a shaky smile as he escorted her up the stairs to their room. "Thank you, Jason. You couldn't have given me anything I would treasure more."

"The best is yet to come, Leanna." He smiled mysteriously, then shooed her into the bedroom. He went to the armoire, pulled it out from the wall, and reached behind it for a large package.

His pleased grin set her heart to pounding. He led her to the bed, set the package at her side, and grinned at her wide-eyed reaction. "I have no designs on that luscious body," he claimed virtuously, then spoiled the effect by leering at her outrageously. "For the present," he amended with a wink. Leanna reddened and looked down at the package, missing the tender look in his eyes as he enjoyed her confusion.

She opened it slowly, almost warily. Her fingers dug under several layers of paper to reach the soft, gray velvet of a habit. Leanna gasped at its elegance. She held the jacket up to her, entranced at its unusual design. The cuffs and breast of the coat were ornamented with carved silver buttons that repeated the design on the saddle. Black braid banded the neck and jacket lapels.

A lacy white blouse appeared next. It frothed at the neck with ruffles that would cascade over the front of the coat when worn under it. The skirt was unlike any Leanna had seen. It was slimly cut and seamed down the middle so she could ride astride. Tall black leather boots and quirt were decorated with the same silver relief as the saddle. The hat was a wide-brimmed cordovan with a braided silver and black leather strap.

Leanna looked ready to burst into tears again, so Jason hastily clasped her at the waist and whirled her in the air, spinning her around until she was dizzy. Gasping for breath, he collapsed onto the bed, then tickled her unmercifully until she dissolved into helpless laughter. Finally, he stopped, hugged her, and drew her to her feet.

"Try the habit on for me, please?"

How could she refuse? Her eyes soft with love, Leanna complied. Jason played lady's maid, helping her with the in-numerable buttons and hooks that comprised feminine modesty. His gaze grew warmer as Leanna's skin became barer. When she was stripped to chemise and stockings, he couldn't resist kissing the velvety skin revealed at the low-cut bodice.

Leanna flinched as though stung and pulled on the habit. When she was attired, Jason ambled around her, examining her impressive figure's every curve. She looked heartbreakingly beautiful and aristocratic in the expensive habit. The hat lent a mysterious air to her green eyes, the shadowing preventing him from reading her expression as she looked at him intently.

He stepped closer and pushed back the brim until he could look into the dark green depths. Leanna was walking a dangerous tightrope between the desire to express her love and her urge for caution. Jason's sultry eyes were pulling her closer and her caution was teetering when a knock at the door shattered their growing intimacy.

Jason groaned and cursed. She had been close to admitting the love he so needed and longed to hear, but when the knock intruded, she straightened like a puppet coming to life and pulled away with obvious relief. Struggling to regain her breath, as though she had just come out of a drug-induced torpor, she pulled the hat off and called for entrance.

Sarah looked distressed when she saw Jason's frustrated expression and Leanna's relief. It was apparent she had interrupted something. She gave Jason a repentant look before offering Leanna a small package. "A little something from Quincy and me," Sarah smiled. She watched almost shyly as Leanna opened it.

A lovely, rainbow-hued woolen shawl was revealed, touching her almost beyond words. She kissed Sarah's cheek softly. "It's lovely, Sarah. Did Quincy help loom the wool?" At Sarah's nod, Leanna added, "I will thank him myself when I see him, but please convey my gratitude in the meantime. Thank you both so much."

With a last apologetic look at Jason, Sarah left the room. Leanna ignored Jason as she sat down on the bed to remove the boots. When she lifted her eyebrows at him expressively, as though questioning why he still remained, Jason almost snarled in frustration. Without a word he wheeled and headed for the door.

Leanna called after him, after fitting her guard into place. "Thank you again for the gifts, Jason. Everything is beautiful and I am most grateful." Jason gave a curt nod and retreated, shutting the door behind him with an eloquent bang.

Leanna curled into a ball on the bed and rested her chin on her arms. While Jason's gift showed understanding and concern for her, he had made it clear he still wanted her emotional submission, now that he had dominated her physically. Leanna closed her eyes. She was unutterably weary and depressed. No matter the path or byway, her thoughts always reached the same distasteful end: Jason did not, and probably never would, love her. She would not be a burden or unwanted responsibility, to be discarded at will. She would be the center of his existence, as he was hers, or she would be nothing. The hot tears flooded down her cheeks. She admitted nothing had changed, despite the thoughtfulness of his gift. She had no option but to leave. Exhausted and despairing, she struggled to sleep.

By the time Leanna had to get ready for the party, she had made preparations for her departure. Jason supervised the outdoor dance floor and helped set up the banquet tables on the lawn while Thomas assisted Sarah with last-minute indoor decorations. Leanna was relieved when her timidly offered help was refused. "Just rest in your room, child," Thomas ordered. "This day is for your enjoyment."

So Leanna was able to steal into the study and take the bag of gold from the desk. Her heart racing, she peeked out the door, then scurried up to her room when she saw the hall empty. There she packed her smallest case hastily with the bare minimum: lingerie and a simple morning dress. She would wear her new habit because she could ride faster while astride. She added the bag of gold to the case, then secreted the small portmanteau under the bed.

By the time Leanna was ready for the party, the air outside was thick with humidity and above the brightly-lit dance floor black clouds amassed slowly. Jason cast them a worried look before going inside to dress.

Leanna examined her exquisite form with detached eyes. The gossamer green silk clung to her seductively, while the low-cut bodice revealed a daring expanse of her bosom. The emeralds draping her throat, ears, and wrists echoed the glitter of her eyes.

Jason stood, a silent admirer, then walked forward to gently kiss the velvety mole just visible on her shoulder. "You are exquisite, my darling. I've never seen you looking lovelier." When he swiveled her around into an embrace, she stepped lightly away, her gown floating around graceful limbs as she moved. She smiled at him brightly. Her cheeks were flushed a brilliant rose that matched the color of her lips.

"Shall we go down, Jason?" To divert his suspicions, she grinned and tossed him a flirtatious look over her shoulder as she moved to the door. Reluctantly, he ignored the pounding of his heart and followed her.

Leanna peeped at him from under her long lashes as he took her arm and led her down the stairs. His green velvet jacket had been deliberately selected to complement her gown. His wide lapels were of the same silk as her dress. He had tied his white cravat simply and had pinned a small emerald in the snowy folds. His knee breeches were of white satin.

Leanna looked quickly away from him. His masculine beauty sent such a shaft of pain through her heart that she stumbled clumsily near the top of the stairs. Jason snatched her to him, and for an instant her guard slipped at the sting of his touch. She stared at him with barren agony in her eyes. His voice sharp with concern, he barked, "Are you hurt?"

Leanna quickly pulled away and took a deep breath to compose herself. Her eyes again unfathomable, she smiled at him. "I'm fine. Thank you; you saved me from a nasty tumble." She ignored his searching look and descended the stairwell to the hall.

Thomas smiled proudly when he saw her. He kissed her hand, then drew her into the study for a fortifying glass of sherry. Leanna didn't hear his compliments, nor did she notice the stunned looks of the guests when they saw her beauty for the first time. Most of that long, painful evening passed in a merciful haze that was assisted by the innumerable glasses of champagne she drank.

The sea of faces, the smiles and congratulations barely penetrated her consciousness. Even Rian's jovial greeting, unusually elegant figure, and flirtatious conversation failed to reach her. Vaguely Leanna sensed she must be making the right responses because the people opposite smiled at her with approval.

The only reality through the laughing, dancing, and drinking was Jason's protective figure. She felt enveloped in a warm world where his scent, his feel, and his caressing gaze shielded her from the unpleasant future. She forgot all but the piercing pleasure of being held in his arms when they opened the dancing with a waltz. Leanna held back nothing in the poignancy of that moment. She met his smoldering gaze with equal ardor, making his heart race.

When the dance ended, Leanna followed him almost absently to meet some late arrivals. She paid little attention to the introductions until an uncomfortable note in Jason's voice as he introduced a seductive redhead alerted her.

Her name was Vivian, her hair was luxuriously auburn, and her figure was voluptuous in clinging gold silk. Leanna met her pale blue eyes and froze at the spite directed at her. She looked from the woman to Jason, who stared stonily ahead, then back to the woman. Vivian smiled in a way that confirmed Leanna's suspicions. When Jason hurried her away, Leanna's last doubt was removed. She knew with a dull certainty that she had met her replacement.

Her warm cocoon became suffocating as reality once more intruded. Jason found his formerly receptive partner stiff in his arms.

"Leanna, are you ill? What's wrong?" he asked anxiously. Her face was pale and beaded with sweat, and she looked ready to faint.

Her reply was hoarse. "I feel slightly dizzy. May we please sit down?" He cradled her to him in a protective hold and led her to a chair off the dance floor.

"Sit here while I get you something to eat," he said gently.

Leanna nodded stiffly, then veiled her clenched hands in her lap. His tender concern seemed false when he had all but flaunted his mistress in her face. It took every ounce of control she possessed to pretend all was well and to remain seated. She longed to scream her anguish and sense of betrayal. She shivered despite the oppressive humidity. Her emotions were so chaotic she was almost hysterical, so it was some time before the murmured conversation penetrated her dull senses.

Since her back faced the tall shrubs outside the house, she didn't see the malevolent look thrown her way. Vivian confided to her frizzy blonde friend, "What a child! How does an innocent like her ever expect to hold a virile man like Jason Blaine?" Jason's name fully alerted Leanna, and she strained now to hear the remaining conversation. She turned her head to see who was talking. The two figures were shadowed by the bushes, but she could see that one of them had auburn hair.

"I am certain he's bored with the little chit already. Why, he confessed as much to me only the other day." The woman's voice mellowed into a deep, rich purr of anticipation. "In fact, we're to meet this very evening. I understand there's an old cabin on the edge of Whispering Oaks that's perfect for an intimate little tryst." Her voice grew throaty with genuine longing. "My dear, I can hardly wait. I've never known a lover as skilled as Jason Blaine."

The throb in Vivian's voice was utterly repulsive. Leanna had felt a similar longing too often not to recognize the hunger of desire. Leanna's last, faint glimmer of hope was extinguished. She leaped to her feet and ran, oblivious to the malicious pale blue eyes that watched her fleeing figure with satisfaction.

When she reached the sanctuary of her room, she buried her head in her pillow. Her anguish was not in the slightest lessened by the harsh sobs that rent through her slender frame. If she had harbored a tiny, valiant hope that Jason's tenderness today was the result of genuine affection for her, it was snuffed out by Vivian's words. "In fact, we're to meet this very evening ... an old cabin ... perfect for an intimate little tryst ..."

The mere idea that Jason could besmirch the place where they had been so happy with that auburn-haired witch revolted Leanna's every nerve. Her frantic feelings climaxed into a realization that Jason would never change. The bitterness ran too deep for her to reach him. Thomas was wrong.

Paradoxically, with this final certainty, a sense of release engulfed her and her tenacious spirit relinquished its last hold on Jason. A deep, unnatural calm descended on her as she realized she could do nothing but leave him and seek a better future. Somehow, she would forget him.

Leanna stopped sobbing. She wiped her tears and bathed her face. She felt only thankful that after this evening she would never see him again.

Calmly, she went back down and played her part until the guests at last began departing. She responded easily to Jason's worried inquiry. "I needed to make a small repair to my coiffure. I'm not hungry, and I'm fine now."

The only crack in her composure came when Vivian approached to say goodnight. Leanna refused to meet her eyes, so she didn't see the woman's triumphant gleam when she searched Leanna's pale face. Vivian deliberately held Jason's hand a fraction too long. "Until later," she whispered loud enough for Leanna to hear.

Leanna stared straight ahead with her face frozen into an expression of politeness, so she didn't see Jason's perplexed look as he ushered Vivian out the door with a sigh of relief.

When all the guests were gone, Thomas and Jason gratefully loosened their cravats and slumped into chairs in the study. Thomas smiled at Leanna tiredly. "I hope you enjoyed your party, child."

Leanna returned a strained smile, but she didn't reply. Thomas's half-closed eyes sharpened.

"I'd like to speak with you, Leanna, if you're not too tired. I have something of import to discuss with you." Leanna rose from her seat by the fire and kissed Thomas's cheek.

"In the morning, Grandfather?" she asked huskily. "I am bone weary." The room was shadowed, so neither man noticed the moist sheen covering Leanna's eyes when she kissed her grandfather's creased brown cheek.

Thomas smiled at her with understanding when she finally straightened. "Certainly, child. It can wait. Sleep well."

Leanna moved to the door. When she turned with her hand on the knob, she looked at Jason for a long time. Her green eyes were shadowed and unfathomable. "I want to sleep in the south bedroom this evening, Jason," she finally said quietly.

Jason's brow darkened, but she forestalled his protest. "Only for this evening. I need privacy tonight. Tomorrow . . . well, tomorrow it won't matter."

Jason opened his mouth to refuse, but Thomas held his arm. "Let her rest, boy," he mouthed.

Jason nodded shortly. "Very well, Leanna, but only for tonight. And tomorrow, we must have a long talk."

Leanna didn't reply. She looked at him a moment longer. She seemed to examine him from head to toe as though imprinting him on her memory, then she opened the door. "Goodnight, Jason," she whispered almost inaudibly, then the door closed softly behind her and she was gone.

Both men sat quietly after she left. Each felt an inexplicable but disturbing uneasiness. She had been so quiet and subdued, Jason thought, as though her spirit had been snuffed. He shook off the fancy. Ridiculous. She was just tired. His tight mouth softened as he remembered the look in her eyes while they danced. Soon, she would admit she loved him. The last barrier between them would be gone, and their marriage could be as happy as Thomas's had been.

He longed for Leanna's love more than he had ever wanted anything in his life. In the quiet of that moment, he at last admitted to himself that she had found her way into his heart. Strangely, he felt no distress at his new vulnerability. He could not quite force himself to name this new, warm feeling; he only knew Leanna was as essential to his existence as the air he breathed. Her well-being and happiness were of paramount importance, and he would do whatever was necessary to keep her with him.

Thomas's angry mutterings finally distracted Jason from his thoughts. Suddenly buoyant, Jason focused on the older man and teased, "More problems with the accounts, Grandfather?"

Thomas grunted an assent, then he gestured at a stack of letters on the edge of the desk. "I almost forgot, Jason. The post from England arrived today, and I believe there's a letter for you."

Jason reached for the pile, then he withdrew the one addressed to him. He read at first desultorily, then rapidly, his eyes sharp with concern as he read on, then cursed. Thomas interrupted his mumbling to demand, "Well? What is it?"

Jason finished the letter quickly, then clutched the missive in a balled hand. "The bastard. If Sherry dies..." He looked at Thomas's puzzled face. "That dog Redfern I told you about has shot Sherry. His fiancée is not sure he will live. She warns me Redfern sailed for Boston and will probably sail down the coast to Georgia next."

Thomas slammed his account book shut. "Boston, eh?" he finally said, his nails drumming softly on the desk.

Jason threw him an angry look. "Yes, Boston. What possible difference can that make?"

"None, lad, none." Thomas took a breath and ordered, "You are not to go anywhere alone until this rascal is found. If he's stepped so far out of the bounds of the law once, he'll do so again. This time, he must be caught. Until that time, you must take precautions."

When Jason began to examine his elegant boots and didn't respond, Thomas hardened his voice. "Understood, Grandson?" Jason nodded shortly, then bolted to his feet.

"I believe I will retire also, Grandfather. Goodnight." Thomas nodded, then sat motionless for a long while, watching the dying fire. Finally, he pulled some heavy writing paper from the desk and began to write.

Leanna locked her door after she had fetched her habit and portmanteau from the other room. She stripped to her chemise and climbed between the sheets to get a few hours' rest in preparation for her journey. She had decided to go to Charleston and rest there while she calculated her next move. Savannah was too close, and unless she could obtain a berth immediately, she would be found before she could depart. She had no doubt Jason would look for her. His pride would be hurt, if nothing else.

She would need Rian's help and would have to ride to the handsome man's cabin to seek it. She didn't know whether to ask for his help in escorting her from there or not. She would have to wait and see.

Leanna shut her eyes, courting sleep fiercely. She refused to let her traitorous mind picture Jason as she had last seen him: relaxed, handsome, and heartbreakingly dear to her, despite everything. Her bruised emotions had so drained her that she soon fell into a restless sleep that at least offered some relief from her anguish.

The sound of thunder startled her awake several hours later. She still felt exhausted, but she forced her leaden legs out of bed. She attired herself in the new habit, her movements calm and deliberate. Grabbing her bag, she draped her heavy velvet cloak over her shoulder, then pressed her ear against the door to listen.

Except for the wind's roar, she heard nothing. She eased out the door and crept down the stairs on stockinged feet. She didn't put on the boots she carried until she reached the front porch.

Outside, the air was oppressive and the storm was in full force. The ancient oaks groaned and swayed under the cruel force of the wind. When Leanna left the shelter of the porch, she was almost blown off her feet. She lowered her head and pushed doggedly toward the stables. She never considered waiting until the next evening. Her instinct for escape was so strong, any doubt was drowned out.

She was gasping for breath when she reached the haven of the stables. With difficulty, she saddled the nervous mare, who had been frightened by the repeated booms of thunder. Leanna had to give her a lump of sugar to quiet her down. When she was ready, with her portmanteau and a small sack of victuals strapped over the mare's hindquarters, she led Morning Mist to a nearby stall and climbed into the saddle.

She blew out the lantern, then spurred the reluctant horse into the fury of the wind. For the first time, Leanna had to use her quirt on the frightened mare to get her to move. When Morning Mist finally moved into a canter, Leanna had no difficulty urging her faster. Footing was treacherous on the muddy road, but with the wind at their back, they made some progress.

Leanna scarcely felt the slash of wind-driven rain. With every mile she traveled, she felt the blood draining further from her heart. Despair and unhappiness ate at her like acid. She was so upset she almost missed the turn to Rian's cabin on the road to Charleston.

When she took the fork toward Charleston, the wind changed until it battered them head-on. The mare strove on until three brilliant flashes of lightning were followed by ear-splitting rolls of thunder. The gray shied in fright, jolting Leanna out of her daze. She bowed low over the mare's neck and soothed her in a low voice. It seemed to be working until a large tree was struck by a savage bolt of lightning. The aged giant fell with a loud groan and a crash that made the earth under them vibrate.

The mare whinnied in terror and reared. Leanna held on easily, her years in the saddle standing her in good stead. But when Morning Mist clamped her bit and ran toward the road's edge, then into the forest, Leanna didn't have the strength to curb her. All she could do was hang on and duck her head under the swooping branches.

She pulled repeatedly at the reins, to no avail. When her hat blew off, her hair soon came loose and was tossed about by the wind. Leanna was blinded and never saw the branch that smashed across her forehead. Nor did she feel the jolting force that reverberated through her body when she crumpled to the ground. She lay there lifelessly, pelted by stinging bullets of torrential rain, unaware of the blood slowly spreading in a widening pool beneath her.

Chapter Twenty

JASON TOSSED AND turned in his lonely bed. He missed Leanna's soft, warm body against him. He finally sighed and pulled on his dressing gown, then went outside to the veranda. The violent wind and rain increased his unease, for he could not shake a sense of impending disaster. He shifted from one bare foot to the other, breathing in the rain-scented gale to calm his overactive imagination.

"Leanna," his lips formed. He could not dismiss the haunting image of her hurt green eyes as he had last seen her. His unease increased when he remembered her unusual moodiness during the party. She had vacillated between gaiety and an almost eerie calm. She had seemed eager to please him until the end of the party, when she became remote and disturbingly quiet. Jason paced the room, his fear that Leanna was in danger growing stronger. He tried to dismiss his unease and give Leanna the privacy she asked for, but finally, with a muffled curse, he acknowledged defeat and went determinedly to the door.

She would surely be asleep by now, so it wouldn't hurt to peek in on her. He would never rest until he assured himself of her safety. He eased her door open, then walked to the edge of her bed. His eyes widened in stunned disbelief. He yanked the huddled covers back, refusing to believe his eyes. He stood frozen with anguish before the empty bed. It seemed evidence that he had driven her away.

His thudding heart broke the spell. He ran to his room and threw on the first clothes at hand, unaware and uncaring that he would ruin his magnificent evening attire. He grabbed a blanket and heavy cloak, then rushed down the hall to Thomas's room.

He shook his grandfather's shoulder urgently. Thomas groaned, but he raised slitted eyes to him. He came awake instantly at the white, agonized look on Jason's face. "What's wrong?" he exclaimed.

Jason had to clear his throat before he could force the words out. "She's gone. I'm going to look for her. Rouse the servants and send them along as soon as possible." The last words were yelled over his back as he hurried to the door.

Thomas jumped out of bed and dressed hastily, his movements jerky with urgency. He inwardly cursed his own stupidity for not reading Leanna's earlier behavior. With a muttered prayer, he rushed toward the servants' quarters.

A quick glance in Morning Mist's stall confirmed Jason's certainty that Leanna had set out on horseback. For a moment a rush of anger inundated him. What possessed the chit to set out on such a night? His fingers fumbled with haste as he saddled Night Wind. He swallowed and tried to dampen his powerful emotions.

Jason used his quirt on Night Wind mercilessly. For the first time the fleet-hooved stallion seemed to creep along at a snail's pace. When he finally arrived at the cross in the road between Savannah and Charleston, he reined the panting horse to a stop. He was oblivious to the cutting wind as he surveyed the scene. Unless he took the right fork, he might be too late to save her. He clenched the reins in his fists and forced himself to reflect carefully. Unless she had slipped into Savannah without his knowledge to book advance passage, she had probably gone to Charleston. Cursing the rivulets of water that obscured all tracks in the sodden road, he plunged Night Wind on the trail to Charleston and prayed his intuition had been right.

Jason had not ridden far along the trail when a terrified, pain-filled whinny came to his ears. He yanked the stallion to a halt and listened tensely. There it was again, off to the right among some trees. He picked his way cautiously through the treacherous forest, ducking his head to avoid the reaching arms of thick tree branches tossed about by the wind.

He narrowed his eyes and followed the agonized sounds until he spied a vague form ahead. It was Morning Mist and she whinnied again. Night Wind answered. She struggled weakly to rise to her feet, but then collapsed in pain. Jason tied Night Wind to a tree, then he examined the riderless mare. The pleading look in her soft brown eyes when he felt her hind leg indicated her affliction. It was snapped almost in two, and her velvet hide was covered with welts and scratches. She had apparently run wild with terror through the forest. His mouth dry with dread, he pulled out his pistol and with a quick, clean shot, Jason put the lovely mare out of her misery.

Then, urgently, he remounted and guided Night Wind through the forest, calling at the top of his lungs, "Leanna! Leanna, please answer!" He was thankful that the storm had at last spent its fury and the wind and rain had died to a whisper. Jason searched in a widening circle around where he had found the mare. Hours seemed to pass. He was almost demented with despair when noises near the river chilled his blood.

He recognized the fiendish sounds of two wolverines in battle and galloped in the direction of the noise, heedless now of the trees. He was both relieved and terrified to see Leanna huddled on the ground in a small clearing. He leaped out of the saddle and ran to her still figure. His throat closed in horror when he saw the dark pool of blood under her skirt. He breathed a heartfelt prayer of thanks that he had found her before one of the vicious animals emerged victorious and claimed its prize. The smell of her blood must have drawn them.

Jason quickly disposed of the wolverines, then he turned to

her gently. He slit her skirt with his knife and lifted her chemise. He was perplexed when he could discover no wound. The blood seemed to be coming from within her.

A pain-filled moan broke from his lips as he realized why she had been sick of late. She was miscarrying their child. Jason lifted her as gently as possible into the saddle, then climbed up behind her. He wrapped her in the heavy blanket he had shielded behind his cloak and cradled her crosswise in his arms.

He forced himself to keep Night Wind to a steady, smooth course, even though his nerves screamed for him to hurry. She was still bleeding. He could feel the warm, sticky stuff soak through the blanket. He clutched her to him and buried his face in her drenched hair. His tears mingled with the rain and streamed down his cheeks. He had never felt so helpless in his life. Even his boyhood anguish at losing his mother paled beside what wrenched him now.

He whispered her name over and over under his breath, pleading for her forgiveness. He no longer tried to deny the love he had struggled to evade for so long. He raged at himself, so full of guilt and remorse he barely saw the plantation out-buildings coming into sight. How could he have been so cruel? He had known long ago his life was meaningless without Leanna, but he had been too arrogant and demanding to admit it. If she died now because of his stupidity, he could never forgive himself.

The shouts of the servants as they saw them coming pulled Jason out of his miserable condemnation. He dismounted and carefully lowered Leanna into his arms. He carried her into the house. When Sarah rushed forward, he choked, "She's losing the baby. Do something Sarah, I beg you! Don't let her die!" The look in Jason's eyes reminded Sarah of a trapped, helpless animal as it awaited death—doubly shocking on such a normally confident, arrogant face.

"Carry her to her room," she commanded gently, pushing him up the stairs. She ran back to the kitchen and fetched hot water, laudanum, and herbs. When she hurried upstairs she found Jason waiting tensely at the side of the bed, his eyes glazed as he looked at Leanna's pale face. Sarah stripped Leanna and sponged the blood away, then she spread a foul-smelling mixture she had concocted on a clean rag and strapped it against Leanna. All the while, Jason stood like a stone statue, never taking his eyes from Leanna's face.

When Thomas came back from searching for Leanna, he sagged with relief when he heard Jason had found her. He was saddened to hear she was miscarrying. He leaped up the stairs in time to witness Sarah covering Leanna warmly after she had dressed her in a thick flannel gown. Sarah shot him a relieved look when he entered, then she threw a significant glance at Jason. Thomas nodded and tapped Jason's arm.

"Come, lad," he ordered calmly. "You can do nothing further. Leanna is a strong girl. She will recover, don't you worry." He literally dragged Jason from the room. He forced him into a chair in the study, then poured him a hefty shot of brandy. Jason clutched the glass tightly, his eyes blank and fixed straight ahead.

Thomas took a reviving sip of his own brandy, then coaxed, "Come, lad, don't take on so. You'll be able to have other children."

Jason looked at him and the depth of despair and pain in the dark blue eyes made Thomas catch his breath. Jason shuddered, then buried his head in his hands. The brandy snifter fell to the carpet and spilled its contents, but neither man noticed. Thomas had to strain to hear the muffled, disjointed words Jason was crying. "It's not the child. Don't you see? It's all my fault. If I hadn't driven her away, none of this would have happened." He shuddered, then looked at Thomas with pure terror in his eyes. "What if she dies? I love her more than my life, Grandfather. If she dies, she'll take my will to live with her."

"Nonsense!" Thomas reproved. "Leanna would not thank you for this maudlin guilt. She will not die. Sarah is most experienced in this kind of thing. You know her skill with herbs." His voice softened. "Besides, you must be strong, for Leanna's sake. She will need comforting when she recovers, and your own fear and guilt will do her no good."

Thomas rose to grasp Jason's shoulder. "I'm glad you finally admitted you love her. Those words will be more of a curative to Leanna than any potion Sarah can devise."

Jason's eyes flickered with a returning spark of vitality. "Do you really think she loves me, Grandfather?"

Thomas smiled. "I know she does."

Jason leaned back in his chair, somewhat comforted. He had almost lost Leanna, but due to the grace of God, he would be given a chance to give her the happiness she deserved. He vowed he would devote himself to that cause.

When Sarah at last came down, she found Jason still white, but he was more composed and impatient for news. "Well?" he demanded.

"She will recover, but she has lost the baby." She watched with compassionate eyes when Jason lowered his head and heaved a sigh of relief and sorrow. He leaped to his feet and started to rush up the stairs, but Sarah's voice was imperative. "Wait!"

He turned back impatiently. Sarah's eyes were gentle. "Leanna has lost a great deal of blood, and she is weak and distraught. It might be better if you wait to see her until she has slept for a while. I've given her some laudanum, and it will take effect soon."

Jason hesitated, but he was desperate to reassure himself of Leanna's safety. "Just for a minute, Sarah?" he pleaded.

Sarah bit her lip, then sighed and nodded reluctantly. "Very well, Jason. But just for a moment, mind."

As Jason took the stairs three at a time, she looked at Thomas with deep concern. "When the pains were tearing at Leanna, I asked her if she wanted me to send for Jason. She looked at me with a bitterness I have never seen and replied, 'Why? He doesn't care what happens to me. No, I don't want to see him.' And she gritted her teeth at the pain and refused even the touch of my hand."

Thomas frowned as he listened. His lined face was drawn with weariness and worry. "We must hope her bitterness is the result of losing the baby. Surely when she fully recovers, she will realize how much we all love and need her? Especially as

Jason has at last admitted he loves her?"

Sarah's eyes were cloudy as she recalled the look of almost hatred in Leanna's eyes and the girl's total withdrawal. "I hope so, Thomas," she responded slowly. "I hope so."

Upstairs, Jason pried the door open, shut it behind him, and walked, soft-footed, to the bed. Leanna had her face turned away, so he whispered very quietly, "Leanna?" He didn't want to wake her if she slept. His eyes noted a slight tensing of her body, so he knew she was awake. But she didn't respond. He sat down next to her and clasped her hand.

It lay pale and limp in his strong brown palm. He caressed her tenderly, his eyes shining with love and remorse. "I regret more than I can ever say that we lost the child." His voice deepened to a rasping whisper. "Please forgive me, Leanna. I have loved you for an age, but I was too stubborn and frightened to admit it."

When she still didn't respond, he said sharply, "Leanna! Are you all right?" He turned her to face him with a gentle but insistent hand and she at last looked at him. He was shocked at the scorn and rejection glaring from her virulent green eyes.

Her voice was low, but the harsh contempt in it sent chills up his spine. "I thought you could do little else to insult me, but I was wrong. Do you honestly think I want or need to hear your insincere protestations of love to salve your guilt?" She lifted her head slightly from the pillow to emphasize her next words. He shrank from the piercing look she cast him. "Make no mistake. You killed my child as surely as if you had personally wrenched it from my body. I ran from your cruelty and indifference to shield *my child* from your heartless influence. You have taken the last thing I value!" Her voice became more tortured with each syllable.

When she cried, "Get out! You disgust me! I never want to see you again!" Jason backed away from her on leaden feet. The anguish in her voice matched the anguish in his eyes. Sarah and Thomas heard Leanna's raised voice and rushed upstairs to take in the distressing scene. Thomas hustled Jason down the stairs and Sarah tried to draw Leanna into her arms.

Leanna shrank away, almost frightened. Sarah looked at her

with such sweet compassion that Leanna's throat closed and for an instant she almost threw herself into the housekeeper's comforting arms. She crushed the impulse ruthlessly and reminded herself of the vow she had made when she could no longer deny she was losing the baby. In the midst of her pain, she swore she would never again give her affection to another living creature. She might lose all chance at happiness, but neither would she experience the excruciating pain and sorrow she had lived through in the last few years. Her need for love had brought her nothing but grief, so she would smother these impulses until they died and she could find peace.

In her anguish, it didn't occur to Leanna that she was responding with the same bitterness she had so condemned in Jason. Ignoring Sarah, Leanna buried her head in her pillow and mercifully drifted off to sleep as the drug took effect.

Sarah stroked the soft blond curls, pain and sadness in her dark eyes. She blew out the wall sconces, leaving only a candle by the bed burning. She trailed with tired steps down the stairs. Leanna's grief filled her own heart.

Thomas was sitting next to Jason, clasping him by the shoulders as he spoke forcefully. "It's an extremely anguishing experience for a woman to lose a baby, Jason. You must be patient with her. As her body heals, so will her mind. A woman who loves as Leanna loves you cannot dismiss the feeling so easily, no matter what the cause."

Thomas's words failed to reach Jason. He stared fixedly over his grandfather's shoulder, his dilated eyes seeing nothing but the twisted look on Leanna's face when she shouted, "You disgust me! I never want to see you again!" Thomas became alarmed at the look on Jason's face and shook him impatiently.

Jason's dazed eyes focused on Thomas who had at last penetrated his trance. The concerned look on his grandfather's face let loose the torrent inside and he collapsed into sobs on Thomas's shoulder for the first time since he was a boy. Thomas sighed heavily and rocked him back and forth, cradling him close as though he were a child.

After a brief bout of weeping, Jason pulled away, wiped a handkerchief over his eyes, and blew his nose fiercely. Then he straightened his shoulders with resolve. The unusual release of tears had reasserted his usual determination.

"Well, by God, she hasn't heard the last of this. She loved me once, and she'll do so again." His mouth quivered a moment. "I will give her another child, and this time she'll be cherished and protected until she thinks I'm smothering her."

Thomas was relieved at the fierce look on Jason's face. Perhaps all would be right yet. He had never met anyone stronger than Jason in a test of wills when that arrogant, determined look appeared in his grandson's eyes. He swallowed as he remembered seeing a similar look on Leanna's face. It would be a long, bitter fight.

For days, Leanna lethargically did as she was told, eating and sleeping when commanded. Her physical wounds slowly healed, but the agony in her mind did not diminish. She had not realized until she had lost it how much she had wanted Jason's child. If the tragedy had come at a different time, or if she had felt less unwanted by Jason after discovering his tryst with Vivian, she might have been able to cope with the shock. It was bitterly ironic that she had at last accepted defeat and given up all hope of winning him only to have him confess the love she had striven for, longed for. The belief that his avowal of love was false, made only to absolve his guilt, compounded her bitterness tenfold. That her rejection of her husband caused Leanna almost as much misery as it did Jason, she did not consider.

Jason waited almost a week before attempting to see her again. It was spring planting time, so Thomas gave him plenty of work to keep him busy. Jason was so exhausted at night that even his nagging guilt could not keep him awake. However, his slumber was haunted by dreams, so he did not wake rested. He lost weight and his handsome, virile face became drawn and strained.

He at last decided he had given Leanna long enough to recover. He was anxious as he climbed the stairs to her room. His forceful nature did not tolerate uncertainty well. He realized he had a long, wearying fight ahead of him, but anything was better than this damnable doubt.

Sukey was brushing Leanna's long hair when he entered. He stopped to stare at the picture she made with her hair flowing down her back and her smooth flesh gleaming through her thin gown. Leanna sensed rather than heard his presence, and the sad look on her face was immediately wiped clean. She met his searching look calmly. Her eyes were not bitter, they were not condemning. They didn't spit rage or disdain. Worse, they expressed absolutely nothing. She might have been looking at an inanimate bedpost, for all the interest her eyes bespoke.

A shaft of pain pierced Jason, but he gritted his teeth and said as pleasantly as possible, "I wanted to see how you were doing, my dear. Is there anything you need?"

She shook her head, her eyes staring through him. He tried again. "You are looking well. Perhaps you would like to ride with me one day soon, when you are better?"

That caught her attention. Her eyes narrowed on him with glittering dislike. "How can I ride? You murdered my horse." Even Sukey gasped at the unfairness of this accusation. Jason dismissed the maid with an imperative gesture. She went with relief, glad to escape what she sensed would be a bitter argument.

Jason returned Leanna's glance with a dangerous look of his own. He forced patience upon himself. "I had no alternative but to shoot Morning Mist, Leanna. She was in a great deal of pain. You wouldn't want her to suffer, would you?"

She looked away under his direct gaze, but she bit her lip to avoid screaming at him; "No, it's you I want to suffer! Why won't you leave me in peace?" But she merely knotted a tassel on the bed hangings and kept silent.

Jason's voice hardened. "Leanna, what do you want me to do? Plead with you on my knees? I can't bring the child back, though I swear I would give my own life if I could." There was such anguished sincerity in his voice that Leanna's eyes slowly, reluctantly, lifted to meet his. The painful earnestness in his eyes convinced her.

He may have wanted the child as much as she. But that did not excuse his abominable behavior and cruelty. Her heart hardened again, and she returned to her perusal of the bed hangings, her face once more remote. A violent wave of frustration overcame Jason. He longed to shake her until her teeth rattled, but he refused to give her the satisfaction of knowing how her indifference hurt him.

He released his pent-up breath slowly through clenched teeth, forcing his body to relax by sheer effort. "Very well, Leanna. I will leave. But I will be back." He walked inexorably to the bed. He was aware that Leanna had stiffened with alarm. He grasped her firmly by the shoulders and said, "And I want to leave you with something to think about." He lowered his face, and she struggled in panic when she realized he was going to kiss her. She turned her head and his warm lips brushed her cheek, but even so, the contact jolted through her like lightning.

Jason whispered in her ear, "Remember that I love you. I will not let you hold yourself from me if I have to fight you until we are both gray with age." Leanna closed her eyes in mingled fear and pain. Her barricaded heart fluttered briefly with hope, but stilled when panic overcame her. He was lying, despite the seeming sincerity in his voice. She must remember his cruelty and his tryst at their cabin. She could picture Vivian's triumphant face.

Jason released her, then he gave her a gentle, sad smile as he realized she was still closed against him. He cast her a lingering look, then strode to the door and closed it softly behind him.

Leanna clutched the pillow to her fiercely. She shut her eyes and clenched her teeth in an effort to forget the ringing sincerity in his voice and the earnestness shining in his eyes when he said, "I love you." The cherished words surfaced again and again until she buried her head under the pillow to stifle their echo.

Sarah and Thomas had no better luck coaxing Leanna. Sarah's gentle inquiries were met with a stony, guarded look. "It's no comfort to tell me I can have other children, Sarah. I doubt I shall ever again let a man close enough to get me with child. If I do conceive, it will certainly not be with Jason." The grim certainty in her voice made Sarah despair, and when she confided the conversation to Thomas, there were tears in her eyes.

Thomas tried to soothe her. "She doesn't mean it, Sarah. Her bitterness will fade with time. Jason will reach her eventually." He sounded so confident that Sarah was comforted, but when she left, the worried look that had marred Thomas's handsome countenance of late returned. With a grim mouth, he decided it was time he talked to Leanna himself.

Leanna was out on the veranda, fully dressed, watching the river. She was still pale, but her skin was smooth and her hair its normal shining self. Spring had gently arrived. The luscious scents of magnolia, dogwood, and greenery permeated the air. Thomas watched Leanna sniff the air and bask in the sunshine, and he smiled. No one so receptive to the intoxication of nature's scents and sensations could withdraw herself from life forever. He began to believe his earlier words to Sarah, so his smile was genuine when he went out to meet her.

He had visited her several times a day since her illness, and she was always polite, but remote. The vivacious spirit that had reminded him so of Jenny seemed snuffed forever. Today was the first time he had seen even a glimmer of her former self. Leanna tensed at the sound of footsteps, then sighed with relief when she saw it was Thomas.

She relaxed against her chair and nodded. "Good morning, Grandfather."

"And good morning to you, my dear. I apprehend you're feeling beter today?" His gently knowing look disconcerted her.

She looked back toward the river, replying colorlessly, "Indeed, I am well. Was there something in particular you wished to discuss with me?"

Thomas's optimism faded a little as she seemed to withdraw into herself. The gentle approach hadn't been effective, so he decided he would poke and prod until he angered her, if necessary. "Yes, my dear, there was something I wanted to discuss with you," he said.

Leanna stiffened, her defenses alerted at the tone of his voice. She slowly turned her head to watch him when he began, "First, I want you to know I grieve deeply for the loss of my great-grandchild." Mindful of Sarah's failure, he made no mention of the fact that she and Jason could have another child, though he longed to do so. "Your life is even more precious to me, my dear, and it concerns me to see you so unlike yourself."

Leanna could no longer hold his gaze when such tenderness shone from his warm blue eyes. To maintain her composure, she clasped her hands in her lap and stared at her interlocked fingers.

He was silent for a time, then he probed gently, "Leanna, do you remember a conversation we had not so long ago, when I told you how much I longed for a grandchild?" At her guarded nod, he went on, "You may also remember we discussed something else that day."

Leanna doggedly persisted in evading his eagle-sharp eyes, but she couldn't block his words. "You were afraid Jason would never love you, and I disagreed. I told you it was just a matter of time until his pride could no longer stand before the force of his feelings for you."

Thomas was surprised when she at last looked at him. There was a bitter twist to her mouth. "And you want me to know that you were right, and that my oh-so-virtuous husband does indeed love me."

Jason had even convinced Grandfather of his sincerity, she thought incredulously. When Thomas narrowed his eyes at her with mingled concern and surprise, she turned wearily. "Well, you have so informed me. Your duty is done. Now please leave me be." She rose and walked to the end of the veranda, her stiff shoulders indicating she had rejected his words.

Thomas was deeply disappointed. It almost seemed the child no longer cared for any of them. Remembering the glow in her eyes when she spoke of Jason before the accident, Thomas simply could not believe she no longer loved the lad. Then what was the matter?

He was tempted to probe further, but she was in no mood to continue the discussion.

He decided she needed more time before he pushed her harder, but he had one more question to ask. "Leanna, where did you plan to go when and if you reached Charleston?" He knew Jason had assumed she intended to book passage to England, but Thomas was not so certain.

"I'm not certain. Find work there, or return to England," she replied, her voice muffled.

Thomas nodded. He gave her shoulder an encouraging pat, then he touched his rough cheek to hers. "Rest now, my dear. Do you feel well enough to start taking your meals downstairs?"

"No, I prefer to eat in my room."

He knew she was avoiding them, but perhaps that might be best for now, at least. "Very well, child. Let me know if you need anything."

Leanna was once more left in her self-imposed exile, where she longed only for a peace that eluded her.

Bella ripped open the letter with trembling fingers. She had not heard from Thomas in some time, and she was eager for news of her son and the bride she had only just heard about. She read the first few words, then paled and slowly perused the rest of the letter. When she finished, she let the paper float to the richly carpeted floor. Her gray eyes were dark with worry and concern.

She had long suspected the aristocratic Sir Gavin Redfern embodied the worst of England's corrupt upper class. He and his kind were the very men her own people had struggled so violently against.

Her husband was deaf to her warnings. He would bluster in response to her criticism, "Redfern's a good chap. Damn me, you've just got to look at him to see breeding in every line. Why, he told me his family crest dates back to the time of William of Normandy." When he refused to listen, Bella ceased to object, but she quietly tied up the majority of her holdings so he couldn't draw on them. Whether Jason wanted her money or not, she would leave him something of her.

Bella was not the least surprised to find her suspicions confirmed about Gavin. She was terrified to learn that the festering malignance she sensed in him was turned toward her son. She rose to pace up and down, searching for some hold she could use on the man. As Thomas had intimated, perhaps there was a way to discover something to have him jailed for, at least for a time.

Bella idly wound a valuable Sevres clock on the mantel. Her fingers stilled when she recalled a conversation she had not paid much attention to at the time, but she now searched her memory. One of society's most proper matrons had aired disapproval. "My son saw that little chit Ellie slip into his room when she thought no one was looking."

The woman shook her gray head in pity. "Poor Mr. Hawthorne. He's done his best with the child since her mother died, and this is how she repays him. That man Redfern is handsome enough, but something in his eyes chills me. And she's such a child! He must be heartless indeed to encourage the chit when he certainly has no intention of marrying her." The kindly woman's mouth turned down when she finished. "Someone should do something about him. Ruining Boston's innocents like that. The girl might not be gentry, but she deserves a better fate than to be cast off when Redfern's done with her."

Bella recalled this conversation now. Pete Hawthorne was a loving, but strict, father of considerable authority among his peers. He would be furious to learn his daughter had fallen under the influence of the city's latest foreign visitor who had spent some time wheedling into Boston society, Gavin Redfern. Perhaps he would be willing to keep an extremely close eye on the man. Possibly they could catch the Englishman at some unsavory dealings. Society's upper echelons already disapproved of him, and maybe some of the men he had repeatedly bested at the tables would be willing to prove him guilty of some crime.

Bella ordered the horses brought round and fetched her cloak. Now was as good a time as any to see Pete Hawthorne. When she arrived at the Hawthorne Inn, Bella was alarmed to find that Pete had just learned of his daughter's involvement with Redfern from a well-meaning friend. The angry father was determined to evict Redfern immediately after dealing him a sound thrashing.

Bella arrived just in time to put a sympathetic hand on his arm and halt him before he ferreted out Redfern. He started and turned to glare at her angrily. Pete Hawthorne was an enormous bear of a man with a thick, curly thatch of brown hair and a huge, broken nose. His imposing physique combined with his pugnacious face gave him a menacing look that Bella knew to be quite deceptive. Their fathers had been friends, and consequently, Bella knew Pete's appearance did not at all reflect the inner man.

Pete's fierce gaze softened when he saw her. "Evenin'," he growled. "I have some business to attend to, Bella, then I'll be with you."

Her soft, insistent voice halted him. "I could use some of your wonderful cider to warm the chill in my bones. I have something urgent to discuss with you."

Pete cast an angry look toward a closed door, then he heaved a heavy sigh and shrugged his massive shoulders. "Very well, Bella. But please make it quick."

Bella did not have an easy time convincing Pete to let Redfern remain unmolested for a while. When she first informed Pete of her idea, he retorted angrily, "I'll not have such offal as Redfern stinkin' up me inn. I run a respectable place. Consortin' with me own daughter!"

The poor man's anguish and disappointment were apparent, and Bella's tender heart nearly broke. They were deep in conversation, so they barely noticed when the solitary barkeep kept inching closer to their table, polishing the already shiny bar. He was a lean, straggly youth with a missing front tooth and straight, lanky blond hair. As he listened, his face lit up and a satisfied smile emphasized his rotted teeth.

By the time Bella left, she had convinced Pete to hold off evicting Redfern a little longer. He agreed to watch the man closely. Perhaps they could prove the blackguard culpable of some crime. He would do everything he could to help her, Pete promised fiercely. But he added the warning, "But I ain't a patient man, as you well know, Bella. If nothin' turns up soon, I'll take matters into me own hands."

Bella was satisfied, for the moment. She went back home to another solitary supper. Her mouth twisted when she had her uneaten plate taken away. It seemed her husband Edward once more had plans for the evening.

Edward was indeed busy. He was getting ever deeper into debt with Redfern every time they played. The two had met at the city's most exclusive inn several weeks ago. They had begun having private games because fewer and fewer men would consent to sit at the same gaming table with him.

With no watching eyes to constrain his ruthlessness, Gavin fleeced Edward time and again. When luck was with him, he smiled and raked in his winnings. When it was not, he skillfully cheated. When Edward signed a growing stack of I.O.U.s while he tried to recoup his losses, Gavin accepted the debts gracefully. He knew Edward's wife was one of the wealthiest people in Boston.

When the promised funds still did not appear, however, Gavin made discreet inquiries as to why. Edward at first tried to bluff his way out. "A temporary shortage, my friend. I'll come about, I assure you." However, Edward was growing nervous. The allowance Bella gave him each quarter was long gone. He had sold some of his jewels to meet part of the debt, but he couldn't settle the whole until next quarter.

On this night, when Gavin requested his money again, Edward sensed a deepening impatience in the elegant blond figure. Edward's mouth tightened angrily as he remembered how much money Bella had banked away. She tied up her funds so he couldn't touch a farthing without her consent. When a speculative look narrowed Gavin's clear blue eyes, Edward broke out in a sweat. His sense of ill usage exploded into rage.

"My miser of a wife has cut off my funds! I can't pay you until next quarter," Edward sneered. "She admits to investing her money for that damn ungrateful brat of a son in Savannah." Edward took another swig of port. He missed the arrested expression in Gavin's alert eyes. Redfern's slim white hand played idly with a ruby pin in his snowy cravat.

It had taken him an age to replenish his wardrobe to the style he was accustomed to. The tailoring he required was extremely dear in this uncouth colony. If it hadn't been for the huge drain on his winnings, he could have left Boston long ago. In truth, he was becoming bored with the prim disapproval that seemed to be directed at him from every quarter. Only the still fresh charms of Ellie and the easy mark of Edward had kept him this long. That and his elaborately-made plans to get back at Jason. His seedy London contacts had revealed that Jason had a rich mother in Boston who was married to a rather weak-kneed man. Not only could Gavin drain the family of funds by fleecing Edward; he could rebuild his own wardrobe, which he'd had to leave behind in his mad escape from home.

He could also take time to set the next stage of his scheme to exact final revenge on Sherry, his age-old rival.

Gavin took a dainty sip of his own wine, then asked idly, "And what might this man's name be?"

Edward belched behind his handkerchief, wiped his mouth and responded glumly, "Jason. Jason, er, Blend . . . Blake . . . dash it, it escapes me."

Redfern smiled. His eyes ignited into a brilliant, fiery blue. "Jason Blaine?"

Edward nodded. "That's it. Know the fellow?"

Gavin didn't reply. He tapped his fingers gently on the table. This might be the opportunity to start unfolding his plan. He had made furtive inquiries at the docks about Jason's standing among seafaring men, and he was not pleased to learn Jason and his grandfather were well-liked and of considerable influence around Savannah. But now . . .

A loud knock at the door made Edward start, but Gavin merely covered a delicate yawn with a polite hand. He called drowsily, "Enter."

They were ensconced in the inn's finest private room, and the lad who entered looked about nervously. He was the barkeep from the taproom. He threw a wary look at Edward. Gavin asked pleasantly. "May we call it an evening, Edward? I am quite fatigued."

Edward gave a short nod. He had no desire to go home to his wife, but he couldn't avoid her forever.

When he had gone, Redfern's sleepy manner evaporated. He barked, "Well?"

The boy's nose twitched and his voice lisped through his gapped teeth when he burst out, "Somethin's happened yer

honor might be interested in. Concerns Mr. Hawthorne 'n a
fancy lady what come by today." He looked expectantly toward
Gavin as though waiting for approval. His lean face was admiring as he looked at Gavin's elegant figure. Gavin waved
him on with an impatient hand. He had hired the idiot for
information, not as an admirer.

"They didn't know I's listenin'. It seems the lady wants to
have yer put away. Mr. Hawthorne found out about Ellie, 'n
he's right put about. He was goin' to make yer leave after
thrashin' yer, but the lady convinced him someone needs to
keep an eye on yer."

Gavin tossed the boy several coins. The boy grabbed them
up eagerly, but the absent, approving smile Gavin bestowed
on him pleased him far more.

"What did this lady look like?" Gavin wondered aloud.
When the boy gave a perfect description of Bella, Gavin nodded
grimly. Blaine and his kin seemed to take a fiendish delight in
making dangerous enemies. Well, let her do her worst. He
would be gone long before they could come up with anything
against him. He would just have to be extremely cautious for
the remainder of his stay in Boston.

Gavin gave a sleepy, satisfied smile as he climbed the stairs
to his chamber. Yes, he could probably wind up his affairs
within the month. Then Bella Forrester and her cursed son
would rue the day they ever interfered with him.

PART FOUR

"I will requite thee, taming my wild heart to loving hand."
—Much Ado About Nothing, Act III, Scene I

Chapter
Twenty-One

JASON GALLOPED THROUGH the night, his panting breath as harsh as the laboring stallion under him. He urged his mount to an even more punishing pace as he frantically tried to outrun his demons. No matter how far or how hard he rode, he couldn't still the mocking voices: "Don't touch me . . . I never want to see you again . . . You disgust me . . . *Murderer!*" When Night Wind stumbled, reason finally penetrated his thick, whiskey-soaked brain.

They had lost one valuable horse, and he would not injure Night Wind because of his unforgiving, stubborn wife. Jason's brows met in a fierce frown as he turned the stallion toward the plantation, letting the weary animal set his own pace. Leanna remained cold and distant despite the concern lavished on her by the whole household. Jason had humbled himself to her repeatedly, to no avail.

He had reiterated his love, but her reaction to his avowals was always the same: a bitter curl of her lip as she looked at him coldly, if she looked at him at all. Jason couldn't rid himself of the suspicion that she didn't believe he loved her, but when he questioned her, she only responded with a cynical smile.

Jason was vaguely aware his rage and frustration were building ominously. He was finding it extremely difficult to keep his hands off her. One moment he longed to shake her senseless, and the next he wanted to fling her on the bed and take her until passion rammed down the barriers. Stubbornly, he refused to admit, even to himself, that he might have alienated her forever.

Jason had set in motion inquiries about Redfern. He had a man keeping watch over the Englishman. He wanted to be alert and waiting when Redfern came after him. He hoped his foe would find plenty to occupy him for some time. Until Leanna put him out of his misery, he would be too preoccupied to deal effectively with a man of Redfern's malignance.

Jason had received no further news from England. He had sent a response to Abby's letter, but he knew it would be months before he could get an answer. The first missive had been delayed by several months due to the vagaries of storm and war, so by now Sherry was either long dead or fully recovered.

Jason was jolted from his thoughts when Night Wind suddenly halted. The black turned his sleek neck and peered back at Jason with a jaundiced eye as he stood waiting patiently for his master to dismount. Jason reddened under what he felt to be an accusing stare. They had apparently been standing outside the plantation for some time, but he had been too lost in thought to notice. The stallion's eyes expressed exasperation.

Glaring at Night Wind, Jason dismounted and roughly led the black in the direction of the stables. Night Wind whinnied softly, and to Jason's ears the sound was crudely mocking. He held out a lump of sugar as a peace offering. Night Wind took it delicately, then Jason stroked the stallion's velvety nose, his mouth rueful and his temper stabilized. Would that he could appease Leanna so easily.

Jason unsaddled the black, rubbed him down, and served him a large bucket of oats. He patted Night Wind's hindquarters, then slowly walked to the house. His nerves were slightly calmer than when he had set out, but some of his tension returned when he entered the house.

Jason climbed the stairs slowly, trying to keep his eyes straight ahead, but with a will of their own, they shifted toward Leanna's door. The blue depths narrowed when he saw a strip of light under the portal. So she couldn't sleep, eh? It was high time he brought things to a head. Jason pushed the door open so hard it crashed against the wall.

Leanna gasped in fright at his shadow looming in the doorway. The door slammed and he came further into the light. She was not in the least relieved to see Jason fully. She would have preferred a ghost. The grim look on his face was one she had not seen for a long time. He was disheveled, tired, and angry. The kid gloves he had handled her with since the accident were flung off with a vengeance.

She clutched the book to her bosom as though it would protect her from him. Her stare was filled with disdain. "Yes?" she said haughtily.

Jason's rage flared hotter than ever. The idea that he had to beg for an audience with his own wife infuriated him. He grabbed the book out of her hands and flung it violently across the room, knocking a vial of perfume from her dressing table. The sound of shattering glass added to the tension growing between them. Then the sweet, seductive scent she had not used in an age filled the air, intoxicating his senses. The disheveled beauty of her disordered hair and flushed face only goaded him further. Her bestirred fear satisfied him.

He walked casually to the bed, then propped his hip against the mattress while he raked her body with insulting eyes. "What's the matter, sweet wife?" he taunted. "Having trouble sleeping?"

Leanna stared stonily ahead, then she crossed her arms over her breast. Her indifference was powder to his already explosive rage. He snarled and swore viciously, then he jerked her to her knees on the bed and crushed her in a bruising embrace. The wild gleam in his eyes terrified Leanna and she began to shake.

Jason felt her trembling. The primitive side of his nature exulted, but the deep, abiding force of the love he now admitted he felt was stronger than his rage. The kiss he had intended to bestow with brutal force landed on her lips as light as thistle-down.

Leanna was so relieved to see the murderous glint in his eyes soften that she leaned weakly against him. Even when his mouth covered hers, she made no attempt to escape. The coaxing warmth of his lips on hers fanned her pleasure, but she was still too lost in her cocoon to respond with her former passion.

Jason's heart thudded against his ribs. It had been so long. . . . He groaned deep in his throat at the ecstasy of holding her in his arms. The softness of her lips, her warmth, and the damnable scent that seemed to grow sweeter by the moment overcame him like a magnum of champagne. But gradually, against his will, awareness of her dry response seeped through his senses. He strove for a moment longer, his lips searching. When she remained limp and unresponsive, he at last drew back.

His eyes were moist with tears as he realized his formally potent weapon of the senses was dull against her armor of indifference. Leanna looked at him sadly. Her rebellious heart somersaulted at the wounded look in his eyes.

Without another word, Jason backed away and left her room. He clicked the door shut behind him and went down to the study to drink himself into a stupor. It was the only relief he could think of for the intolerable pain coursing through his body.

Leanna lay where he had left her. She bit her lip to keep the tears at bay. She had not cried since losing the baby. She feared the release of tears would rip away her veils until she was once more vulnerable to the pain Jason could inflict on her.

She took deep breaths to calm herself, but she could not blank out the memory of his eyes when he left the room. She lay there, poised between the painful return to life and the still enticing protection of her safe cocoon, staring into the darkness until dawn.

Thomas was weary when he went down to breakfast the following morning. He had not slept well for days since this latest trouble between Leanna and Jason. He was far later than usual when he entered the dining room, and he expected to find that Jason had eaten hours before and had left to work about the plantation.

But when he queried the houseman, the man responded, "No suh, we ain't seen him yet this mohnin'."

Thomas frowned and ate his usual breakfast absent-mindedly. When he finished, he went to Jason's room, only to find the bed empty and unslept in. With alarm stirring, Thomas stomped down the stairs and sent a boy to the stables to see if Night Wind was in his stall. The boy returned with the news that the stallion was enjoying his morning hay.

Thomas knocked lightly on Leanna's door, and when there was no response, he pushed the portal open. Leanna had finally fallen asleep around dawn, and the soft sound of the door closing failed to wake her.

His alarm growing, Thomas strode to the study on the chance that Jason might be there. He recoiled from the heavy smell of brandy that poured from the room when he opened the door. Jason was sprawled untidily in the large wing chair near the dead fire. His hair was standing on end, indicating he had run his fingers through it repeatedly. His shirt hung open to the waist and his unshaven chin sagged against his bare chest.

A half-empty bottle of brandy stood at his elbow, another empty bottle at his stockinged feet. A brandy snifter lay on the carpet under his limp hand. The liquor it contained had soaked the expensive rug. Thomas sighed and shook his head. He hoped he was not to see a repeat of Andrew's self-pitying destruction in Jason.

Half-impatiently, Thomas shook Jason's shoulder. When there was no response, he shook him harder. "Wake up, boy," he ordered gruffly.

Jason gasped and opened reddened eyes to see what had disturbed the oblivion he had fought hard for. Thomas's reproving face swam before his reluctant gaze. Memory returned. Jason groaned and buried his pounding head in shaky hands.

Thomas left for a moment. "Send a large pot of strong coffee to the study," he ordered the houseman curtly.

Thomas tapped his foot while he waited. He opened his

mouth to remonstrate with Jason, then snapped it shut. The boy was so insensible he probably wouldn't heed him anyway until he had been revived.

It was a long, wearying job forcing the blistering coffee down Jason's reluctant throat. He tried to shove Thomas away, muttering, "Go 'way. Leave me alone." When the hot coffee spilled on Thomas's wrist, he lost all patience.

Without hesitation, he removed the flowers from a vase on a table and splattered the water over his grandson. Jason gasped and straightened. "What the devil is wrong with you?" Then he winced and inched back very gently against the chair, as though his head was as fragile as crystal.

After half a pot of coffee, Jason's wits had fully returned. Thomas demanded, "What happened to make you try to drink yourself to death? Using my most expensive brandy, too." The aggrieved note in Thomas's voice struck Jason's uncertain temper as funny.

Thomas watched stonily, his arms folded across his still broad chest, as Jason burst into laughter. "I'm glad you find me funny," he said. "Now tell me what happened *this instant.*"

Jason's laughter died. He returned Thomas's gaze with a diamond-hard stare of his own. "I don't want to talk about it," he retorted. In anger, as much at himself as at Leanna, Jason rubbed his scratchy beard and stood unsteadily to his feet.

When his face grimaced in pain, Thomas relented. "Very well, lad, we'll save our discussion for later." He put his arm around Jason and helped him up the stairs, shouting for a hot tub to be prepared in Jason's chamber. When Thomas tried to help Jason undress, his grandson snapped, "I'm not a child. I can manage on my own." Thomas left him alone.

After a long, refreshing bath, Jason felt almost human again. His head still ached, but the elf that had been chopping down trees inside his skull had finally stopped. Jason debated taking Night Wind out again, but he knew he was just delaying the inevitable. Thomas would drag the reason for his bout of drinking out of him. The memory of Leanna's indifference was a raw wound in his heart that he was loath to reveal, but Thomas would give him no peace until he knew what had happened.

Jason shut the study door behind him, then went to prop his foot against the fireplace grate. Thomas waited patiently, but when no explanation was forthcoming, he probed, "Well? I take it your evening activities were because of something that happened with Leanna?"

Jason turned from his perusal of the empty hearth to face Thomas. Despite his best efforts, he was unable to stifle the memory of Leanna's indifference to his kiss. His eyes dark but inscrutable, Jason explained huskily, "I came close to losing my temper with Leanna last night. When I came back from a ride very late, her candle was lit and I found her reading. When I confronted her, she treated me to her usual disdain, and suddenly I could no longer bear it." Jason looked away. He was unable to control the mist that came to his eyes.

"I kissed her with all the love and passion in my heart, and—" his voice broke "—she lay in my arms as lifeless as a beautiful statue." Jason shivered. "She felt warm and soft in my arms, but inwardly she was as cold as ice." He looked at Thomas again, and now the pain coursing through him was bare to see.

"I don't believe she'll ever soften to me, Grandfather. I've lost her. The night she miscarried the baby, the Leanna I fell in love with retreated, and I don't think I'll ever see her again." Jason looked at Thomas with such anguish that Thomas's mouth quivered. He longed to comfort his grandson, but he was no longer certain himself that Leanna would ever forgive the boy.

Thomas paced agitatedly up and down. His mind was forced to consider a solution to the deadlock he had rejected before. He finally stopped in front of Jason and considered his grandson's downbent head with compassionate eyes. He cleared his throat and suggested gently, "It might be best to let Leanna go, at least for a while."

Jason's head snapped up and his dull eyes ignited into flames. "No!" he shouted. Then, calmer, "She stays. Whether she ever forgives me or not, she is my wife and we belong together."

Thomas nodded. "Certainly you belong together. I only suggest you live apart for a couple of months to give Leanna a chance to recover mentally, as well as physically. Distance is a great teacher, Jason. I believe Leanna still loves you, deep inside, but she has retreated from the pain you caused her. If she is isolated from your disturbing presence, she will realize how she still needs you." Thomas stopped when Jason shook his head with granite determination.

"Or she might decide life without me is far more comfortable. No, Grandfather, she stays." Jason clenched his hands and his voice became low and piercing. "As God is my witness, she responded to me once against her will. She will do so again, whether she wants to or not. What we felt for one another is too special to die so easily." So saying, Jason strode out of the study to begin his long-overdue duties about the plantation.

Worry still ate at Thomas. If Leanna's resistance persisted, Jason might lose patience entirely and do something he would later regret. The situation was becoming increasingly explosive, and Thomas hadn't the slightest idea how to defuse it.

Late that evening, Jason wiped his muddy boots on the front carpet, then stomped wearily into the hall. He had not just supervised the planting today. He had actually helped plow in an effort to exhaust himself and bludgeon out all thought. Long after the work crews had stopped, Jason stayed busy.

He oiled the already greased gins. He fixed some of the fencing on the north property line. After it became too dark for him to see, he worked in the stable. As he climbed the stairs to his room, he was surprised to see Leanna's door open. She peered out at him, a question in her eyes. His jaw quivered at the beautiful picture she made with her flowing hair silhouetted against the dark wood door, illuminated by the candles glowing behind her. She asked softly, "May I speak with you, Jason?"

His heart jumped with hope. Was she finally softening? He tried to read her face, but her eyes were shadowed. He cleared his throat. "Certainly, my dear. But I would like to bathe first. I am not fit company for anyone at the moment. I'll come to your room when I have changed."

She nodded and shut the door quickly. She paced up and down as she waited. She finally went out on the veranda and clutched the railing so hard her knuckles stood out. During the long hours of the night after her confrontation with Jason, Leanna had decided it was best that she leave. Despite his cruelty to her, Leanna wanted to cause Jason no more pain. Of late, she had been forced to conclude that maybe he really did care for her, in his way. The pain she had seen in his eyes the previous night couldn't be totally bogus.

Her heart leaped with jubilation at the notion that Jason really loved her, but her cautious instincts still held her in a tight grip. She was too afraid of betrayal to risk opening herself to him again. She instinctively knew that as long as she remained, she would succumb to him again.

Leanna stiffened when the door opened. Jason's firm tread drew nearer until he stood so close she could feel his commanding presence. Leanna turned and met his blue gaze with a shuttered look. She gestured to the chairs on the veranda and seated herself after Jason sat down.

She began firmly. "Jason, I think it best for all concerned if I leave." When his face paled, she looked away and continued doggedly. "All we do is cause one another pain. There is no future for us now, and to be honest, I no longer want a future with you." You are too much of a threat, she added to herself. She glanced at him, then looked quickly away when he stared at her with probing intensity.

She was not telling him everything. Why did she want to leave now, after all this time? "Do you want to go back to England?"

Leanna returned to the rail. "I don't know," she replied sadly.

"Then where?"

She hesitated. "Maybe Charleston," she admitted. "After a time, I may go back to England. I am not certain of anything at the moment except that I need to leave. Rian has offered to help."

He grimaced at the mention of his friend's name, but chose to ignore it for the moment. "*Need* to leave? Why do you *need* to leave?" He must get to the truth of why she wanted to leave, so it was best to leave Rian out of the discussion in order to avoid another bitter argument.

Leanna bit her lip at the mistake. She whirled away. "I need peace and solitude. There are too many bitter memories here."

Jason's heart pounded. If he was ever to reach her, he must do it now. He stood slowly to his feet and walked up behind her.

Leanna did not shrink when he turned her to him. She met his searching look calmly. Jason massaged her delicate shoulders while he framed his words with great care.

"Leanna, I cannot let you leave. It tears my heart in two to see you so unhappy, but if you would only forgive me, I know we can recover the happiness we tasted so briefly." Leanna stood silent while his words hammered her eardrums. He was so eloquent and pleading. Surely he was sincere? She longed desperately to believe him, but panic filled her at the memory of the soul-destroying despair she had experienced when she listened to Vivian exult about her tryst with Jason. Her heart hardened.

She pulled away. Jason despaired as he watched the uncertain trembling of her mouth. "I can never forgive you," she said fiercely. "If you don't let me leave, I'll make your life as miserable as you have made mine."

Jason's pain exploded into anger. He turned and left her before his rage grew to uncontrollable lengths. He paced angrily up and down his room. Back and forth he prowled, but he could find no relief for his frustration. His face was black with the fury and torment constricting his heart. He went to the armoire and searched inside with trembling hands for his boots.

He must get out of the house and clear his head or else he would do something he would later regret. He felt like he was struggling in a deadly mire. The harder he tried to appease Leanna, the deeper he sank into her disdain. His abject pleading had been ineffective, and he had been tempted to try a more violent way to reach her. He fought hard to smother the impulse, for he knew she would probably never forgive him. God dammit, where were those riding boots?

His weary brain finally remembered he had given them to a boy to clean. Jason searched in the top shelf for an old pair, but his impatient movements dislodged a different box. It fell at his feet and dumped its contents. Unwelcome memories crowded his mind as he looked at what had pooled around his feet: beautiful beaded Indian leggings and knife.

He wrenched a smile as he remembered his boyish joy when his mother had defied his father and presented him with the leggings on his last birthday before her departure. Andrew and Thomas had scoffed at Jason's wish to dress in the leggings and creep about the forest like a savage.

But Bella had smiled at him tenderly. On his birthday, he had been astonished to find the leggings he had asked for and a genuine Indian knife. He had whooped with joy and flung himself on Bella's neck; then he dressed in the garments and went hunting with Rian. Jason was unaware of the bitter argument that followed between Andrew and Bella. Nor did he know that shortly afterward, Andrew began seeing a mulatto girl on the plantation. Two months later, Bella was gone.

Jason slumped down on the floor and picked up the soft doeskin to rub it between his fingers. The memories flooded in an irresistible tide to sweep away his anger and bitterness. Now, when he was on the verge of losing Leanna, he could at last understand the depths of despair to which frustrated love could plunge. Bella fled because she could no longer bear the bitterness of a once happy marriage gone sour. Andrew's pride drove her away and Andrew's overweening stubbornness kept him from asking her back. For the first time, Jason sympathized with Bella. He wondered if she felt the pain on leaving them that he felt now at the thought of losing Leanna.

Jason buried his face in the soft skins. He felt paralyzed with fear and helplessness. "Leanna, my darling," he whispered. "Don't let pride and fear destroy us as it destroyed my parents." Briefly, he wondered if Thomas was right. Maybe if he let Leanna go, she would realize what they meant to one another and come back of her own accord. But what if she didn't? His head bowed in indecision, he stayed on the floor for a long time. His mind was trapped between memories of his past and fear for his future.

Only the servants stirred the next morning when a knock sounded at the door. Sarah answered, and she looked stunned as she peered at the face of the tall, black-haired man. He waited patiently with a small, lovely brunette clinging to his arm. He bowed courteously and smiled, "You must be Sarah. Jason has told me much about you. I am his cousin Sherry, and I am come from England to see him."

Sarah blushed and stammered an apology when she realized she was gawking instead of inviting them in. She stood back in welcome. "Please forgive my manners. I'm amazed at the resemblance to Jason," she explained, still staring at Sherry's handsome face.

Sherry smiled mischievously. "Yes, amazing, is it not?"

Sarah seated them in the salon and ordered a tray of coffee and tarts.

"Sarah, this is my wife Abby. Perhaps Jason told you I was to be married?" he introduced.

"Yes, he did. I'm most pleased to meet you, ma'am," Sarah smiled as she poured them both a cup of steaming, fragrant coffee.

"And I am glad to meet you, Sarah. Tell me, how are things between Leanna and Jason?" Abby gave Sarah the sweet, confiding smile that set everyone immediately at ease. She was disconcerted to see Sarah's face crumple.

The housekeeper looked at them with scared, worried eyes. "Thomas and I are at our wits' end. Terrible things have been said between Jason and Leanna." Sarah pulled a handkerchief out of her pocket to dab at her tears. "I don't know what's going to happen unless someone can knock some sense into them. Do you think you can help?" She looked hopefully at them, for Thomas had told her of the couple's stabilizing influence on Leanna and Jason.

Sherry and Abby frowned, looked at one another, then Sherry patted Sarah's hand. "We shall do our best, Sarah. But first we need to know what has happened."

Sarah went immediately to the door. "I'll get Thomas."

Abby and Sherry sat quietly while they waited. "Could this have anything to do with Gavin, Sherry?" Abby worried.

"We'll have to wait and see, Abby. But if I know my stubborn cousin and my no less stubborn ex-ward, there is more to this dilemma than Gavin's interference."

As usual, Abby discovered, Sherry was correct. Thomas was downstairs in a trice. Aside from less than smooth hair and a slightly wrinkled neckcloth, he looked like the gentleman he was. He shook Sherry's hand in a hearty welcome.

"I'm so glad to see you again, my boy. You were but a babe when I left. You've grown into a man your father would have been proud of." Thomas looked sad when he mentioned the old earl.

"I'm glad to meet you, Uncle Thomas. Jason spoke of you often. Now, what's this about trouble between Jason and Leanna?"

Thomas sighed and poured himself a cup of coffee. He took a few sips, then he told them everything that had happened since Leanna's arrival. He ended with the conversation between himself and Jason last night.

"The lad has told her repeatedly he loves her. She either doesn't care, or she doesn't believe him. Last night, I suggested that Jason send her away for a few months to give her a chance to recover from her bitterness, but he wouldn't hear of it." Thomas set his empty cup down and clasped the arms of his chair.

"He's afraid she might find life more comfortable without him. I don't know what else to suggest." The worry edging on despair in Thomas's gruff voice troubled Sherry and Abby.

Before either of them could respond, the parlor door burst open and Jason entered the room. A wide, delighted grin split his tired, drawn face at the sight of Sherry.

He hauled his cousin to his feet and enfolded him in his arms. "You old devil, I knew you were too mean to die," he joked.

Sherry twinkled, "It will take more than the venom of Gavin Redfern to put me under." He drew Abby forward. "Especially now that Abby is my wife."

Jason lifted Abby off her feet and kissed her cheek loudly. "Well, dear Abby, what do you think of the wilds of America?" he teased.

Abby reddened when she realized he had heard one of her comments to Leanna. "Everything I've seen so far is lovely."

When Jason beamed, she looked at him sidelong and finished, "Primitive, but lovely." He pretended to be affronted, and Abby's delightful laughter filled the room.

Sherry looked at Abby with such a world of adoration in his eyes that Jason could not control a twinge of envy, especially when Abby returned the look in full measure. Jason turned away to the window, the horns of his dilemma more troublesome than ever. If Leanna could never forgive him, then what right had he to hold her? He was lost in thought, so he didn't hear Thomas suggest that Abby go up and surprise Leanna. She gladly complied, for she was eager to see the girl she considered the sister she had always wanted.

Leanna was half-awake when the door opened. Expecting it to be Sukey, she didn't open her eyes. When she felt a presence standing beside the bed, she stiffened in alarm. Jason again? Her eyes opened warily. She was stunned to see Abby's beautiful face smiling gently at her.

"Abby," she cried, springing upright in the bed. Abby laughed and sat down next to her and hugged her tightly. The two girls held one another for a long moment, then Abby drew back and smiled.

"It's wonderful seeing you again, my dear." Her voice grew soft with sympathy. "I was very sorry to learn about the child."

The bright light that had been missing for so long in Leanna's eyes abruptly dimmed. "Yes," she replied coolly. "It was a most painful experience." Leanna threw back the covers and dressed. When she was finished, she looked at Abby directly.

"Why are you here, Abby? Is Sherry with you?"

"Yes, Sherry is with me. As to why I'm here. . . . My dear, didn't Jason tell you Gavin escaped and shot Sherry? He has gone to Boston, and it's our belief he will be after Jason next."

A chill made Leanna shiver. She shook it off and refused to acknowledge the terror that filled her at the thought of Jason's danger. Her soft mouth tightened. "No, he didn't tell me," she responded grimly.

Abby looked at the closed, withdrawn young face before her. They certainly had their work cut out for them this time, she thought sadly. She took Leanna by the arm.

"Come, my dear. Sherry is eager to see you." She smiled at Leanna in obvious pride. "He is my husband now. We were married several months ago." Leanna murmured congratulations. When Abby tried to pull her out the door, it seemed for a moment that Leanna would resist, then she followed Abby down the stairs.

The men rose when the women entered the salon. Leanna avoided Jason's eyes. She smiled wanly in response to Sherry's delighted, "Leanna, my dear, how marvelous to see you! Abby and I have both missed you greatly." Sherry drew Leanna down beside him on the couch. Leanna returned his warm smile, but cautiously.

Then she studied her clasped hands while everyone broke out in excited conversation.

"Your plantation is huge, Uncle. And you seem almost entirely self-sufficient, judging from the buildings we passed."

Thomas nodded. "Yes, we produce most of our foodstuffs and cloths, though of course we have to import certain items like salt and spices."

Thomas asked curiously, "How did you arrive so quickly? We only had your letter a few weeks ago. It was delayed by a storm, apparently."

Sherry looked wry but unsurprised. "Luckily, one of His Majesty's man-o-wars is rather more reliable. We were given special passage because of my work in the War Office."

Abby was seated on Sherry's other side, and Leanna was painfully aware of how his arm encircled his wife's shoulder while they talked. She restlessly laced and unlaced her fingers in an effort to distract herself from Sherry and Abby's obvious happiness. She strove to ignore Jason's intense stare, but the tension in her grew until her head began to ache. The desultory conversation between Sherry and Thomas dimmed and receded as the battle between her fears and her desires hammered her confused mind ruthlessly. Her throat dry and her head pounding, she choked back a sob and ran from the room.

Jason leaped up to follow, but Abby was faster. Jason found the portal closed firmly in his face. Abby followed Leanna's racing figure slowly. When the girl went outside to lean against the enormous oaks, Abby walked up and seated herself calmly on the ground without a thought for her modish morning dress.

Leanna bowed her head in her hands as she tried to still her trembling. She was a prey to emotions she had hoped were dead. Envy, jealousy, pain, and the old familiar longing for love she had never totally subdued all beat inside of her.

Abby pulled Leanna down beside her and lifted her chin. "My dear, this attempt to smother your natural inclinations is unhealthy. What has Jason done that is so terrible?"

Leanna's head jerked up. "How can you say that? He tormented me endlessly. He knew I loved him, but that wasn't enough. He wanted to humble me, to see me grovel at his feet." Her mouth twisted with bitterness. "That was bad enough, but to make a tryst with that woman at the very spot where we first—" Leanna's voice choked and she clenched her hands to still the tears that threatened to fall.

Abby's eyes narrowed. So there was more here than Jason or Thomas knew of. "What woman, Leanna?" she asked insistently.

Leanna turned away. "Never mind. Go to your husband and enjoy what happiness you can find. It may not last long. I don't believe there's a dependable man left in the world." Leanna ran toward the river with her hair streaming behind her like a gold flag.

Abby walked slowly back to the house with her brow creased in thought. Leanna's angry taunt had hurt, but she knew her friend was too upset to think rationally. Before the bitterness festering in Leanna like a gangrenous wound could be drained, she would have to be convinced there had been no other woman. Abby had seen the hungry look in Jason's eyes when he looked at Leanna. He was too much like Sherry to give his love with less than his whole heart.

The men broke off their discussion of Gavin when Abby entered the salon. Jason leaped to his feet. "Is Leanna all right?"

Abby eyed him as though she were trying to see into his soul. He met her intense look with a puzzled frown. "What is it?"

"I need to speak with you privately, Jason," Abby replied calmly.

Jason immediately led her into the study. "Out with it, woman," he snapped. "Where is Leanna?"

"She's outside, but I have spoken with her. I don't believe she has ever told you of the true reason for her bitterness." She watched his face intently as she asked, "Have you been unfaithful, Jason?"

Jason looked stunned, then his eyes narrowed as Leanna's behavior was at last explained. "Never," he answered with ringing sincerity. Abby nodded, convinced.

"Nevertheless, she believes you have been unfaithful to her. Apparently the place of the supposed meeting has some special meaning to her."

Jason paced restlessly up and down as he wracked his brain. He started to shake his head in despair when he remembered Vivian's mysterious remark the night of the party. He had sensed Leanna's tension when the woman insinuated, "Until later."

Jason's eyes darkened to the ominous, stormy blue they became when his fury was aroused. Abby watched in alarm. He reminded her of a kettle bubbling ominously. He could boil over at any moment. He wheeled and strode out of the room with Abby at his heels.

"What is it, Jason?" When he didn't respond, she insisted, "Now is not the time to lose your temper. You must be gentle with Leanna if you don't want to alienate her further."

Jason snorted in fury. "Gentle, hell! That's the problem, I've been *too* gentle with the spoiled brat. What she needs is a good thrashing, and I'm just in the mood to give her one."

Abby grabbed his arm and dug in her heels to halt him, but he flung her off as though she were a fly he could swat aside. Abby stumbled, then ran back to the house to get Sherry and Thomas. Jason was in a dangerous rage, and God only knew what he would do to Leanna.

Jason was vaguely aware that Abby had gone for help. Well, he would have this out with Leanna uninterrupted. And then, by God, if she still wanted to leave, let her! He would gladly pay her passage to Alaska if she asked for it.

Leanna was soaking her legs in the water. She watched the ripples swirl around her slim calves. She concentrated fiercely on the tiny waves to avoid thinking of the man who was advancing toward her like a man pushed beyond control.

Leanna was concentrating so acutely that she didn't hear him come up behind her. She shrieked in fright when huge hands pulled her to her feet. She was at first relieved when she saw Jason, but when she took a good look at his face, she swallowed. The scathing remark springing to her lips died.

His teeth were clenched, his nostrils flared, and his eyes shone with the bright, deadly glitter of sunlight on steel. He shook her angrily, once, twice, then he jerked her along behind him toward the smokehouse.

Leanna stumbled after him. She gasped, "Have you lost your wits? What have I done to merit this treatment?" When she stumbled again, he impatiently threw her over his shoulder. He could see Sherry and Thomas hurrying toward them, so he sprinted the last few yards to the smokehouse.

Once inside, he threw Leanna unceremoniously on the ground while he bolted the thick door behind them. There was no other exit. Leanna scrambled to her feet and faced him defiantly, some of her old spirit ignited. She rubbed her aching posterior as rage bubbled up and invigorated her numbed mind.

Jason jerked her toward him. He sliced her face with his razor-keen eyes. "You stupid little nitwit, what's this I hear about a tryst with Vivian?"

Leanna paled, then she met his eyes with a malignant gleam of her own. "Surprised to learn I know of your little infidelity? Tell me something, dear husband, was she better than I? Did our cabin ring with her cries of ecstasy as you writhed in our bed together?"

Jason drew back his hand to strike her, but when she flinched, he threw her to the ground in disgust. He was pale with the effort he expended to control his temper.

He leaned down and took a handful of hair to yank her head back. He ignored her wince and said, "I'll say this but once. I have not made love to any woman but yourself since we married, I have never met another woman at our cabin, and I long ago lost all interest in that fat cow Vivian."

Leanna met his inflamed eyes steadily. "Can you give me

one good reason why I should believe you?"

Jason's control snapped. His cry of rage was primitive in its guttural intensity. He took Leanna by the shoulders and shook her unmercifully until he was breathless and her hair was a tangled mass of soft gold. Finally, he stopped and pushed her away with a contemptuous look.

"I have humbled myself to you repeatedly, but no more. If you want to throw away what we had because of your twisted bitterness and pride, then that is your decision. I got along fine without you before we met, and I will do so again."

He pulled her close to his warmth. She could feel his body vibrating with rage. "You can leave as soon as you have borne my heir."

At her outraged gasp, he bared his teeth in a taunting smile. "You shall give me the child you denied me by your careless refusal to trust me"—here his voice quivered for a moment before it hardened again—"that Vivian's words weren't true. You owe me that much."

Jason gestured toward the loud, angry voices that came through the door. "Your champions will not save you, dear wife, because, like it or not, you are mine to do with as I will."

Leanna flew at him in a rage, but he crushed the hands she would have used to scratch his face. Smiling with enjoyment at her impotent fury, he held her arms behind her back and leered at her. "So eager to begin, lover? I'm shocked you could want me in such conditions as this."

Leanna opened her mouth to blister him with curses, but he smiled even deeper and crushed his mouth against hers. Her struggles waned, then ceased as the old magic that had so enchanted each of them reasserted its power. Jason's mouth coaxed when he felt her reluctant response. Leanna groaned and struggled to free her arms. He released her wrists and she brought her hands up to push him away. But somehow, her arms crept around his neck and her mouth opened to the famished, deliciously familiar thrust of his tongue.

The knocking and voices had ceased some time ago, but neither of them noticed. The passion that always flowed between them was rushing through each like a hurricane-fed torrent, so the creaks at the door took a moment to register. Jason lifted his head to listen.

He smiled wryly, then dropped a last kiss on one of Leanna's closed eyes. "My darling, we are about to be rudely interrupted. We must save this for later."

Leanna's eyes opened reluctantly. The rage in his eyes was gone now. The light of love shone sweetly at her, warming the last of the ice away from her wary heart. She returned his smile and he heaved a deep sigh of relief. She could no longer deny her heart the love it yearned for despite her fervent counter-efforts. Leanna sniffed, a tear glistened in her eye, and she gulped on a sob. Soon, she was weeping copiously in his comforting arms.

Such was the sight that greeted the frantic trio that rushed inside when the sturdy door was at last pried from its hinges. The three stood stunned with mingled relief and exasperation. They had expected to see Jason hurting Leanna, and here he was cradling her in his arms with a soft look in his eyes. His arrogant features had been transformed.

Thomas sighed so deeply his chest almost met his chin. He sank down on a nearby hitching post. "Thank God," he said simply.

Sherry and Abby held hands as they watched the moving sight. Abby turned her cheek to Sherry's caressing palm when he smiled, "My darling, I don't know what you said to Jason, but I confess I was afraid he was going to murder Leanna. I should have known better. You are a born statesman."

Abby's eyes swam with happy tears. "I am much happier being your wife." And their tender embrace mirrored the one taking place inside the smokehouse between Jason and Leanna.

Chapter
Twenty-Two

THE LONG, WEARYING drought of bitterness had ended. The kernel of love planted in passion on their first meeting had germinated despite their anger and distrust of one another. The sapling that had taken root from that first attraction now blossomed into a hardy tree that offered them sustenance, shade, comfort, and strength. The roots of love entwined and bound Jason and Leanna together as surely and strongly as the old oaks clung to the warm, rich soil of home.

No longer was Jason the arrogant possessor. His eyes watched her over the rich luncheon Sarah had prepared in celebration with such tender, cherishing warmth that Leanna's breath caught in her throat and she could scarcely force herself to eat. The love shining from his eyes justified the pain she had borne to win him; it affirmed and celebrated her womanhood and fulfilled her dreams of love. The joy that filled her was so poignant it was almost painful.

Jason, too, was barely aware of the others. He didn't notice the proud look on Thomas's face as he watched Jason watch Leanna. Sherry and Abby held hands under the table, their own happiness heightened by the emotion emanating from the other couple.

When the last dish had been taken away, Jason rose and drew Thomas aside. They spoke briefly, then Thomas nodded his head in agreement with Jason's words. Jason went to Leanna, put his arm around her, and drew her tenderly to his protective side. He felt the tremor that shook her with a mixture of wonder and delight. An answering trembling began deep within her own body.

Leanna barely heard his comment to Sherry and Abby above the thudding of her heart. "Leanna and I wish to thank you for your efforts on our behalf. If you hadn't come, we might have drifted even further away from one another." Unaware, he tightened his arm around Leanna at the terror of the thought.

"We owe ourselves a brief, belated honeymoon. I'm taking Leanna to a private spot we've shared once before, but please stay. Grandfather can show you around. We'll return in three days."

Sherry winked at Jason, but Abby dug him in the ribs before he could make the ribald comment she could see leaping to his lips. He said simply, "Have a good time, you two."

Leanna flushed even rosier and Jason laughed. The pair went up the stairs, arms around each other's waists. Thomas turned to Sherry and Abby with gratitude and relief softening the rugged creases of his face. "I owe you both more than I can say. Is there anything at all I can do to repay you?"

Sherry drew Abby close. Their eyes met with perfect accord, then Abby answered for both of them. "The look in Jason's eyes and the happiness on Leanna's face are all the satisfaction we need." The three were silent for a moment as they thought of the couple that had gone up to pack. Then Thomas bestirred himself to escort his guests on a tour of Whispering Oaks.

The day itself seemed attuned to Leanna and Jason. No clouds marred the bright blue sky. The heady scents of spring thickened the air. A meadowlark trilled at them as they drove under its perch. And the sun, bright, warm, and ennobling, beamed on them with approval.

Leanna leaned on Jason's shoulder and rubbed her cheek against the rough texture of his jacket. He grasped the reins in one hand and encircled her shoulder with his arm, dropping a gentle but emotive kiss on her gleaming blond head. "If you don't quit snuggling against me so, my fiery vixen, we may not make it to the cabin," he teased.

Leanna reddened, but she merely burrowed deeper into his body. She put one hand over his heart and was satisfied to feel its strong thumping against her palm. She grinned impishly into his shoulder, but her voice was innocent when she replied, "Oh? Did you have something in particular in mind for us to while the time away? I'm not certain I have healed sufficiently for us to be so intimate."

Jason slumped and stifled a groan. He took several deep breaths and cursed himself for forgetting her condition. He slowed the carriage to a snail's pace.

He was afraid to look at her lest he show his disappointment. "Forgive me for being so imprudent, Leanna. I assumed you had healed long ago. Under the circumstances it might be best if we return to the house. It would be pure torture for us to be so secluded but unable to embrace." His voice shook a little and he prepared to turn the carriage about.

Two little hands tightened on his and halted his action. Jason almost reluctantly turned to face Leanna. His eyes widened at the slumbrous, sensual look on her face. She had released her hair and the rippling waves of golden light seemed to have caught the sun.

She leaned close to whisper, "I was but teasing, my darling. I am perfectly well, and my body hungers for yours. Hurry to our cabin so we can begin work on our heir." Jason's drooping mouth curved upward in a jubilant grin.

He whooped in delight. He crushed her in his arms and punished her with a brief, hard kiss, then he growled, "You shall pay for your teasing, dear one, when I get my hands on that gorgeous body."

Leanna peered up at him contentedly as she once more

leaned on his shoulder. "I shall pay, and gladly, dear husband."

This provocative exchange heightened their already soaring passions. While Jason unharnessed and stabled the horse, Leanna went inside to ready herself. She felt as excited as a bride and slipped into a revealing nightgown that Abby had given to her. In truth, their coming together would be a new beginning for them. With love finally admitted on both sides, their passion would have a new, fuller meaning. Leanna lay down on the bed and closed her eyes in a brief prayer of thanks for being given another chance at happiness.

Jason was slow returning to the cabin. His hand trembled slightly as he opened the sturdy door. His stomach churned with nervousness, love, and, most disconcerting of all, fear. He leaned back against the door and gulped down deep breaths, trying to quiet his pounding heart.

A wry grin formed on his lips as he realized he hadn't felt so gauche the first time he had taken a woman. The poets always said love made one feel strong and invincible. How wrong they were. He had never felt so weak and humble in the whole of his thirty years. For the first time in his life, he would be a lover in spirit as well as in name. It had never been so important to please a woman, but he was afraid when he first set hands on her silken flesh, his self-control would shatter. Shaking his head in an effort to clear the cobwebs of fear, he straightened his shoulders and strode into the cabin, his turmoil successfully hidden.

Jason froze and his breath whooshed from his lungs. Leanna's beautiful body was an exquisite test to his will as she lay on her side. Her figure was molded closely by the flesh-colored gown.

With acute male hunger, he devoured her lush breasts, trim waist, and the brown triangle at the junction of her legs. He recognized the seductive gown that had so excited him when he saw her in it once, a long time ago. The surge in his body then was gentle compared to the tide of feeling that flooded him now. He coiled his hands for control. He had hungered for her forever, it seemed, and to see her beckoning in all her glory, ready to receive him, was almost unbearable. He was afraid to touch her and put his strength to the test. What if he couldn't give her the gentle ardor she needed on this, her first time since the accident?

Leanna was mystified at his hesitancy. She was trembling with eagerness, but still he stood at the door as though frightened. Finally, with a tender smile on her face, she rose and went to him. She never would have believed it, but her arrogant lover was nervous. She was touched and aroused at the realization that she must be the cause.

She loosened his cravat and rose on tiptoe to pull it from his neck. She forced his jacket off his stiff shoulders and flung it in a heedless heap on the floor. She unbuttoned his shirt slowly, deliberately scraping his bared chest with her nails as she descended. She added his shirt to the growing pile.

When she licked his flat nipple like a hungry kitten as she unbuckled his belt, a tremor shook him. Groaning almost in pain, he encircled her waist and fastened his mouth on hers. The unreserved sensuality of her response enflamed him further. She nibbled his lips playfully while her hands roamed over his bared torso. Jason's hands shook as he tried to force their eagerness to a gentle stroke when he released her breasts from the low-cut bodice. He pulled her off her feet and consumed the peaks that yearned for his kiss.

The soft pants that issued from her reddened lips broke the last of his control. He lowered her to the bed and flung off the rest of his clothes. Leanna just as eagerly removed her gown and lay waiting, quivering with need. Jason mounted her immediately and tried to force himself to gentleness as his manhood once more felt the warmth of her most secret part.

But Leanna was as excited as he. She had no need of gentleness. When he still hesitated, she grasped him and urged him inward. A moan escaped their lips in unison as he made one famished plunge. Leanna arched against him, crying, "Oh, my darling, I love you! It's been so long . . ."

As he began to move, Jason gasped, "Leanna, my love, my only love . . ." And then, under the fierce onslaught of passion, there was no need for words. Jason reached endlessly, but still he couldn't get enough of her. Leanna savored his hard warmth buried in her and moved about him to hold him deeper.

Jason nibbled and teased her breasts as he thrust hungrily.
The first tremors of fulfillment were quick to invade her. She
bit her lip to keep from screaming when the friction of his
lunging set off her first spasms. Jason relished the dazed, shattered look on her face, and he thrust harder, faster, his own
need clamoring for release. Leanna cried out when her senses
escalated to a dizzying height she had never suspected she could
reach. She almost fainted as the waves of pleasure reached her
every pore and nerve.

Jason felt her hard convulsions grip him. He groaned in
triumph and withdrew one last time, throbbing, before he
plunged to the hilt. He shook with a shattering feeling as he
spent his seed in her clenching, welcoming warmth.

The incredible sensations were slow to fade. Jason pulled
Leanna on top of him, but he remained nestled within her. He
had proclaimed his love and possession in the most elemental
way possible, but he was not yet able to relinquish his oneness
with her. Their panting breaths slowed, and finally, Leanna
raised her limp head to look at Jason with an adoring light in
her face.

"Do you see how marvelous it can be between two people
in love, my darling? You have never given me such joy. I felt
I would die of pleasure."

Jason nibbled her throat and the tip of each soft breast before
replying. His voice was muffled when he admitted, "If I had
known what awaited us, I would never have struggled against
you so long, Leanna." He quit nuzzling to meet her eyes and
reflect a look that approached humility. "I am ashamed I doubted
you, my love. Never again will I question the existence or the
power of love. Joy so sweet surely comes only to those in love.
I have certainly never felt such pleasure, even with you, though
I thought our lovemaking could never be more delicious."

He whispered in her ear, "You have broken down my last
barrier and stormed the castle of my heart, my proud warrior.
I will be your faithful vassal always."

Leanna's face glowed brighter and she scattered light, loving
kisses over the strong planes of his face. The realization that

their pledge of love had almost come too late made the moment all the sweeter. The time for talk would come. They still needed to exorcise the painful ghosts of their past mistakes, but neither wanted to spoil this perfect unity yet. So Jason stroked Leanna's smooth back and she bowed her head and rubbed her cheek over his hairy chest. Each relished the physical and emotional empathy that seemed a kinetic force between them.

Feeling lucky, feminine, and totally fulfilled, Leanna fell asleep. Jason listened to her slow breathing with a soft, happy expression he had not worn since boyhood. His fears had been for naught. Their union could not have been more satisfying. Yawning as weariness muted his exhilaration, he pulled the covers over them both and fell into a deep sleep. Leanna was still atop him.

Leanna woke slowly with a feeling of well-being and happiness. She stretched on her unusually hard, warm bed, then started when she felt the bed shift beneath her weight. Fully awake, she stared down at Jason's relaxed face. She giggled as she noticed how sleep could not obliterate the satisfied look around his firm mouth. She savored his features for a full minute, then her sprite's expression became an impish grin.

Jason swam up through a warm pool of sensation as his pleasant dreams crystallized. He awoke to the feel of Leanna enveloping him with her warm, full lips. He groaned. "My dear, where did you learn such tricks?"

Leanna stopped only briefly to smile, "It's amazing what one can learn by reading, my dear husband. Of course, my parents never knew the Duke of Chester had a risque taste in literature . . ." She continued with her beguilement until Jason soared. Then she lowered her loins on his erect manhood and began a slow, languorous ride until her passions caught up with Jason's. Her speed increased until Jason had to grit his teeth to force himself to wait for her. Galloping now, they rushed up the peak of fulfillment to reach the summit together.

Leanna flung her head back in exultation as Jason cried out. She felt a glorious sense of power when she realized the potent force of her womanhood. His superior masculine strength was helpless before the age-old might of her femininity. Headiest of all was the knowledge that only she could bring him this apex of pleasure. Sweating and gasping for breath, Leanna collapsed against him.

Jason stroked her creamy neck, then raised her chin so she could meet his shining, tender eyes. "My lovely vixen, my beautiful lover, I think I must have loved you almost from the beginning. Can you forgive me for my stubbornness?"

Leanna returned his loving look with a soft, glowing warmth in her pine-green eyes. "I have nothing to forgive, for I am not blameless. My pride almost separated us forever."

Jason pulled her convulsively to him. Their embrace was fierce as they reflected how near they had come to losing each other. If Jason hadn't checked on her that night, or if he had taken the wrong road . . .

Jason played with her hair, wrapping it around her neck in a gleaming rope. He gave a pained laugh. "It's not true that women are the weaker sex. You riveted each thought and desire from our first meeting, but I was too frightened to admit it. It seems I was torn between rape and tenderness for most of our married life. And always, until near the end, you seemed so self-possessed, so unaware of your power over me. It fair drove me mad. I think that's why I struggled so violently against you. I certainly had no desire for anyone else."

With a rueful smile on her lips, Leanna flung her head back to look up at him. "How odd that our fears were so similar. I felt helpless before the strength of the feelings you aroused in me, and I was certain they were writ for all to see." Her voice trembled with remembered hurt. "It seemed so cruel for you to insist I humble myself to you and admit my love, when you appeared willing to give nothing in return."

Jason gave her a quick, comforting kiss. "How we misunderstood one another. I needed to hear you confess your love, my darling, not because I wished to be cruel, but because I had to be certain you cared for me. In my inmost soul, I knew I loved you fiercely, but until I was assured of your love, I couldn't force myself to admit it. However, the night you left, I could deny the truth no longer, with or without a confession from you."

He smiled into her startled face. "Even before I found you bleeding in the forest, I knew I loved you. Surprisingly, I felt no alarm or resentment. It seemed right and inevitable that I should belong to you, as I had always felt you belonged to me, even on the night we met."

It was Leanna's turn to look humble. Her delicate features winced with regret as she asked, "You mean you really did love me all those times you said so, when I was ill?"

Jason nodded, his eyes shadowed with the painful memory of that dark time. "I think it was the worst memory of my life, that evening when I kissed you in your chamber and you lay lifeless in my arms." He shuddered, but relinquished the memory gladly when Leanna smothered his face with kisses and stammered words of love and regret.

They were silent for a time, then Jason asked eagerly, "When did you know you loved me?"

"Do you remember the night you were wounded in the storm?" He nodded. "I saw you fall, and I have never felt such helpless terror before, or after. When I realized I would gladly give my life to save you, I could fool myself no longer."

Leanna's smile was wistful at the memory. "At least it explained my physical response to you. It's odd, but my body knew how I felt long before my mind would admit it." Each thought back to that stormy time between them, and the conflict that had troubled them so was now a memory they would cherish.

Jason continued her train of thought. "From the first, I sensed the danger you presented to my emotions. That's why I was so reluctant to marry you. And when you refused to share my bed, my desire grew even more uncontrollable." He shifted his head restlessly. "Ah, what a curse pride is. If only we had bared our hearts, what pain we could have saved one another."

Leanna kissed the frown from between his brows. "True, my darling, but now we appreciate what we have even more, and it's made our joy all the sweeter."

When they finally dressed and prepared a light supper, their eyes met in silent communion over the meal. Their verbal confession had been as healing and rejuvenating as their phys-

ical union. By unspoken agreement, they had put the past
behind them and savored their happy present. They were free
to anticipate the future. When they had eaten, they held hands
and returned to bed to make love through the night.

The two halcyon days that followed were full of golden sun,
joyful laughter, and ecstatic lovemaking. Leanna and Jason
rode, swam, pranced through the forest like children, and, on
one memorable day, Jason taught her how to fish. He watched
sidelong as she tried to thread the worm on the hook. Her nose
was crinkled with distaste as she tried to skewer the slimy,
squirming creature. Finally, she glared pugnaciously at the un-
cooperative worm and cast a woeful, pleading look at Jason.

His gaze was bland as he looked at her winsome face. How
beautiful she was with the sun glittering in her golden hair and
her cheeks flushed with heat. How fun she was to tease. With
a smile and a shrug, he drawled, "Sorry, my dear, that's the
first thing an angler must learn. If you can't bait your own
hook, you can't catch anything. And if you can't catch anything
. . . well, I doubt I'll land enough for us both. I feel quite
hungry."

And so saying, he dropped down onto the grass and pulled
his hat over his face. If Leanna had looked closely, she would
have seen his grin, but she was too outraged at his arrogance.
She fumed in silence for a moment, then a wicked smile lit
her face.

Moving slowly, carefully, she inched down to the water and
retrieved his line. Grimacing, she pulled the worm off his hook
and threw the line back in the water. Taking a deep breath, she
doggedly worked with the worm still wriggling on her hook
until she had it anchored. She flung her line in the water and
rinsed her hands, then sat down to wait with an innocent look
on her face.

Watching, Jason was hard put not to laugh at the satisfaction
emanating from her, but he played along. When her line bob-
bled, he coached her on the best way to pull the fish in. He
held the large trout up for her inspection and congratulated her.
"There, now wasn't that worth it? You'll get used to baiting
your own hook, and you'll wonder why it ever bothered you."

Leanna smiled at him sweetly and again baited her hook without the shudder of distaste this time.

Jason let her catch two more fish before he frowned and wondered aloud, "What could be wrong? I haven't even had a nibble." Leanna couldn't suppress a soft giggle, but she puzzled at the smile that played at his lips when he pulled his line from the water.

Looking directly at her, he purred, "Now, how do you suppose that happened?" Leanna raised her brows and looked innocent. Laughing heartily, Jason flung his pole aside and pulled hers from her hand. He shoved her back on the soft grass and lowered himself on top of her. Still laughing, he ignored her breathless protests and threatened in her ear, "You must pay for your perfidy. Since you saw fit to purloin my bait and let me go hungry, you'll have to be my dinner instead."

He drew back and examined her from head to toe rakishly, as though trying to decide where to begin his feast. Leanna squirmed under the lecherous look that made his face seem almost menacing, then she responded to his teasing with an act that would have made Mrs. Siddons proud.

"Oh, please, sir, spare me. I will gladly share my meager catch with thee." Her tragic look brightened into the spirited Leanna for a moment as she added a sarcastic aside, "Besides, I smell of fish."

Jason leaned so close his breath stirred her eyelashes. He sighed with pleasure, "No, you smell of woman." And he pulled nonchalantly at her buttons until her dress fell open to the waist, then he unlaced her chemise and bared her beautiful, heaving bosom. His hands cupping each perfect mound, he rubbed the tips with his thumbs until they stood up in rigid excitement. Leanna lay quietly, staring at his intent face, her eyes as green as the crushed grass under them. As he lowered his mouth over her breast, she sighed and arched upward into his working lips.

Soon her hands tore impatiently at his shirt. When he lowered his furred chest over hers, a sensuous moan escaped her lips. Each explored the area both were most interested in. Grasping her hips, Jason thrust within her and began the rocking motions that never failed to arouse them. The warmth of the sunshine lay like a soothing blanket over them and the singing of the birds sounded a melodious blessing as Jason and Leanna pledged their love in the age-old way.

Jason fell to Leanna's side and held her in a tender, possessive embrace until their sledging hearts slowed to a patter. He teased, "You can steal my bait anytime. You're much more delicious than fish." They were interrupted when a squirrel scampered pell-mell down the tree over their heads and stopped when he saw them. Cheeks puffed, it chittered in vexation, then, with a disdainful flick of its tail, it ran back up the tree and ignored the invaders. Jason and Leanna laughed together, chuckling even harder when they spied a bright little face peeking cheekily at them through the branches.

Almost giddy with happiness, they gathered their fishing equipment and, hand in hand, walked back to the cabin. It was difficult to force themselves to leave the next day. Their happiness had been so idyllic they were loath to share it with anyone. When their clothes were packed and the cabin was clean, they stood at the doorstep of the little home and savored a last, tender embrace. After a long, satisfying kiss, they cast a regretful look back and started for Whispering Oaks.

They rode in silence at first, then Leanna voiced the fear that troubled them both. "When do you suppose Gavin will appear?"

Jason shrugged. "I don't know, but I intend to be ready when he does. I've sent a friend to follow him, but I've yet to hear from him unless there has been word in our absence."

They found Sherry, Abby, and Thomas at lunch when they arrived. The three exclaimed in delight when they saw them. Leanna touched her cheek to Thomas's, then sat down opposite Abby. Jason ignored protocol and sat down next to Leanna.

Sherry and Abby watched with a smile as they ate the roast beef, squash, and corn with gusto. Sherry winked at Thomas. "They seem fair starved. Do you suppose it really is possible to live on love?"

Leanna flushed and Jason threw him a quizzical look. Abby frowned at Sherry, then smiled at the honeymooners. "You both look much better than when you left. You missed this delicious plate of cornbread. I'd never tasted such a dish, but I confess

I've become fond of it in the short time we've been here."

The conversation was light and desultory for the remainder of the meal, and none mentioned the man uppermost in their thoughts. Sarah waylaid Leanna after lunch. Abby watched as the housekeeper put her hands on Leanna's shoulders and searched her face with anxious eyes. What she saw seemed to reassure her, for she drew a deep, relieved breath.

"You are happy, child?"

Leanna returned her gentle smile with a grin that illuminated her face. "I've never been happier, Sarah." Leanna kissed Sarah's soft cheek and whispered, "Jason and I both love you and we're grateful for your concern."

Sarah watched Leanna climb the stairs with Abby trailing close behind. Her lips trembled a little as she thanked God for giving Leanna and Jason their chance at happiness, and, if in her heart of hearts she couldn't stifle envy, she thought God would understand and forgive. No one else would ever know. Giving herself a little shake, Sarah returned to her duties.

Abby watched as Leanna prepared for her bath. When the younger girl had leaned back in the hot water with a luxurious sigh, Abby twinkled, "Well, my dear, was I right about Jason's possibilities as a husband?"

Leanna lounged at ease against the tub, but she opened her eyes to radiate such joy that Abby was touched. Her cheeks flushed, she admitted, "You were right beyond my wildest dreams. Sometimes I want to pinch myself to be sure I'm not dreaming." And, with a secret smile, she began to wash herself. "I don't believe Jason has ever been happier, either." Her soft glow dimmed a little when she added, "I hope we can have a child as the expression of our love. Grandfather so wants a great-grandchild."

Abby soothed, "That will come, my dear, be patient. Cherish this time together, because a child will occupy a good part of your day, when one comes."

Leanna sighed. "Yes, I know, but I desperately want Jason's child growing within me. It's something only I can give him, and he's made me so happy I want to make him happy in return."

Their eyes locked in warm, womanly agreement. Abby

touched her flat stomach. "Yes, my dear, I understand."

Downstairs, the mood in the study was less cheerful. Jason looked grim when Thomas informed him there had been no word from Boston. "Robbie has had plenty of time to send a message with a coastal cutter. Something must have happened." He explained to Sherry, "One of my crew has been following Gavin. He was to send word of his findings after a few days."

"What other precautions have you taken?"

Jason seemed lost in thought, so Thomas replied, "The servants are alerted to inform me or Jason immediately if strangers appear on our property. Jason has asked Ben and some of his other crew members to keep an ear peeled for word of a stranger's arrival from Boston. We've heard nothing as of yet."

Sherry warned Jason, "You had best carry a weapon at all times. It would probably be wise if you didn't travel about alone."

"Yes, I've carried one since we got the news. As for the other, well, I'll not let Redfern or anyone else interfere in my life." His mouth was stern and unyielding.

Thomas met Sherry's eyes with a wry look and an unspoken plea. Sherry nodded imperceptibly. "Very well, Jason."

It was his turn to look immovable. "But please remember, this is my fight. Redfern is my enemy, and I want to be the one to deal with him when the time comes. So I think it best if we stay together."

Sherry's usually mild blue eyes were molten with anger as he added in a savage undertone, "He'll think the fiends of hell have come back to haunt him, before I'm done with him. He's used up all his luck, and he'll not escape this time. It's time Sir Gavin Redfern learned retribution comes to each of us, before we die."

Chapter
Twenty-Three

A WEEK EARLIER, Gavin strolled down the dark, fetid lane near the wharf with apparent nonchalance, but his agile muscles were tensed for action. He was aware of the stealthy footsteps that followed, as he had been aware of them for the last few days. He had a strong suspicion that Blaine knew of his presence and had sent a man to follow him. He must eliminate the pursuer, because his plans were close to fruition and he had no intention of letting Blaine thwart him again. So he had deliberately walked down this deserted street that reeked of rotten fish. He could afford no witnesses to what must be done.

Gavin sauntered to the corner, then he ducked inside a doorway. The footsteps hurried, as though the man who shadowed him feared he would lose his quarry. Gavin frowned in concentration as he tried to judge the height and weight of the man behind him. His quick glance earlier had shown him little as the man was hidden in the night's murk.

Gripping his heavy cane like a bludgeon, he suspended the

gold-headed stick over his head as the footsteps hurried around the corner. The sailor felt the swoosh of air as the cane crashed down and he tried to leap back, but his reflexes were too slow. Redfern felled him with one hard blow. Bending at the waist, he turned the man over and examined him carefully in the poor light. He saw a youngish man with dark blond hair and an angular, strong face. A sailor, eh? He'd wager he knew who the bastard's captain was.

Gavin dragged the limp weight over to the wharf, where he cut two lengths of rope from a coil he found in a nearby skiff. He bound the sailor's arms and legs, all the while listening for approaching footsteps. He used the man's hat to pour some of the sewage-infested water over his face. The sailor choked, sputtered, and blinked. His eyes widened when he felt the cold threat of steel against his throat. The look on Gavin's patrician face was no more reassuring.

Gavin smiled grimly as the man struggled against his bonds. When the sailor opened his mouth to scream for help, Gavin pricked his throat with the blade until a bright dot of blood appeared. The man shut his mouth and glared at Gavin with a defiance that successfully hid his fear.

Gavin flicked the knife with a feather's touch against the pulse at the man's throat. "If you want to live, you'd best confess who ordered you to follow me." The man glared at him with contempt but remained silent.

Suddenly, Gavin was furious. How dare this stinking tar think he was better? Gavin scraped the knife along the man's vulnerable Adam's apple and grinned when he winced in pain. "One more chance. *Who sent you?*"

The sailor swallowed in fear, but he looked away from Redfern's threatening blue gaze and remained stubbornly silent. Gavin shrugged. "No matter. I know Blaine sent you." The sailor couldn't control a start of surprise. It was enough. Gavin twisted the man's head around.

"You would have died anyway, but my thanks for confirming my suspicions." Gavin watched emotionlessly as terror filled the sailor's eyes.

For the first time, the man spoke. "No, please, I admit it

was Cap'n Blaine. I know nothing..." The words were the last he uttered. Gavin hit him again and shoved his unconscious bound body in the water. He watched the bubbles rise and waited until they stopped, then he walked slowly back to his lodgings.

He grimaced when he saw the light under his door. Ellie had been a nice little dalliance, but she was becoming a damned nuisance. He hated little worse than a clinging woman. He'd hoped to avoid a scene and slip out with her none the wiser.

Ellie looked up eagerly when the door opened. Her joyful face fell when she saw the impatient look on his beautiful features. "I'm extremely weary tonight, my dear. Even your abundant charms can't tempt me."

Her lip pouted and her pretty face looked petulant. "But Gavin, it's been over a week..."

"Yes, yes, but not tonight." He lifted her from the bed and wrapped her discarded robe about her. "Now go to your room and let me get some rest. Perhaps tomorrow..."

But now her pride was hurt. *"Perhaps?"* she sputtered.

He waved a commanding hand for silence. She flounced to the door. "You can get your favors elsewhere, my fine gentleman. Now you've had your fill, I'm no longer good enough for you, is that it?" Her voice rose, but there were tears in her eyes.

"I'm in no mood for a scene, Ellie," Gavin responded grimly. "No one else has my favors at the moment, though I don't precisely see why that's a concern of yours. Now go to your room. We'll talk later."

She was slightly mollified. With a last reproachful look at him, she went to her room on dragging feet. Gavin wasted no time. He flung his belongings into one large case, his thoughts racing ahead of his nimble fingers as he packed.

It had really been ridiculously easy taking Blaine's mother. When she had left from her weekly meeting with Hawthorne, Gavin had closed the trap. Her aged coachman and young, frightened footman had been easy to knock unconscious and leave trussed in the carriage. The two drunken louts he'd hired from a dockside tavern were matched in strength only by their

brutality. They would have gladly sold their own mothers for
the gold he had paid them. Their captain was as easy to bribe.
His small sloop should make the trip to Savannah in a se'-
n-night or so, and when they arrived, the man had promised
more help would be available for the "right price."

Gavin flashed a last look around, then he hefted the case
and slipped out into the hall. He left the lantern burning and
locked the door. The longer before his absence was discovered,
the better. Pulling his hat low to shield his features, Gavin
eased down the stairs and left by a side entrance. The streets
were deserted at this late hour, so no one observed when the
elegant gentleman kept up a brisk pace until he reached the
wharf.

When he climbed aboard the sloop, he glanced around with
narrow eyes. The deck could have been cleaner, but she seemed
sturdy enough. Striding over to Captain Strope, who stood near
the helm, he demanded, "Where is the woman?"

"In me cabin, below."

"Get under way immediately." He ignored the man's sour
look and went below.

Bella recovered consciousness bit by bit. She shook her
head and tried to clear the rhythmic pounding in her ears. She
only slowly realized the sound was not in her aching skull.
She sat up and put a hand to the lump on her forehead, then
she forced her eyes open. She whitened when she saw the spare
furnishings of a cabin. My God, the sound was waves slapping
against a hull. She was being taken to sea! Two fierce faces
swam before her eyes and her memory returned.

She was frantic with worry about the condition of her servants when the door opened and Gavin entered. Bella whitened
still more when she saw him. Of course. How stupid of her
not to be prepared for this. She sat up and forced herself to
meet his jeering eyes calmly.

"What have you done to my servants?" she challenged.

Gavin lowered his lean frame into a chair at the table. He
stretched his legs before him in an insultingly negligent pose
and rested his chin on his hands, all the while letting his eyes
roam over her body. Pity she was older than he. She still had

quite a figure and face. In some ways, brutalizing her would feel highly satisfying.

Bella gritted her teeth to keep from shuddering with distaste at his look. She kept her stare level and unafraid and her voice even. "Have you killed them?"

Gavin flung her a mocking look. "I? Do such a dastardly thing? My dear, you shock me." He watched her effort to hold her temper and fear in check with amusement.

She sat straighter and met his eyes steadily. "It won't work, you know."

Gavin's eyes narrowed. "What won't work?"

"I presume you hope to use me to get to my son. You've overlooked a major flaw in your plan." Bella knew it was unwise to taunt him, but suddenly she could not control her fury. "Jason hates me. You can kill me with his blessing, he'll not lift a finger to stop you." She borrowed some of his own mockery as she smiled at him.

Gavin clenched his fists in rage and leaped to stand over her, quivering with fury. She drew in a sharp breath, but she refused to shrink away.

He jerked her head back. "You bitch, you and your damned son think you're so clever. Do you think I don't know what your little meetings have been about with Hawthorne? I've known from the beginning, and I've taken care to stay strictly within the law."

He flung her head away in disgust and retook his seat. His chilling, genial smile appeared again. "Until today, that is. But it should be some time before I'm connected with your disappearance. I was seen by half of Boston in the inn tonight, during your capture."

His eyes hooded and he reminded her of a cobra about to strike. "Your son will be cold in his grave before you're found." He smiled sweetly. "If you ever are."

He sauntered to the door, his temper restored by the stark fear on her face. She would take her life with her own hand if her stupidity caused Jason's death.

He paused with his hand on the knob. "By the by, your little homily about how your son hates you doesn't hold water.

Whether he cares for you or not, he will never let you die. Of that I'm certain." His lip curled in a sneer. "The Blaine men are too officious about their duty. He'll come running when he hears I have you." He laughed and gave her a courtly bow before the door muffled the sound of his satisfied mirth.

Bella stared with blind eyes straight ahead. Her body was chilled from head to foot and her heart was leaden with dread, but her mind was frantic as she tried to think of some way to foil him. There had to be a way, and she must find it. Her son's life would depend on it.

Bella was nauseated for most of the trip. The passage was rough as the sloop took advantage of the coastal winds for a speedy voyage. Bella had hoped to bribe the crew to betray Gavin. Men that could be bought for gold once could be bought again. However, Gavin brought her frugal meals and saw to her wants himself. He taunted her with a sneering smile when he saw her disappointment.

"Did you think to bribe my loyal crew, my dear? I'm afraid they have no idea you're one of the wealthiest people in Boston. Nor are they likely to learn, so you'd best accept the situation."

When he turned to leave, in desperation she pleaded, "I will gladly cede you half my holdings if you turn this ship about and forget your vengeance."

Gavin turned to face her, and his beautiful face was so ugly with hatred that she drew a sharp breath. "You can't tempt me for all the world's gold. The Blaine men have twice ruined my life and I will not rest until your blasted son breathes his last. He's too much like his dead, arrogant cousin for my taste. Men such as they think their wealth can buy them anything." He muttered to himself, "My blood is far bluer than theirs, but that's not enough for society. Well, if I can't have respect of one kind, I'll have respect of another."

His eyes unclouded as he beamed another cannibalistic smile. "Wealth can smooth the way in this world, but there's one thing no one can bribe." He purred, "You can't bribe death." And so saying, he turned and left her in miserable solitude.

When they neared Savannah, the winds calmed. Bella was

so nervous that she paced a continual, agitated trail, up and down, up and down the small cabin until her feet hurt, but the activity provided no solace for her terrified mind.

Abby, Leanna, and Sarah were chatting comfortably on the veranda when Benjamin galloped to the house and leaped off his horse. His bright hair was matted with blood. Leanna broke off in mid-sentence when she saw him and exclaimed, "Benjamin! Are you all right?"

He stammered in his haste to get his words out. "Aye, ma'rm, I be fine. But the Cap'n's mum is in danger."

Leanna's eyes widened. "What on earth do you mean?" she cried.

Benjamin slumped down on the porch steps and gulped down several deep breaths. Sarah ran inside to fetch some lemonade and hot water. Benjamin's eyes filled with tears when he explained, "They jumped us from behind. We hadn't a chance. Oh, ma'rm, I's so sorry..." And he dissolved into tears, his thin shoulders shaking with anguish.

Leanna was frantic, but she sensed Benjamin must have a moment to compose himself before he became coherent. When Sarah rushed back out, Leanna poured Ben a big glass of lemonade with a shaking hand while Sarah gently cleaned the boy's wound and wiped his dirty face.

Leanna clenched Ben's shoulders after he had swallowed the liquid. "Tell us what happened from the beginning," she commanded with a firmness of which Thomas would have approved.

Benjamin explained, "I be playing cards with a friend on deck when those two brutes I told you about, Dan and Pete Duggan, jumped us from behind and put the lights out on us. When we come to, a purty blond-haired gent was standing over us with the meanest smile I ever seen." Abby and Leanna's eyes met in mutual dread.

"He kind o' sneered, like, and said I should fetch my Cap'n right away if he ever wanted to see his mum again." Benjamin's voice broke as he added, "He said his men were eager to 'make the lady's acquaintance' and he would give her to them if the

Cap'n don't arrive within a few hours." Benjamin's high quaver didn't resemble Gavin's musical tones, but the words chilled each woman to the marrow. Benjamin concluded dully, "He said if I alerted the port authorities and anyone tried to stop him, he'd kill her himself. They followed me out o' Savannah to be sure I didn't tell nobody."

Leanna had heard enough. As she ran to the stables, she moaned to herself, "Dear God, what a time for the men to go hunting." She barked at the startled head groom, "Silas, do you know where the master hunted today?"

The startled man shook his grizzled head. "No'm. Should I send someone to look for him?"

"Gather as many hands as you can, and send Gus to the house immediately. Also, harness our fastest team to the light curricle." Leanna ran back to the veranda.

Sarah had sent Benjamin inside to lie down, and Abby was tapping her foot impatiently while she waited for Leanna. Her fears were confirmed when she saw Leanna's face. "So no one knows where they went?"

Leanna's mouth was white around the edges as she bit off, "No, apparently not, and God knows how long it will take to find them. Jason has hunted with Rian sometimes clear on the other side of Savannah."

The two women looked at one another again with grim eyes. Each knew the other's thoughts, and finally Abby nodded briskly, as though Leanna had asked her a question. "I don't see that we have a choice, Leanna. It may be a bluff, but God," she shuddered in horror, "we can't take the chance. Do you know how to shoot?"

Leanna shook her head ruefully and Abby sighed in exasperation. "Neither do I." They were trying to decide what to do when Gus ran up to the house.

His face was dark with concern. "Yo sent fo' me, Miz Leanna?"

Leanna was relieved to see him. "Gus, when Jason, Thomas, and Sherry are found, tell them to go directly to the *Savannah*. Gavin Redfern has kidnaped Mr. Jason's mother and has taken control of the ship. He apparently has quite a sizable group of men and he has threatened to, er, harm Bella, if Jason doesn't appear within several hours."

Gus's eyes widened. "Yo' mean Miz Bella is in Savannah?"

Leanna nodded. "Yes, Gus, and she is in dire danger. Abby and I are going on into town to see if we can help."

Gus frowned at this. He said hesitantly, "That ain't wise, Miz Leanna, if you'll excuse me fo' sayin' so. Mistuh Jason will be powuhful angry."

Leanna once more met Abby's eyes. Only a woman can understand the horror of the threat of rape, and if they could do anything to save Bella, they must. Leanna looked back at Gus. "We're merely going to try and round up some help, Gus. We won't go aboard, I promise."

Gus was still disturbed, but he saw the stubborn set of Leanna's mouth and he knew it would be useless to protest further. He touched his forehead and said fervently, "God go with yo', Miz Leanna. I'll lead the search fo' Mistuh Jason mahself." He hurried back to round up his men.

By the time Abby and Leanna reached Savannah, almost two precious hours had passed. Leanna urged their weary team through the busy streets and went directly to the docks. She stabled the horses in the storage building Jason had used when they arrived in Savannah, then she and Abby proceeded to the rowdiest bar on the wharf, the Ship's Landing. She had heard Rian tease Jason about the good times he and his men had spent there. Leanna prayed some of Jason's crew were still in the area.

It was early afternoon, but already the smoky taproom was crowded with men. The raucous din slowly died down when they entered. Leanna and Abby squirmed under a score of interested appraisals that varied from surprise to admiration to blatant lust.

A gigantic sailor strode with an arrogant, rolling stride toward them, a wide grin splitting his face. "Well, ladies," he boomed, "lookin' fer a good time? I'll gladly oblige . . ."

A curt voice and rough hand cut off his gleeful invitation. "Stow it, mate. That's Cap'n Blaine's wife." Leanna drew a huge sigh of relief as she recognized Jason's bo'sun.

He surveyed her sternly, then reprimanded, "This is no place for you, ma'am. Cap'n Blaine would have my hide if anything happened to you." He was shepherding her toward the door as he spoke, but Leanna resisted.

She explained in an urgent undertone why they had come. The man frowned as he listened, but when she asked how many of Jason's crew were available, he shook his head grimly. "Not many are here, ma'am. The Cap'n told 'em he'd not be sailing for a while, and most of 'em hired out on other voyages."

When Leanna's face fell and she bit her lip in frantic worry, the man comforted, "Mebbe I can help. The Cap'n's a respected man hereabouts, and I can probably round up some friends. Wait outside for me."

Leanna dazzled him with a brilliant smile. "Thank you. Any help you can provide will be greatly appreciated." Leanna and Abby retreated with relieved alacrity into the sunshine.

No one noticed the large, ham-fisted brute who had slipped out the door when he heard the bo'sun identify Leanna. Soon after, he returned, along with three other men. Leanna and Abby were preoccupied in a worried conversation, so they paid no attention when the four approached them. In a trice, the four surrounded them like a hulking wall and forced them behind the tavern. Leanna and Abby had time for one choking scream before they were knocked unconscious with a quick uppercut to the jaw. Like supplies, they were bundled in sacks and carried down the docks.

Bella was almost in tears of anger and fright when the cabin door slammed back against the bulkhead. She started and watched in amazement when two bundles were carried in and dumped unceremoniously on the bunk. The sailors left as soon as they had deposited their burdens, ignoring Bella's plea of "Wait!"

Bella eyed the two motionless bundles with misgiving, but the odd, elongated shape alerted her. Frowning, she hastened to the bed and opened the sacks. She gasped when a small, dark head was revealed. Quickly, she slipped the sack down and off Abby, then she opened the other one. Gleaming blond hair spilled over her hands, and she stopped her fumbling with an arrested look. Thomas's description of Leanna rang in her ears: "Small, but spirited, with the most beautiful head of golden hair I've ever seen. She has a dimple in her determined little chin and slanted green eyes."

Her heart pounding heavily, Bella tore a strip from her petticoat and dipped it in the pitcher of water by the bed. She dabbed at the lump on Leanna's jaw, and her suspicions were confirmed when dazed, slanting green eyes looked up at her. Smiling with mingled joy and pain, Bella murmured huskily, "Hello, my dear. I am your mother-in-law. I am overjoyed to meet you at last, though I deeply regret you are embroiled in this mess."

Leanna shook her head to clear the haze before her eyes, then she winced in pain. She squinted up at Bella, searching for some sign of Jason in the calm features. Except for a wide, full mouth that mirrored Jason's, Bella bore little resemblance to her son. But the steady, fearless look in the dark gray eyes was decidedly familiar.

When her thoughts cleared, Leanna blurted, "Ma'am, are you unharmed?"

Bella understood her meaning. "Yes, Leanna, I am fine. However, I fear my son is doubly in danger now that Redfern has you. He is now much more apt to lose his temper and act recklessly."

Leanna watched as Bella clenched and unclenched her hands. "You love him, don't you?"

Bella looked surprised. "Of course, my dear. I will love him until the day I die, whether he hates me or not." She tried to disguise the distress in her voice, but it was obvious.

Leanna's mouth tightened at the agony Jason had put his mother through by not trying to reconcile. She sighed heavily. Now was not the time for anger. But if they all came out of this alive. . . . With brisk movements, Leanna dabbed at Abby's face until she came to. Introductions made, the three women stayed quiet and listened for some sign of action above.

Finally, Leanna's patience wore thin and she leaped up and went to the door. She rattled the knob, then bent down to examine the lock. She moved about the cabin, looking for some kind of pointed instrument with which to pick the lock.

Bella watched sympathetically. She shook her shining dark head. "It's useless, Leanna, there's nothing. I've searched this cabin countless times."

Leanna brushed against a chair on her dispirited way back to the bunk, and Abby exclaimed, "Look, Leanna, the chair is loose!"

Leanna wiggled the ladderback chair and, indeed, it rocked from side to side. Her heart beginning to pound, Leanna bent down and examined the chair's moorings. One huge, metal spike bobbed up and down when she yanked at the legs.

Abby and Bella jumped up and dropped to their knees beside Leanna. The women took turns rocking the chair back and forth, harder and harder, until the spike tore loose. With a triumphant smile, Abby displayed the long, angled nail. The three rushed over to the door and tried to slip the nail into the lock. It was too large.

Leanna examined the door frame closely. There was a minuscule gap between the door and the frame. She held out her hand for the nail and scraped it along the edge where the lock was embedded in the frame. Abby and Bella kept their eyes glued on Leanna's steady hand. When Leanna tired, Abby took over, and so on, for what seemed hours. All three women prayed soundlessly to themselves for the safety of their menfolk as they took their turns at the lock.

Chapter
Twenty-Four

JASON WAS TAKING careful aim at a large pheasant when Gus and three hands stomped into the clearing, scaring the unsuspecting bird away. Jason swore under his breath, but his exasperation evaporated when he saw Gus's worried face. "What is it, man? Why have you come all the way here to find me?"

Thomas, Sherry and the handsome giant, Rian, heard the voices and the sharp concern in Jason's voice and came running, their muskets at the ready. They sighed with relief when they saw Gus, but then they caught the gist of the conversation and the relief changed to alarm.

"My God, Gus, how could you let them go?" Jason cried, his face red with anger and fear. He turned to Sherry and Thomas. Rian looked beside himself. "Did you hear that?" he barked.

Sherry verified as though he couldn't believe it, "Leanna and Abby have gone into Savannah to try and save your mother. My God, how foolish they are!"

The raging fear in Sherry's voice had a benign effect on Jason's anger. Above all, they must keep a cool head. "Gus, come with me. Silas, you and the other hands go back to the plantation."

Jason turned to Thomas, but his grandfather knew what he was going to say. "I'm coming," he said savagely. "I'm not in my dotage yet." He stalked toward their horses, but Jason was pleading with him.

"Grandfather, I'll have my hands full worrying about Leanna and my mother," Thomas looked at him sharply, for he had not called Bella by that name since he was a boy, "without having to worry about you." When Thomas still looked unyielding, Jason exploded, "Blast it, be reasonable! We've only four horses and one of us must go back with the hands if Gus is to come."

With a sigh, Thomas gave his disgruntled consent. "I'll go with the hands, boy. Now get moving. If I know my granddaughter, she's in the thick of things." Jason and the other men leaped on their mounts and galloped hell-for-leather toward Savannah.

Thomas climbed into the wagon with the hands and met Silas's eyes. "Well, Silas, the boy thinks we're too old to be of any help. Shall we prove him wrong?"

With a delighted grin, Silas answered, "Yassuh!" and whipped the team on the road to Savannah.

The riders stabled their horses in Jason's rented wharfside building. Jason's heart leaped to his throat when he saw the curricle tied to a post. The team was still harnessed, as though Abby and Leanna had left in a hurry. He jumped from his horse and ordered from the side of his mouth, "Gus, take care of the horses and meet us at the Ship's Landing as soon as you can." Sherry and Jason, with Rian trailing behind, had discussed what to do on the way, and they had concluded that Leanna had probably gone there to enlist help. She knew that Jason's crew caroused at the tavern in their free time. It would also be the best place to muster up a gang, if she didn't recognize any faces.

Jason, Rian, and Sherry ran the short distance to the pub, but before they reached it, they were hailed by Jason's bo'sun.

"Cap'n, thank God! I think they've taken yer missus and her friend." The three men whitened at the news, even though they had been expecting it. Their hands clenched in rage as they listened.

The man's face was red with chagrin and anger. "They came in the Ship's Landing and asked for help to save yer mum, and I sent 'em outside to wait while I tried to recruit some men." His eyes were wet when he apologized wretchedly, "I'm sorry, Cap'n, I should've been more careful. They were taken while they waited for me outside."

Jason waved him off. "Forget it. My stubborn wife would have gotten involved anyway." His voice grew brisk as he once more started for the tavern. "How many of the men are in town?"

"Barely a handful, Cap'n, but when I told the others what the louts had done, taking over your ship and kidnaping yer mum and wife, I got plenty of volunteers. I was coming in search of you when you arrived."

"Do you have any idea how many we're up against?"

"Naw, but I think they're a mean bunch. Pete and Dan Duggan are among 'em."

"All right, round up as many as you can, discreetly, if possible. I'll be in in a moment."

Jason met Sherry's stern eyes. "Well, cousin, tell me what you think of this approach. I go aboard, alone, as ordered. I'll keep Redfern involved as long as possible, and give you and the men time to slip aboard. It will mean a dunking, of course, but I don't think the men will mind. You and Rian can climb up the anchor chains."

Rian started, but held back his impulse to offer himself as the distraction. He knew this was a matter between the two cousins, that he would have to follow along, and restrain his own impulse to avenge Leanna's kidnaping. These two men were strong in their own rights.

Sherry nodded. "It might work, but I'll go instead of you."

Jason shook his head with the unyielding look about his mouth again. "No, Redfern will want to taunt me first, but you he'd probably kill on sight."

Sherry grated his teeth in frustration, then he gave a curt

nod. "Very well, Jason, but remember one thing. He's mine. I want him."

Jason asked irritably, "What the hell difference does it make who kills him, as long as he dies?"

When Sherry's eyes remained implacable, Jason shrugged with ill grace. "Oh, very well, I'll save him for you, if I can."

"Good. Let's get started." They went to the tavern and were greeted by a rousing cheer. Many of the sailors had been land-locked for too long and they had been spoiling for a fight.

Jason explained the plan. "Above all, get to the poop deck and release the prisoners. It's vital that we reach them as soon as possible. Follow these two men," he said pointing to Sherry and Rian, who nodded when their names were mentioned.

Jason peered at the brown, rough, eager faces listening to him intently, and he felt a wave of affection for the group. Aye, there was no one better in a fight than a seafaring man.

Jason rowed steadily to the ship, and if his heart was black with rage, it wasn't apparent on his face. When his head topped the ladder and he jumped aboard, he held his hands out to his sides so the men could see he was unarmed. Rough hands grabbed him and held him to the deck. He was searched thoroughly, then hauled to his feet.

Jason cast a casual look about. A dozen of one of the toughest lots of men he had ever seen surrounded him. He saw no sign of Gavin. He spied a familiar face and smiled gently at Pete Duggan. "Where are they?" he asked in a soft drawl.

Pete felt uncomfortable under the veiled menace in those dark blue eyes, but he shrugged and blustered, "Ye ain't in command here, Cap'n. *I* be givin' orders fer now." He swaggered up to Jason and met him stare for stare. "Where's yer men, *Cap'n?*"

Jason's eyes narrowed and a chill ran up his spine. Duggan was a little too arrogant, a little too confident. Something was wrong. He threw a surreptitious look toward the poopdeck, and Pete smiled in satisfaction.

"That's right, Cap'n, they ain't here. The gent expected you to try somethin'." He pulled his pistol out and quite coolly shot Jason in the shoulder. "That should keep ye quiet fer awhile."

Jason staggered back under the force and for a moment, a

red haze of pain clouded his vision. Then all hell broke loose on the deck as the first of Jason's men came aboard, led by the savage whooping cry and muscular frame of Rian, and the fight began. Jason was vaguely aware that Pete was herding him toward the ladder. Several men formed a wall around them to shield their retreat.

Jason saw Sherry's dark head and shouted with the last of his strength, "They're not here! Follow!"

Pete cursed and slammed his pistol down on Jason's head. He lifted him over his shoulder and carried him down the ladder effortlessly. Once in the rowboat, he dumped Jason's unconscious body and rowed quickly, strongly, toward the innocuous-looking little sloop that was berthed nearby. Pete threw a sneer of satisfaction at Jason as he noticed the blood on his wounded shoulder.

Sherry watched in frustration, then he shouted to Rian, who was engaging three embattled men, "I'm following Jason! They're going aboard that sloop, it appears." Sherry dove in the water and swam underneath the waves as much as possible. Pete kept throwing wary glances behind him, but when he saw no boat, he assumed the fight was keeping Jason's men too busy. He flung Jason over his shoulder and climbed aboard, unaware of the dark head that broke the surface of the water beneath him.

Gavin was striding impatiently up and down the deck. A glittering, triumphant smile played at his mouth when Pete carried his burden aboard. "Excellent!" he congratulated. He turned to Strope, who stood at the helm. "Get under way. We have what I came for." He gestured for Pete to bring Jason below, and led the way. Only Strope and two other men were on deck when Sherry slipped aboard.

Shielded by the rail's shadow, he fell to his knees and crawled toward the helm. The captain opened his mouth to give the order to ship anchor, but the words never left his lips. Sherry felled him with a handy belaying pin and trussed him securely. The remaining two hands were busy in the trees and when, one by one, they dropped to the deck, they were surprised to see no one standing at the helm.

Wariness prickling their necks, they approached the helm

cautiously. They had no time to reach the pistols in their belts before Sherry sprang from behind a gunwale and knocked them out. He tied them up also, then he grabbed their weapons and went below and listened at the cabin door.

The women had almost chinked enough wood from around the lock to pry it loose when they heard footsteps. Leanna amused Abby with a curse that was scarcely ladylike. Leanna hid the spike, and all three women had leaped to the bunk and arranged themselves in varying poses of innocence when the door crashed open. Gasps left their lips in unison when they saw Jason.

Pete dropped him on the floor, and the jarring pain roused him. He groaned and moved feebly, but his eyes flew open when he heard Leanna's beloved, tearful voice, "Jason, darling, what have they done to you?" She tore a strip from her petticoat and dipped it in water to begin cleaning his wound. She shot a look of hatred toward Gavin's negligent figure.

Bella swayed on her feet with such a paper-white look about her mouth that Abby pushed her gently on the bunk. Her dazed eyes stayed glued to Jason, but for the moment, he was only aware of Leanna.

He reached up a shaking hand to touch her cheek. "Little fool, you almost frightened me to death." Leanna kissed his hand and tried to probe around his wound as gently as possible as she felt for the lead. She tore some fabric from her dress and matted it against the wound. Then she used a strip to tie the other in place.

Gavin's mouth twisted as he watched Leanna's tender concern. "Don't bother, my dear. He'll not live out the hour, anyway."

The words roused Bella from her stupor. Her whole body seemed to ignite into a pillar of fire. She leaped at Gavin and tore at his face like a wildcat. Pete grabbed her by the shoulders to haul her away, and in that tense moment, the door burst open.

Abby radiated joy when she saw Sherry. Gavin had his back to the door, but Pete flung Bella to the ground, and went for his pistol. Without hesitation, Sherry shot him through the heart.

Gavin reached for his own gun and whirled to face the intruder, but Jason put out a foot to trip him and the gun went off, spending its shot harmlessly in the bulkhead. From the floor Gavin looked up at the doorway. His face froze into a disturbing amalgam of disbelief, hatred, and rage. He cried out and tried to get to his feet, but Sherry waved a pistol in his direction, forcing him to halt.

He stared at the man who had thwarted everything including death, and he choked out laughter. It was an ugly, distressing sound and Abby winced to hear it. She looked at Gavin almost with compassion, but the contempt in the others' eyes did not lessen one whit.

Gasping for breath, Gavin finally quit laughing and lounged back at ease on his elbow. "Well, old friend, what's it to be? Pistols or swords?"

Sherry's eyes had lost some of their blood-lust, and he was now quite cool. "Swords, I think." He cast a leisurely look about. "Is there such a gentlemanly weapon available aboard this scow?"

"I doubt it. I have some fine blades in my cabin. Shall we repair to the deck?"

Sherry bowed a courteous assent. "Certainly." His smile was mocking. "You'll forgive me if I go last?"

The women looked at one another in bewilderment. They seemed almost . . . friendly. What happened to the hatred they had displayed only a few moments ago? Gavin led the way to his cabin, then out on the deck into the sunshine. Jason ordered Leanna, "Help me to my feet."

Aside from one brief glance at Bella, he had yet to acknowledge his mother's presence. It was not apparent even to Leanna what he was thinking. Bella met his look with a brave serenity in her eyes. When he caught her gaze, he was struck by the lack of guilt there. Waves of emotion flowed over him, but he dismissed them. There was no time for talk now. He'd not miss this fight if he bled to death getting on deck. It was a long, wearying task assisting him up the steep stairs, and he and Leanna were gasping for breath when they emerged into clear air.

Sherry and Gavin were already stripped to their shirts and

testing their blades. The spectacle had attracted dockside observers. The fight had been won by Jason's men, and, bloodied but jubilant, they climbed aboard to watch. Jason smiled ruefully when he saw Thomas and the other hands. Thomas examined him with anxious eyes. The bleeding from his wound had stopped against the rough bandage they had applied. He felt less dizzy, so Jason nodded to his grandfather that he was all right. Thomas turned his attention to Bella.

- She was still watching Jason with inscrutable eyes. Thomas walked to her side and put his arm around her. She smiled up at him, then the duel began and claimed everyone's attention.

The salute was brief. With a hiss of steel on steel, they began. The earlier friendliness was banished entirely. Fierce determination lit the two faces. Sherry let Gavin set the pace, giving ground while he studied the rhythm. They had fenced often as boys, and they had been evenly matched, for Sherry's superior advantage of strength and height had been equaled by Gavin's lightning swiftness. However, Sherry had had an exhausting day, and Gavin was fresh and ignited by hatred.

Abby bit her lip so fiercely she tasted blood as she watched Sherry give ground before the flashing menace of Gavin's rapier. Sherry at first made no effort to attack; he merely parried Gavin's thrusts. His feet shuffled as he stepped backward, as though he felt weary. Gavin sensed his weakness and redoubled his efforts. He tried a dazzling series of feints and thrusts, but always, in the nick of time, Sherry slapped away the wicked death wand with his own sword.

Gavin's brow beaded with sweat and he began to tire, but his eyes only glowed the brighter. No wavering was apparent in his rhythm of cut and thrust, cut and thrust. Instead, with each lunge he seemed to get a little closer to Sherry's breast. Once, Sherry's blade barely deflected the tip of Gavin's sword, and the sound of ripping cloth electrified the watching audience. They sighed with relief when only a trickle of blood appeared in Sherry's torn sleeve.

The incident gave Gavin confidence. Ignoring his tiring arm, Gavin increased his ferocity, jabbing with such menacing swiftness that Sherry had to turn his body to parry the thrust. He whirled around and suddenly advanced with such viciousness that Gavin had to give ground. Sherry's blade seemed a wall of steel and for a moment the sweat of fear, rather than exertion, clouded Gavin's eyes. His old foe had advanced some in the art since the last time they engaged.

Gavin was beginning to stumble with weariness now, and the ragged breathing of both combatants was the only sound in the still air. Abruptly, after a series of thrusts that seemed to send shockwaves through Gavin's body as he parried them, Sherry lunged from the deck so powerfully that Gavin's delicate wrist could not deflect it. With a sickening sound, Sherry's rapier plunged almost to the hilt in Gavin's chest.

The glow in Gavin's eyes dimmed as he fell to his knees, then slumped to the deck. He smiled up at Sherry with twisted lips that made Sherry wince. His breath rattled, and Sherry had to bend low to hear the tortured words, "You win, dear fellow. As always."

Gavin wheezed and blood trickled from his lips. He twitched, once, twice, then he was still. The ringing shouts of admiration, relief, and joy failed to reach Sherry's ears as he gazed down at his enemy. The beautiful blue eyes were sightless as they stared at the sky. Bending down, Sherry closed the eyelids and choked back a gag of regret as he noticed that Gavin's features were, at last, wiped clean of all bitterness.

A gentle hand touched Sherry's arm. He turned to meet Abby's tearful eyes. He clasped her fiercely to him and buried his face in her hair until the sympathy and love emanating from her gave him strength to pull away. He smiled at the group around him and went to help carry Jason down the ladder.

The group that rode back to Whispering Oaks was silent and somber. They had stopped in town so Jason could see a doctor. The bullet had passed through and the wound was clean, so the doctor expected no complications.

Leanna rode in the back of the wagon with Jason, while Thomas and Bella sat up front. A somewhat tousled, bruised but triumphant Rian said he would follow later after he delivered Gavin's men to the right authorities.

Leanna whispered angrily to Jason. "You jack-ass, couldn't

you see how much she loved you when she attacked Gavin?"
She watched without sympathy when Jason flinched when they
jounced over a hole in the road. She leaned close to stare him
in the face.

"You will be polite and courteous to your mother, or by
God, I will *still* go to Charleston." And with this ultimatum,
she sat back, folded her arms, and stared, sphinxlike, straight
ahead.

Jason was angry at her insistence, but he finally sighed and
pulled her into his good arm. "Very well, hellcat, you win."

When they reached the house and Jason had bathed and
changed, he felt much more comfortable. Leanna followed him
as he went in search of Bella. They found her in the study with
Thomas.

She sat straighter in her chair when they came in. She met
Jason's wary eyes calmly. Thomas glanced from one to the
other of them, then he took Leanna's arm and led her from the
room. Jason sat down opposite Bella and asked stiffly, "I hope
you suffered no excessive harm from your ordeal?"

"I am fine, Jason." Son, she longed to call him, but held
her impulse in check. Her heart raced with hope. At least he
talked to her.

Jason shifted, then winced as his wound protested. He rushed,
"I'm sorry you were kidnaped because of me. I would have
warned you if I'd had any inkling of Gavin's intent."

Her composure slipped as she studied his earnest face. In
that moment he reminded her irresistibly of the boy he had
once been. She couldn't resist the temptation to smooth his
hair from his brow. Her smile was so tender his throat closed
for a moment.

"I would have borne almost anything for the opportunity to
see you again," she said simply. She no longer tried to shield
the love in her eyes, and suddenly, without his being aware of
it, Jason was in her arms. Tears of regret, pain, and love filled
their eyes and washed away the bitterness.

Jason whispered into her shoulder, "Forgive me, Mother. It
hurt so terribly to lose you, and then to watch Father destroy
himself . . ."

Bella set a finger to his lips to stop his apology. "The past is dead, Jason. I want only to build for the future and enjoy getting to know my son again."

When Leanna slipped back in, her face lit with joy to see them talking to each other. She would have edged out again, but Bella drew away from Jason and held her arms out to Leanna. It was like homecoming for Leanna to embrace her mother-in-law.

Jason felt a great load lift from his heart. He knew now he had always loved his mother. His violent rejection of her had been caused by pain, not by hatred. The sight of the women most vital to his world holding one another filled the last void in his life.

He looked at Bella. "You'll stay a while." The words were not a question.

Her jeweled eyes smiled at him tearfully. "You won't be able to drag me away."

Arms linked, the three left the room and went to find Thomas.

Chapter
Twenty-Five

WHISPERING OAKS HAD never seen such festivities. Every meal was a joyous occasion made brighter by the fact that Sherry and Abby also decided to stay for a visit. Bella wrote and invited Edward to Savannah. He replied that he wanted to stay in "civilization," but he would be glad when she came home. Perhaps they could find contentment together yet.

For now, however, her energies were devoted entirely to her son. Her love deepened as she grew to know both him and Leanna. Her eyes misted with tears when she watched her children put their heads together and whisper or exchange a passionate embrace when they thought no one was looking. As she watched the love grow stronger between them by the day, she often thought of Andrew. She hoped he knew, somehow, that the happiness that should have been theirs had been found by their son.

The handsome giant, Rian, was seen often around Whispering Oaks, sometimes soused with ale after a drinking bout with fieldhands, or the family. At one point, in the study, Rian strode toward Leanna and lifted her slim frame up, then hugged her fiercely. Leanna, somewhat surprised but pleased, returned the affection.

"Well, little lady," he said in a deep basso voice, his eyes glinting with more than a little envy. "You never took up my offer and visited me to escape this rascal," he said, nodding his curly head toward Jason. Jason, standing nearby, frowned.

He set her down gingerly as she gave him a wicked smile. "No, but you came when we needed you most, and for that you'll always be welcome at Whispering Oaks," she said, glancing toward Jason for approval. He gave a nod, though his expression indicated he wasn't thrilled at his best friend's proximity to his exquisite, vivacious wife.

"As a guest only," Jason said gruffly, though he broke the tension with a grin. He had developed a sense of humor about his own passions, and he would exercise it in the coming months.

The big man roared laughter, clapping his childhood friend on the back heartily. "On that you can count on, my friend. But remember, Leanna," he said, looking back at her once more. "I'm here if this big fellow gets out of hand."

Leanna smiled, while the rest of the party joined them and, exuberant, linked arms to follow the couple into the dining room for another supper together at Whispering Oaks.

Sherry and Abby stayed for several months, even after Bella had departed. Sherry decided they deserved more of a honeymoon than they had had, and Abby was certainly not eager for him to return to the War Office. After a particularly boisterous dinner, they strolled down to the river. As they stared down at the somnolent water, Sherry pulled Abby back against him with his hands clasped at her waist. She asked in a dreamy tone, "Do you think I'll get fat?"

Sherry was puzzled at the abrupt question. "I doubt it, dearest, but even if you do, I'll love you anyway." He dropped a light kiss on the top of her head.

Abby seemed not to have heard. "They say you're hungry

all the time, and it's hard not to eat. Still, I think the benefits outweigh the risks, don't you?" She nudged him teasingly in the ribs, but Sherry was too stunned to notice her play on words.

Slowly, he turned her to face him. He opened his mouth to question, but one look into her tender, brimming eyes was all the answer he needed. He grinned in delight and lifted her high into the air, only to blanch and lower her down again as gingerly as possible.

She smiled at his unnerved face. "I won't break, dearest. Let me tell Leanna, um?"

Sherry gave her a reverent kiss. "Whatever you say, darling."

Abby told Leanna that evening in the privacy of her chamber. She was upset to see the shattered look Leanna couldn't quite hide under her genuine joy for her friend. "I'm delighted for you, Abby. Sherry must be overjoyed."

Abby searched Leanna's face with gentle eyes. "Of course. My dear, don't worry, your time will come. Sarah thinks you can conceive, doesn't she?"

Leanna nodded, but her lip trembled. "What if she's wrong? It's been months since the accident, and after a miscarriage . . ."

"It is perfectly natural for it to take even years, Leanna. Worrying will only make the time seem longer." She grew brisk. "We've decided to leave soon, and I would enjoy your assistance in helping me think of a name for the baby."

Leanna was touched. The request emptied her mind of all else, as Abby had intended. On the day Sherry and Abby departed, Jason found Leanna on the veranda, crying. He lifted her into his arms and sat back down with her in his lap. He kissed her tear-wet mouth and soothed, "Don't take on so, darling. We'll see them again. I usually sail to England every year or two."

She sniffed and gave him a watery smile. "I know. Forgive me for being so silly." She buried her head in his chest and mumbled, "I'm so afraid I won't be able to give you an heir."

Jason sighed heavily. They had discussed her fears before, but he had yet to find a way to reassure her. Nevertheless, he tried again. "My love, I don't doubt it for an instant. It hasn't been that long. Please try to be patient." When she didn't reply, he changed his tactics.

Lowering his mouth over hers, he whispered, "Maybe we haven't been trying hard enough. Shall we pursue this conversation in a more appropriate manner?"

Leanna giggled when she felt his hardness under her. As he carried her up to the bed, she whispered back, "It's not for lack of trying, as you well know, you randy thing..." But when Jason lowered his naked body over hers, all her fears and, indeed, all clear thought, fled.

About nine months later, Jason strode up and down the study, pausing occasionally to take a distracted sip of brandy. He set the glass down and went to stand at the window. A moment later, with jittery movements, he lifted the same glass, still half-full, and poured in a large measure of whiskey. He took a sip and was so upset that he didn't even notice the atrocious taste.

Thomas watched with amusement as the procession of glasses seemed to multiply as the night wore on. When he could stand it no longer, Jason cried out in frustration, "To hell with it! I'm going up."

His long strides ate the distance up the stairs, but when he heard a shrill, pained scream, he sagged against the banister and fell to his knees. An instant later, he heard a loud squall that wiped the dazed look from his eyes. He scrambled up the rest of the stairs and burst into the bedroom. Leanna was white but triumphant. She smiled at him proudly as Sarah held up a wad of blankets.

"A handsome, strong boy," Sarah congratulated him. Jason peered cautiously at the squirming little bundle. Dark hair, dimpled chin, and slanted eyes.

Jason hastened to the bed and fell to his knees beside Leanna. He cradled her face tenderly and looked with alarm at her swimming eyes. "Are you all right?" he asked.

She sighed and caressed her cheek against his hand. "I'm marvelous. You've given me a beautiful son, my darling. Thank you."

Jason barely heard her. Even with circles under her eyes, she had never seemed so lovely. Their eyes locked in a gaze so intimate and loving that Sarah slipped from the room after depositing the baby in Leanna's arms.

Jason watched the child's frustrated nuzzling at Leanna's bosom, and suddenly he smiled. "I know exactly how he feels," he whispered fervently. Leanna opened her bodice and guided the famished mouth to her breast. She smiled up at Jason. The last months of her pregnancy had been harder on him than on her. She had spotted frequently, and Sarah had thought it best that they abstain from lovemaking.

As Jason watched his child taking nourishment from his wife, he felt a rush of emotions: pride, satisfaction, happiness, but, deepest of all, love. He put his hand on Leanna's other breast and stroked her satin flesh with a deep hunger that was reflected in his darkened eyes. He lowered his mouth over hers, and the passionate kiss they exchanged was witnessed only by their son. Breathing hard, Jason drew back.

"Get well soon, Leanna," he pleaded.

Love encircled them in a warm embrace as Leanna returned his desirous look. "Yes, soon, my dear love. Soon." They exchanged another kiss that was full of promise and joy. Neither of them noticed when their son gurgled at them as though to share in their happiness.

A STIRRING PAGEANTRY
OF
HISTORICAL ROMANCE

Shana Carrol

___ 0-515-08249-X Rebels in Love $3.95

Roberta Gellis

___ 0-515-07529-9 Fire Song $3.95

___ 0-515-08600-2 A Tapestry of Dreams $3.95

Jill Gregory

___ 0-515-07100-5 The Wayward Heart $3.50

___ 0-515-08710-6 My True and Tender Love $3.95

___ 0-515-08585-5 Moonlit Obsession $6.95
(A Jove Trade Paperback)

___ 0-515-08389-5 Promise Me The Dawn $3.95

Mary Pershall

___ 0-425-09171-6 A Shield of Roses $3.95

___ 0-425-09079-5 A Triumph of Roses $3.95

Francine Rivers

___ 0-515-08181-7 Sycamore Hill $3.50

___ 0-515-06823-3 This Golden Valley $3.50

Pamela Belle

___ 0-425-08268-7 The Moon in the Water $3.95

___ 0-425-07367-X The Chains of Fate $6.95
(A Berkley Trade Paperback)

Shannon Drake

___ 0-515-08637-1 Blue Heaven, Black Night $7.50
(A Jove Trade Paperback)
